Stephen Palmer was ~~~~~~~~~~~~~~~~~~~~~~~~~~~~~~
Wales and Shropshire. He was educated in Shrewsbury
and at the University of London, and currently works
as a media technician. His main non-literary interest is
music, and his own ambient group have released
several albums. He is married with no children, and
lives in Bedfordshire. He likes cats.

Glass is his second novel, following the widely
acclaimed *Memory Seed*.

Visit Stephen Palmer's World Wide Web site at:
http://www.geocities.com/Area51/2162

Also by Stephen Palmer

MEMORY SEED

GLASS

STEPHEN PALMER

ORBIT

An *Orbit* Book

First published in Great Britain by Orbit 1997

Copyright © Stephen Palmer 1997

The moral right of the author has been asserted.

A CIP catalogue record for this book
is available from the British Library.

ISBN 1 85723 475 8

Typeset by Solidus (Bristol) Ltd
Printed and bound in Great Britain by Clays Ltd, St Ives plc

UK companies, institutions and other organisations wishing
to make bulk purchases of this or any other book
published by Little, Brown should contact their local
bookshop or the special sales department at the address below.
Tel 0171 911 8000. Fax 0171 911 8100.

Orbit
A Division of
Little, Brown and Company (UK)
Brettenham House
Lancaster Place
London WC2E 7EN

For Amanda

Acknowledgements

Many thanks to Amanda, Dave Norman, Steve Kett, Jim England, Pete Wyer, Paul Thompson, and also to John Moore and Karen Sayer. Special thanks to George Cairns and Paul Hannington, and to Tim Holman for remaining invaluable.

1

DYING OF GLASS

The Reeve of Cray lived in a spherical chamber located in the heart of the Archive of Noct. It was split into two hemispheres, the upper containing electronic apparatus coagulated into lumps set here and there with screens, the lower, malodorous below the grille that was the floor, of less apparent purpose. Furniture was spartan – a desk, a chair, a black statue dedicated to the perpetually nocturnal – and the atmosphere seemed poisoned with fumes.

The Reeve, Umia, looked at home here. He was of medium height and weight, his large head topped with cropped white hair, a pair of small blue eyes overshadowed by wild eyebrows. He wore a cloak of glittering blue salmon leather, and a kirtle embroidered with crimson thread. His left lower leg and left forearm had been replaced, the leg a node-encrusted lump like a steel sea urchin, the forearm a polished orb with dangling cable. These prosthetic limbs in addition to the vexed manner made Umia seem like an afflicted old soldier oppressed by memory.

The door to the chamber opened, and he saw his

First and Second Deputies, Heraber tall and saturnine like an evil siren, Ciswadra small and bent like a crone. The pair walked in.

'Are the other two here yet?' Umia asked Heraber.

'They are inside the Archive and will be here in seconds, Reeve.'

'Good. I hate wasting valuable time.'

Umia frowned and looked at the still open door, hearing the sounds of bootsteps, and then seeing the other two members of Cray's ruling Triad, Querhidwe the Lord Archivist of Selene, dressed in clothes so dusty and unwashed they might be those of a street beggar, and Rhannan – cursed Rhannan – of the Archive of Gaya. Gruffly Umia welcomed them, though his words were traditional and held no sincerity.

Since only Umia had a chair, all except he were forced to stand.

'We are gathered here this morning,' Umia began, 'to discuss the threat to Cray of the invader gnostician creatures, with specific reference to the plague of glass that is spreading. I have been thinking on this topic, and I have come to the conclusion that some sort of purge would help—'

'Purge?' Rhannan interrupted.

'That is what I said.'

'Has this been discussed with Heraber and Ciswadra?'

Umia found himself irritated by her question. 'Of what relevance is that? My methods are my own. These gnosticians I believe to be the menace that has deprived us of our security, since they populate the Earth in its entirety, and are unlike us. This is obvious. The question is, do we actively pursue them or merely banish them from the city?'

'Talk of a purge of gnosticians is indecent,' Rhannan said. 'They are harmless. Any link with the glass plague would be disputed by my Archive.'

'Yes, yes,' Umia said, 'but you are of Gaya. Heraber . . . ?'

'The glass is spreading, my Lord Archivist. I now suspect this plague to possess an exponential vector. If we take the age of Cray to be five hundred years and extrapolate from what we know, then little time remains, perhaps less than a year. The fact that until recently it has been eating at the foundations of Cray, rarely appearing above ground, has also confused our calculations. But there can be no doubt now that you have a serious problem.'

'I? You mean all of us in the Archive of Noct.'

'You are the Reeve,' Rhannan pointed out. 'Noct is forever in charge because the Lord Archivists of Gaya and Selene are not allowed to bring deputies to the Triad, unlike yourself.'

'What then do you suggest?' Umia asked with poor grace.

'A purge is pointless. We must first see to the appalling conditions suffered by the general populace, many of whom live in the streets. Then we must create shelters and homes away from those districts worst affected by vitrification. The people suffer grinding poverty, and this is why they care for little other than their predicament in the city. Certainly an emergency Triad consisting of the Lord Archivists of all seven Archives must be set up, and discussions begun. Will you do this, for the Crayans you rule?'

Umia sighed. 'Heraber and Ciswadra would agree to a purge, so you are outvoted. We three will decide how it is to be managed. You two need not contribute. I will discuss the matter with my advisers.'

At this point Heraber and Ciswadra exchanged uncertain glances. Umia did not miss this. Abruptly he stood up and began declaiming, as if to conceal a mistake. 'Why is it that only Cray seems to matter to us? Are we solipsists? No. It is because of these gnosticians and the glass plague they spread, for it is well known that foreign bodies bring diseases. Whoever heard of disease at home? I say – we here at Noct say – that humans have been ousted. Yes, *ousted*. We must have the courage to act against that which threatens Cray. There will be a purge, once suitable methods have been decided. Good! This meeting is now at an end.'

Silent and with grim faces, Rhannan and Querhidwe departed the chamber. For a few moments Heraber, the more decisive of Umia's two deputies, looked at her Reeve as if with malice. Then she said, 'What of the other Archives, my Lord Archivist?'

'What of them?'

'Rhannan at least will stir up trouble amongst the masses.'

Umia waved her away. 'I will discuss the matter with my advisers.'

'But surely we must consider Tanglanah of the Archive of Safekeeping, and Ffenquylla of the Archive of Wood?'

'The Archive of Wood? Do you jest? It is but the home of the nostalgic and the terminally unrealistic. And likewise for the other two minor Archives.' He hesitated, then said, 'Tanglanah at least has some charisma, and if the reports are correct a certain popularity.'

'The reports are correct,' Ciswadra said, 'for I collated them.'

'Well,' Umia frostily replied, 'investigate her if you must, but do not let your work on the plague and the gnosticians suffer. It is paramount. I will not go down in history as the Reeve who could not recognise an enemy.'

'Very well,' the deputies said in unison, turning to leave.

'Wait,' Umia said. 'Rhannan has angered me with her foolish criticism of the Triad's constitution. We will deal with it in the usual way. See to it.'

At last the chamber was silent. Umia put one ear to the wall, to hear the faint booming of innumerable feet on plastic and metal, and below that, like the echo of a sonic boom, the din of the city outside.

He sat in his chair. Perhaps it was time to talk with the voices.

2

THE PYUTON

When the two orange-suited enforcers barred her from walking further along Red Lane, Archivist Subadwan began to worry. The din of the city, groaning and clashing all around, and the inebriating effect of the jellies she had eaten conspired to confuse her mind. It was late at night. And both of them were armed with serrated scimitars.

'Halt!' one bellowed through a megaphone. 'You're one of the Gaya girls, ain't you?'

Subadwan leaned against a scuffed copper wall. Because she was small and slim, some of the Triad's more officious servants found their zeal difficult to restrain. Yet tonight she wore no Archive clothes, dressing instead in red and yellow striped breeches, a blue jacket embroidered with bells, and a black scarf. Her dark, braided hair was streaked yellow, the glossy locks reaching down to the small of her back. Four opal earstuds glittered as white mote storms passed through the perspex paving below her feet.

Subadwan stood erect and with an effort raised her hands for sign language. *I am Subadwan of the Archive of Gaya. I am no child. I have done nothing illegal.*

'Ha!' came the inevitable response through the megaphone. 'Show us your fishtail, girl.'

A shocking thought entered Subadwan's mind.

'Um ...' she said, hands in pockets, apprehension draining away some of the lethargy she felt. The men approached until they were close enough to hear her voice over the hundred-decibel babble that the Rusty Quarter produced. 'Um, I seem to have left it at home.'

'At home? And you so high in Gaya's estimation? Dear Subadwan, consider yourself under our jurisdiction 'til we can stand you up in front of our top orange.'

'This is just harassment,' Subadwan retorted. 'You were waiting for me. Gaya save us.'

'Say, quiet, girl.' Their sweating, Cray-grimed faces leered down at her, framed by dangling black fuzzlocks. Each of them grabbed an arm.

She was forced to move, but when she showed herself able to walk they relaxed their grips. 'Where are you taking me?' she asked.

'Enforcer House.'

Subadwan tried to stop. They tugged her into Feverfew Street. 'All that way? Why? I've got my 'tail at home. We can go there and I'll show it to you.' To this the brute pair just laughed.

Feverfew Street was golden bright, illuminating the plastic houses on either side to their upper storeys. Some of the taller towers were shadowy up high, their turrets and spires indistinguishable from the dusty night air unless some blue flickering aerician should swerve around one, or the halogen lamps of an aeromorph, far, far higher, happened to be occluded. Subadwan, as she was marched down the street, tried to avoid the glances of other nocturnal folk, feeling ashamed that once again she – her Archive – had become the target of Triad callousness. Huddled groups of outers lay among cables and ducts stretched along the street, their filthy, dusty bodies clothed in rags. A few lessers, many dressed in the official uniforms of their masters, ran by on errands. A clerk of the Archive of Selene sped by, her white gown rippling.

After a few minutes they reached the part of Feverfew Street that had become vitrified. To Subadwan's right, panes of glass, bent into spikes and bubbles glittering blue and white, reflected and refracted the light of the street; houses to her left seemed to have avoided the infection. But even from the street she could sense an inner darkness to the glass – its black heart, where luminophages multiplied unchecked. 'That's what you should be fighting,' Subadwan shouted to the enforcers. 'Why aren't you doing anything about our city turning to glass?'

'Say, quiet,' they responded.

'Glass can cut people,' Subadwan continued. 'Why don't you get on with clearing it up?'

'We said *quiet*.'

They hurried on into the Blistered Quarter. The noise was deafening. Subadwan had not had a chance to put earmuffs on. The two enforcers wore radio transceivers over their ears and so were spared much of the din but, as they made south, the screeching, crashing, cacophonous tumult of the Blistered Quarter in collaboration with the sweltering heat reduced Subadwan to tears. 'Give me earmuffs!' she yelled.

Casually, as if humouring a lesser or humiliating an outer, one of the enforcers produced a pair of greasy earmuffs, which he then offered to Subadwan upon the point of his scimitar. The gesture was not lost on

Subadwan. With poor grace she snatched the covers and put them on.

Entering Ficus Street they passed the Water Purification House, crossed the river into Eastcity, then made up Deciduo Street, a bright alley sparkling red and gold on to which Enforcer House abutted. Here they stopped. A tall figure wrapped in orange approached from the gloomy building, steel boot heels clacking on the perspex street, a fish mask covering the upper half of her face. Subadwan knew this to be a pyuton fellow of the enforcers. 'What have you got there?' said a whirring voice.

'Subadwan of Gaya,' came the smart response. 'Caught out without ID.'

'I'll take her in.'

The pyuton, producing a two-foot revolver from a holster slung over her back, gestured Subadwan into the building. This being the latest of many infractions, Subadwan knew what to do: walk along the stuffy, black-carpeted, so-silent corridor to the door at the end marked 2F1 and then wait – standing, not seated, for if you sat somebody would poke your arm and make you rise.

At the door a pyuter voice said, 'Enter.' Subadwan opened the door to room 2F1 then walked inside.

Silvery light greeted her, a light that emanated from the walls and the roof. As ever, the small pyuton with the matted ginger fuzzlocks, the steel tooth brace and the calm, round face that looked as if it had never known a feeling sat at the room's only desk, sheets of plastic in front of her. 'Subadwan,' she said, her voice harsh.

Know your rights, Gaya's knowledge taught. Subadwan knew her rights. 'Call Rhannan,' she told the triader official. 'Call her now and she'll speak for me.'

'You think Gaya's *lone* Triad member will help you?' came the reply. The pyuton pressed grey pads, inlaid as an arc in the desk melamine. 'The *only* representative of Gaya on the Triad?' she continued.

Sensing that the pyuton did not want her here, Subadwan suppressed her own irritation. Maybe it would be best simply to accept this incident and swallow her pride.

'Show me your identification fishtail,' the pyuton demanded.

'I can't. I accidentally forgot to put it in my pocket.'

'That is a transgression. Archivists of Gaya must carry a fishtail at all times.' The pyuton looked at her desk, a portion of which was flickering with information; lines and diagrams of blue and black within the white. 'I see this is the thirteenth time you have stepped across the Triad's boundary.'

'Might be, yes.'

'It is logged. We shall decide what to do with you within seven days. You had better depart.'

Subadwan left the room, returning to the front of Enforcer House, where she was expelled. A group of jeering enforcers demanded back the earmuffs.

What would happen now? Of course, she did not know: and that was the point. Sometimes there were penalties, other times there were not, but every time, as the Triad knew, the miscreant suffered by not knowing what was in store. Subadwan however, despite her youth, had developed a method of avoiding this subtle mental torture, and that was to follow tenets of personal indifference to the Triad. She did not care. Lord Archivist Rhannan and Archivist Aswaque, Gaya

love them, were her only superiors, and so short of
assassination she was safe even from Cray's Reeve,
repugnant Umia of the Archive of Noct. She did not
care.

Subadwan's home was a cool house made of bronze
and copper in the Rusty Quarter, where Cray's most
ancient metals had been forged into dwellings,
courtyards and cloisters. But just walking the streets
had stained her clothes black – and her skin, she knew
from experience, would be as grimy as any street
outer's. It was late, almost midnight in fact, but the
Baths never closed.

She hurried across to Lac Street, followed the road
leading around the Swamps – that putrid black heart
of Cray – then made south for Peppermint Street.
Glass shards crunched under her boots, making her
slip and slide. Crossing the bridge into Eastcity she
noticed that even this far downstream the river
remained a sooty gel, thick enough for a pair of scribes
of the Archive of Vein Extraction to walk along it on
gridiron shoes. Hastening into the Plastic Quarter, she
soon found herself at the Baths. Far above, in the dis-
cordant sky, sheet lightning flashed between hovering
aeromorphs.

But here stood Cray's most beautiful building: and
it was soundproofed. The clamour of aerial vehicles,
plastic buildings, heat exchangers, groaning architecture, electronic devices and speakers, cables and
pipes choking every street – the ceaseless noise of Cray
– all this was here reduced by means of felt padding
and pyuter-controlled anti-sound. Here, at last,
Subadwan could remove her head-band and not risk
damaging her hearing.

Here also she would find one of her closest friends,

Liguilifrey the blind masseuse, who with Calminthan the Laverwoman ran the Baths. Liguilifrey was a little older than Subadwan and beholden to the Archive of Perfume, but these differences had done little to weaken their decade of friendship.

The Baths were twinned domes of blue-veined marble. Passing through the only entrance, a double door of finest polythene, Subadwan walked along claustrophobic corridors until she reached a set of changing rooms not unlike the cells of a hive in their cylindrical form. She undressed and, following ancient tradition, folded her clothes inside a niche in the polished wall, knowing they would be washed by Bath pyutons then replaced.

At this time the Baths would be almost empty. She heard only a few voices echoing, and entered the bathing chamber, two linked circular pools of steaming water with great domes for their roofs, then made for the nearest pyuton. 'What is the temperature?' she dutifully asked.

The pyuton was sitting on the crumbly stone edge of the pool, its amputated legs in the water. 'Two ninety-four,' it replied. Subadwan glanced at the other thirty pyutons, sitting around the pool, gazing into the water. Cables linked their spine vertebrae to the Baths' power source. Tradition required them to sit here for years at a time, the biomechanical transducers hanging from their ruined legs heating the water.

Subadwan walked into the water by way of limestone steps. Happily naked, in her favourite place, she relaxed, lying against the side to let her muscles loosen. Some people liked massage, but she preferred the anonymous touch of water. Few sensations surpassed water.

' 'Dwan?'

The voice reverberated above gurgling water. Subadwan, dozing, turned around to see a figure she knew, dim against the gleam of discharging glow-beans.

'Aquaitra. What are you doing here?'

Aquaitra entered the pool and, after hugging Subadwan, lay back until her head was above water. Her skin was dark, her black curly hair damp around her scalp, and she wore as much bakelite jewellery as all three of her superiors put together.

'I was searching for you,' Aquaitra replied. 'I looked all around the Archive—'

'I've not been there since this afternoon.'

'—then I went up to your house, then down to my house to see if you had passed by, then I went all the way down to the Water Purification House, because I knew you had business there today.'

'Only some independents in need of shriving.'

'Then I thought of coming here.'

Subadwan nodded, causing ripples to spread out. They were almost alone, just two men and a sleepy old woman at the far end. 'What's so important that you needed to do all that?'

'There was a pyuton to see you.'

Subadwan looked into her friend's eyes. 'What pyuton?'

'She said she needed to converse with you. I said you might be here, or possibly at the Damp Courtyard.'

'I *was* at the Damp Courtyard. I expect it's some Triader pyuton come to annoy me. I got arrested today.'

'Oh, no!'

'A couple of enforcers dragged me down to Deciduo Street.'

'What happened?'

Subadwan splashed her feet at the water's surface, as if to mask the slight shame she still felt. 'On a seven-day notice. They'll probably leave me be. I'll tell Rhannan, she might put in a word for me.'

'Was it genuine?'

Subadwan laughed. 'They were waiting for me, the morons. They knew where I was. Happened I'd forgotten my fishtail.'

'Oh. But you're all right now?'

'Yes, thank Gaya.'

A voice said, 'That is good!'

They both turned to see a tall pyuton wrapped in a brown shawl that offered little to disguise her voluptuous figure. With a pale oval face and spiky black hair, the eyes were menacing violet, almost fierce under thick eyebrows. Despite the pyuton's position towering above them at the side of the pool, Subadwan was not going to be threatened. 'What do you want?' she asked sharply.

'You are Subadwan of the Archive of Gaya?'

'Yes.'

'I wish to speak with you.' The pyuton turned to Aquaitra and added, 'In confidence.'

Aquaitra splashed about as she tried to stand up. 'I'll go—'

'No,' Subadwan said, trying to grab her friend's arm.

'I have to, 'Dwan. I have an early morning tomorrow. We can meet after breakfast.'

Aquaitra walked off but turned to glance back, and sign, *I'll stay to listen. I'll lipread.*

'Let us make for the other pool,' the pyuton said. 'It is empty.'

'I'll swim there,' Subadwan replied.

Menacingly, the pyuton walked at her side as she swam without haste through the narrow channel joining the twin pools. Her bare plastic feet, she noticed, were clean. She must have worn boots, must have taken them off before entering the water chambers. So she was following Crayan tradition. This was not official harassment. Most likely the pyuton did not want to cause a disturbance. Interesting.

At the far side of the Baths, Subadwan sat in shallow water, ensuring that her face and that of the pyuton, now crouching beside her on the pool's edge, were visible from Aquaitra's position. 'What do you want?' she asked for a second time.

'I have been instructed to arrange a brief private meeting between you and a pyutonic colleague of mine regarding some work that my colleague would very much like you to do.'

'I'm too busy.'

'This is important. It is not official work—'

'Who is this colleague?' Subadwan interrupted. 'What do they do, for Gaya's sake?'

'The person does nothing for Gaya's sake. I speak for graceful Tanglanah of the Archive of Safekeeping.'

Now Subadwan wished Aquaitra were here. Why should that sinister deviant, Lord Archivist though she was, require a secret meeting? 'With me?' Subadwan said. 'Wouldn't it be better to meet Rhannan or Aswaque?'

'The graceful pyuton wishes to speak with you also. You possess certain qualities.'

Amused at this hammer-blow flattery, Subadwan laughed out loud. 'What qualities would those be?'

'Being but an adjutant, I have not been informed. Will you meet graceful Tanglanah?'

'What's the meeting about?'

'I am but an adjutant—'

Subadwan nodded, saying, 'All right, I know. I'll have to think about it. Call me tomorrow at my Archive, a couple of hours after dawn, and I'll tell you then.'

The pyuton considered. Her purple eyes seemed to narrow, though her pallid face showed no expression. No human expression, at least. Plastic visages animated by plastic emotions, that was what Subadwan had been taught. She did not hate pyutons, but she did hate the regime that allowed every pyuton such elevated status – a status that was owed to beggarly outers and enslaved lessers.

Eventually the pyuton said, 'Very well. I shall call tomorrow morning. Farewell until then.'

She stalked off, and Subadwan swam back to the other pool. Climbing out into chilly air, she reached for a towel off a heated copper rail attached to the marble wall. The towel was green, and Subadwan paused to look at her reflection in the polished marble. In superseding Crayan law, Bath law had created a place where even the Triad's most fervent achloricians could not practise their ancient art.

A shout broke her reverie: Aquaitra. The pyuton was gone, and Subadwan led the way back to the changing rooms, ducking where the tunnel ceilings forced her to.

'Do you think this is anything to do with those enforcers harassing you this evening?' Aquaitra asked as she took her clothes from the niche wall.

Subadwan had not considered this. 'Doubt it,' she replied. She dropped the towel to the floor and, using talc from an alabaster bottle, powdered her body. As Aquaitra handed over ambrosia-scented underwear, then breeches, then waistcoat and jacket, Subadwan dressed, all the time thinking what motive might be behind the appearance of the pyuton. Eventually she said, 'I'll have to ask Rhannan about all this. I suppose it can't do any harm if she and Aswaque are going. But let's keep it secret for now, eh?'

'I would be careful, 'Dwan.'

Subadwan nodded. 'Perhaps they want us to join their Archive.'

'I hope not.'

'Me, too. What could be worse than pyutonic safekeeping? But they are planning something.'

3

THE LORD ARCHIVISTS

Gaya's Archive was set in a yard of bronze. Turquoise verdigris covered many parts, especially the outer sections, but where people had over the centuries walked into the Archive from Lac Street, or from surrounding alleys, there were eroded paths glittering gold, twinkling, reflecting lights above; the lamps of the aeromorphs, of the occasional flying carpet, and of azure aericians with glow-bean nets strung from their wings. The Archive's conical bulk lay central.

Subadwan stood in the yard. Through the noon gloom, even with her antique wooden lumod in one hand, she found it hard to make out the faces of people leaving the Archive. There had been a meeting and hundreds of smiling citizens were departing. Some independents – for no Triader or pyuton paid attention to the memoirs of Gaya – had left their pedicians tied to rusty iron posts, and were now mounting these beasts of burden, sitting uncomfortably behind the knobbly stumps of their shoulders. One man sat upon a woven brass rug and rose into the heavens.

After waiting ten minutes, Subadwan entered her

Archive. The outer public chamber – the only entrance for citizens – stood cavernous, its honeycombed aluminium skeleton entirely hidden by flesh which here and there grew ginger hair, wrinkled up, or even produced deformed nails, tentacles, and unidentifiable orifices. But the deepest mystery was why this flesh was purple and not pink: purple, the skin colour of the invader gnostician creatures who lived outside the city, inhabited the land all around, and indeed flourished across the Earth to its furthest corners.

Subadwan hastened up the central staircase in the direction of those chambers at the tip of the cone, some three hundred feet above ground. There she hoped to find the Lord Archivist. As she ascended, the flesh of the Archive grew more leathery, became holed in places exposing aluminium, elsewhere shrivelling to dried wisps shining with fat. The upper chambers, where she, Rhannan, Aswaque and other important Archivists had their quarters, were created from plastic, metal and in one case chewed paper hardened with gum.

Rhannan was in. Much relieved, Subadwan entered the gold illuminated chamber and touched her superior on both shoulders in the ancient mark of respect. Rhannan seemed flustered, her bobbed blonde hair dirty, her face grimed, the clingfilm robe that sheathed her rotund body street-stained. She had just returned from the city.

'I'll be as quick as may be,' Subadwan began. They sat here at the apex of the cone, Subadwan conscious of a dull thump from Cray's myriad buildings, for at this height much noise rose up from the heat exchangers on every roof. 'Last night a pyuton asked me to meet—'

'I thought this was about your being arrested?' Rhannan said in her husky voice. She frowned.

Subadwan continued. 'Oh, that was nothing. I wanted to ask you about a meeting with Tanglanah.'

Rhannan frowned again. 'She asked you to meet her?'

Subadwan knew something was awry. The direct Rhannan would not, as she was now, saunter across to a table and pour two tankards of foaming caramel brew. 'Are you well, Lord Archivist?'

Rhannan smiled, offering one of the tankards. Subadwan took it, knowing its nutritional content would last her the rest of the day. 'I've heard bad news, I must admit. But it doesn't concern you.' Subadwan received a few seconds of Rhannan's intense gaze. 'No doubt you have cleverly spotted my flustered state and surmised . . . well, enough of that.'

'This meeting?' Subadwan prompted.

'Both Aswaque and I have been entreated by *graceful* Tanglanah's personal minion, but neither he nor I offered a reply. The memoirs of the Archive of Safekeeping need not bother us, I think, not when the Triad does nothing to save people expelled from their vitrescent homes, nor even lifts a finger to combat the luminophage plague.'

'Is that true?'

'The Triad is a bad regime. It is a cyberocracy. So I have taught since Gaya made me Lord Archivist. It is in fact a Monad, almost a dictatorship, with me the junior member. Reeve Umia and his two Noct cronies make up three of the five. Ridiculous! He controls *three* votes of five. Querhidwe and I might as well leave Triad politics now.'

Subadwan shrugged. Her superior was in poor

mood. 'You both being Lord Archivists means you cannot.'

Rhannan nodded. This fact she knew. 'You had better go now,' she told a disgruntled Subadwan, brushing fingers through her hair. Subadwan stared. Could that be a wig Rhannan was wearing?

'Are you leaving or not?' Rhannan enquired.

Subadwan returned to her home on Dusk Street. The short walk was marred when she triggered wall-clinging chromium blisters to burst and discharge their tapeworms. With light provided only by her lumod and mote storms passing below her feet, she bound her cut arm with a strip of cloth.

It was worse elsewhere. Citizens of the Blistered Quarter habitually wore an extra layer of clothes as defence against tiny airborne splinters, while some lanes in the Empty Quarter were so choked Triader gangs swept them daily, collecting shards in sacks and dumping them outside the city walls. Upon these glass hillocks moccasin-shod gnosticians, bent double, swayed and pounced as they collected fragments.

Back at home, Subadwan tried to recall the nuances of her conversation with the pyuton, until a call redirected by Archive networks made her pyuter chime. 'Hello?'

It was the pyuton. 'Subadwan, I await your reply.'

'Am I speaking in strictest confidence?'

'Of course.'

Subadwan was tempted. The fact that Tanglanah had made representations to Rhannan and Aswaque made her imagination fill with possibilities. The urge to know what was going on was too much. Surely one meeting could do no harm.

'Where would we meet?' she asked.

'If not at our Archive, then any venue of your choice offering private chambers.'

'How about the Damp Courtyard?'

Immediately the pyuton replied, 'When?'

'Half an hour?'

'Lord Archivist Tanglanah will be there. Please arrange her entrance so that nobody is alerted.'

The link was cut. Dressing in thick breeches and coat, pinning up her hair and pulling a floppy hat over it, Subadwan departed her house and ran down to the Damp Courtyard.

The Damp Courtyard, though not one of Cray's more salubrious hostelries, was Subadwan's favourite. After submitting at the door to a check for technological parasites, luminophage debris, and other Crayan flotsam, she walked into its lush interior. In form it was a quadrangle based on the ancient design of the cloister. An outer ring of luxuriant blue vegetation rose ten, twenty feet high, touching meshes slung across the quadrangle that were laid to trap city dust and grime and to halt the descent of metal fragments. Some plants grew from the ground, others were potted in earthenware bowls shaped as trepanned human heads. It was a design also used in the Baths, and so known to be old. Scattered around this annulus were black iron tables set with silk cloths, and this was where the clientele sat. A pool of clear water lay centrally, home to aquatic spiders, monkeys augmented with fins and gills, and, inevitably, an array of nuisance life, such as purple pipe creatures, and a breeding pair of violet stalkers, which were related to the lumbering pedicians.

As Subadwan entered the courtyard and looked around, adjusting her eyes to the illumination provided by glass bowls of glow-beans, she was surprised to see a lone gnostician sitting cross-legged at a table. Gnosticians, though not aggressive, were considered a problem by many, and at best were tolerated. However it was Gaya's policy to nurture the creatures, some of which showed intelligence.

The gnostician glanced at her. The tentacles under its chin twitched, and its low-set eyes, above which a moist mouth burbled, widened in some unfathomable gesture. Though dressed in chunky cotton shirts, the garments were not enough to disguise the hunchback, the double-jointed limbs, and the deep violet tone of its white-haired skin.

Subadwan glanced at the windows edging the courtyard. These faced rooms owned by Yardkeeper Merquetaine, a friend and a follower of Gaya who enjoyed much business provided by Archive students. She spotted the yardkeeper, carrying a tray of biscuits to a couple sitting at the edge of the pool, and called her over.

Merquetaine approached. She was six feet tall and elegantly dressed in skin-tight breeches partly enclosed by a knee-length black jacket featuring diamante lapels. She enjoyed a reputation as the lover of many men, and some women, but those who came to know her more deeply discovered that her wisdom was only a little less than Rhannan's.

'Have you got a minute?' Subadwan asked.

'One minute only,' Merquetaine replied.

Subadwan led Merquetaine under a cloister arch, where it was cool, and where lipreaders were defeated by sprays of leaves. 'I need to borrow a private room for an hour. Do you mind?'

'Use the red room at the top of the stairs.'

'Gaya praise you. Now, my guest wants to remain anonymous. Can I borrow the key to the wicket gate?'

In reply Merquetaine handed over a fishtail, then hurried away. Subadwan left the courtyard by its main entrance and waited, bandanna covering her mouth, earpads in place, just off Red Lane. Ten minutes later Tanglanah appeared.

She was taller even than Merquetaine. Wrapped from head to toe in a grey robe edged with crimson, Subadwan could make little of her features, even when a burst of light flashed through the alley perspex. She unlocked the wicket gate, led the way up a spiral staircase, then entered the red room. This was a small chamber furnished with chairs, a pyuter console, air conditioning fans, and a wine butt, all these items, as well as the wall plastic and floor vinyl, being some shade of red.

Tanglanah unwrapped herself and sat. With undisguised interest, for this was the closest she had ever been, Subadwan studied her. The Lord Archivist was a dark-skinned pyuton with a large head and rainbow-irised eyes, each one seeming to change from second to second like the twinkle in a glass pane. Her clothes were of the richest twill. A silver brooch shaped as a lizard and as long as Subadwan's hand clasped her undershirt.

When she spoke, her voice was husky, lacking the metallic twang of cruder pyutons. 'I'm glad you were able to come, Subadwan, so first let me thank you.'

'I came out of curiosity.'

'That is an excellent motive.'

Subadwan nodded. 'I expect you wish that Rhannan and Aswaque also possessed my curiosity,' she crisply replied.

'When you said you came out of curiosity, you seemed to imply that this was a lesser motive. But curiosity is one of the greater motives of the conscious being. Didn't you know? To answer your point, though, I expect to see them at a later date.'

'I talked to Rhannan about meeting you.'

Tanglanah did not reply.

Subadwan said, 'What exactly did you have to say to me?'

'Have you ever heard of abstract countries?'

'No.'

Tanglanah smiled. 'Good.'

'Good, why?'

'Because you therefore have no preconceptions. But allow me to continue. An abstract country does not exist as a physical place, yet it is possible to feel there, to feel trees and rocks, and water on the hand. One can feel the sun's heat on the face. I want you to experience an abstract country.'

'Why?'

'How did I guess you would ask that question?'

Subadwan laughed, disconcerted by Tanglanah's attitude. 'Gaya love me, it's reasonable enough.'

'Have you ever loved a man, Subadwan?'

Stranger and stranger. 'Um, yes, I have. More than one, actually.'

'Then you'll know that love is unquantifiable. It is a feeling that one can describe, experience and understand, but never quantify.'

Subadwan leaned forward. 'You sound like you've never loved anybody.'

That seemed to take the Lord Archivist by surprise. But she replied, 'What do you mean by love?'

Subadwan sat back. She had expected talk of plots,

strategies, secret operations. 'Are we getting a little out of the light, here, you and me?'

Tanglanah considered. 'No.'

Subadwan nodded. 'So you really want me to say what I mean by love?'

'Your understanding has no small bearing on my proposal.'

Again Subadwan nodded. 'Well, it's ... you said love was a feeling?'

'I did.'

'I don't think it is. It's not an emotion. Love is the source of emotions. When you're in love you *feel* joy. When I loved my last man, Gaya praise him, I felt all sorts – joy, happiness, excitement. Lust. Bit of anger.'

'Yes.'

'Love,' concluded Subadwan, getting the thoughts clear in her head, 'love is wanting to get somebody inside you, almost. Or maybe get inside *them*.'

Tanglanah nodded in agreement. 'When we love, we want to map a person into our conscious mind, map them as deeply as we can. True love and true understanding are one and the same thing.'

This sounded like a conclusion, but Subadwan did not want the pressure to let up on Tanglanah. 'We?' she asked. 'Then you've loved somebody?'

Tanglanah paused once more for thought. 'People and pyutons are both creations,' she said. 'The creation I love is abstract. I want to understand it as best I can. But I have one problem.'

Another pause. Subawan felt that here she was meant to ask what the problem was. She remained silent.

'That problem,' Tanglanah continued, 'is familiarity. One feels a kind of ennui sometimes.

Somebody who is free of familiarity needs to experience my abstract country, to understand its strange moods.'

'You mean me?'

'Possibly. I have not yet decided if anybody is to help me.'

'Does this have anything to do with your Archive?' Subadwan asked.

'No.'

'I don't believe that.'

'I would not expect you to.' Her eyes took on a sinister, yet fervent expression. 'But if ever you experience this place, Subadwan, then you will as sure as black is black believe that my offer has nothing to do with my Archive.'

Subadwan sat back. 'That's all?'

Tanglanah nodded. 'Think on this first discussion. It is a private matter, concerning neither your Archive nor mine. I will call you. Or you can call me at my Archive, although you will not want to identify yourself—'

'Gaya love me, certainly not.' Subadwan hesitated. She was intrigued, but ... 'You might as well know now that I'm not interested.'

With easy movements Tanglanah stood, then walked to the door of the red room. 'Give me a few minutes to leave, please.'

Subadwan assented with a vague gesture, and then the Lord Archivist, wrapped tight, was gone. After five minutes Subadwan left the room, returned the locking fishtail to Merquetaine, and departed the courtyard.

The pall covering Cray had lifted somewhat, letting through a weak solar glow while the moon was also visible. Subadwan paused to study it, knowing that at this moment the telescopes and monoculars of the Archive of Selene would be trained upon the faint shape, looking for signs of change on its surface. Subadwan, who considered Selene's memoirs vulgar, walked on.

4

LENS

Sitting at his desk, Dwllis, Keeper of the Cowhorn Tower, surveyed the fifty or so fragments of metal and plastic before him. They ranged in size from one no bigger than his thumbnail to a monster as large as his fist. These were antique memories, their collection and investigation being the task that took up most of his time, though why they were appearing remained a mystery to him and to the authorities he served. They could be found like cankers on street walls, as if they were being exuded by the city itself. Dwllis's theory that they were the echo of an earlier city, he kept to himself.

He stood up and began to walk around his room, hands clasped at his belly. He was a tubby man of medium height, balding at the brow with brown fuzzlocks too long down his back. A pair of pale blue eyes were dominated by thick eyebrows, and there were dark rings underneath them. His mouth was small. With large flat feet, but extravagant jacket and kirtle, he looked like a fop trying to impress but not quite succeeding.

So he considered his position in Cray. Without him, the information carried by the antique memories would stay buried in the labyrinthine worlds of abstract data present in Cray's networks, data so profuse that the libraries of Noct stood by it as a speck of dust before a cliff. He, a historian at heart, could not complain of their existence. Without him the reification of Cray's memories would go unexamined, unnoticed even. Yet in the mass of ancient administrative minutes and undated weather reports he was sure he had found something important. How could he convince the authorities of this?

Perhaps he should use the tradition surrounding the Keeper of the Cowhorn Tower, an ancient position, with himself the eighteenth incumbent. Alternatively, he could point to the fact that some Crayans brought him antique memories, and thereby stress his relevance to the city. Or he could just carry on being ignored.

He glanced at the thousands of disks, blocks and pyramids lying dust-covered on the shelves of his study. The collection was the work of centuries. He and previous Keepers had tried to explore the historical knowledge contained in these lumps of memory. Surely that must be worth something? It upset him that his position as guardian of Cray's history was ridiculed, and although he dimly perceived the status of academic research in a city threatened with destruction, he nonetheless thought people should value tradition.

At length, unsettled by his inability to raise his spirits, he departed his study. From the hall of the Cowhorn Tower he heard a tapping. He stepped outside and looked up at the tiled exterior of the tower, to see that the tapping had been made by a family of dust-birds nesting where the rightmost extrusion met the main body. With irritated gestures their chisel beaks pecked at the tiles, in one place exposing the polythene superstructure. Tutting to himself, Dwllis searched the blue sward below the nest and retrieved three tiles, each a square of white and brown plastic with the texture of canvas. He pocketed these, glared up at the birds, then returned to the hall.

Inside, door shut, he paused. 'Etwe? Etwe?' he called in his cultured baritone voice. 'Etwe, those damnable birds are pecking off the tiles again. Three of them this time.'

No reply. The Cowhorn Tower was silent. Twenty yards above him, where the bulk of the tower swelled out into an array of galleries served by a central staircase, Etwe should be building a memory interface.

'Etwe? Are you there?'

There came the sound of a door opening, and then, leaning over the wrought iron rail that ensured safety on the lower levels, he saw Etwe, a slim, striking beauty dressed in mauve silks. Free flowing blonde hair tumbled around her pale face as her grey eyes gazed upon him.

He blew her a kiss. 'Look,' he said, exhibiting the tiles. 'It's those birds again. I'm tempted to requisition a team of Triader lackeys with a ladder, I am. Get them to put the tiles back and get rid of the pests.'

'You do that,' Etwe said.

'Damnable birds.'

There came a clunk from the entrance, and the thrum of the city penetrated the tower's sound-proofing. Somebody had opened the front door. Dwllis turned, and was astonished to see before him a gnostician carrying a knobbly gourd.

It was a young male gnostician, fiery purple of skin with a fine coating of ginger hair. His chin tentacles

were limp, like drooping whiskers, and his eyes were
hooded, the round mouth above both these features
clamped shut. His body hair had been shaved into a
herringbone pattern. Gnosticians, apparently following bizarre mating rituals, shaved patterns on to
themselves with remarkable precision. Dwllis knew
that under the loose, grey shawl that the creature wore
the pattern would continue. This one also wore wicker
sandals and a floppy hat that, when he looked closely,
seemed to be present for no other reason than to
conceal a number of recently healed scars.

The gnostician approached with the characteristic
loping gait of its kind. Knowing that some were
intelligent enough to follow simple signs, Dwllis
signalled to a cup of water, then made drinking
motions. 'Good morning, my fellow. Drink, drink?'

Dumb, the gnostician glanced between man and cup
before offering up the gourd. Dwllis accepted it, then
heard a rattling sound. Something inside. It was a
pencil of silicon punctured by twenty metal insert
points: an antique memory. This was the first time a
gnostician had brought him one. It must be a magpie
creature, copying the actions of human beings.

He smiled and said, 'I shall call you Crimson Boney,
on account of your colour, and being so thin.'

The hairs on Crimson Boney erected and he dipped
his head. Diffidently, he glanced around the hall in
which they stood. When Etwe began to descend the
staircase he backed away, but he did not leave when
she approached. The gnostician remained before them,
alternately bowing and bobbing his head.

Dwllis turned to Etwe. 'This charming gnostician
has brought me an antique memory.'

Etwe took the device. 'Standard silicon, probably

found in the Old Quarter. I could manufacture an interface for that.'

Dwllis nodded. 'If you wouldn't mind.' He returned his gaze to the creature. 'What are you doing here, mmm? I've not seen one of your kind in here before.'

'Do you think this is an intelligent one?' Etwe asked.

'Possibly. Go and carry on with your work.' Dwllis took the hot hand of the gnostician and led it gently into his study, where he indicated the antique memories lying on shelves. Once Etwe's footsteps had ceased, he tried to interest Crimson Boney in the memories, shaking and rattling them, even connecting one up to a liquid screen in order to show a display of architecture. The gnostician seemed to comprehend that it was attending a show, and Dwllis found himself both mortified and excited that at last he was not being treated as an eccentric. If only his fellow Crayans could cultivate such an attitude. In conclusion, he took the gourd, rattled a few antique memories inside it, then firmly handed back the emptied gourd and led the creature to the door, and outside.

'Go find more!' he said. His voice was deep and loud enough for it to penetrate the moderate din. He possessed a good pair of lungs, as many friends had pointed out. 'Find more, Crimson Boney. Good boy.'

Crimson Boney hesitated, and gazed out over the expanse of the Rusty Quarter. From this altitude it stretched out in shadow, pulsing veins of light marking the wider streets, here and there a cluster of pink or yellow lamps. Then he loped off down the track to Sphagnum Street. Dwllis wondered which of the colonies outside the city it had come from.

Perplexed, he returned to the Cowhorn Tower.

Gnosticians had appeared on Earth some five hundred years ago – so suggested the little historical information that he had so far collated – and the sanctuary of Cray had been built in response to what was perceived as their threat. But the creatures were peaceful and only xenophobes attacked them. Yet Dwllis found himself troubled by Crimson Boney's appearance. In those deep parts of the Earth from which gnosticians had sprung, were there leaders with enough intelligence and malice to desire war? Was war even a concept they understood?

The afternoon passed by quietly enough.

It was because he never expected to see the gnostician again that he was taken aback when, at dusk, as diurnal shadows fled under a fiery evening, there stood inside his front door a hunched figure carrying a gourd.

'Crimson Boney?' Dwllis switched on a lamp and walked across to the gnostician. 'Good evening, my friend . . . it really is Crimson Boney, isn't it?'

Dwllis took the proffered gourd and extracted another antique memory, a lump of gallium arsenide this time, only two wires visible for connecting an interface. Dwllis, amused, rather impressed, crouched in front of the gnostician and shook him by the hand, saying, 'Good boy. This is really fine. We could make a team, us two, we could make a damned good team.' He sighed. 'If only you could tell me where you stole these from, eh? What are you up to, loper?'

He rose to his feet. Crimson Boney scampered about then stood waiting at the door. Dwllis found himself intrigued by this gnostician. He must find out what was going on.

Keeping the gourd back, he visited Etwe's work-shop. 'Etwe,' he said, handing her the memory, 'look what Crimson Boney's brought us. Listen, I'm going to follow him when he leaves, see what he does, where he goes. You'll deputise for me.'

'You're going out into the city?'

Dwllis frowned. 'I'm not tied to this place.'

Chastised, Etwe looked at the floor. Dwllis busied himself before a mirror, dusting off his black brocade jacket and blue kirtle, arranging his fuzzlocks to his satisfaction, then applying a little powder to spots on his face.

At the door he gave Crimson Boney the gourd, and the gnostician departed. 'Do I look well?' he asked Etwe.

'Very nice.'

Dwllis peered through a slit in the door, to spy his quarry speeding down the gravel path that led into Sphagnum Street. He put on earmuffs, slipped out, and began to follow. Suspecting that the gnostician would use back streets, Dwllis was glad when this guess was proved correct. He soon realised, however, that Crimson Boney was not making for the west wall, but hugging the boundary of the Swamps and heading for the river. People in the street paid Dwllis no attention, but their heads were turned by the sight of the gnostician. Dwllis followed Crimson Boney's every step. After almost half an hour of wandering, the gnostician began to slow and look about him, forcing Dwllis to hide more than once. The affair was pro-voking in him an intense curiosity.

They crossed the river. Crimson Boney picked up Marjoram Street, took an alley off Broom Street, then loped south. Dwllis followed, pushing aside cables and ducking under pipes, tripping over the wasted legs of sleeping outers, crunching across heaps of glass. At length, the speed of his flight reduced to a walk, the gnostician scanned an alley both ways – Dwllis was hiding in a doorway – then darted into a passage. Dwllis almost missed it, for here the ground perspex was dim, dead, and there were no house lights. In fact, Dwllis was not entirely sure where he was.

He crept up to the passage and looked around its corner. Crimson Boney, if that shadow amongst shadows was the gnostician, seemed to be standing in front of a door. It was impossible to hear anything through the earmuffs. But then there came a flash of light as somebody opened the door from the inside, and the gnostician was illuminated for brief moments before he leaped inside the building. The door was shut.

After a minute, Dwllis walked up to the door. Above it there lay inscribed a luminous crescent moon.

It was the sigil of the Archive of Selene. This must be the rear of that place. Not a little appalled at what he had discovered, Dwllis walked back to the alley and followed it around to Onion Street. The broad vinyl steps at the front of the Archive of Selene were bustling with those beholden to the moon. Dwllis, waiting at the lower step, found himself studying the arcane designs of luminous plastic stapled to the Archive's fascia: crescents, circles, even some faces. Mythical stuff, of course, to be taken lightly. Above these he saw the tips of telescopes poking out from the roof.

One of the last to enter, he sat at the back of the public auditorium – a chamber a hundred yards in diameter with a lunar dais at the front and rows of chilly seats to the rear – where he was forced to endure a discourse about the moon changing shape. Dwllis, by nature a follower of traditional tenets, yawned and scanned the galleries, chambers and doors around him for signs of gnosticians, but he saw nothing. When Lord Archivist Querhidwe finished her speech, moving out of the sickly light of Selene's orb, he tried to slip away before the crush began, but he was stopped by a pyuton who had been standing behind him.

'You are a new face to our Archive,' she said.

Dwllis bowed to her. 'Good evening. Yes, I have never been here before.'

'We are always glad to entertain new citizens. I could take you to a quiet chamber and give you leaflets, books – maybe a plastic moon on a stick to take home.'

The exits were crowded, offering no chance of escape. 'That is a most generous offer,' Dwllis temporised, 'but I need time to think about it.'

'But you must be inclined to the lunar to have come here.'

'The moon is interesting.'

The pyuton smiled. 'Selene is changing shape. Soon the streets will be choked with excited citizens.'

Dwllis nodded, eyeing the exit. He had heard this statement many times before. 'How remarkable.'

'You do not believe me?' The pyuton whipped out some laminated documents from the pocket at the front of her white gown. 'This is Selene thirty years ago, full face. And this is Selene ten years ago.'

'Exactly the same,' Dwllis said, glancing at the pictures.

'But this is Selene last year. Do you not see how the face is becoming compressed?'

Dwllis did not.

'And this is Selene last night, waxing. Look now for the compression, and the extension and division of one of the cusps.'

Dwllis took the picture, and there did seem to be changes. 'But these,' he pointed out, 'could easily be produced by refraction effects of the atmosphere. Recall the shadow covering the city. How can you be certain that it does not distort the images received by your telescopes?'

'We are certain because Selene's memoirs describe similar changes.'

Dwllis nodded. The nearest exit was clearing. He said, 'Thank you for your time, but I must depart now.'

'Wait,' the pyuton said, grasping the cuff of his jacket. 'Don't you work in the Rusty Quarter, at the Archive?'

Dwllis coughed, embarrassed, but also annoyed that he would now have to divulge his identity out of politeness. 'Madam, I am none other than the Keeper of the Cowhorn Tower, Senior Historical Adviser to the Reeve.' He bowed and left the Archive.

Thoughts bothered him as he walked north along Feverfew Street. Had the pyuton really not known who he was? That pricked his esteem. It must be that she was toying with him, making him state his own identity. Well, the Keeper of the Cowhorn Tower would not be going there again.

Back home with Etwe, having heard that no more gnosticians had appeared bringing antique memories, he decided to go to bed early. By the light of a glow-bean he read a pamphlet distributed by the Archive of Gaya, advocating rights for lessers. But sleep did not come easy. At midnight he rose from his bed at the top of the Cowhorn Tower and descended to the lower bowl, wandering the galleries there for ten minutes before, irritated and wishing for tranquillisers, he hurried down to the base of the tower, and the outer door. There, wearing thin earmuffs, he took in the sights and sounds of the city.

Night impenetrable covered the southern quarters, but he was able to glimpse pyrotechnics along Sphagnum Street, the cosy pink lamps of his local courtyard, the Copper, and, at the edge of vision, that macabre, glutinous light that emanated from parts of the Archive of Gaya.

Then he looked east.

At first it seemed some freak of the seething atmosphere, but it was too spherical. It came closer, and it seemed to Dwllis that he watched a glass lens of awesome dimensions rolling through Swamps fog; and yet he could see through it, to some other place that was bright, yet softly illuminated. The thing came near. Huffing and puffing he stepped backwards. Through it images started to form, then were lost.

Suddenly a man's leering face appeared. 'Noct save me!' Dwllis yelled before he slammed the door shut, locked it, and, gasping for breath, clambered to the top of the tower. Fear had taken control of his limbs. Etwe had heard his cries and was standing dressed in a gown at her workshop door. He hugged her.

'What is it?' she asked.

'I saw a thing over the Swamps,' he muttered. When he recalled the scene, he trembled. 'Damn it! I saw a thing rolling in off the black slime, against the wind.'

'Let's check,' Etwe said in comforting tones. She ran to fetch a shallow tray, and poured in a few drops of liquid, then attached pyuter wires. The tray became a glowing screen, which she activated using the fishtail code-key strung around her neck. Speaking the names of pyuter routines she turned the door camera eastward.

'Nothing,' Dwllis said, peering at the screen. He looked up at the wall of the chamber. 'What a relief this tower has no windows.'

'You must have imagined it,' said Etwe. She took him by the shoulder, in a light grasp. 'Shall we go to our room?'

Dwllis hesitated.

Coyness took Etwe. 'Have you been chewing . . .?'

'No,' he said sharply. He glanced at her, then looked away.

'I believe you.'

'It is the truth. Etwe, retire to bed. I am just going to check the front door of the tower.'

Dwllis descended to the ground, taking his time, trying to think of a useful weapon, for he intended peeking out into the night to see if the apparition was still abroad. He knew he had not imagined it. But as he shivered by the front door both hands were as empty as his mind. He opened the door.

The sward outside, like the air and the sky, seemed clear and calm. With no earmuffs Cray's clamour attacked his eardrums, though being so close to the Swamps and the Cemetery the noise was of medium level compared to that of southern districts. His ears reported no otherworldly sounds. No rank smells, as allegedly accompanied spectres, spoiled the air. Moving slowly, he left the safety of the tower and stepped out.

Still nothing.

He followed the polythene wall for half its circum-ference before spotting something. Away north shimmered a sulphurous blur. It was the lens, images flickering in its lensing centre. As it returned south Dwllis swore and with thumping heart ran back to the door, which again he locked.

Etwe was waiting. 'There is a . . . a lens-like object in the Cemetery. Don't go out. It saw me. It may return.'

'It *saw* you?'

Irritated, Dwllis waved a hand at her. 'So it seemed to me. May I not have my perceptions?'

'We're safe in here,' was Etwe's cool reply.

He nodded. 'We need protection,' he said. 'I need to make a picture of the object to show the Triad officials.'

'Will you do that tonight?' asked Etwe.

'I must, I must.'

Feverish, determined to capture the apparition's image, Dwllis hunted drawers and cupboards for a portable pyuter with a lens, which Etwe linked to one of her pyuters by radio. He was ready. For the third time he stood quaking by the front door of the tower, listening. He commanded Etwe to remain at the opposite side of the room, beside her pyuter. Creeping out, he first ascertained that the lens was not close, then made around to a position from where he could survey the Cemetery. There the object shimmered, drifting south. Starting to tremble, he fed images to the pyuter as the apparition closed, moved east, then with a sound of clanging bells surmounted the Swamps wall and disappeared into the gloom. He ran back.

The images were good. They stored them then made for bed. It was almost dawn when Dwllis dozed off, but three hours later he was awake and ready to depart for the Nocturnal Quarter, where, at Triad Tower, an official had agreed to meet him.

Dwllis did not approve of either pedicians or aericians. A flying carpet being beyond his means, his only option was to walk. But he would wear no filmy cover. There was such a thing as style.

Today he wore clothes he imagined suitable for the interview, a brown and blue striped kirtle, a black velvet frock coat and a red shirt. His fuzzlocks he caught up in a sack hat in order to offer respect to officialdom. So attired, he walked down the main streets into Eastcity, arriving hot and bothered at a building in Eel Row attached to Triad Tower, where he announced his name to a fish-masked guard.

'Wait here,' he was told.

Some minutes later a genteel officer dressed in a brown cloak with a dorsal fin arrived to lead him into an ante-room. As he sat, another Triader, of high rank judging by her orange carpskin-trimmed robe, arrived, waving away the first with a fluttering gesture. She drew up a chair and sat opposite Dwllis so that their knees almost touched.

'Good morning, Madam,' he began.

'Good morning, Keeper. We received your message. You have been troubled during the night?'

'I have,' Dwllis replied. 'I'm here to ask for protection.' He handed her the sheaf of images. 'I took these last night, and they very clearly show an object. I could be in danger. Anything could emerge from the Swamps, Madam, anything, and being so close I feel I need some sort of . . .'

Dwllis ran out of words. The pyuton looked sympathetic. 'I quite understand. Of course you are an official of the city and so may demand your right, but you may find that too many of our Triaders are out performing their civic functions.'

She rose and left the room, taking the images with her. Unsure of how well he had performed during the brief interview, Dwllis waited impatiently, tapping the floor with the toes and heels of his boots, walking around it twice, then sitting and brushing dust off his coat. When an achlorician came to remove some leaves that were turning green (for autumn was approaching), he watched the process.

Fifteen minutes later the pyuton returned to say from the open door, 'We'll send protection up. It'll be along presently.'

'Thank you,' an uncertain Dwllis said.

The pyuton disappeared and the brown-cloaked officer arrived to show him off the premises. A little surprised, Dwllis found himself standing alone back in Eel Row. Perhaps it was just the manner of officials. Before heading back, he decided to make a detour east.

The Copper Courtyard, the smallest in Cray, was little known, its position by the Swamps bringing a ghoulish reputation to those who had heard of it. But Yardkeeper Cuensheley had cooked and brewed for Rhannan's predecessor, her mother being a recorder of Gaya, and the quality of her provisions was unsurpassed. In addition, she knew few equals as a singer.

Dwllis stood upon the burnished copper floor. The quadrangle around him was set with dwarf trees in pots, the edges of their leaves turning from blue to green just like those of the plant he had seen earlier. Soon, the city would be swarming with achloricians.

Amidst cushions, low plastic tables were set, while above there hung a net, and below that were strung lamps on wires. A score of Crayans presently relaxed at the hostelry.

Dwllis, spotting Cuensheley, waved at her. She approached. She was of slender build and medium height, but her long blonde fuzzlocks tied with rainbow ribbons, and her round, blue eyes set slightly too close elevated her out of mediocrity. Her skin was poor, though, too wrinkled for a woman of forty. She wore pale flowing garments that trailed along the floor.

'Dwllis,' she said in her fluting voice, 'it's been too long since I saw you.'

She pointed out empty cushions where they could sit, but Dwllis sternly refused, saying, 'Good evening, Cuensheley. No, I am not staying tonight. I wondered, though, have any of the regulars mentioned seeing anything unusual last night? Or this morning? Has there been talk of odd things?'

Cuensheley smiled. 'Nothing. Is there a mystery? Tell me!'

She seemed sometimes like a girl to Dwllis: too enthusiastic. Occasionally she would laugh and clap her hands out of joy at some happening or experience. Dwllis, who only laughed when somebody told a joke, found there were times when he recoiled from her almost as though her vibrancy were a physical force.

He nodded, as if this was what he expected to hear. 'I would consider it a favour if you would listen out for talk of apparitions.'

'All right,' she said, smiling. 'You sure you don't want a quick spearmint julep?'

'Wholly sure.'

'Are you getting short of—'

'Hush!' Dwllis said, glancing at the nearest people. 'Do you want my reputation in tatters?'

Cuensheley laughed. 'Please! Are you sure I can't just get you a small drink? Free, of course, as it's you.'

Dwllis made to leave the courtyard, waving Cuensheley away.

No events of significance had stirred the peace of the Cowhorn Tower so he spent the rest of the day trying to tease information out of antique memories. At dusk, feeling a little restless, he decided to give up the struggle, but before he had cleared away his work a knock on the door startled him.

It was a short, solid man, a Triader guard dressed in an orange cloak, the belt around his pot belly boasting a scimitar. He wore a fish helmet and plastic boots. Any hint of power was ruined by the man's unshaven cheeks and by his ears, which stuck out under the helmet rim.

'I's sent to guard you. Name's Coelendwia, sir.'

This was his protection? Dwllis stared at the man. 'Good evening to you. You're here to protect me against Swamp dangers?'

Coelendwia produced what seemed to be a pair of bellows from the pack on his back. 'This here's a spark rifle, sir. Known efficacy against dangers.'

Dwllis nodded. This was some official's idea of a jest. The fellow must once have been a street urchin, since he was no pyuton. The Triad had considered his appeal and must have found it less than worthy. But Dwllis could not go back now since the humiliation would crush him. This person would have to do.

'What are your hours, my good man?' he asked.

'Dusk to dawn, sir, by the clock.'

Dwllis found the ring of that word 'sir' pleasing. It was a word with the sort of sound he could bask in. He could even like the stubby little fellow. The rifle at least would be worth keeping. Of course, Coelendwia was lacking intellectually, but that no doubt informed his career choice. 'Good,' he said. 'Dusk to dawn it is. Do you own a razor, Coelendwia?'

'Several, sir.'

'A freshly shaven face impresses the opposite sex, I have found.'

Coelendwia seemed puzzled. 'Yes, sir.'

Leaving the tower door ajar, Dwllis asked Etwe to give copies of the lens images to the Triader, so that he knew what to aim at, before sending a message of thanks to the Triader authorities. He returned to tell Coelendwia, 'The thing we have seen is large, some variety of apparition from the miasmas of the Swamps. It's nothing weaponous, you understand, but damnably fearsome. It is fifty feet in diameter, Coelendwia, and floats like a bubble.'

'Is it something you recognise?'

'No.'

'Then knowledge be your best weapon, sir.'

'Yes, indeed, that is the case,' Dwllis murmured, gazing down on his new aide. 'Now, good night. Awake me only if the lens approaches the tower.'

'Yes, sir. Goodnight, sir, sleep well.'

Dwllis locked the tower, then retired with Etwe to their chambers, where he ate supper and read books. Later he manicured his nails and brushed the clothes that he had worn during the day. An hour before midnight they retired to bed.

'Are we safe here?' Etwe asked as they lay side by side under thin blankets.

'Of course we are,' Dwllis replied. 'The Triader owns a spark rifle. Besides, do we not lock up every night?'

Dwllis turned to stroke Etwe's blonde hair, which lay flowing over her pillows. Her grey eyes were closed, but he knew she was faking repose.

'Are you cold tonight?' she asked. Her voice seemed to quaver around the silent room.

'What do you mind?' Dwllis replied. He took one arm in his hand. 'There are temperature receptors in this, but no blood. Does a bit of cold hurt you? Or do your polymer nerves relay it just as figures?'

'I was concerned for you.'

Dwllis lay back. 'I am well enough. Good night.'

5

AEROMORPH

Some days after the meeting with Tanglanah, a few hours before midnight, Aquaitra arrived at Subadwan's front door. Subadwan looked out in great surprise. 'Aren't you meant to be at your special council group?'

'Yes I am,' Aquaitra replied, clearly agitated. 'That's why I *ran* here when you called. What's—'

'I've not called.'

'You didn't call? Yes you did. What's the matter, 'Dwan, what's happened?'

Subadwan laughed. 'Nothing.'

'You called me, frightened—'

'I didn't call you.'

Aquaitra grew angry. 'You did! We spoke, 'Dwan, you said it was desperately urgent, those were your exact words.'

'I didn't call you.'

'You *did*.'

They stood bristling at one another. Subadwan shrugged, then said, 'You'd better run back, else your group'll think badly of you.'

'Do you mean I've come all this way for nothing?'

'Gaya love us, I didn't call you, Aquaitra!'

Without another word, she turned and ran off. Puzzled, and worried at the anger shown by her friend, Subadwan retired into her house.

At the Archive next day Aquaitra remained distant until the afternoon, when she told Subadwan that her council group, at which she was being considered for special honours, went badly. She accepted that Subadwan had not called, but took no blame, and seemed wary when the topic of the call came up. To make matters worse, Subadwan accidentally smashed a memory fishtail belonging to Aquaitra, which for some reason had moved inside its cubby hole so that when the door opened it fell to the ground. Seething with frustration, Aquaitra left early. It seemed to Subadwan that somebody was trying to cause friction between them.

There came a final blow. Rhannan had arranged for herself, Aswaque and Subadwan to meet Lord Archivist Tanglanah later that night to discuss Archive relations. She shrugged. She would have to go.

This bad day left Subadwan in no mood for further intellectual jousting with the suave pyuton, but as early evening merged into late she found herself waiting with her superiors on waste ground by the Ulcerated Courtyard, between the two Archives. 'Did Tanglanah give you any hint as to what she wanted to discuss?' she asked.

Rhannan grumpily replied, 'I only agreed to it to stop her and that cursed adjutant of hers, Laspetosyne, from bothering us. Once this is over I'm going back to the Archive, and we'll have no more wheedling calls from oh so *graceful* Tanglanah.'

Aswaque added, 'No, she did not set an agenda, except to remark that relations between our two

Archives were frosty enough to need thawing.' He nodded to himself.

'Whatever that means,' Rhannan muttered.

Subadwan noted two tall, cloaked figures walking up the lane toward them. 'Well, here they are.'

'Mind your tongue,' Rhannan said. 'I'll do the talking.'

Tanglanah's face was impassive as she approached, and her manner calm, but Laspetosyne's spiky hair seemed ruffled, as if she had run.

Tanglanah spoke with a haughty air. 'I am glad we could find neutral ground on which to discuss our future,' she began. Pointing at the door of the building next to them she said, 'Let us retire inside, there to talk.'

Rhannan suspiciously appraised the one-storey metal house. 'Is this some hide of yours, Lord Archivist?'

'Please call me Tanglanah. We are friends here, or at least not enemies.'

'You haven't answered the question,' Aswaque grunted.

Tanglanah walked to the door and opened it. 'It is perfectly safe.'

'For humans as well as your kind?'

'For all. The public city map, as you well know, refers to it as a warehouse for articles of toughened clothing. It is not property of mine.'

Subadwan followed her superiors into the house. Tanglanah led the way, while Laspetosyne closed the door. They found themselves in a single room lit by glow-bean chandeliers, dust on the floor, cardboard boxes all around. Various small creatures scuttled away as they moved in. Tanglanah placed five boxes in an exact pentagon, then sat on one. Laspetosyne followed suit. Subadwan waited for Rhannan and Aswaque to sit before taking the final box.

A curious and rather embarrassing silence then followed. Tanglanah gazed at all of them with her mesmeric eyes, before glancing to Laspetosyne. Subadwan imagined telepathic messages being sent. She shivered.

'What was that?' Aswaque asked, glancing at nearby holes nibbled into the walls.

'Just ferrophagic vermin,' Laspetosyne said.

'I heard nothing,' said Tanglanah.

'You have good hearing?' Rhannan asked, adding a sarcastic edge to her voice.

'I have the most perfect hearing in the world,' Tanglanah answered. 'It has been tested to seventy thousand cycles per second.'

'What does that mean?'

'It means I can catch the encrypted conversations of bat gliders as their pilots hover above the city simply by angling my head in the correct direction.'

Rhannan laughed as if giving this no credence, but the boast clearly made her nervous, as no doubt it was intended to. 'Can we get on with whatever it was you wanted to discuss?' she said. 'Then perhaps you can leave us to our work.'

Tanglanah nodded. 'It was a question of status.'

Abruptly, Laspetosyne stood and shuffled a pace towards Rhannan, who sat at her side. 'Excuse me,' she said, 'is that an attachment you are wearing?' And with one swipe she pulled off a wig.

Rhannan exploded. 'What do you think you are *doing*?' She snatched the wig and tried to put it back, but in her anger she dropped it. Subadwan, who had before now idly speculated on Rhannan's scalp, sat in astonishment, mouth gaping. Aswaque was his usual unemotional self.

Rhannan stood and pushed Laspetosyne back to her box. 'That is enough! No more of this nonsense. I forbid you and any of your pathetic cronies ever again to contact my Archive. All the systems will be set to bar you.'

They looked at her as if uncaring.

'Did you *hear*? Nothing more!'

With clicking fingers she gestured for Aswaque and Subadwan to join her departure. They made for the door. But as Rhannan reached out for the handle Subadwan felt her body tip forward. The metal floor was breaking into fragments. Suddenly she felt cold air at her face and it was dark – too dark for an ordinary street.

Subadwan was hundreds of feet in the air. The metal building must have risen as they talked.

Falling. Falling fast!

She was plummeting to the Earth.

Rhannan and Aswaque fell at her side. Screeching voices reached her through the tearing wind.

Smells of burning, soot and dust.

The city lay in darkness below her, only its streets visible, like the irradiated veins of a supine creature. Subadwan could see great areas stark black, where no streets led.

Clawing, cycling at the air, she fell, trying to paddle in a motion that must have been wired into her brain, trying to push the air away from her.

If only she could fly!

She groaned as an invisible mass pressed against her chest. It knocked the air from her lungs.

The rushing at her ears lessened. She understood without thought – just from the feel of pressure upon her torso – that she was not free-falling any more.

Like suddenly weighted scraps of cloth, Rhannan and Aswaque dropped into sooty clouds below her, and vanished. Subadwan had no time to consider upon what part of Cray they would meet their deaths.

Unable to determine why she was not falling with them, Subadwan instinctively stretched out her arms and legs, and after a few seconds of flinging her limbs into contorted positions she found a face-down posture that allowed her to descend as gently as a piece of tissue paper.

There was too much fear inside her to think. Below, her superiors already lay smashed.

After a minute she saw that the city was near. Before she knew it she was trying to avoid the flat roof of an alley building.

Too late. Curling into a ball she hit the roof.

She passed through it.

Her feet felt heavy as lead. Blood rushed from her head; or seemed to. She staggered, held out a hand, and found a wall to lean against.

She was standing at the door of the warehouse, Rhannan and Aswaque – white-faced – at her side.

Subadwan turned and ducked, expecting attack, but the building was empty. A noise above her made her look to the ceiling. Something arachnid and pyuter-metallic scrabbled through a hole in the roof, then, like an aerician, spread polythene wings and flew. She knew it must somehow have created the illusion they had just experienced, or at least been the channel along which the illusion had passed.

Rhannan walked out into the street, Subadwan and

Aswaque following. Rhannan looked up at the flying device. 'Some pyuter spy,' she said. 'Bat spawn most likely. Well, that is the last time any of us will have contact with the Archive of Safekeeping. They are a cult of lunatics. Aswaque, you will return to our Archive and instruct all systems to repel any network tainted with the Archive of Safekeeping. Subadwan, return home and prepare a report for internal viewing.'

Subadwan respectfully placed her hands upon Rhannan's shoulders, then dropped them, and asked, 'What happened?'

Rhannan hesitated, then said, 'Doubtless some trick of Tanglanah's. We may never find out.'

'Tanglanah is a bully,' Aswaque echoed.

Subadwan saw then that neither of her superiors had any understanding of the brief period they had just spent in an artificial country, and the realisation made her feel both frightened and emboldened. She asked Rhannan, 'What will you do now?'

'I am going straight down to the Archive of Noct to demand a meeting with the Reeve. This anti-human harassment has to stop. I won't leave until I have assurances, whether he likes it or not.'

Tanglanah returned to the Archive of Safekeeping, walking into a room whose walls were padded plastic, glowing gold and silver as if veins coiled and writhed underneath. At a wave of her hand these images cleared like evaporating mist, to reveal a Crayan landscape, dark, motionless and gloomy.

In a plaza, a hemispherical shape lay, insectoid feet outstretched, mandibles extended, as if it was a tank of war in repose. Tanglanah looked at it for a few moments, then said, as if to the wall, 'Bring constructive interference!'

The picture came to life. Feet scraped the resin of the plaza ground, and mandibles quivered. What was two dimensional acquired depth. The black creature twitched, then moved.

'Tanglanah?' it said.

'Greckoh. I bring news.'

'What happened?'

'We have found our subject.'

A shiver seemed to pass through Greckoh's chitinous body, as if its ahuman mind had caused an electronic ripple. 'Good. Was it one of the superiors?'

'It was Subadwan.'

'What ability did she show?'

'She has the imagination necessary to fly. She was very quick, as if she flew by instinct, but I had already detected something of her vigour during our earlier conversation. The irony is that Subadwan is the one we require, yet her potential marks her out as dangerous to us.'

'She is but a human.'

'Yet a human we need.'

Greckoh paused before remarking, 'The long wait is over. Now the flaw in Cray has fully manifested itself and we have chosen Subadwan, we can start to work in earnest.'

6

THE CEMETERY DRUID

During the week after Coelendwia's arrival the lens appeared most nights. It would emerge from the mists of the Cemetery or the Swamps, sometimes floating up to the Cowhorn Tower as if it wanted to get inside. Brave Coelendwia stood his ground by the door, but the object harmed nobody.

The attraction of the lens to the Cowhorn Tower was unmistakeable. Furthermore, it soon became apparent that only Dwllis could see the spectral images it showed. These images were of a dark, urban landscape occasionally the setting for the figures of women. Once or twice Dwllis saw these figures in detail, but he recoiled from their baroque, sometimes macabre images. Coelendwia stared at the lens for hours, squinting to see in the darkness, but he could make out nothing. Despite its silence, Dwllis felt that the lens was taunting him with its presence, goading him to act. Until he understood its origins, however, he had no idea what he should do.

Dwllis's troubles were legion. Crimson Boney was bringing antique memories every other day, leaving Dwllis with the unsettling feeling that here was an intelligent gnostician. When Crimson Boney burbled and purred at him it was as if the gnostician were speaking – actually trying to converse. Dwllis was shocked by the thought that the gnosticians might be more advanced than people had realised. The fact that Crimson Boney seemed to have some connection with the Archive of Selene only made things more baffling – and far more worrying.

Added to this was the problem of Cuensheley. One day Dwllis met her at a food parlour. The only other person in the parlour was its owner, Belh.

He had been buying provisions – apple bricks, gums of basil, rosemary and spearmint, jars of orange foam, and a good number of mushroom powdercakes, to which he was partial. Cuensheley must have followed him in. If only she would leave him alone. Finding himself short of triad tokens, he heard Cuensheley offer to pay.

'Good day, Cuensheley,' he said, 'it really is no trouble.' He realised that he would lose face whether he put food back or asked for credit. Her presence bothered him.

'I must, I must,' she insisted, laughing at his confusion.

Dwllis felt his face become hot. 'The Triad runs the food parlours and gives us their tokens,' he said stiffly. 'Would you have me break the law through an accidental oversight?'

'Why are you so worried?' Cuensheley replied, taking his basket. 'I'll pay for these.'

Dwllis looked at Belh. He wanted to stop Belh accepting Cuensheley's tokens, but that would be impolite. He struggled to control himself.

Belh asked, 'Is there anything else, Dwllis? We've got some nettle bars—'

'Does he like them?' Cuensheley asked.

Dwllis felt anger welling up. Thickly, he replied, 'That will be all, Belh.'

'Where do you think this food comes from?' Cuensheley asked him. 'It's made in Triad factories and distributed by Triaders. You surely don't think they're going to notice if you pay over their own tokens a day or two late?'

Dwllis, as embarrassed as he had ever been, said nothing.

Cuensheley then said to Belh, 'Put in a few nettle bars.' She turned to Dwllis. 'Don't worry that somebody's being nice to you.'

Dwllis caught Belh looking at them. Immediately Belh looked down at his token register. The atmosphere of the parlour was too tense. Dwllis walked outside.

A minute later Cuensheley stood at his side. He had to lip-read what she said because of the noise. Their hands loaded with baskets, sign language was impossible. 'This is too much for me to carry,' she said. 'Would you help me back to the courtyard, please?'

Dwllis was a master of etiquette. He could not refuse. He wondered if she knew that fact, and was deliberately shaming him. 'With pleasure,' he said, taking two of her baskets. They walked along Sphagnum Street side by side. People will notice this, Dwllis thought, and wonder if they were having an affair.

'Can I ask you a question?' said Cuensheley.

'Certainly.'

'I'm having a music evening at the courtyard tonight, and I want you to come. Consider that an official invitation.'

Dwllis said nothing.

'You're not afraid to come, are you?'

'Afraid?'

'You don't seem to like me.'

'I am partnered,' Dwllis said, hoping that was enough.

'To a pyuton,' Cuensheley pointed out.

'Etwe and I love one another.'

'I often wonder why you live with a pyuton,' said Cuensheley. They had reached the Copper Courtyard, and he gave her the food baskets.

'I have just explained why,' Dwllis said. This line of questioning he did not like.

Cuensheley favoured him with a smile, then, as if on a whim, kissed him on the cheek. Surprised, Dwllis had no time to jump back. Hair ribbons flapping she turned and walked into the courtyard, leaving Dwllis to suffer the glances of smirking passers-by.

He returned to the Cowhorn Tower in poor mood. As he fretted in his study he imagined many excuses for not attending the musical evening, but all seemed artificial, and he knew that if he offered any to Cuensheley she would see them as false, which would cause more difficulties. The woman was a problem, nothing but a problem, with her airy ways and probing questions. He could not imagine why she played these games, unless she was considering blackmailing him over his addiction.

If there was anything truly feared by Dwllis it was arguments. He could not stand the thought of arguments. Anger to him was the worst human failing. So when he announced to Coelendwia that they would that night be making a survey of the Cemetery, and when Etwe then approached at speed, he feared the worst.

'Do not try to stop me,' he told Etwe, hands raised.

'You can't enter the Cemetery,' she said. 'It's too dangerous.'

Coelendwia nodded. ''Tis, sir—'

'Don't stop me!' Dwllis yelled. For a moment, the force of his own voice shocked him. 'Coelendwia, we both will explore the Cemetery for clues to this damnable lens. My mind is quite made up. We shall go tonight.'

'The idea is absurd,' Etwe said. 'Have you taken leave of your senses?'

Dwllis would not tolerate this dissention. Leaving the wide-eyed Triader to gape at Etwe, he hurried into his study and began noisily to prepare a sack of equipment. He knew the plan was risky, but he had decided. He was the Keeper of the Cowhorn Tower, after all, a man of the Reeve himself.

As evening became night, he calmed. Midnight arrived, and he went to see Coelendwia at the front door.

'I am ready. Let's go.'

Coelendwia looked up and down at Dwllis's attire.

'What is it?' Dwllis asked, wondering if he had failed to tie his laces, or somewhere missed a button . . .

'Will you be dressed like that, sir?'

Dwllis looked down at his blue kirtle, silken socks under loafing shoes, and at his splendid azure smoking jacket, which tonight he wore over a ruffled shirt. 'Do you consider it too vulgar for the Cemetery?'

Coelendwia seemed in a dilemma. 'Sir, I must advise you. The Cemetery is a filthy, muddy place choked up with barrows and druidic accoutrements.'

'You think the druids would prefer something paler?'

Coelendwia took a deep breath. 'Sir, I'll be going in tough Triader orange, with big boots and a woolly hat. Follow suit, and . . .'

He left Dwllis to form a conclusion. Dwllis without a word saw that the little man had a point, and offering no alternative view returned to his room to change into hardy clothes, choosing cotton breeches belonging to Etwe, a thick coat and a hat. As an afterthought he put on earmuffs loaded with speech amplifiers.

Thus dressed, they walked down to Sphagnum Street and then north, up Crimson Street until the Morte Street gate appeared.

'We shall enter from this point,' Dwllis said.

'Very good, sir.'

Dwllis paused. 'You had better lead, Coelendwia, on account of your Triader skills.'

'Right you are, sir.'

The gate – two basalt uprights with a monolithic lintel – had no bar, and so they walked through, carefully and with trepidation. Morte Street, petering out at the Swamps wall, was not an illuminated way, and so the only light they had this gloomy night leaked from their hand lamps – wire mesh filled with glow-beans on the end of a string. It did not bode well.

'Do you have any plan, sir?' asked Coelendwia.

'Of course. We shall proceed directly to the centre of the Cemetery, then inch eastward.'

'As you say, sir.'

Since only pyutons were interred here Dwllis knew he would encounter nothing grisly. That left living denizens, including the druids, lone soothsayers declaiming their epigrams from the Cemetery wall, and minions of the Reeve's deputies. Following Coelendwia's hunched figure Dwllis peered to either side, raising and dropping his lamp as the occasion demanded.

Great barrows rose up all around. Mud squelched underfoot. The granite structures were close packed, and soon Dwllis found himself squeezing between chilly blocks until it was difficult to see where they were going. Sometimes he noticed limbs emerging plant-like from the mud, and once he trod on a head. Claustrophobia became intense. When Coelendwia led the way into a dead end, Dwllis spun on his heel: to see a figure standing under a six-foot red lumod, blocking their retreat.

The sight froze him. 'Who are you?' a deep voice said.

The man was wearing a belted cloak and a hood, revealing no clue to his identity. The red light made him seem supernatural, while dust blown off the barrows looked like drizzle floating around him. Dwllis, heart thumping, replied, 'Travellers. Who are you?'

'Are you outsiders?' came the reply.

Dwllis looked at Coelendwia, then returned his gaze to the man. 'We hail from the Rusty Quarter.'

'Outsiders,' the man grunted. 'What are you doing in this realm?'

Truth was probably the best defence. Dwllis said, in the most authoritative voice he could muster, 'We seek the glass lens that of late has been floating from the east.'

This made the man start. 'You seek it?'

Dwllis nodded. 'I am the Keeper of the Cowhorn

Tower, given that honour by the Reeve of Cray. I claim and accept the right to investigate all that troubles my locale.'

'Then you had better follow me. The lens is a swamp object, but wedded to the technology buried here. Your name is?'

'I am Dwllis and this is my manservant Coelendwia.'

The man thought for a moment. 'My name is unimportant.'

'We must call you something,' Coelendwia ventured.

The hooded man laughed and turned, waving for them to follow him. His sleeve fell loose and Dwllis saw a hairy arm scabbed and scarred like a street beggar's. A real man, then.

The man led them up a flight of steps made of quartz blocks, great chunks that must have been settled by machine. The steps led upwards between two barrows twenty feet high or more – barrows that Dwllis noticed were marked with spirals, dots and leaf-sprays of red ochre.

Upon the roofs of the barrows they hopped, following the man, who often would utter a laugh as he performed especially long leaps between stones, until they found themselves at a clearing lit by crescent lumods stuck into the mud. A number of people in pale cloaks milled around below them.

Dwllis took off his earmuffs. The city din was reduced here, composed mostly of aerial noise.

All three men lay down to watch the events below. Very quickly Dwllis realised that the dozen or so people were scribes of the Archive of Selene, circling around something, fuzzlocks bouncing, their white robes muddied and torn. The primitive earthiness offended his sensibilities, but he had to look on. He saw no sign of Querhidwe or any of her deputies.

The man rolled over to Dwllis's side. Dwllis caught the odour of qe'lib'we on his breath. He must be an addict. 'These aliens have been here many evenings since the longest day,' he whispered. 'They bring their dubious symbols and their foul knowledge. It is an abomination.'

'Why do your people not eject them?' Dwllis asked.

'We are permitted by our craft only to touch pyuter species. Besides, battle is dangerous.'

Dwllis knew then what he had half guessed before, that the man at his side was one of the pyutonic undertakers, an awful man of mud, cold, dismemberment and electronic decay. No wonder he considered this place his realm; it was conceptually separate from the city, thick with dread, technologically putrefied. Dwllis was afraid, now, for he realised that here he dealt with something massive and unforgiving: rituals of the electric departed.

He asked the druid, 'Do you believe it is these rituals that have disturbed the object?'

'I think so. The aliens disturb the electronic substrate linking the barrows, but because they have no craft they blunder and bash like infants. But the lens is no ordinary apparition. I have never seen its like.' At this, the druid took from his pocket a chunk of spongy matter, and Dwllis smelled a yeasty odour. His mouth watered and his hands itched.

Heedless of Coelendwia, he said, 'I'll have some of that.'

The druid ripped off a chunk and handed it over. Dwllis popped it in his mouth and began chewing. In moments a warmth rippled through his body, and he felt pure confidence, as if nothing could hold him back. He told the druid, 'These damned scribblers must be stopped. What can you do?'

'We can do nothing.'

'There must be something.'

Dwllis returned his gaze to the scribes. Around a mound of mud they were pacing, chanting, lunar symbols in their hands. Dwllis looked up to see an almost full moon hazy behind city dust, and he could see that it had lost its circular shape. Two lumps were forming at opposite ends, and the body as a whole seemed to be extending.

'Yes,' said the druid, 'Selene is transforming again.'

'Again?' Dwllis asked.

'Many centuries ago Earth possessed a different moon, and that also transformed itself. History is repeating itself.'

Dwllis was stunned by these simple words. Sensitised to historical niceties, he immediately saw their significance. The other Cray that he believed had once stood on this land must somehow be exerting an influence over current events, like the spirit of a dead leader hanging over a congregation.

He asked the druid, 'How do you know all this?'

'Centuries ago my kin lived amidst the Archive of Gaya,' came the reply. 'Although we have split, our tribal memories recall some old stories that the Archives conceal. Do you not see a balance in Cray, city-man? Three Archives support it: that of Selene who is tied to the Earth, that of Gaya, who is but an incarnation of the Earth, and that of Noct, who represents the night that blankets the Earth. A cosmic decision is approaching. Selene transforms and change is mooted, while the people of the Earth fall under a transforming pressure. Truly one will have to stand forth to lead the leaderless.'

These words, spoken in tones ever more doomy, made Dwllis shiver. This druid was no fool. Though isolated from Cray, he possessed vision: he saw, and he thought about what he saw.

'Look now,' said the druid. 'The ritual climaxes.'

Dwllis looked down again. All the scribes were staring into the Swamps mist, as if waiting for a sign.

'What's happening, sir?' Coelendwia asked, his voice tremulous.

'They have twisted the electronic substrate,' answered the druid, 'in an attempt to see images of its interior. The aliens interfere with the realm of the dead. See! The lens appears.'

From the Swamps – not far off – the lens appeared, drifting towards them, then making towards the southern wall of the Cemetery.

'Does it always come from the Swamps?' Dwllis asked.

'Always. It is an object of that place. But few can see the deathly images it focuses.'

Dwllis grimaced. 'I can. Perhaps I should journey into the Swamps to find and understand this lens.'

The druid glanced at him. 'No. Many dangerous folk have their abode there—'

'The Swamps are lifeless,' Dwllis claimed.

'Outsider, they are not. Where the river makes a bend there lies the Isle. I myself have not visited the Isle, but others of my dear kin have. The Swamps themselves are a shifting morass of biochemical traces and self-generating information packages, all set in gel. It is thought by some older druids that the whole area is a pyuter of unimaginable compass. Think on that if you will. Now do you see the depths that you so heartily wish to explore?'

'I did not wish to insult you,' Dwllis said. 'But I am thinking that this lens shows great interest in my tower.'

'What then is inside your tower?'

Dwllis chuckled. 'Memories. Nothing but memories.'

The druid considered this for some minutes, while below, the scribes, having peered into the lens and then banished it, wandered away from the site.

'What do they do that for, sir?' Coelendwia asked.

'I understand little of their ritual,' the druid replied, 'but it seems to me that they seek guidance from the denizens of the lens. Oddly, they do not fear it.'

'Who are these denizens?' asked Dwllis.

'I have seen three. One is a grotesque creature of black with a bag body and chin tentacles like those of the gnosticians, while the other two are human, or almost so.'

'Do the denizens say anything?'

'No. Come, you have seen the origin of the lens. It is time for you to leave this realm and return to your own.'

As they headed back Dwllis felt he had seen too much. Clambering over the Cemetery wall, he stood still and tried to formulate some suitable question that the druid might answer. Eventually he said, 'We have not seen the origin of the lens, rather we have seen it swing in from the Swamps. Do you know more than that?'

'The Swamps are home to many things,' the druid observed.

'You are not being candid with me. Have you seen an image of me inside the lens?'

'Never. But you have?'

'I may have, once or twice. It is difficult to be certain.'

The druid turned away. But before he vanished into the mist Dwllis heard him say, 'We shall meet again.'

Next day, under a flaming dawn sky, Dwllis was once more confronted by Cuensheley. He had intended visiting the Archivist of Selene with whom he had previously spoken, but Cuensheley had other plans. Standing at his door she made plain her grievance. 'I've heard you went out last night. Is that why you didn't come to my evening?'

'Good morning, Cuensheley. I am afraid my manservant and I were out last night, yes.'

'Gadding about,' Cuensheley muttered. 'Where are you going now? You don't usually tramp about the city.'

'Your assessment is inaccurate. I am going to see a friend at the Archive of Selene.'

'I'll come with you.'

Dwllis stepped back. 'As you wish, but be sure that you cannot worm your way into my life by force.'

'I don't want to,' Cuensheley replied with a grin. With her blonde fuzzlocks, crimson and blue ribbons down to her waist, and crisp cream garments, she looked delightful. But Dwllis felt only apprehension over what she might do or say. She handed him a pouch saying, 'That's the week's qe'lib'we.'

Dwllis glanced this way and that like a fugitive. 'Thanks.'

Was this the hold, this simple drug? Illegal it was not, but only lessers and outers succumbed to its narcotic embrace, and the social fall following any revelation of his addiction to the citizens of Cray would be fatal.

They began their walk south. Both wore earmuffs without amplifiers, and so they talked in sign language. Dwllis suspected that Cuensheley would tire of the journey soon, for there was a limit to the time she could be away from the Copper Courtyard. He was not overly worried, though it was embarrassing to be seen in public with her.

He signed, *Who looks after the courtyard?*

Ilquisrey.

Your daughter cannot oversee it for long.

Cuensheley laughed. *She is eighteen and no idiot.*

Dwllis had not made it his business to meet Ilquisrey, and so knew little of her, though rumour had it that she was if anything more vivacious and flighty than her mother.

What troubles you? she asked.

People make problems.

She laughed again. *You prefer gnosticians and pyutons to human beings, do you not?*

If that is a jibe, it is low and impolite.

Manners are not everything. We must seize the passion of the moment.

Dwllis looked at her in surprise. She seemed serious. *Murderers kill out of passion, and I would not follow them.*

You're such a calm, well-mannered man.

Thank you.

Except when you've been on the—

He grasped one of her hands, then signed, *We need not mention that.*

You like it though. Your passions come out from hiding when you chew it.

So you may think.

Cuensheley laughed as if she had scored a point. It struck Dwllis that there could not be two less alike people in Cray. Of course, his interest in pyutons and gnosticians stemmed from his position, and the alleged dislike of people was professional detachment and in no way a symptom of misanthropy as had been suggested. Cuensheley surely knew that. As for the qe'lib'we, he only chewed that once a week, although he had noticed that the pouches had recently been fuller than usual, allowing two portions instead of one.

I like a man who is interested in clothes, she signed.

Dwllis glanced down at his own costume: black frock coat with cream shirt, blue kirtle and black long-socks under purple boots, the whole giving the impression of sober sophistication. He replied, *Do you think it suits me?*

Very much. The boots set it off well.

Dwllis nodded, confirming that her view was correct. They had already reached the Archive on Onion Street, and he signed to her, *I am going in to speak with an acquaintance. I may be some time.*

I am coming with you.

Dwllis shook his head. *I would rather you did not.*

I am coming.

So be it.

Dwllis, Cuensheley a pace behind, entered the cool

and quiet interior of the Archive of Selene and asked a
door flunkey whether any Archivists might be
available.

'Only the Lord Archivist is here of the superior
staff,' Dwllis was informed.

'I shall see her briefly.'

'That will be difficult—'

'Ask her if you please,' Dwllis replied, waving the
flunkey away with a limp-wristed gesture. 'Damnable
lessers,' he said, glancing at Cuensheley.

'I used to be a lesser,' Cuensheley said sharply.

'I apologise, I did not mean—'

'Don't prejudge people and they may like you
better.'

'I am liked well enough,' Dwllis complained.

Cuensheley offered no further observations, and
when the flunkey returned to say that the Lord
Archivist was available, they walked in silence
through the columns and passages of the inner
Archive, until they reached a red plastic door. This was
opened for them.

The chamber they entered was long and narrow,
painted white with lunar decorations picked out here
and there in yellow. A blue stellar carpet lay on the
floor. At the far end sat Querhidwe, partially visible
amongst a pile of crescent cushions also decked
yellow. She looked up from the book she was reading
to gesture them forward. Dwllis took the lead, until he
stood a few yards away.

'Good day, Lord Archivist,' he said. 'Thank you for
this audience. This is Yardkeeper Cuensheley of the
Copper Courtyard.'

Querhidwe was a ragged-looking pyuton, dressed
in a one-piece suit of unbleached material, her dark

hair tousled, her boots dusty. Rumour claimed she was of unstable character. She put down her book and said, 'Why have you come today?'

Dwllis coughed and rearranged his coat to make his speech seem more important. 'Madam, I have witnessed two peculiar events, both related to your august Archive. In my noble capacity as Keeper of—'

'Get on with it, man, for Selene's sake.'

'Indeed. The first involves scribes and recorders of Selene making trouble in the Cemetery, and the second is the astonishing disappearance of a gnostician into your building.'

'You said this has something to do with you?'

Dwllis nodded. 'Madam, even one as genteel as I hears rumours. Folk speak of factions emerging within the Archive of Selene.'

Querhidwe grumpily replied, 'Let them. Is this all you had to say?'

'It is a matter of concern.'

Querhidwe waved him away. 'I suggest you limit your concerns to the Cemetery and the Swamps.'

Thus chastised, they departed. Dwllis said to Cuensheley, 'There is something afoot. The Archive of Selene is experiencing difficulties. Unless I am much mistaken we have just been brushed off.'

Cuensheley nodded. 'I wonder what's going on?'

Dwllis took a deep breath. 'It is my duty to find out.'

Under night gloom the surface of the Swamps twinkled.

Bubbles popped as gases rose from the pulsating depths. Through the biochemical glitter on the surface a multitude of tiny creatures scurried, some insectoid, others pincer wielding, still others hopping on padded feet, so that a maze of dark trails was left entangled amongst the rushes and broken stalks. Occasionally a purple glider would drop on silent wings to snap up the unwary.

Elsewhere, cloaked gentlemen on punts pushed their weary way from an island in the centre of the Swamps to certain outposts, secret and disguised at the perimeter wall.

Free of fog, to the south, a dark and bubbling morass lay surrounded by twitching reeds.

These reeds began to thrash as if something was gnawing their roots, and the bubbles came thick and fast, spurting gel into the air and creating a symphony of squelching slaps. The gaseous eruption brought a smell of musk and cinnamon. Nearby animals fled.

From the depths a creature rose. Emerging between two flanks of gel, with liquids trickling from the hole, its streamlined head first thrashed, then calmed as it stared with yellow eyes at its surroundings. Struggling to be released from its womb, it pounded the gel until it managed to crawl on to a low line of hillocks, where, breathing heavy like a machine exhaust, it rested.

It was a man with a fish head: seven feet tall, muscled like a fighter, a baleful beast. As it lay panting its unblinking eyes gleamed with jaundiced cunning. The cloak it wore crinkled, expanded, and dried, like the wings of an insect emerging from the chrysalis, to become a voluminous garment covering polished armour, thick breeches, and boots shod with metal.

With a great inhalation the creature stood upright. Nearby lay the Swamps wall, and flickering lights from houses off Platan Street. Grunting with exertion it waded across to the wall, climbing it easily, before stamping off Swamps debris.

It strode south, for in that direction was the Archive of Selene.

7

THE ARCHIVE OF SELENE

Autumn settled upon the city, and with it came hordes of achloricians. These scarlet-suited Triaders armed with slicing implements, secateurs, hoes, forks and spades prowled the eight quarters of the city with zeal, cutting down and trampling the dying plant growth, removing even those leaves with only a hint of green. On every street, in addition to glass and grime, great clods of soil were dumped where the achloricians had dug up profusely verdant plants, and many of these clumps crumbled to expose grubs, worms, platelets and springs; but despite their hunger the gasping outers could not eat this food, for all was indigestible, and only mewing flocks of aerician chicks with their hooked teeth and forked tongues took advantage of the feast. Achloricians were not indiscriminate, however; everblue foliage they left undamaged.

But these were not the only groups on the streets, for even the short-sighted agreed that the moon was changing shape, and many Crayans left their houses to look up at the sky and wonder what was happening. From the Archive of Selene there emerged evangelical mobs proclaiming the new age of the moon, and many heeded these words, becoming beholden to Selene's memoirs since they did not doubt the evidence of their eyes. So the hours during which the moon arced from horizon to horizon became giddy street demonstrations, and often it was difficult to walk from one place to another. Amidst the cables, valves, hissing pipes and other street detritus it became common to find discarded lunar sticks, pamphlets lauding Selene's virtues, and softly glowing vinyl crescents, all items manufactured at frantic rate by Archive factories. Many outers took the opportunity to better themselves by declaiming from pedestals, and some acquired fame by this method. Others were cast down, castigated by their friends, or even shot.

After a week of lunar madness there came a response from the Triad. It was unpleasant.

The squads were known as noctechnes. They dressed entirely in black. Each was armed with one truncheon, one energy rifle, and a serrated scimitar. To further intimidate the populace they painted black images of fish skulls and saw-toothed daggers on their cheeks. Fins sewn upon the spines of their costumes were steel spiked. It soon became clear that their task was to dampen the lunar ardour of ordinary Crayans, for they would threaten Selene's clerks, even when these unfortunates were speaking in public, and sometimes they would arrest citizens at random. Nobody was killed or injured, but the experience was gruelling. A silent hatred began to form against the Reeve Umia and his Archive of Noct. But the noctechnes carried out their duties as if ignoring the world.

It was only the more observant who noted, with sinking hearts, that Cray's gnosticians also suffered harassment from the noctechnes, and wondered what horrors such barbarism presaged.

Dwllis became frustrated. Events of late – the appearance of the lens, his Cemetery jaunt, trouble with gnosticians, and events surrounding the Archive of Selene – had caused him grief, and often he found himself, at dead of night, pacing the chambers in which his antique memories were kept, wondering if the knowledge they contained mattered at all. The pain of Querhidwe's rejection had in particular disconcerted him. And since seeing Crimson Boney enter the Archive of Selene by a back door, he had been tormented by his inability to make a link between the Archive and the gnosticians. Then of course there was the question of the transforming moon. Somehow, the calm, rational, *plebeian* life that he had led seemed a shadow in the past. He felt almost an obligation to act. He *needed* to go out, go out into the city and discover things. Sitting reading ancient scripts no longer seemed enough. Etwe tried to dissuade him, but he ignored her and demanded that she continue manufacturing interfaces.

Luckily he possessed stocks of qe'lib'we. He found that spongy substance useful when concocting plans. It was in such a mood, mechanically chewing, his mind a fecund haze, that he conceived the idea of breaking and entering.

Immediately he realised he could not do it alone. Etwe was useless: so was the rather dense Coelendwia. He required somebody loyal and intelligent.

Cuensheley? No, she would take advantage of him.

But further chewing failed to provide inspiration. There was no alternative. Galling though it was, he would have to ask Cuensheley for help. No longer could he sit here and vegetate.

He found it almost impossible next morning to

speak to her. For some minutes he wandered the alley outside the Copper Courtyard, turning over in his mind certain phrases, suggestions, particular ways of asking her for help, before entering and settling at his usual table. When Cuensheley saw him she hurried over.

'You already run out of—'

'Good morning, Cuensheley,' he interrupted. 'Do you have a moment to listen to a proposition?'

Immediately he regretted that word. Her eyes shone.

'A suggestion,' he said, 'that is what I meant.' He lowered his voice. 'I have been thinking about the Archive of Selene. We have got to discover what is going on in that lunar place. Do you agree?'

'I agree, and it worries me, but what can we do?'

'I need an accomplice – no, an assistant. An assistant. I think it is time we . . . well . . . what say we wander around by ourselves when there's nobody there?'

Excitement was plain on her face.

'I'm serious,' he said. 'It would be no walking party.'

'I realise that,' she replied. 'Of course I'll help. I want to know why all this trouble's started too.'

'I'll pay you for your trouble, so the relationship is not one of favours.'

'I'm not accepting money,' Cuensheley protested. 'I'm your friend.'

Dwllis tried to smile, but it came out as more of a grimace. 'Tomorrow it is new moon, and the Archive is empty when Selene is empty. We must go inside tomorrow night.'

'Without fail,' said Cuensheley, a gleam in her eyes. 'Thank you for asking. I won't ruin it, don't worry. Before I had Ilquisrey, I used to be look-out for a drug-running gang.'

Startled, Dwllis sat back. 'You did?'

'Oh, yes.'

Now Dwllis did laugh. 'In fact, being look-out was what I wanted of you.'

Cuensheley reached out and put her hand on his. 'It's nice when you laugh. You don't laugh often.'

Dwllis withdrew his hand. 'I am not often amused.'

'You must have some sense of humour to have hatched this plan.'

'You think it a joke?'

Cuensheley shook her head. 'It's inspired. But it's too eccentric for you to have thought it up. No, you *dreamed* it up.'

Dwllis was silenced by these words. She was alluding to the drug, he knew, but in her fanciful way she was making light of serious affairs. He just did not know how to deal with her: she was serious, and yet frivolous; profound, and yet . . .

The next day he spent inside the Cowhorn Tower, interrupted only by Crimson Boney bringing more memories. He took a walk in the afternoon gloom, a brief jaunt around Sphagnum Mews. It was so dark, dark as night, that he had to increase the power on the lumod he carried, though he was able to reduce it once he reached the glittering Sphagnum Street.

At dusk there developed a blood-red sunset that lit the city for a while, creating a myriad of crimson sparks from the vitrified buildings of the Blistered Quarter, sparks that, in columns of dust, seemed to float like fire motes into the heavens, rising on thermals then falling back again, ever cycling, following the convection patterns of hot and cool air.

That evening Dwllis and Cuensheley, dressed in dark clothes and carrying backpacks, walked down through the Blistered Quarter, past Westcity Power Station, across into Eastcity and along Hog and Broom Streets, leading them to the alley upon which the rear of Selene's Archive abutted. Here, Dwllis pointed out the grilles through which he intended making an entrance. Cuensheley nodded. The alley, a narrow passage with perspex dimly lit, was occupied only by them. Its nearer end was visible from the Archive wall, and that end Cuensheley watched while Dwllis eased free the rusty grille. Soon he and Cuensheley had squeezed into a low-roofed chamber, the grille loose but upright behind them.

Dwllis uncovered his lamp – pink glow-beans in a mesh – and, after brushing the dust off his clothes with a sharp *tsk, tsk*, he looked around.

They were in a simple store room. Cheap gimmicks of glowing yellow were scattered about. The floor showed a faint luminosity, gleaming dust and scraps. One door led out and this they opened: it led into a corridor.

From his records, Dwllis had a mental picture of the Archive plan, but he suspected that he ought to go *down*. Seeing steps, he indicated with exaggerated gestures that they should descend. He was not so simple as to think the place wholly empty, but he knew they had little chance of meeting anybody.

He shrugged. Descending further, he saw he had taken the correct route. Twenty feet or so below ground level, where the steps opened out, he saw a plastic door on which the silhouette of a gnostician had been glued.

'This could be it,' he said. 'We begin here.'

'Be careful, Dwllis.' Cuensheley whispered.

'Keep a look-out while I investigate.' But the door was locked. Dwllis glanced at Cuensheley, and she produced a roll of lock picks. This was a disconcerting sensation for Dwllis, since he was used to people not understanding him. With quick flicks of the wrist she picked the lock.

'Easy,' she remarked.

The door was heavy – heavier even than the door to the Cowhorn Tower – and it took both of them to make a gap wide enough for Dwllis to slip through.

The room looked like a laboratory of some kind. It was a hundred feet long and half as wide, a cold chamber thrumming bassy with city reverberation. One side was laid out with metal tables, the other a jumble of apparatus, empty pyuter screens, pyuter rigs stacked haphazard like boxes; and everywhere wires. There were thousands of wires. The place was unlit. Dwllis's glow-beans threw fluttering shadows black as Noct breath.

On the metal tables, of which there were eight, gnosticians were laid out. They were alive but unconscious. Bizarre, as if belonging to a lunatic's dream, they lay insensible. Dwllis couldn't bear to look at their faces, and it was all he could do to stop himself running out. A stack of pyuters lay tempting, linked to a large screen laid flat on a desk, and Dwllis felt he had to operate it. From a clay pot standing next to the screen he poured a measure of fluid, covering the miniature joints of the base, the liquid expanding like warm gel with a rainbow static following its leading edge. Seconds later an opening screen flickered into view, upon it twenty small boxes shaped as lips; the entrances to pyuter routines. Noting one set of lips labelled 'gnos', Dwllis opened it with a mounted needle.

A holograph screen surrounded his head.
Information was dense and not labelled for the
uninitiated, and so he found it difficult to absorb what
was present. Most of it seemed to be reports and documents concerning mental augmentation performed on
gnostician subjects from the west of the city. But
when, with mild shock, he noticed a document
labelled with Crimson Boney's image he knew he had
found a data nugget.

Mild shock became horror. Crimson Boney had
been mentally augmented by Selene's Archivists.
Worse, the gnostician had been deliberately sent into
the city to find memories and take them to the
Cowhorn Tower. There, nestling at the bottom of the
report, was Dwllis's own picture.

The feelings Dwllis felt turned his stomach.
Repulsed, he ducked out of the holograph screen and
leaned over one of the gnostician tables. These
creatures were almost sentient: perhaps they were
sentient, conscious like human beings. All this time
everybody had considered them little more than clever
animals. The clerks of the Archive of Selene had guessed
this after much research, and now were using their
knowledge to further their own interests, whatever
those might be. The medical reports mentioned no
goals. These poor creatures had been violated, had been
forced to accept veins of biotechnology into their heads.
Dwllis felt an upwelling of sympathy and pity in his
body, and as he leaned over the table he also felt great
anger at what had been done. He did not know what to
do with his emotions, and so, for a few moments, he
just stayed put, breathing quickly. Amazed.

A shadow moved – something at his side. He stood.
The gnostician was quick as a light mote. It grabbed

his hand and bit with its mouth. The bandages around its head flapped. It screamed, a hideous though muffled noise like an engine overstretched.

Dwllis pulled back. His right hand felt numb.

He heard somebody at the door, but looked at his hand. His thumb, first finger, and part of his palm were gone. They were in the gnostician's mouth. It was rolling around on its table.

Blood spurted.

Throat constricting, Dwllis grabbed his right hand, trying to stop the blood. He was too shocked to breathe.

He wailed like a child. Cuensheley was at his side.

The blood stank. He missed what happened next. He stood in limbo, clutching his hand. Cuensheley was doing something, yelling for him to keep still.

A tourniquet at the wrist. She was pulling him from the room.

He found himself outside the room. A thought took him: he yanked himself out of her grip.

'My hand!' he managed to gasp. 'They'll find it! They'll trace me!'

Swearing, Cuensheley disappeared back into the room. Dwllis heard voices above. Archive folk. They were discovered.

'Hurry!' he whispered.

She reappeared.

'Turn the pyuter off—' he began.

'Fool!' she hissed at him. 'Shut up. There's somebody coming.'

Dwllis, panicking, looked around for something to hide behind. Cuensheley pulled him. He tripped, hardly able to see where he was going. She caught him, tugged him on.

The voices were near. The sound of his own breathing seemed to fill his world. He was convinced they would be caught. Dark faces would appear, eyes would see him.

Reality seemed to be notched. Consciousness was cracking. He could not feel his hand. He found himself stumbling up stairs, Cuensheley at his side, the sound of harsh breathing in his ears. His arm ached.

'Shush!' Cuensheley hissed. Somebody walked past. He did not know if he was hiding or awaiting capture.

Then they were in the room through which they had entered. Cuensheley put boxes at the grille and pushed him up. With great difficulty he scrambled out through the gap, aware that he must not knock his right hand – the reeking Crayan air had brought him around – and that he had escaped. Almost. He heard the crash and squeal of heat exchangers and local electronic installations, and he wished for silence. Staring, he surveyed the alley for passers-by: nobody. Cuensheley was at his side.

'Can you hear me?' Cuensheley said, her mouth at his ear. 'We haven't got long. I'm going to have to loosen that tourniquet. Stand still.'

He submitted to her expert aid. The ache in his hand became an unbearable throbbing, deep inside his flesh it seemed, a bone-ache that made him want to shake his limb off to free himself. He groaned, bent double. He felt Cuensheley adjusting the tension of the tourniquet.

'Quick,' she said. 'We've got to get to the Copper Courtyard as soon as we can. Can you walk?'

He could not answer; his jaw was clamped. He nodded. There was no pain, just the ache, the worst ache he had ever felt. He smelled blood again. When a light mote storm passed through the street perspex he saw pools of red, lit like miniature sunsets. There was blood everywhere.

'They'll follow us,' he managed to gasp.

Cuensheley wrapped his wounded hand in her jacket, then pulled him away from the Archive wall, hurrying him to the end of the alley, checking for crowds – there were no mobs, but some groups of people walking to and fro – then, with the injured hand slung as well as was possible in Dwllis' coat, leading him along the street. Nobody paid attention to them. They were too busy watching Selene's clerks in dispute with the noctechnes. As they hurried along Hog Street and Culverkeys Street they saw a great variety of people; lone demagogues, crowds listening to the lunar clerks, sinister noctechne squads with their cloak-fins erect, Triaders out with shovels and cloths attempting to clear up the piles of glass. As they followed Platan Street around the Swamps, Dwllis noticed that vitrification was beginning to attack houses even here, and there were many pitch black alleys where luminophage clumps had done their worst.

They stumbled into Sphagnum Street, mercifully quiet, then made along the passage leading to the Copper Courtyard. It was midnight, and nobody remained inside the quadrangle. Dwllis collapsed.

Then he heard Cuensheley and Ilquisrey at his side. The tourniquet was loosened: the ache became unbearable and he rolled and groaned, a rhythmic motion, unable to stop. The bandage was off. He felt blood soak his clothes.

He felt faint now, aware that he was being saved, knowing the two women were to his left and right, not knowing what they were doing. He lost consciousness for brief seconds, then came round, then fainted again.

'His gums are white,' Ilquisrey said.

He looked into her eyes. Her jet black fuzzlocks were tied into a bun. Her oval face with its mysterious kohl-circled eyes loomed close over him. Her breath stank of alcohol.

'Hold that bandage,' Cuensheley demanded.

'Has he gone?'

Dwllis hovered around unconsciousness. He realised that he had been transferred to a soft couch, but he did not know where: in a room somewhere. Somewhere warm.

'Chew this,' Ilquisrey said, thrusting a spongy mass into his mouth.

He thought it must be qe'lib'we, but the taste was bitter, painfully bitter, with a throat-clearing burn like bad wine. He coughed, spraying the stuff everywhere. They thrust more into his mouth. He opened his eyes to see Ilquisrey carrying a large tray full of coloured lumps.

'Drugs!' he croaked.

'Shut up!' Cuensheley replied.

'We're experts on drugs,' Ilquisrey said. 'You'll be all right.'

Dwllis relaxed. 'Don't be angry at me, please,' he said.

Cuensheley bent down and hugged him. 'What has that beast done to you?' Her tears wetted his face.

Dwllis could not look at his hand, lacking the strength. 'Bit it off,' he gasped. 'Where am I?'

'Home,' Cuensheley said: and even in his state Dwllis heard the sourness in her voice. He chewed, glad he did not have to say anything.

The hours until dawn – he knew it was dawn because the walls and roof of the room in which he tossed and turned grew crimson – Dwllis spent slipping between consciousness and unconsciousness, aware that women were sitting near, remembering now and then who they were, but never able to ignore the ache in his hand. The throbbing ebbed and rose. The substances he was given reduced the pain, but they robbed him of sleep and made him hallucinate. Once, he imagined that he was back inside the Archive, chased by glass-wielding gnosticians, and fat, lolloping agnosticians with infant papooses on their backs.

Nor was he ever able to forget the scream of the gnostician that had attacked him. The sound echoed through his mind like a wail in a cave.

Shortly before midday, Ilquisrey entered his room carrying a tray on which a large mug steamed. 'Tea,' she said. Her throaty voice sounded sympathetic. Dwllis felt a sudden urge to know her. He had not realised it until now, but, alone with his nightmare, he was desperate for companionship.

'What is it?' he asked.

'Strawberry tea laced with morphino and aq'ailbar.'

'What are those substances?'

'An analgesic and a relaxant.'

'I see.'

'You need relaxing,' Ilquisrey said, opening his mouth and making him sip the tea. Some minutes later he had finished it. The fire of it burned his throat and stomach. 'Yes, it is strong,' Ilquisrey said.

He asked her, 'Was that qe'lib'we you gave me earlier?'

'Oh, no, something much more dangerous.'

'What?'

She stroked his sweating forehead. 'You're so pale. You lost a lot of blood. But Mum thinks you're brave.'

'Does she?'

'She often talks about you.'

'What does she say?'

With a sly grin Ilquisrey answered, 'I think you'd better ask her yourself.' She stood, loosened her black fuzzlocks so they tumbled down her back, thrust her hands into her pockets, then left the room humming to herself.

8

Umia's Advisers

Umia knelt on the floor of his chamber, peering into the lower hemisphere. Was this where the voices came from? He examined the riot of mud, sand and weird white plants of local origin, plants that did not need the light of the sun to create food but instead used the energy of sound and vibration. The light of pink glow-beans showed nothing suspicious.

Now he stood alone. And yet two disembodied voices counselled him, arguing this way and that.

'What should I do about the glass?' Umia said out loud.

Gaijin, the lighter, more reedy voice said, 'You can do naught about it, O Reeve. Glass comes inside your Cray, like the wind through open bars, and an overcoming is inevitable.'

Lune, whose voice chimed deeper in Umia's mind, like an old bell, said, 'Do not listen to Gaijin, for she spouts the counsel of the desperate, the desolate. Your Archivists work night and night to create the bacteria that will remove the luminophages from the world, and they are close to success. Umia, you listened to me when I advised you to create the sonoplasts, and you did right. Do not ignore me.'

But Gaijin said, as Umia in an agony of indecision leaned over a table and cradled his head, 'O Reeve, you listen to Lune, yet the selenic pervert natural justice. The noctechnes do hale work, do they not? O for the memoirs you have to rule over all.'

'Yes,' Umia said, 'Noct must prevail, but what about my people? They scream and crush in the streets, they are slashed by glass, they are attacked by metal tapeworms and silver grubs emerging from the very walls. What of my people?'

Lune replied, 'The important thing is to rid Cray of the luminophages. The flaw in the city must be understood. But hark, someone comes.'

Umia stood straight. There was a single knock at the only door into the chamber. He called, 'Yes?' and a young officer walked in, a chief Triader administrator in orange breeches and a grey cloak with two dorsal fins, her brown fuzzlocks tied back with a black ribbon. She said, 'Reeve, I bring the report as promised.'

Umia waved at her impatiently. 'Read it, read it.'

She took a scroll from an inner pocket and began to read. 'Reeve, the report reads as follows—'

'Get on with it!'

'Second Deputy Ciswadra reports that a sonoplast has been engineered that uses fifty per cent of ambient sound to produce energy. The bacteria into which these sonoplasts were injected lived two minutes and thirty-six seconds before dying. The DNA of these sonoplasts has been analysed and a short section of the end group of bases is being altered. The new DNA will be tested inside the pyuter environment before being manufactured by micro factories. The side effects are that the equipment in which the bacteria lived was transformed to yellow plastic. However, the glass was transmuted successfully. First Deputy Heraber is of the opinion that in a few weeks a bacterium will be created that can be released into the city.'

Umia waved away the administrator. Alone, he sat at a desk, chin on hands, a dejected expression on his face. 'What shall I do?' he said to himself.

Soon he heard the voices again. He could not tell from where they came, or even if they were real, though they seemed real. Lune said, 'Umia, your great time is approaching. If the sonoplasts are efficient enough the glass wave can be turned back and Cray can be saved. Doubt not that the luminophagi units create this glassy plague in their dark night masses, create transparency in their luminophagous frenzy, thereby to bring more light to themselves.'

But Gaijin responded, 'You I advise otherwise, O Reeve. Lune is not to be trusted. Gnosticians are evil beasts. They work with glass. They hold one of the keys.'

Umia said, 'Lune, glass becomes opaque if it is thick enough! Why should I believe you, why should I believe this story of making transparency to pass more light?'

'This is the heart of luminophage strategy, Umia. Light is energy. If it is halted, the organism dies. In creating an almost completely transparent environment the organism makes conditions that are most beneficial for itself, thereby to survive and pass on its silicon genes. Cray is a city overpowered by noise. Since you cannot use light energy, you must use sound, and if you succeed you will halt the glass and create day from night.'

Gaijin scoffed at this, saying, 'Noct is our epitome, O Reeve, and you are tied to Noct. May you never leave this chamber while you are Reeve and the scion of Noct? No you may not! There exists a hierarchy of people to do your will – stern, tough, so there is no softness. For softness kills, O Reeve. Noct and you are hard as night.'

Umia paced around his chamber, before turning to the black statue and staring up into its ebony face. Only the opal eyes and lips were not black. 'Save me, Noct!' he cried. 'Each new Reeve kills the previous Reeve. I killed your previous servant and chucked her body down below for the plants to suck on. I did that. Save me now and never let anybody enter this chamber carrying a weapon.'

'Hands strangle,' Gaijin pointed out. 'Boots kick heads in. Teeth rip out throats, bite eyes. Hands stuff tongues down throats, cave in windpipes—'

'Noct,' Umia said, ignoring Gaijin, 'I am not afraid of somebody coming for me, but I do fear being unable to carry on. Succour my talent, Noct, let me continue, let me remove the accursed loping purple invaders for ever.'

Umia walked away from the statue and collapsed into a chair, exhausted.

Lune said, 'The two Archivists below you in the hierarchy, Heraber and Ciswadra, will never hatch plots to become the new Reeve of Cray.'

Umia retorted, 'How do you know?'

'And what of Querhidwe?' said Gaijin. 'You, O Reeve, must do something about her Archive or it will control your city.'

But Lune said, 'Fear nothing from Selene. Fear only the plots of Gaijin, for she is a hater of human beings. And do not fear Gaya!'

'Distrust Gaya,' Gaijin said.

'Embrace her,' suggested Lune.

Umia stamped his foot. 'I'll *never* embrace her!'

9

IN THE ARCHIVE OF GAYA

One day, Subadwan had to visit the Water Purification House in Feverfew Street, on account of brown water trickling from taps and standpipes throughout the Archive. Having been told that the problem was due to glass fragments and dust choking the lower sewers of Westcity, and that she and all the other residents of upper Westcity would have to wait until Triader aquanauts cleared the tunnels, she could do nothing but return to the Archive. She had half expected to get nowhere, since city pyuter networks had refused to connect her with the Water Purification House. As she passed through the Blistered Quarter she saw some houses half-plastic half-glass, patchworks of darkness and twinkling light set with polythene bricks chewed by silicon grubs. Street cables, some of which she had to swing aside to pass, were also succumbing to heat damage, and under these no outers lay. Where vitrification was bad it was often the case that pipes, cables, wires and tubes were twisted together and pegged to one side, out of danger, so that Subadwan had to crouch and slide to make progress. But the street was not only choked with cables: piles of white glass dust glittering with

larger fragments lay everywhere, causing many
citizens to don masks as well as their earmuffs.

Subadwan looked up into the sky. It was noon, yet
dark. Through grimy air she could see the moon, an
oval now with one triangular end. All around her
stood awe-struck Crayans. They even gazed up from
the crowded roofs of the city, braving the fantastic din
there. Subadwan settled her earmuffs over her ears
more comfortably and hurried on, the manic sparkling
streets lighting her way, while, above, the inde-
pendently moving twin searchlights of bats created
shifting columns of sickly light.

The Archive grounds were thronging, bustling
pedicians jumbled up with cloaked folk, lumods
everywhere creating a kaleidoscope of light, the golden
ground invisible. Subadwan had no alternative but to
forge a way through, signing with impetuous hands,
*Make way. I am Archivist Subadwan. Make way for
me.*

Inside, the public chambers were crowded, smelling
of dust, sweat and pedician manure. Subadwan
hurried upstairs to her own chamber, grabbing her
clothes – blue gown and boots, with a sheaf of golden
ribbons for her fuzzlocks – and putting them on. In
front of a mirror she washed her face, clipped speech
amplifiers to both ears, replaced the opal studs with
blue sleepers, drank a shot of spearmint alcohol, then
tied back stray fuzzlocks. Minutes later she was
standing with Aquaitra on the podium of the public
chamber, a great hall packed with three or four
thousand people, Rhannan and Aswaque nearby.

Aquaitra sidled over to her. 'Everything all right,
'Dwan?'

Subadwan nodded. This was not the time to

mention the encounter with Tanglanah and Laspetosyne.

'Rumours of trouble at Selene's,' Aquaitra said.

'Trouble?'

'Some ghastly creature's muscled his way into the Archive, bullying the elder Archivists. Very strange.'

Subadwan grimaced, then nodded. 'I heard something about that. A warrior with the head of a fish. Must be a pyuton mutant. Gaya save us from such vermin—'

Rhannan held up her arms and signed to the crowd, *Quiet*.

Aswaque, at her side, signed, *It is Gaya's time*.

A twin detonation from the rear of the hall made the assembled laity gasp and look behind them. Two smoke trails in the air. Something flying over.

Subadwan glimpsed two black faces flashing by.

Rhannan screamed. Aswaque yelled and sank to the floor. Before Subadwan could turn to see what had happened somebody at the front of the hall screeched, 'Headbreakers! Headbreakers!'

Scant seconds had passed. Subadwan turned, saw Rhannan and Aswaque on the ground, their heads capped by a black hand, or so it seemed.

The crowds screamed and panicked. Everyone was shoving for the doors at the back.

Subadwan stared petrified at Rhannan and Aswaque. The headbreakers were clasped to their skulls. With a splintering crack both skulls split along the crown. Blood and brains spilled out. Subadwan stood mere yards away. Blood splattered her clothes.

Aswaque's body lay still: Rhannan twitched.

Assassination. Subadwan stood rooted to the

ground. She could not even scream because her tongue was stuck to the roof of her mouth. Assassination.

Aquaitra must have run towards her. Subadwan was knocked to the ground, a screaming voice in her ear. Galvanised, she sprang to her feet and ran to the edge of the podium, as far away from the bodies as possible, then turned to stare at the carnage. The din of the panicking crowds almost made her panic, but she was too fascinated by the bodies to let herself go.

The black creatures melted across the podium, becoming two puddles of stinking tar. Aquaitra was standing over the bodies.

Aquaitra turned. 'What—'

Using Archive cant Subadwan signed, *Quiet*.

Aquaitra nodded. 'Yes, Lord Archivist.' It was said without sarcasm – naturally, automatically. Subadwan stared at Aquaitra, horrified. It was true. She *was* Gaya's Lord Archivist.

Then she looked down at the brains and gore, and felt numb.

Still the people were screaming in flight. The hall was half empty but strewn with bodies, some motionless, some struggling, some jerking like electric puppets. There was nothing Subadwan could do to stop the crush. Twenty, thirty bodies she could see.

Subadwan ripped down the curtains at the back of the podium and covered both bodies. She caught sight of a plastic-armoured doorwarden. 'Open all doors,' she shouted. 'Get the other doorwardens. Issue emergency orders, everyone out of the Archive. Take anybody living to the hospice wardens. Take the bodies outside, cover them. Find two plastic coffins. Quick, do it!'

'At once Lord Archivist.'

'And don't call me Lord Archivist!' Subadwan yelled after the man.

'Subadwan, you *are*,' Aquaitra insisted.

'Leave me alone,' Subadwan said. She now felt an urge to leave the podium, leave the chamber, so that nobody would be able to stare at her. 'Direct the doorwardens,' she told Aquaitra.

'But the assassin—'

'Gaya's love, the assassin's long gone! Now do what I say.'

Aquaitra nodded – it was almost a bow – then ran off. The hall was quietening, only a few hundred people clustered to the rear, some still shouting, others staring back at the stark scene.

Hardly able to breathe, Subadwan ran all the way to the apex of the Archive, where she stumbled into Rhannan's room and slammed shut the door.

She sat, not in Rhannan's chair but in the chair that always stood on the opposite side of her desk. Golden light shone bright. Subadwan had no idea how to dim it. At the table of brews she poured herself more spearmint alcohol, but then found herself unable to drink it. She did not know what to do; what to feel. She worried that she felt nothing. Then, walking around the chamber in a circle – not realising this was what she was doing – she worried what people were thinking below.

They would be thinking of her, of course. All thoughts would ascend to this chamber. But Subadwan just wanted to remain alone. She scribbled a note on a sheet of plastic and stuck it to the outside of the door: *No entry. I will appear shortly. Do not knock. No pyuter messages*.

But as she sat down again, a husky pyuter voice said, 'The Reeve is on line, Lord Archivist—'

'Don't—' Subadwan stopped herself.

'The Reeve wishes to speak.'

Subadwan sighed. 'Let him through.'

A vertical gel-screen became illuminated, tiny imperfections giving the face of the old man depicted there an aqueous image, distorted in waves. The age of the screen made his skin sallow and his wrinkles brown.

'Lord Archivist Subadwan,' he said, 'I have just heard the terrible news.' He paused. 'I am talking to the Lord Archivist of Gaya, am I not?'

'You are, Reeve.'

'Of course, we must make immediate arrangements for you to be inducted into the Triad—'

Subadwan uttered a single laugh. She felt sudden anger. 'Gaya praise us, don't think you can inveigle *me* into your web of corruption. I refuse utterly.'

Umia seemed surprised. 'Do I hear aright?' For some seconds the sound transmitted from the Archive of Noct seemed to die, before a hum returned, and Umia said, 'The law states that the Lord Archivist of Gaya be a member of the five. You have no option but to become one of the Triad. Doubtless you are shocked, and that is why your manners have temporarily failed you.'

Subadwan, the anger within her making her voice quaver, replied, 'I shall never be one of the Triad. Never, *never*. It's an organisation of partisans and fools. I shan't attend a single meeting, even if you name me the fifth member against my will.'

'This cannot be,' Umia said, shaking his head.

'Do you think I don't know what this is all about? You're afraid of our Archive. And you're afraid what will happen if you can't control it. That's why you're making this call.'

'I will leave you for now,' Umia said with dignity. 'You have not heard the last of this matter, be assured.'

The call left Subadwan with raw nerves, numbness already departed. She felt no sorrow, only anger. And in her mind there formed an inkling of pressures to come.

'Lord Archivist Querhidwe wishes to speak with you,' said the pyuter. Its throaty voice, designed to soothe, only irritated her.

Subadwan's defocussed gaze traversed the chamber. Though it had been created from plastic, fat lumps carried accidentally from walls lower in the Archive had formed greasy spots, so that parts of the chamber looked diseased. The furniture was of clumsy design. Subadwan felt an urge to recreate the entire place.

Frustrated, she sighed. 'I suppose I'll have to hear what the pyuton's got to say.'

Querhidwe's face appeared on screen. 'My dear Subadwan,' she said, 'a minion has just informed me of what has happened. My commiserations. Terrible, quite terrible. Is there anything I can do?'

'Nothing.'

Querhidwe nodded. 'As I thought. Rhannan and I had many agreements, Subadwan, and I expect these to be continued—'

'Expect nothing,' Subadwan snapped. 'I'm not Rhannan.'

Again the inscrutable pyuton nodded. 'You are Subadwan, of course. Still, you are a function of your Archive, an official figure, the mortal figurehead in fact—'

'I should have thought you had enough problems with bullying freaks in your own Archive, never mind harassing me!' Angrily, Subadwan slapped her hands on the table. 'Pyuter, terminate this call.'

Querhidwe's face vanished.

'There is a call from the Senior Administrative Officer of Triad Tower.'

With a yell Subadwan flung a tankard at the screen, but it bounced off. 'No more calls!'

'Lord Archivist,' said the pyuter voice respectfully.

Yes, the numbness had gone. Already shock was over. Subadwan felt immense anger, and fear at what this anger might do. The assassinations had propelled her, a twenty-five-year old, into a position she did not want. Responsibility could oppress.

First, she had to stop people calling. The pyuter voice emanated from a stack of rigs. She initiated a recording for general release to the networks. As she spoke she signed, for non-lipreaders watching on public city screens.

'Crayans. Rhannan and Aswaque have been assassinated by headbreakers at the Archive of Gaya. There is no news on those responsible. In due course the investigation will become public. I, Subadwan, am the Lord Archivist of Gaya. Aquaitra is Second Archivist. The Archive of Gaya will reopen tomorrow.'

As Subadwan finished she heard the sound of boots outside her door: people reading her note. She waited, but nobody knocked. They were shuffling around outside, though, and she did not want that.

'Tell the people outside to go away,' she told the pyuter.

A muffled voice relayed her commands. Footsteps sounded, then receded. Breath held, Subadwan listened. Nobody there. She was alone again. It was what she needed.

Until the scarlet clouds of sunset dissolved into

purple gloom Subadwan stayed in the apex chamber, thinking of what had happened, drinking enough alcohol to calm herself though not enough to dull her thoughts, letting her mind sort out its own chaos. After dusk, she knew she was the Lord Archivist. The truth lay in her mind and shock could not blunt it any more.

People looked at her askance when she reappeared. Doorwardens and recorders prowled the deserted, echoing building, but many of the Archivists were also present, typically talking in small groups as if with nothing to do. They fell silent when Subadwan approached. 'Carry on,' she told them, not stopping.

It was Aquaitra she wanted. She needed to talk with her deputy, and there was the matter of the Third Archivist to appoint. That would have to be poor Gwythey, middle aged and shy, who like herself would not want the sudden responsibility.

Aquaitra appeared from a door. 'Over here,' Subadwan called.

Aquaitra approached, placing her hands on Subadwan's shoulders in respect. Unexpected, the gesture embarrassed Subadwan. They stood alone in a low-roofed chamber. She found that she was trembling. She had thought that all her feelings were done with, gone, expressed, but it seemed not.

'Who did it?' asked Aquaitra.

Subadwan had thought little on that question, just as she did not want to think about the black faces, the blood, those moments of shock. 'An assassin,' she replied.

'What will we do?'

'Appoint Gwythey. Put the bodies in the coffins. I'll

arrange their interment, you deal with the Archivists and the rest. You tell them what happened.'

Subadwan felt hot tears falling down her cheeks. The emotion made Aquaitra cry. Together, hugging each other, they wept. It was the knowledge that they were in charge that brought the emotion. Subadwan thought she had accepted it all, but she had hardly started. She had witnessed an atrocity. Shock had numbed her, now pain had arrived, and loss, and a strangely precise sense that she was somehow alone and socially isolated.

After a few minutes Aquaitra departed and Subadwan dried her tears. She knew there were more to come.

Finding Gwythey, she appointed the pale woman Third Archivist, ignoring formal rhetoric apart from the ubiquitous shoulder-salute. This laying on of hands she would have to get used to, since Gaya demanded it. Gwythey was too shocked to say very much, not even asking for details of the assassination. She accepted her appointment with a nod and a frightened expression. Subadwan wept again.

The rest of the day passed with speed. Subadwan tried to organise her tasks, but it was impossible with people arriving all the time – this to do, that to do – and the memory of what had happened hanging over everything. It was an hour after midnight before she realised the day had passed.

She hardly slept that night. Only as the first light of dawn appeared in the east did she doze off for a few hours.

Much had been accomplished. No bodies remained inside the temple. Every trace of blood had been cleaned away. Rhannan and Aswaque lay in their

coffins, already sealed by glow-torch into their
biodegradable final resting places, ready for Gaya to
reabsorb them back into her body during decades to
come. A crowd of some two hundred Crayans stood in
the Archive yard, curious, voyeurs all of them, but
they learned nothing from the well-muscled
doorwardens who stood like doom statues at the
public entrance.

Thirty-six people had been crushed to death in the
public chamber. All had been returned to their families
except one unidentifiable woman. Her face was too
disfigured to recognise, and she had been carrying no
fishtail. Some said she was the assassin, a suicide, but
Subadwan immediately silenced such talk and had
Gwythey give the unfortunate a pauper's burial.

The daily dissemination was due at noon.
Subadwan, expecting a full house, was surprised when
only a few hundred people turned up, though when
she considered events from their point of view she
realised that fear must have kept them away. In
tremulous voice, aware of her tiny figure, of her
inexperience, and her youth, she performed the
speaking as best she could. The worst moment came
when she dropped her goblet of water. Aquaitra
jumped to her assistance, saving a few drops, which
Subadwan, red-faced, drank.

Time seemed to slow. Still battered by tasks she had
to perform, now and then weeping in silence,
Subadwan nonetheless could look at the assassination
from a distance – as an event that lay in the past and
did not embrace her with arms of terror. The Archive
she imagined as a hill of miniatures below her. So
much to do. So much activity. She decided she would
be a delegating Lord Archivist.

She dozed during the night. Still she had not been home to her own house. She had lived hour-to-hour.

In the morning Rhannan and Aswaque were due to be buried. Subadwan called Aquaitra to the apex chamber.

Aquaitra, if her dark-encircled eyes were a symptom to be judged, had also slept little during the past two days. Seeing this, and the expression of lost hope on her face, Subadwan fell to crying, and for some minutes both Archivists were unable to speak. But Subadwan knew that grieving was unavoidable, and that it was bad to repress it.

'The burial,' Subadwan began, pouring them both an iced drink.

Dubiously looking at the blue brew, Aquaitra said, 'Should we be drinking alcohol on this particular day?'

'One won't harm,' Subadwan said. 'The burial will start at noon. I'll have to lead it, with you and Gwythey—'

'Is she coping?'

'Gaya save me, I've hardly had time to see her. You noticed anything?'

Aquaitra shook her head. 'She's always been quiet.'

'She been crying?'

'I don't know, 'Dwan.'

Subadwan sat down in the seat behind Rhannan's desk. Her desk. 'I'm going to change all this,' she said.

'I will help you.'

'Thanks. Do you want to stay in your own room?'

'I think—'

'You can if you want to,' Subadwan said. 'We could put Gwythey in my old room.'

Aquaitra nodded, saying, 'That would be best.'

'It's bad, isn't it, us talking logistics, room changes, when Rhannan and Aswaque are in their coffins?'

'The work of administration has to be done, I suppose.'

'Yes. But it's bad.'

Silence fell upon the chamber. Both women sipped at their drinks.

'Aquaitra?' said Subadwan, cautiously.

'Yes?'

Subadwan could not quite decide how to phrase the question. 'Um, do you know anything, any snippets of gossip, about who did it? You heard anything—'

'Not one word, 'Dwan, not one single word. Everybody is as shocked as we are. I saw nobody at the back of the hall, only the smoke trails.'

'I saw them flash by.'

'Did you? Oh, 'Dwan . . .'

Subadwan shrugged. 'Done now. Gaya's love, but headbreakers are expensive pyuters, aren't they? Whoever fired them didn't want mistakes. Those things don't fail, do they?'

Aquaitra, face blanching, murmured, 'I imagine not.'

They finished their drinks. 'Come on,' Subadwan said. 'Time to bury them.'

Arm in arm they walked down the central staircase. Both had dressed in ceremonial blue gowns upon rising. Gwythey and all the other clerks joined them as they descended, followed by a train of scribes and recorders, forming by the time they stood at the lowest level a throng of a hundred and twenty people. There, each guarded by a doorwarden, lay the two white coffins.

Subadwan turned and indicated which clerks should

lift the coffins. Subadwan leading, the coffins behind her,
behind them the rest of the mourners, a single-line
procession formed heading east along Lac Street, the
short lane terminating at the Swamps. It took only ten
minutes. Gloomy Crayans lined the street on both sides,
their faces lit only by glittering motes in the perspex
under their feet. Above, the sky was night dark, and the
coffins seemed to glow in contrast, as though Gaya was
already absorbing vital essences.

The Swamps were Cray's natural system of corpse
removal, but it had been noticed that bodies were not
sinking as once they used to. Many said this was
because there had been an overload.

At the Swamps there lay a low wall. On the other
side black gel bubbled in a few liquid places, a layer
of dust and grime on top criss-crossed with animal
tracks. To Subadwan's left two bodies lay half
submerged, limbs and head visible, skin black as
soot. The vermin of this place ate only each other,
never touching human flesh. These corpses were
pristine.

Subadwan looked at the faces of the chief
mourners. There was Reeve Umia's representative,
Heraber pyuton of Noct; there stood Querhidwe, just
behind her two leaders of the lesser Archives, Arqu of
the Archive of Vein Extraction and Drellalleyn of the
Archive of Perfume; and just arriving Ffenquylla of the
Archive of Wood.

Subadwan glanced at other faces. All wore
linguistic decoders over their ears so that none of her
words could be lost to city clamour. 'Where is
Tanglanah?' she called.

No reply.

A few people looked around as Subadwan called

again, 'Where is Tanglanah of the Archive of Safekeeping?'

Nothing. Just noise.

Then Subadwan said, 'We'll give her five minutes.'

The minutes passed like hours. Everybody was embarrassed, studying their boots, checking their pockets, whispering to their friends, comrades and kin. Subadwan stared over the Swamps, not angry, but sad that Cray's ancient code had been flouted. Far away, like a single glow-bean floating on a breeze, she saw a lamp emitting purple light. She wondered how that light forced a way through the sombre mists, how it navigated the gloom. Then, briefly, she saw the silhouette of a figure on a punt. It looked human, cloaked and hooded. Dark fog closed in. Had that been one of the druids?

A voice at her ear: Aquaitra. 'Your five minutes have passed.'

Subadwan blinked, left her reverie. She looked around. 'Is she here?'

Aquaitra shook her head.

Subadwan turned to the coffin bearers and said, 'Drop them in the Swamps.' As the clerks did this, she intoned:

> 'Gaya, we bring bodies
>   for you to eat.
> Gaya, we bring sentience
>   for you to keep.'

The ritual was short. Had Rhannan and Aswaque been even a little less important they would not have been inside coffins, and then the ritual would have been still shorter.

The coffins lay slowly sinking upon the gel as the mourners dispersed. Gaya required Subadwan to leave last, and so, ten minutes later, she departed the Swamps and followed Aquaitra and Gwythey down Lac Street.

'I wonder what could have made Tanglanah stay away from the burial?' Aquaitra asked, not addressing her question to any particular listener.

Subadwan answered. 'I don't know. Doubt it's significant.'

Gwythey seemed uncertain. 'It's a new cult, Safekeeping. She's not important.'

Subadwan said, 'I think she's very important.' And she gave Aquaitra a lingering glance.

Back at the Archive, Subadwan was able to relax for an hour in her chamber. Determined to remove Rhannan's aura from the place, she changed the position of every item of furniture, except the vertical screen and the great stack of pyuters that stood immovable by the door. For a moment she stood before these pyuters, stroking the rough slabs of protein, the prickly interfaces, wondering what lay inside, wondering why they remained unconnected to the Archive systems and the city networks.

'I'm Subadwan, the Lord Archivist,' she said.

The husky pyuter voice replied, 'I accept that.'

'I must have access to all Rhannan's secrets.'

'You are Lord Archivist. You have access.'

Subadwan paused. 'Are there pass-verses? Secret codes and colours?'

'I recognise your voice,' said the pyuter, 'and your image. I see you now, standing puzzled before the stack.'

'Are you the Archive pyuter?'

'I am one of many.'

Subadwan had never before considered this pyuter. Did it have an identity? Did it run the Archive? 'So there's nothing secret for me to learn?' she asked.

'There is a secret colour. It is green.'

'Green?'

'Green is the colour.'

Subadwan frowned. This was autumn, the season of green to be destroyed, the season of achloricians. 'But green isn't a colour you can show. It's banned.'

'Green is the ancient colour of Gaya. Rhannan and those before her understood that green is suppressed for a reason. Green is an ancient horror too painful to experience, yet it epitomises what it is to be human. Have you not wondered why there are so many pyutons in Cray and why Gaya alone is the human home? Gaya's blue is a new colour. Blue leaves and blue stems are like your blue, the blue you ritually wear, but in ages past they were green.'

All Subadwan could think of was the Baths. 'Green is allowed in the Baths,' she said.

'That is true.'

'Why?'

The pyuter answered, 'I do not know. Subadwan, be aware that there are many secrets unknown to me, and some of them exist in this room.'

A little frightened, Subadwan glanced around the room, regretting now that she had so clumsily moved everything about. 'In this room?'

'On the pyuter stack.'

The top of the stack was six feet above the ground. Subadwan could not see the top. Standing on a chair she brushed her arm across it and almost knocked off what seemed to be a plastic sack. It was a greasy mask made of the thinnest neoprene, a full mask that looked as if it would envelop an entire head.

Initially repelled, for it felt slimy and looked macabre, Subadwan realised how easy it would be to put it on. She ought to try it. The pyuter would not allow her to come to any harm.

Wincing, she pulled the mask over her head. Something tickled her ears, her temple, the back of her neck, and then something passed over her eyes. When her sight returned she knew that she had put on a different world.

In the golden room at the Archive of Safekeeping, Tanglanah and Laspetosyne stood before the image of Greckoh. Tanglanah said to Greckoh, 'The deed has been done. Subadwan is elevated to Lord Archivist of Gaya.'

'Good,' Greckoh replied. 'How tractable do you think she will be?'

'I wouldn't like to guess,' Tanglanah replied. 'Her elevation will change her perception of Cray and everybody in it. For a while there will be shock.'

'Shock,' Greckoh scoffed. 'The defence of weaklings!'

Tanglanah said nothing, as if considering some abstract point. After a considerable silence, Laspetosyne said, 'Our test showed Subadwan to be unusually imaginative. Humans are difficult to work with, Greckoh. Do not expect the plan to run without problems.'

'The plan must succeed! For five hundred years we have waited for a suitable moment to begin our rescue. We must save ourselves. I will not countenance failure.'

To this Tanglanah said, 'We will succeed. But we will need time. I cannot go to Subadwan and continue where I left off after the test. She must settle into her new role and acquire all the accoutrements of her position. Only then will she be ready for the next phase.'

'You sound in awe of her,' Greckoh said. 'I trust your embodiment as a pyuton has not dulled your intellect.'

Again Tanglanah hesitated, and Laspetosyne looked at her, then back at Greckoh. As if to fill an embarrassing void, Laspetosyne told Greckoh, 'Living as a body presents certain difficulties, but our intellectual capacities have not been reduced.'

'Our enemy *must* be defeated,' Greckoh insisted.

At last Tanglanah spoke, and with intensity. 'Greckoh, listen to me. Our enemy is as brilliant as we two. Something exists in the Archive of Gaya that bears the mark of our enemy, and that thing I believe will lead Subadwan, now she has access to all of Gaya, in the direction we wish. But you must have patience. We are in a delicate situation. The gifts Subadwan possesses made her our choice, but they may also work in her favour. I will not have haste ruin everything. I will take my time. I will cajole Subadwan. And then, when she is where we want her, the mark of Gaya will lead her to our enemy. You need not doubt that it will happen. Subadwan will lead and we will follow.'

10

INTERMENT

Dwllis awoke.

He did not recognise the room in which he lay. It was small, dark, with one window looking out into the infested sky. The skyline was silhouetted against blood-purple streamers; dawn or dusk, then. Like a meteorological spectre the moon shone pale through grimy air. Dwllis watched that satellite as it rose into the sky, watched it fully fifteen minutes without glancing away, hardly blinking, to see if it would squirm, glimmer, or otherwise transmute, but it did nothing. It looked bigger however. The window through which he gazed was perspex, possibly with a lensing action, and so Dwllis put the anomaly down as explained.

This room was stuffy and warm. It was packed with furniture, but there was no pyuter stack. In place of paper, nylon tiles had been glued to the walls, pastel blue, gold and white, each tile a square as big as a plate, with a tiny gouge in the top right corner where the application tool had bit. The room was worn, time-eroded, but clean.

He lay with right arm bandaged to the elbow. He remembered his wound. It throbbed, but it was bearable. He noticed a bitter taste in his mouth, and he wondered if it made his breath smell.

'Hello? Is anyone there, please?'

He heard footsteps ascending a creaky stair, and the door opened. It was Ilquisrey.

'Evening,' she said. On the tray that she carried was a tankard full of a steaming liquid, which she offered to him.

'What hour is it?'

'Dusk,' Ilquisrey replied. She stared down at him with something approaching curiosity, though it might have been contempt. 'You've been out of it for almost a day.'

'The Cowhorn Tower,' Dwllis said. He tried to sit up, but his body was weak. He could just lift the tankard.

'It's in the capable hands of Etwe.'

'I must order her to remain put,' Dwllis said. 'People may bring in memories. Gnosticians, too. I must send out the order.'

'I think you treat her real bad,' Ilquisrey said. 'I'll tell Mum you're awake, though, and you can argue it out with her. Personally I don't know why she bothers.'

Five minutes later Cuensheley was sitting at the foot of his bed. Dwllis said, 'Your daughter was quite rude to me just now.'

'She's only speaking her mind. You listen and you might learn something.'

'There is a difference between ill manners and forthrightness.' Dwllis could see from the amused expression on her face that she thought his point irrelevant. He began to worry about Etwe again. 'I must send out a message to Etwe at the Cowhorn

Tower. She is incapable of running it without me.'

Cuensheley sighed and began to play with one of her longer fuzzlocks. 'We've been there today, Dwllis. She's fine.'

'She cannot stand in for me!'

'Well she is. I'm not lying, Dwllis.'

Dwllis lay back. 'I am the Keeper of the Cowhorn Tower. I cannot be away for long. The Reeve may have asked for me.'

'You've got to stay out of sight,' Cuensheley pointed out, lifting the wounded hand. 'If anybody lunar sees this, they'll suspect, won't they?'

'What did Etwe say to you?'

'She's very pretty, isn't she?' came the reply. Cuensheley was gazing out of the window as she spoke. 'What sort of personality does she have? It must be quite something to have attracted you and kept you.'

Dwllis fidgeted on the bed. 'She is essentially normal,' he said, unable to think of any other description.

Cuensheley laughed, long and loud. Then she bent down and kissed Dwllis on the lips.

Fighting down his anger, Dwllis said, 'I am in precisely the position you want, am I not? You only wish to take advantage of me, not help me.'

Cuensheley, as she walked to the door, said, 'Position? Do you mean supine?'

'Why not go the whole way?'

Cuensheley stood at the door. She shook her head.

'Laugh at me then,' Dwllis said.

The door shut.

With no other option, Dwllis tried to analyse what Cuensheley had said. He felt certain that she was taking advantage of the hold she exercised over him. True, she had saved him from a ghastly fate, and she had been brave enough to accompany him in the first place, and shelter him now. She thought he was handsome. Clearly she liked him, that being the only explanation for all this coy banter. But there seemed to be a deeper layer of motive, one more suspicious, and he began to wonder if she could be working for some agency of the city. Perhaps one of the Archives, or maybe even the Triad itself. He had a sudden mental picture of her stripping off to reveal a skintight orange one-piece.

Then he realised he had an erection. The shock made it go away. Heart thumping, fearful, he realised that she was invading his mind. That worried him. His subconscious mind was rebelling. What dreadful thoughts. He tried to force himself to become calm. But his heart still pounded.

Etwe: she was placid, industrious, attractive of course – though that was just a bonus – and she was fond of him. Cuensheley: she was courageous, hardworking, a successful courtyard keeper, but frivolous, demanding, exhibitionist, and a singer to boot.

Dwllis could not stop a laugh from escaping his lips. The two were alike in many ways. Yet Cuensheley, with her compulsive passions, was not safe – unlike serene Etwe.

He could not accept that something about Cuensheley attracted him. It must be an aberration, all these drugs, or a result of lying in Cuensheley's bed.

Was this her bed? It was double. No, this cluttered chamber could not be her bedroom.

Dwllis examined the bed. It was steel with a soft

mattress and cotton sheets, a sumptuous affair tinted grey and gold, the sort of bed to sink into.

He caught himself: no more of this idle day-dreaming. He reached underneath and lifted a bundle of pamphlets loose bound with string: *The Erotic Exploits of Gaya's Daughters (Illus.)*

He lay back. He felt soiled by the personal details that he had discovered. It was revolting. He replaced the pamphlets and decided that this must be Ilquisrey's bedroom, for she was a wastrel, lascivious too, a half-wild devotee of Gaya's more unruly aspects. Cuensheley could not be susceptible to such nonsense.

Just to be clear of the facts, however, he picked up the pamphlets and riffled through their pages, reading a passage here and there and noting the quality of the pen-and-ink illustrations. He looked for a printer's mark, and there it was: Grebbequ's of Ash Lane, in the heart of the Old Quarter. Amazing that such material could be published.

Dwllis sighed. He felt sleepy. Suspicious, for he had been asleep most of the day, he examined the dregs of his brew, to notice amongst the undissolved mushroom granules a number of red capsules part-dissolved.

When he woke again the sky was pink as a warm cheek, dark clouds brushed across it, higher up the final shimmers of midnight's noctiluminescent cirrus.

Today he felt stronger. Getting up brought the first problem: clothes. Dressed in somebody's gown and a pair of slippers he encountered the second problem: although he felt stable and his hand only throbbed, the door was of that type requiring two hands to open. This gave him his first glimpse of difficulties to come. His injury was forever.

With his left hand he knocked at the door, and soon he heard Ilquisrey's brisk tread approaching. She opened the door. 'Mercy save us, if you're not up.'

Dwllis smiled. 'You thought of that sentence some time ago, didn't you?'

Ilquisrey smiled back. She seemed in a good mood. 'Don't you castigate me after all we've done to help you. Mum's downstairs in the kitchen.'

Dwllis descended the staircase, but turned and said to Ilquisrey's back, 'Is that your bedroom I slept in?'

She turned. Her kohled eyes seemed very full, as if she had endured a thousand secrets. Then she tossed her fuzzlocks and the illusion of mystery was shattered. 'You think I'd let you in mine? It's Mum's, of course.'

Dwllis continued his descent. At the bottom of the stairs he realised that he stood in the rear hall of the Copper Courtyard's living quarters, to either side lounge rooms, ahead a short corridor leading to the kitchen and the pantries and then out into the courtyard. Entering the kitchen, he discovered Cuensheley alone, flash-frying parsley cakes over a flickering flame. Surrounding her in the crowded kitchen were numerous bottles of cooking alcohol.

'Hello,' she said, a wide grin brightening her face. 'How are you?'

'Good morning.' Dwllis looked down at his bandaged arm. 'It is well enough. It does not hurt.'

'So it shouldn't after everything we've pumped into your bloodstream.'

'Yes, the drugs,' Dwllis said tentatively. 'I hope you know what you're doing.'

'I know.'

'Is that my breakfast?'

'It could be. Aren't you going back to let Etwe cook you a nice meal?'

Dwllis felt again that familiar knotting sensation in his stomach – and the acid taste at the back of his throat, as if he had indigestion. He bit back harsh words, then said in a quiet voice, 'What do you want from me, Cuensheley?'

She tossed the cakes onto a herb griddle, grabbed a bottle, and took a swig. 'I want to know why you live with a pyuton and not a real woman, that's what I want to know.'

'Have we not had this damnable discussion already?'

'Not to my liking.'

'Etwe and I are very fond of each other.'

Cuensheley slammed the bottle on a table and returned to her cooking. 'I've seen what she's like. She's a husk. She's all flesh and no bones. She's a pyuton stack with no innards.'

'And what do you think of me?'

She could not look him in the eye. 'I think you're interesting, desirable, friendly. But there's this constant backing off that I'm getting to hate. I can't stand it much more. I've done so much for you.'

Dwllis detected a threat. 'That you have done of your own will. You can claim no reward for services rendered.'

She turned, eyes flashing, and shook her finger at him. 'I don't want any reward!' Dwllis took two paces backward. 'Why should I want a reward? This isn't a game, it's real life.'

Dwllis coughed behind his hand to indicate his embarrassment, though Cuensheley ignored him. He said, 'I am aware of what you think of me—'

'Oh, are you?'

He paused. 'I think so.'

'Think some more.'

Dwllis nodded. 'Very well. Now, where are my clothes?'

Cuensheley took a bag hanging from a hook on the kitchen door and handed it over.

Dwllis returned to his room to change, then left the Copper Courtyard, deciding that etiquette must bow to circumstance. He could not return to bid Cuensheley good day. He wondered from what sickly recess of his mind his insight had come. He knew himself poor with people. He was a man of words: a scholar. Swiftly he walked down to Sphagnum Street, then along to the Cowhorn Tower, all the time thinking these dangerous thoughts. The tower looked the same. No changes. Nothing had collapsed.

Dwllis entered. 'Etwe? Etwe? Come here at once.'

There she stood at the upper railing. 'Dwllis?' She hurried down the stairwell, hair floating behind her. 'Are you well?'

He showed her the bandaged hand. 'Injured.'

'Is it bad?'

'Never mind that. What have you been doing? I hear rumours that you have taken over.'

'I had no choice,' Etwe replied.

'What exactly have you done these last two days?'

'Nine memories were brought in by the gnostician,' she said, 'and I've classified—'

'You *classified* them?'

'Yes. They were clear cut.'

Dwllis paced around her. 'Your task is to construct interfaces. How can you classify city memories if you are not the Keeper of the Cowhorn Tower?'

Etwe nodded. 'That is a point.'

'Indeed it is. What else?'

'I rearranged the upper electronics chambers,' Etwe said, 'since they were cluttered. Also I am in the process of altering the tower's collating services.'

'In the process?' Dwllis spluttered. 'You shall stop that process. I relieve you of duties this instant.'

Etwe, expression bland, looked at him. 'Relieve me? What do you mean?'

Dwllis could not stop himself spitting out the words. 'I mean you are out of this place. You work here no more. You think me fool enough to harbour in my home a pyuton who thinks herself equal to the Keeper of the Cowhorn Tower?'

'But I meant no harm. The work of the Keeper is too important to leave. I had no idea what had happened to you—'

'That is none of your affair. Get out now.'

Though Etwe's face was calm, her twitching hands and dejected posture suggested an unexpressed turmoil. Head bowed, Etwe said, 'I shall get my power packs and outboard devices, then leave.'

'At once!'

Five minutes later she was gone, walking down the path to Sphagnum Street. Gone.

Dwllis watched her go. The moment she disappeared he realised that Cuensheley's influence had plotted inside his mind. She had made him do it. This was not about Etwe taking over, it was about him living with a pyuton. He knew it, and he cursed himself for knowing it.

For the rest of the day, in a vain effort to prove to himself that Etwe had been at fault and not Cuensheley, he surveyed the damage – although it

turned out not to be damage – that his erstwhile
assistant had done, before changing everything back
the way it had been. Come evening, he felt sickened at
himself. He knew that already Etwe would be a
network in some other Triad machine, toiling, speaking, creating. Most Triader pyutons could simply erase
their pasts by effort of will and start a new life. Not
the important ones of course, like Archivists high in
the service of Selene, but then Etwe was not
important. Doubtless Etwe would perform this
erasure, losing the little identity she had built up,
becoming a drone, melting into the pool of faceless
Triader pyutons from which she had been fished. But
there was no going back. Gone: gone forever. What
made everything worse was the anger he had visited
upon her.

Coelendwia appeared for the night shift. Desperate
for somebody to talk with, Dwllis stood awhile
outside the tower, mentioning after desultory conversation that Etwe would no longer be in the vicinity.
Coelendwia took this with his usual equanimity.

Then: 'You heard the news, sir?'

Dwllis shook his head. 'What news would that be?'

'Lord Archivist of Selene has been assassinated.
Fishtail in the back, they do say. Rumours of two
factions scrapping, sir, and a monster come to be a
demagogue.'

Dwllis, recalling how he had last seen Lord
Archivist Querhidwe, said, 'That is most awful
tidings.'

'Makes three in two days, that does.'

'Three?'

'Yes, sir. Surely you've heard what happened at
Gaya's?'

Dwllis shook his head again, mouth open.

'That Rhannan and that Aswaque assassinated by scalpers. Dreadful scenes, sir, makes me shiver just to think about it. Forty-odd people killed in the crush afterwards.'

Numbed, Dwllis leaned against a polythene wall. How much had he missed? 'But . . . but has anybody been caught, Coelendwia?'

'Not that I've heard, sir, no. But I have heard tell of all the other Archivists upping their security. Stands to reason, of course.' Coelendwia stopped chattering to point down the path. 'Who might that be, eh?'

A cloaked figure was striding up towards the tower. Dwllis recognised the rough garment style but could not place it.

'It's one of them druids,' Coelendwia said.

He was correct. Dwllis stepped forward a few paces to meet the man. 'I am the noble Keeper of the Cowhorn Tower,' he said.

The druid stopped just two yards away, but, illuminated only by light escaping from inside the tower, he remained a shadow without identity. When he spoke, however, Dwllis recognised the voice of the druid they had met. 'I am Hedalgwadey. We are known to each other.' He handed Dwllis a small silver fishtail on the end of a chain. 'This is for you. The electronic sister whom we shall soon inter bequested it to you. You are required at the interment, which takes place tomorrow night.'

'Hedalgwadey,' Dwllis mused. 'So you trust me now.'

'You are Dwllis?'

'I am. But how could you know that my attendance is required at the interment?'

Hedalgwadey replied, 'There is more than one channel of communication between pyuterkin. Some channels we eavesdrop upon. Those with sufficiently sensitive ears can hear the soughing of innumerable electronic tides, which are the memories of the city broadcasting their speed of light whirr. That is how we know which bodies to bring to the Cemetery.'

On impulse, Dwllis placed the chain around his neck, so that the chill metal fragment rested between his collarbones. 'And this?' he asked, a forefinger against his breastbone.

'The bequest was made before Querhidwe's end.'

'How do you know?'

'Druids know these things.' And with that, Hedalgwadey was gone.

Dwllis was disconcerted enough by this visit for him to delay his return to work. Besides, he was finding one-handed life difficult: how much easier it would be if Etwe were here to open things for him, to hold things, to stand conveniently by. How much he regretted his temper. He could not quite accept that she really was gone.

Throughout the next day Dwllis found himself troubled by such thoughts, and as dusk approached, the gloom of the day brightening into ruddy haze, he felt he fully understood the consequences of his action. In fact, part of his enlightenment was that action *had* consequences.

When night arrived so did Hedalgwadey. The druid was dressed in a brown robe wire-belted, carrying a wooden lumod and a sickle. Dwllis, nervous for no reason he could think of, brushed specks of dust from his costume and studied the druid's manner and posture for signs of criticism.

After a significant pause, he asked, 'Do you think this outfit suits?'

It was simple grey cotton – his most elegant cuts worn with blue ankle boots. The silver fishtail he wore outside his jacket. Hedalgwadey muttered, 'It'll pass.' Dwllis closed and locked the door to the Cowhorn Tower, lit up the *Absent sign* by touching a button, then, pressing speech amplifiers over his ears, followed Hedalgwadey to the Cemetery. Sphagnum Street, already choked with cables and pipes, was further littered with cheap moons on sticks, the thoroughfare looking as if some surreal tide had left erratically glowing flotsam. But the clerks still prattled and the people still listened, symbols in hands, unless they were harassed by noctechnes. Dwllis noticed that there were two types of moon, waxing and waning, the holders of which seemed to be in opposition, and seeing this he was reminded of Coelendwia's remarks concerning two duelling factions.

He had no idea what to expect in the Cemetery. So far as he knew, only druids and other pyutons witnessed interment, and for a few mad moments he wondered if any augmented gnosticians would be present. Hedalgwadey remained silent.

Inside the Cemetery, walking along muddy paths between megaliths tall as trees, Dwllis asked one question. 'Excuse me, but how do you come to be a druid? How does anybody?'

'We are appointed by elder druids who enjoy access to the secret thoughts of the great country to which the minds of so many electronic sisters travel. These thoughts give clues to the identity of druids to be, these being boys of between eight and eleven years. Such boys are taken to the Cemetery to begin their novice years. Any failing become Swamps fodder, or are thrown to the mercy of the streets.'

'Are only boys allowed to be druids?'

'Just as pyuterkin are almost all female. It is cosmic balance.'

'And what is this great country?'

Hedalgwadey replied, 'Every now and again it imposes itself upon Cray, according to the rhythm of an arcane cycle.'

Dwllis said nothing more before arriving at the stone circle in which the interment would take place. A double ring containing two small rings seemed to be the form, but Dwllis could see little since light was provided only by iron braziers. These braziers emitted the odour of nuts. All around, the standing stones glowed dull red. They seemed like fingers emerging from the sodden ground, he but a toy in some subterranean giant's palm. He felt a chill upon his skin.

There were fifteen, perhaps twenty, other druids present inside the circle, some dressed in brown, some in black, some in white. All carried sickles. Now Hedalgwadey had shown him to his place he could see Querhidwe's body lying on the ground, dressed in a temple gown, the fishtail still in her back. It was ghoulish, as if she had been dropped there without ceremony.

One of the white druids looked into the sky and began altering the controls of a box he carried. Dwllis glanced up, saw aeromorph lights, hazy behind engine fumes, and saw, lower down, bats following mote-storms along Sphagnum Street. There was a rainbow flicker as some unlit vehicle reflected Cray light.

He looked to see who else had been invited, noticing Tierquthay, small and white-fuzzlocked, bottle-bottom spectacles perched on the end of his long nose. He was hunched over as if the weight of his elevation to Lord Archivist had already left its mark. He also spotted Tierquthay's deputy Iquinlass, who had spoken to him at Selene's Archive. Apart from these two the circle contained only druids. Hedalgwadey returned to stand at Dwllis's side.

The white-robed druid took from his box a black object. At first Dwllis thought it was a mask, but when he threw it into the air with a shout it expanded and left a white trail: a headbreaker. Dwllis froze. But the device, as if it were a dud, flopped upon Querhidwe's head and remained still. The druid made a sign and the headbreaker split Querhidwe's cranium in two.

Everybody relaxed and began chatting. Hedalgwadey said, 'The first part of the ritual is over. You have witnessed what very few outsiders have witnessed.'

'I still cannot believe I was asked. What happens now?'

'The cranial pyuter will extract certain veins, from which neural fibres will be grown, fibres that will connect the pyuterkin to a ganglion. Watch as the process begins.'

Dwllis did watch. The headbreaker, falling off the skull like a green leaf in autumn, was collected by the druid, and something tiny that Dwllis could not see was placed into a beaker of jelly. Intense light was shone upon this beaker by means of five lumods thrust into the ground around it. The white druid placed his box close by, then sauntered off.

'Is that your chief?' Dwllis asked.

'We have no chief,' Hedalgwadey replied, a trace of surprise in his voice. 'You outsider folk may need your absurd hierarchies, but we do not. In death we are all equal. When you live with death you achieve an appreciation of equality.'

Neural fibres were now emerging from the jelly, twisting this way and that but growing ever nearer the box, like worms. When they reached the box they paused, but then, invigorated, carried on growing until they reached the plastic-splintered rent in Querhidwe's head.

'And now?' Dwllis asked.

'The fundamental output devices inside the pyuterkin's brain are connected to the ganglion. The veins control the system. Now be quiet, for the moment of connection arrives.'

Dwllis shivered. He felt a necromantic deed was being enacted. It was perverted, sickening, this meddling with brains and self-motivating technology. It could not be right. Damn, why had Querhidwe requested his presence?

The white druid knelt at the ganglion, now a mass of damp tendrils exposing only one part of the box, a grille and a dial. First checking the state of the body and the beaker, he raised his hand to touch it. The druids closed in. Hedalgwadey motioned for Dwllis to move in so that he stood only a few yards away from Querhidwe. Everybody was leaning in, as if to watch. The white druid touched the dial, then turned it.

Dwllis wore high-quality linguistic amplifiers, capable of dragging the quietest mumble out of Cray clamour. He heard a whine, a buzz, and then . . . what was that sound? The druids relaxed, smiled, but listened. Dwllis heard a soughing, the most peaceful, hypnotic ambience he had ever experienced. It was a sound like the crash of waves mingled with the swish of treetops, a sound that brought images small and vast, botanic and universal.

The white druid said, 'The interment is done. This electronic sister has passed away. Bring on the barrow stones.'

Hedalgwadey led Dwllis out of the circle. 'Now we build the barrow,' he said.

'Tonight?'

In reply Hedalgwadey pointed to the heavens.

Dwllis saw a dozen pink lights hanging over the Cemetery. They dropped and became giant bats with rotors, carrying megaliths in nets. Dwllis gasped in a moment of recognition. The Cowhorn Tower stood close to the Cemetery. Many times in earlier years he had seen these lights through night haze and wondered what they were. Even as a teenager, living alone in Cochineal Mews, he had seen them and thought them some foreign breed of aerician.

The bats, under druidic direction, placed their loads, flying off when the nets had been cut. As an operation it was organised to perfection. The noise was loud, but no worse than city din without ear protection. After an hour a barrow had been made around Querhidwe's body, with only the roof and one wall-stone remaining to be added.

Hedalgwadey led Dwllis into the barrow, first allowing the other druids, Tierquthay and Iquinlass to enter. Iquinlass stared at Dwllis when she recognised him, but since Dwllis kept his right hand in his pocket she did not notice his injury. Then the white druid said, 'We shall listen to the sounds of the afterlife.'

He turned the ganglion dial. The soughing sound

surged, then quietened, and Dwllis realised that the druid was trying to maximise its volume. Because he stood at the back he was able to whisper at Hedalgwadey's cowl, 'What is that ganglion?'

'A radio receiving the other side.'

A voice: deep, cracked, old. The barrow stones shielded Dwllis from city echoes, allowing him to hear clearly. It said, 'I speak to the successor of Querhidwe, O new Lord Archivist of Selene. Use the gnosticians! Care not what they are, but extract what you may from them. Though they are a scourge, they hold secret knowledge that must be retrieved. Heed not the tenets of Gaya, for the memoirs of Gaya are fantastical, baroque lies, designed to confuse, misinform, and manipulate. Be one with empty Selene! And now, I must depart, and consider what else to do . . .'

So they filed out of the barrow. Already, bats were hovering above the stone circle with megaliths and keystones for the roof. Dwllis took a deep breath and allowed Hedalgwadey to guide him away.

They stood on a hillock just outside the circle, watching everybody disperse. 'That is all, outsider,' Hedalgwadey said.

'But I still do not understand.'

'Understand what?'

'Who was that speaking to Tierquthay?'

'A spirit of the afterlife.'

'But who?'

'There are a number of spirits. Interference means that the broadcasts are not always of good quality. We are but observers of that other world, not inhabitants, and so I cannot say precisely who it was. However, you will recall the grotesque creature with the black bag of a body that I mentioned in our earlier meeting. It could have been her. Come, you must leave the Cemetery.'

'But I must know!'

Hedalgwadey stood absolutely still. Then in tones almost sarcastic he said, 'Some of these spirits we have seen in the lens. If you truly have seen yourself in that necromantic device then maybe you know more than you realise.'

Dwllis wondered if this druid was hiding the truth. Convinced, now, that the Archive of Selene was at the bottom of all that had happened to him – and of much that was happening to the city – he felt that he needed to find out as much as possible. But in twenty minutes he would be at the Cemetery gate.

Dwllis departed the Cemetery alone, deep in thought. He kicked aside wires, lunar rubbish, clumps of soil and grime, metal boils and blisters from the city's aching walls, ignoring every mendicant outer, until he reached the path up to the Cowhorn Tower. He stopped, then hurried on to the Copper Courtyard.

It being well past midnight the courtyard was locked up, but Dwllis, knowing that Cuensheley would get up for him, persuaded the pyuter system to rouse her. In minutes she was at the entrance, unhappy, dressed in a black gown.

'What do you want?' she asked.

Dwllis glanced behind him. 'Good evening. It is damnably dusty out here. Haven't you got a drink for a parched throat?'

'Do you know what hour it is?'

Dwllis was taken aback by her manner. 'Not exactly, no.'

'Oh, come in.' That was more like it. 'What's the matter?'

Cuensheley insisted on returning to her bed, and so in the familiar bedroom, perched demurely on the end of her bed, Dwllis described what he had seen. She was astonished.

'You look ill,' she said.

'If you had seen what I've seen . . . My life is being turned upon its head. And Etwe is no longer at the Cowhorn Tower.'

'What?'

'I have dispensed with her services.'

'Why?' Cuensheley sat up, a smile now appearing on her face.

A distasteful display, Dwllis thought. Casually he said, 'It is best not mentioned.'

'You *must* tell me.'

Dwllis knew she would never stop asking. 'Later,' he promised, playing along, for he had no intention of telling her what had happened. 'Do you have any qe'lib'we to hand? I need—' He stopped himself. He did not like to admit his need.

As if it were an unimportant issue, Cuensheley said, 'Oh, over there, on that table.'

Dwllis pulled a small lump off the mass and began chewing. 'My hand is beginning to ache,' he said. 'Would you rebandage it please?'

Cuensheley frowned. 'I may as well tell you now, so you know, if there's one thing I hate it's being woken up in the middle of my sleep. I don't mind late nights, early mornings, but I hate being woken up.'

'I am sorry.' The familiar sensation of confidence, like clear water along a dusty lane, seeped through Dwllis as he chewed. 'I mean it,' he added. The effect of the drug made his sinuses pop as they cleared, and he took a deep breath.

Cuensheley stomped out of her room then returned with hot water, bottles and bandaging. Dwllis heard Ilquisrey's faint voice call, 'You all right, Mum?'

Cuensheley did not answer. Unbandaged, the hand was an unpleasant sight. One glance and Dwllis looked away. He could not move the two remaining fingers. With a brush and a squeezy bottle Cuensheley cleaned and dressed the wound, then rebandaged it. 'Happy now?' she asked.

'You seem tense,' Dwllis observed.

'It's the hour.' Bluntly spoken.

'I said I was sorry.'

'What's that thing around your neck?'

Dwllis handed it to her, chain and all. 'I do not know. It is a bequest, an absurd bequest from Querhidwe to me. Why she should want me to keep an item of jewellery—'

Cuensheley groaned. 'It's a key, you fool! It opens something. Obviously she wanted you to have it.' Cuensheley's thoughts ran wild, making them difficult to interrupt. 'She must have known that you and me got into the Archive that night. Maybe there were cameras. Somebody might have seen us. And don't forget you saw an image of yourself in Crimson Boney's memoirs. The question is, what does this fishtail open? It's small. Could be a box. Could be a slab of pyuter memory. Could even be a door key to a house, or a chamber in the Archive. Did Tierquthay see it around your neck?'

'No, I do not think he did. But Iquinlass may have.'

Cuensheley said grimly, 'I think you ought to hide this. I'll keep it. I think Tierquthay will be after it – which means he'll be after *you*.'

'Do you think so?'

'He is Lord Archivist of Selene, isn't he? You'd better move in with me for now.'

'That won't be necessary.'

Cuensheley seemed surprised. 'Suit yourself. But I think Coelendwia might meet an intruder soon. You realise that this means we'll have to get into the Archive of Selene again?'

Dwllis's fears were confirmed by this statement for the idea had occurred to him. 'Perhaps,' he replied.

But she was not listening. She was examining the fishtail. 'Look at the wear marks on this,' she said. 'They're obviously from a mechanical lock, not an electric one, because of these fans of scratches. Somebody's used this fishtail a lot.' She held the chain up to a lamp. 'Somebody pale judging by this hair still caught in it. Querhidwe, maybe. I know somebody who could analyse this hair to see if it belongs to a person or a pyuton.'

Dwllis said, 'As you wish. I am but a historian.'

Cuensheley offered him a piercing look in reply.

Dwllis had no answer. But when she undid the top buttons of her gown, he jumped up, trembling, and said, 'No, no.'

She stood, offering him the locket from around her neck. 'I only wanted you to have this in return for the fishtail. What are you frightened of?'

He laughed – a too-loud laugh that he knew she would see through. 'Nothing. I must go. It is late, as you said.'

He took the locket, and with Cuensheley tailing him departed the courtyard. She managed to kiss him once before he left. 'Don't do that in public even if you must in private.' It was a harsh rebuke that he later regretted.

Cuensheley shrugged, remarking, 'I won't give up.'

Dwllis walked home. Not wishing to speak with anybody else he watched from behind a spray of leaves until Coelendwia, patrolling the base of the tower, was out of sight. He ran for the door, but before entering he turned to survey the city. Hot, dusty and loud it lay spread before him. At that moment he hated it, because it represented something of his torture.

The moon hung above the sea, and Dwllis realised that it was beginning to look something like a fish. He entered the Cowhorn Tower, to find a message. His presence had been requested by the Reeve.

11

EXILE

It was as if Subadwan was floating in dark syrup, surrounded by a hundred suspended panes of glass illuminated along their edges. The panes were of different sizes and colours, each labelled in the top left-hand corner with an abstract symbol. She noticed that, faint as a bleached picture, each was also etched with a pair of human lips. The temptation was to touch one.

She touched one. Nothing.

She kissed one.

'Headmerger welcomes you to its country,' said a voice.

Subadwan understood. The mask was a head-merger, a device so sophisticated it represented a pyuter landscape: but which?

Before her, the glass pane bubbled and billowed. As it enlarged, the others faded away. Subadwan was not frightened, however, for she knew that this Archive pyuter would do her no harm.

The pane was a notepad. Each pane must be devoted to a different topic, this one apparently covering the keeping of order amongst the door-warden ranks. A short summary of points was spoken

by the lips, with accompanying diagrams and portraits
flowing like electronic ponds across the glass surface.
This pane would be useful. Here the shortcomings and
strengths of Archive staff were noted. Becoming
excited, Subadwan wondered what other secrets were
at hand.

Some were pleasant, others shocking. The third
pane she kissed covered secret meetings Rhannan had
had with the Reeve, meetings designed to redefine the
historical limits placed by society upon Gaya. Nothing
had been agreed. Subdued, she read on.

There was a pane devoted to Aswaque, to herself, and
to Aquaitra. The pane on Aquaitra was terrible. There
were reports detailing drinking binges, suspicious
activities in low-life courtyards to the south, association
with substance-crews and rowdies. This was not the
Aquaitra she knew. It was not the Aquaitra anybody
knew, come to that.

More panes. One on that popinjay in charge of the
Cowhorn Tower. He was an odd character, raised by a
guardian independent in Cochineal Mews, unlisted
parentage and siblings. Rhannan had made notes of
his possible uses, mentioning the quantity of memory
accumulated in the Cowhorn Tower, but there was no
indication of her acting on it.

And here at last were notes concerning Tanglanah,
the Archive of Safekeeping, and a certain abstract
country. So Rhannan had known of it. Subadwan was
amazed.

'The abstraction must be explored,' droned the lips,
manifesting Rhannan's thoughts, 'but how? The
Safekeeping Archive is dangerous. Potential for mob
rule.' Diagrams of the position of the Archive scrolled
across the pane, accompanied by images of Tanglanah,

her adjutant Laspetosyne, and then thirteen of the Assemblage of Fifteen. Subadwan added Tanglanah and Laspetosyne to thirteen and made fifteen. Did the two pyutons wish to set themselves up alongside the other thirteen exemplars of their Archive, or was there a deeper kinship? Rhannan had made no notes. And although Subadwan had already guessed that Tanglanah represented not only the Archive of Safekeeping but also a wealth of secrets, it remained a comfort to hear that suspicion from another's lips.

Further exploring the pyuter country, she came upon one pane that was a window upon the external world, allowing her a complete view of her chamber, and a reflection of herself in the dark pyuter screen . . . a reflection like her, and yet unlike. She shivered.

Time to leave. She let herself relax, then raised her hands to peel off the mask. Reality appeared suddenly, just as the pyuter country vanished. In one hand she held floppy neoprene.

'Aquaitra wishes to see you,' said the pyuter voice.

'She's here now?'

'She stands outside your door.'

Replacing the headmerger, Subadwan made to open the door herself. Her scalp felt cold.

Aquaitra entered, eyes wide. ''Dwan!'

Aquaitra was staring at the top of her head. Subadwan felt a bare scalp. Fuzzlocks lay scattered on the floor like snakeskins.

Aquaitra slammed the door shut. 'What's happened?'

'Something of Rhannan's. I can't tell you just now.'

Ashamed, remembering now the wig that Rhannan wore, Subadwan searched for something with which to cover her head. At the rear of a drawer she found a cloth cap which, red with embarrassment, she put on.

Subadwan could not tell whether Aquaitra was tired or nervous, but her friend seemed tense. Guessing the cause, she said, 'Forget I'm Lord Archivist for a moment. It's just me.'

'I know, I know. You will be unhappy if formality intrudes, so I will try to remember you are 'Dwan.'

'I'm still Subadwan.'

Aquaitra nodded. 'I thought you might like to hear news off the streets, news that is strange and worrying.'

'What news?'

'At the Archive of Selene—'

'Not that place again.'

'—that monster has started to assist Tierquthay.' Aquaitra frowned, then sighed. 'A frightening man. I saw him on the steps of the Archive as I walked past on my way from Plash Street back to our Archive. Pikeface they call him. He is horrible, a huge man, seven feet tall.'

'Seven?'

'Seven feet tall, with bulging muscles and black hair on his chest. But he has the head of a fish, 'Dwan, all black and greasy, with staring yellow eyes. And yet he can speak. He is a rabble-rouser – he spoke to a crowd of three hundred as I passed. He wears a great blue and black cloak, and steel boots.'

'Who is he?'

'As I passed by the Archive, I thought I heard that he had been made Tierquthay's Advocate.'

'What is a pike, anyway?' Subadwan asked. 'Pyuter,' she called, 'what fish is a pike?'

'The pike is a voracious species extinct since the arrival of the gnostician and associated species, known for being vicious and for eating other piscine species.'

'Voracious,' Subadwan mused. She recalled the circumstances of Querhidwe's assassination, then said, 'Perhaps this is the Archive of Selene's response to their Lord Archivist's death, converting Crayans away from Noct and the Reeve—'

Aquaitra gasped. 'You mean the Reeve had Querhidwe assassinated?'

'No, no, um, I don't know,' Subadwan said, waving her hands in a firm gesture of denial. 'Gaya love me, it could have been anybody for all I know. But a pike, Aquaitra. A voracious fish that eats other fish. It's got to have some meaning, hasn't it?

Aquaitra shrugged, then glanced away.

'The Archive of Selene wants to eat authority,' Subadwan mused. 'They want to draw everybody in, especially now the moon is changing. It's got to be a direct challenge. This city's going mad. Three assassinations. You listen to me, Aquaitra, that Pikeface won't last long.'

Aquaitra shuddered. 'You have not seen him.'

Subadwan was not listening. 'It's Noct versus Selene. The Reeve must be beside himself, with all this lunar evangelism in the streets. I bet the noctechnes start getting really nasty now.'

Subadwan looked at Aquaitra. There was another matter. 'Aquaitra, I've had some odd reports about you.'

'Me?'

'From reliable sources. It's all a bit strange. Do you know what I'm talking about?'

'No.'

Subadwan tried to laugh, as if it were trivial. But Aquaitra's denial unnerved her. 'Of course you do. It surprised me, I must admit.'

'What did?'

Subadwan grinned, then chuckled. Then her face fell. 'Now I'm Gaya's Lord Archivist I can't really ignore all this . . . carousing.'

'Carousing?' Aquaitra sat bolt upright. '*Carousing*?'

Subadwan did not know how to go on. 'There's been talk of you going into dives, Empty Quarter substance lounges, that sort of—'

''Dwan, what are you talking about?'

Subadwan leaned forward. 'Look, Aquaitra. I know the Empty Quarter. I know what it's like. But I have responsibilities now.' She sat back. 'Not that I really want them. No, that's not right, I *am* taking on the responsibility.'

''Dwan, you're rambling.'

'But this low life has got to stop.'

Aquaitra shook her head, her expression a mixture of revulsion at the charges and surprise at the prosecutor. 'I do not go into the Empty Quarter other than for Archive duties.'

'That's not what I've heard.'

'Well who has told you?'

'People. I can't say, it's secret.'

Aquaitra sat back, exhaling a sigh of frustration. She tapped at the arms of her chair. 'I think that somebody is trying to separate us,' she said, looking directly into Subadwan's eyes. 'This is not the first time that odd things have happened to make you go off me, to make you suspicious of me. And have you noticed that it is only one way? Somebody is deliberately trying to blacken me in your eyes.'

Subadwan remembered the faked emergency call and realised that Aquaitra's points were valid. But the pyuter reports were detailed, coherent, and they had been taken seriously by Rhannan. And yet the name Tanglanah came to her mind.

Aquaitra continued. 'Somebody wants to make me leave your service, perhaps, or not help you so much. Perhaps somebody with ambition who is jealous of our friendship and who wants me out of the way. That's what it is, 'Dwan.'

Subadwan wanted to believe this, but the detail in the reports had impressed her. She wanted Aquaitra to leave, wanted a distance between them, just briefly, while she considered the whole affair. On the spur of this moment only one plan commended itself. 'I've got a job for you,' she told Aquaitra. 'I want you to take charge of the investigation into the assassinations of Rhannan and Aswaque. Gwythey will help. I'll direct. Find out everything you can.'

Aquaitra stood, and Subadwan, heart sinking, knew that her friend had seen this for the distancing manoeuvre it was. 'I will do it,' she said, 'because you are the Lord Archivist.'

But not for friendship, Subadwan thought. 'One other thing,' she added.

Aquaitra turned. 'What?'

'I'll need some sort of wig. If you wouldn't mind . . .'

The conversation had produced in Subadwan a black mood. She felt isolation combined with a dread of pressures and responsibilities to come. Not for the first time she felt she was mistakenly Gaya's chosen – an unpleasant, shaming thought, but one she could not repress, deny, or otherwise excise from her mind. Gaya *had* chosen her, and Gaya made no mistakes – unless dealing with human beings was itself a mistake.

'There is a communication from Umia,' she was informed.

Head in hands, she replied, 'Put him through. Audio only.' She did not want him to see the vulnerability in her face. How easy it would be to drown under this deluge of calling people.

'Lord Archivist?' said Umia.

'I'm here,' Subadwan replied.

'It is time for your decision.'

'What decision?'

'You, Lord Archivist Subadwan, must agree to become one of the Triad.'

'I've got no intention of joining the Triad. Is that clear enough?'

Umia's voice deepened, and quietened. 'Then you leave me with no option. Crayan law demands that the Lord Archivists of Gaya and Selene must be members of the Triad. So it is written, Noct preserve us all. Lord Archivist, there are enforcers outside your building as we speak. They will come for you. Please don't resist because they will use any means at their disposal to coerce you. I deeply regret this, Subadwan.'

The line crackled, then shut down. Subadwan sat back, struck to the core. Then she was on her feet, rushing to the door. She had to escape the Archive. Gaya preserve her, she was about to become an exile from her own home.

She ran out of her chamber, but then returned to collect the headmerger. At the top of the staircase she looked down, seeing nobody, but hearing the clatter of steel-shod boots on aluminium. Here, at the summit, she was trapped. She had to descend.

Near panic, she descended two levels before fear made her stop. The bootsteps were very close.

She looked around. There were three doors on the landing: one her old room, the others pyuter-stacked.

She slipped into one of the pyuter rooms, leaving the door ajar and peering out.

Three orange-clad enforcers leaped up the steps, fuzzlocks bouncing, each armed with smoking black rifles that shuddered like beasts about to pounce. The rifle of one man wriggled as if desperate to kill, until he dealt it a slap across the muzzle.

The moment they were out of sight she ran down a further two flights of stairs. Then she heard the enforcers shouting. They knew she was gone. Legs pumping, lungs gasping, she slipped away from the centre of the stairwell seconds before a column of flame roared down. They knew what she was doing.

But now she was on a level of rooms – a complex level where she could run, hide, play the maze. Only six levels lay below. There would be enforcers at the public entrance, but that was not the only way out.

So far she had seen nobody. The enforcers must have cleared the area as they ascended. But now, entering a store room full of gowns, she came across a pair of frightened scribes, two pale faces, four dark staring eyes. 'Stay put,' she said. 'They only want me.'

'Dear mother—'

But Subadwan was already gone, running along these linked chambers, until she came to a secondary stairwell. It was narrow, and led all the way down to the first level. There came no sound of pursuit. At the first level she ran along a fleshy corridor until a large window appeared. Outside, people congregated. To her left she saw the public entrance, a dark space in which four enforcers stood. The periphery of the bronze yard was crowded with students.

The clamour of the city made Subadwan lose her

concentration. How could she escape? A single shot and she was dead.

One option. At the back of the yard stood a wicket gate.

She ran around the level, flitting from room to room, ordering silence when she came across clerks, doorwardens or recorders, hurrying on with no other word, until she came to another window. Outside there were milling people, but no Triaders.

She opened the window and slid down the fat-stained flesh, landing with a bump, knocking the breath out of her. People pointed at her and called out, but she heard nothing except the clashing din of the city. Running, signing, *Quiet, leave me*, she sped towards the wicket gate. It was open. She slipped through and bolted it. Not that that would do much good against Noct weaponry.

The lane running along the back of the Archive yard was dark, no motes within it, and it was empty of Crayans. A covered passage led from the wasteland at its end to Dusk Street, a tunnel of plastic that Subadwan, panting, slowing because she was tiring, followed until she stepped out into the street. Her home was nearby.

She jumped back. Three enforcers at her door, chatting. Gaya had saved her.

Subadwan quailed. There was only one place for her to go. The Baths. Her favourite place in all Cray. If there was one place even the Reeve could not violate it was the Baths.

Bitterness made her feel sick. Now she was away from Gaya's house she was utterly alone. The tiff with Aquaitra made it worse. How would she live in the Baths? How would she communicate?

But she was not there yet.

Subadwan dared not return along the back-lane. She would have to continue north awhile. Uncertain of managing a flight across the north of the city, through the Rusty, the Stellar, and Eastcity's cursed Cold Quarter, she decided she would have to cling to the Swamps wall, following Platan Street to the river, then creeping through Plastic Quarter alleys until she reached Peppermint Street.

Obstacles infuriated her. The journey was a nightmare. Rag-shrouded outers begged for alms, cables and hissing pipes filled the streets as though they were growing from buildings, and everywhere there were churning crowds of lunar students, as if the waist of the city, from the Swamps down to the southern quarters, was inflamed with Selene's fever, infected by her shouting clerks and her hypnotised converts. Yellow crescents on sticks littered the streets. Noctechnes prowled. Glass shards lay everywhere, crunching underfoot. And the noise, it almost drove her to scream for silence: that hammering din, the unholy symphony of engines, electronics, roaring engines above, thundering heat-exchangers and factory machines below.

When she came to Print Street and the winking lamps of the Indigo Courtyard, she was filthy. Her hands were black. Doubtless her face was too.

The Baths were but a block away. Walking along a passage, she halted at its end to peer out, shrinking back when she saw that the street was busy with lunar traffic. Not far away, on the other side of the Old Quarter, stood the Archive of Selene itself, the source of this chaos. Subadwan spat in its direction then slipped into the street, head bowed, merging with the throng until she could dart through the polythene doors of the Baths.

She was safe. She could relax.

Subadwan disrobed at the first available chamber and walked, body pale but limbs sooty, to the pools themselves. After the ritual question regarding water temperature, she sank into bliss. The water steamed and she felt her ordeal was, for the moment, over.

Awaiting the Westcity visitor, Umia strode around his chamber, the metal of his replacement leg clanging against the grille floor. His right hand he balled into a fist, which, in time to his stride, he smacked into his metal hand. He was frowning.

At last the door announced, 'The Keeper of the Cowhorn Tower is here to see you, Reeve.'

'Send him in, send him in, don't wait around.'

The fop wore a maroon velvet jacket, black boots enclosing tight cream britches, and a curious hat that looked like a cake. He glanced at the digital fob on his lapel, struck a nonchalant pose, and drawled, 'My Lord, your esteemed servant is here.'

'Dwllis,' Umia said without hesitation, 'it's time you did some work to earn your keep. The gnostician creatures, we're thinking of purging them from the city. First, I want you to check for past purges. If any have been made, I want to learn from them. What's that look on your face?'

'My Lord, you mean a purge of all gnosticians? From Cray? Impossible.'

'Don't tell me what's impossible,' Umia replied. He felt anger rising at this insolence. 'Your duty is to serve me with historical data, and I expect only the best service. Is that clear?'

Dwllis looked aside, as if to gather his thoughts, then said, 'My Lord, I fear you do not understand the significance of this. The gnosticians are kindly creatures, and it is only the xenophobic who fear them. They are harmless. What reason could there be for a purge?'

'Reason?' Umia shouted. 'I'm Reeve, you bloody fool! Your reason is that I said so!'

Dwllis stepped back. Again he paused, before saying, 'My Lord, it is my sworn duty to advise you, and my advice is to heed the lesson of history. There have been no purges—'

'How do you know? You haven't looked yet. These loping beasts invaded the Earth. Isn't that reason enough to banish them from Cray?'

'Well, let us not be hasty. That word "invasion" is emotive, and we must at all costs keep our emotions out of this discussion. No, it seems to me, my Lord, that—'

Walking to his chair and sitting, Umia spluttered, 'What are you blathering about? If I say I want information, I get it. Now are you Keeper of the Cowhorn Tower or aren't you?'

'You know I have that honour, my Lord.'

'Then do as I say!'

Dwllis stood still. Incredibly, he seemed to be hesitating. Umia stared.

'Are you deaf, man?'

Dwllis coughed, hand in front of mouth. 'My hearing is first class.'

'You could have fooled me. Keeper, you are wasting time. I want that report sent to me the day after tomorrow. Is that clear?'

'I suppose it is.'

'Good. And don't go telling anybody. There will be a campaign of misinformation set up to control public opinion.'

'Lying, my Lord? Is that wise?'

He was doing it again. 'I'll decide what's wise and what's not,' Umia said. 'How dare you lecture me!'

'But lying, my Lord,' Dwllis protested. 'It . . . it always rebounds upon the perpetrator in the end.'

'Oh, get out, man. Just go and do what I ordered. *Now!*'

Dwllis bowed and retreated. 'My Lord.'

12

ATTACK

During the night after Subadwan's flight from the Rusty Quarter, Liguilifrey the blind masseuse returned from a walk around the Baths, meeting Subadwan at the Osprey Chamber, a small room tiled with sea-blue porcelain and with a very high roof. Light was provided by a single bag of glow-beans hung centrally. The circular form of the room and its complete lack of furniture meant that it was not a popular meeting place, but it was perfect for Subadwan's needs. The pair leaned against a wall, lying on their sides with legs stretched out, facing one another. Subadwan wore a black gown provided by Liguilifrey, who wore a similar gown dyed green and embroidered with blue chevrons.

'What did your eyes see?' Subadwan asked.

Liguilifrey patted the black avian pyuter perched on her shoulder. 'A bat hovers above the Baths. They have guessed already, I'm afraid.'

Subadwan shook her head. 'Umia's agents long ago told him how much time I spend here.'

'The bat has no pilot slung underneath.'

To this news Subadwan had no reply. Autonomous hang-gliders were rare beasts and indicated anxiety in

Noct's highest echelons. Umia may not have seen her enter the Baths, but he knew she was here. She was trapped. 'What else did your eyes see?'

'The sky is full of aericians carrying customers, full of flying carpets taking rich folk from west to east, and back again. The aeromorphs hover low tonight. The stink of their engines actually made me sneeze. If only we had noseplugs that work. You'd think *my* Archive would be able to make them, but their factories are too busy churning out noses on sticks to rival the lunar mob.'

'Did your eyes see any spies lurking around the Baths?'

'No.'

Subadwan sighed. 'They won't be long in appearing. Thank Gaya they won't dare come inside.'

Liguilifrey touched Subadwan's shoulder. 'You're safe here. This chamber can be your headquarters. Feel free to spread papers and pyuters around.'

'Thanks, Liguilifrey. Has your messenger taken that message to Aquaitra?'

'Yes. I'll go and see if she's returned.'

Subadwan stood and stretched. 'I think I'll go and have a soak. What time is it?'

'Gone midnight.'

Subadwan followed Liguilifrey out of the Osprey Chamber and around the nearer pool. When she took off her gown and stepped into the water, she smiled, before submerging herself until she could hold her breath no longer. Then she lay upon the crumbling steps, shallow water lapping around her body. The late hour meant she was the only woman bathing. Somehow, the tranquillity of the water and the warmth of the steamy atmosphere reduced every knot of

tension within her. Even Umia's bat seemed a sur-
mountable obstacle. Subadwan liked time alone, and
only here in all Cray did she find peace.

She felt her eyelids become heavy. Rippling water
surrounded her. It was quiet, no city noise damaging
her ears. No press of people.

'Subadwan of Gaya,' said a voice.

Subadwan jumped, uttering a cry. She turned.
Above her stood the imposing figure of Laspetosyne,
cloaked, barefoot, her hair greased and spiky, her
violet eyes piercing. 'You frightened me,' she said,
trying to stand and painfully aware of her shining
scalp.

Laspetosyne crouched down. 'I am here to tell you
that the graceful Tanglanah wishes to speak with you.'

'I'm staying here tonight,' Subadwan replied
sharply.

'The graceful pyuton awaits. The Baths are empty.
You *can* stay here.'

'Um . . . is it important?'

Laspetosyne replied, 'The hour is very late and
graceful Tanglanah has travelled across half the city. I
would guess that the matter is—'

'Oh, send her in, then.'

Bothered by her nakedness, Subadwan clambered
out of the pool, towelled herself dry, and put on her
gown and the floppy hat that Liguilifrey had provided.
When Tanglanah appeared at the other pool, she sat
with her legs in the water. Tanglanah swiftly
approached. Apprehension started to make Subadwan
fret, and she splashed her feet in the water.

She had forgotten how compelling was Tanglanah's
appearance. Her great height, her poise, the perfect
dark skin and rainbow eyes, the rich grey clothes: all

these features combined to produce a noble figure. In contrast Subadwan felt like a child, pale and tiny, paddling in the pool.

Tanglanah sat on the damp marble. 'You will be wondering why I am here,' she began.

'Of course.'

The pyuton's gaze swept her up and down. 'What has happened to your hair?'

Subadwan chose not to answer.

'You seem ill at ease, Subadwan.'

'After what happened with the abstract aeromorph, is it surprising?'

Tanglanah replied, 'That was an accident for which I have apologised, and for which I apologise again. I must also apologise for Laspetosyne's aberrant behaviour with the late Rhannan, for which there is no excuse. You must understand that we pyutons are not human. We have our own mores.'

'You certainly do,' Subadwan said with some bitterness. 'So why are you here?'

Tanglanah reached into the folds of her serape to produce a copper box, which she opened, revealing on a bed of black silk a glass shell the size of her palm. It twinkled amber and green in the glow-bean light.

'This is a token of my goodwill,' she told Subadwan, 'a present from me to you. Here, take it. It is harmless.'

Subadwan took the shell. She did not want to thank the pyuton, but the words trickled out of her mouth. Reluctantly she glanced up at Tanglanah's impassive face.

'Keep it safe,' said Tanglanah. 'Glass smashes.'

There was silence for a few moments.

Eventually Tanglanah said, 'I would still have you help me with my problem.'

'I don't think that's very likely.'

'Come, Subadwan, it can be a bargain of equals. There are seven Archives in Cray, each a store of memories. In my abstract country a similar situation exists. Gaya lies inside it. I can offer you aspects of Gaya, and you can offer me your unique vision. We both gain and trust does not enter the equation.'

Irritated, Subadwan said, 'Don't talk to me about Gaya as if you know something. Your Archive is only a few years old. Gaya is as old as Cray.'

This remark produced an extraordinary response. Tanglanah seemed to be wheezing, head bowed, the transducers along her neck cords spasming. Her eyes closed. For a minute she remained in this position, an occasional gasp escaping her lips. Then she raised her head to glare at Subadwan and say, 'As old as Cray? And what do you know of Cray? I knew Gaya five thousand, seven hundred and thirty-two years ago, when Gaya was already twenty thousand years old—'

'*Tanglanah!*' It was Laspetosyne, sprinting over from the side of the other pool.

Tanglanah's head jerked up. Subadwan, as frightened as she had ever been, scrambled to her feet. Tanglanah stood to meet Laspetosyne. 'Do not leave,' she told Subadwan. 'We are akin, you and I.'

'Graceful Tanglanah,' said Laspetosyne, 'it is time to leave.'

'Yes, my adjutant, that time approaches.'

Tanglanah turned to Subadwan, who stood trembling some yards away. 'Do not fear, Subadwan.'

Subadwan could not stop herself trembling. She said, 'You spoke in a fit. I know you pyutons pretend to have few emotions, but I said something to upset you.'

Laspetosyne interrupted, 'Graceful Tanglanah—'

But Tanglanah raised one hand, and her adjutant was silenced. Then she told Subadwan, 'I spoke in haste. Indeed I am old. But what of that? Pyuter power internals can last centuries. These pyutons around the pool are extremely old. The truth is that most of my life has been spent in the timeless void of my abstract country, and it is for that reason that I need a young mind to enter it with me and see it afresh.'

'And that young mind would be mine?'

'If you are willing.'

Subadwan shook her head. 'I'm not willing.'

'You may be when you have considered the matter more deeply. Think on it. Remember it will be a bargain of equals.'

'And how would we enter?'

Tanglanah glanced at Laspetosyne, then replied, 'The country is here about us, and yet it is not here. It exists hidden amongst the teeming memories of the city, controlled by an arcane rhythm buried deep in the city's soul, waiting to impose itself upon reality. I have seen much of this country, perhaps too much. That is my dilemma. You, on the other hand, are a fresh pair of eyes, and you have a mind possessed of considerable wisdom. You would be the perfect person.'

'You haven't answered my question.'

'But I have. The country imposes itself upon the reality of the city. One enters simply by not denying its existence.'

Again Laspetosyne interrupted. 'It is time to leave, Lord Archivist.'

Tanglanah nodded, then said, 'You need not decide now, Subadwan. I shall return in a few days.'

The pair departed with no further word, leaving Subadwan cold and confused.

The next morning Subadwan set up a pyuter in the room next to the Osprey Chamber and tried to connect it to the Archive of Gaya. At first the secret codes allowing her a secure line would not respond, but after ten minutes they came to life. Subadwan was left with a feeling of unease. It felt as though somebody at the Archive was making alterations, perhaps emboldened by her absence.

The network systems reported no clerks available, then returned the same result for Aquaitra and Gwythey. Subadwan cursed with frustration. Was she being ignored?

Two hours ensued during which Subadwan found herself bounced around the Archive networks, until Aquaitra was located and a line established. But Aquaitra was in a foul mood, for Umia had called her.

'He said not to appoint any assassination investigators,' she tearfully reported. 'How am I supposed to do my job if I can't appoint any investigators?'

'It's none of his business,' Subadwan replied. 'Simply appoint Archive scribes.'

'Don't you understand? He said not to appoint anybody. I can't investigate anything.'

'He's bullying you to see how far he can go. Follow my orders. Now, Aquaitra, I want you to come to the Baths—'

Aquaitra was shaking her head. 'Oh, no, I'm not giving you away that easily. It is too dangerous.'

'Come to the Baths,' Subadwan repeated.

'No. We can talk by pyuter.'

'Aquaitra, you're ignoring me. I'm still Lord Archivist.'

Again Aquaitra shook her head. Subadwan had never seen her tear-streaked face so determined. 'Things have changed, 'Dwan. Two Archivists assassinated and now the Lord Archivist has run away. People here are terrified. I *have* to stay here.'

'I can imagine what it's like,' Subadwan said, 'but you must follow my orders.'

'I'm not leaving this building.'

Subadwan felt battered and betrayed. The hopelessness of her situation had now sunk in to its most profound depth. Her power was but a fraction of its former state. Isolation was her lot. She had no option but to give in.

'Stay then,' she muttered. 'But I'm still Lord Archivist. I'll make tonight's speech by pyuter. Set up some screens in the public hall.'

'I will do that.'

The link was closed and Subadwan sat back. Was it possible that Aquaitra, embittered perhaps, had turned against her? At this moment she could be preparing to overthrow her. In the eyes of many Subadwan would appear a failure, not Gaya's chosen. Worried, Subadwan found herself stroking the glass shell, which was smooth as oyster skin yet hard as diamond. She put it to her ear, and heard the soughing of trees, the wind over moors, and the distant rippling of many streams.

During the afternoon Subadwan had Calminthan and Liguilifrey wash and massage her, so that by early evening she was relaxed and ready for the telecast ritual. The speech passed tolerably well. She noticed that her students were numerous but that their concentration was poor, as if they were looking at events off screen. Paranoia set in. It was difficult not to imagine Aquaitra – sitting nonchalantly perhaps – making dismissive gestures, or even laughing at the words of her superior, stolid Gwythey nearby in support. Perhaps they were chuckling at the contrast between her diminutive self and giant screen image.

Later, she confided in Liguilifrey, and that made her feel better. Liguilifrey's eyes had been out in the city, reporting vast crowds on the steps of the Archive of Selene, blocking Onion Street and Pine Street. There were two thousand people at least, all waiting for the speech of Pikeface. Subadwan had instructed the avian pyuter to record any such declamation. They listened to its cracked voice in horror. Subadwan cringed at the references to great change, to the Spacefish, as the moon was now called, and to the primacy of Selene.

Shaking her head, she told Liguilifrey, 'No good will come of this. Pikeface is enamoured of the mob and the power they give him.'

'Tanglanah has a similar power over those who wish for safekeeping. Crayans are frightened of sudden change. They want easy answers.'

'There are no such answers available to me,' Subadwan said. 'I want to know why Tanglanah said she had known Gaya for thousands of years – but how can I work when I'm trapped?'

Liguilifrey considered this, then said, 'What about Dwllis at the Cowhorn Tower?'

Subadwan, remembering information gleaned from the headmerger, wondered if Dwllis would know anything of the pre-Crayan era. 'It's worth a try,' she said.

They made the call. A young woman with dark eyes, thick black fuzzlocks, and an insouciant expression said, 'Copper Courtyard.'

'I seem to have the wrong line,' said Subadwan. 'I wanted the Cowhorn—'

The woman had looked off-screen. 'Mum! Some woman for Dwllis.'

The face of another woman appeared, middle aged, blonde, with eyes so faded blue they were almost grey. 'Hello?'

'I was trying to contact the Keeper of the Cowhorn Tower,' Subadwan began.

'He's resting.'

'And you are?'

'His partner. Aren't you . . . ?'

Firmly, Subadwan said, 'If you would have the Keeper talk to me for a minute, I'd be most pleased. I am indeed the Lord Archivist of Gaya.'

Two minutes passed before the pasty face of Dwllis appeared on the screen, a local power drop making his image distort into blocks. 'Good evening, Lord Archivist,' he said. 'I am honoured to speak with you. How may I help?'

'Do you know anything of Gaya before Cray was founded?'

Dwllis scratched his chin, then pulled down his hand as if remembering his manners. 'Knowledge of Gaya, you say. Madam, without accessing my records I can say nothing, but if you gave me a few days I could collate information for you. Would that suit? You see, I have rather an urgent task to complete.'

'As soon as you can,' Subadwan said.

Dwllis nodded. 'Surely your own Archive would contain such information?'

'Not from that long ago. Gaya's memoirs begin with the founding of Cray five hundred years ago.'

'Then I shall perform the work for you. Now, I heard of your difficulty, so where should I contact you?'

'Meet me at the Baths, but don't tell anybody I'm here.'

'Confidentiality is my nature. Good night to you.'

'Good night.'

Next day she spent talking with a stubborn Aquaitra and an oddly quiet Gwythey. Her feeling that these two were planning something became stronger, and she yearned to be back at her Archive, in control, sitting at the apex, her clerks ready to act upon her word. The sense of being trapped grew worse.

Later, she wandered the Baths barefoot in her black gown, enduring the glances of other people, daring them to say something. But not one person spoke to her. Either they were embarrassed or she was a non-person. She knew that many Crayans must have heard of her predicament, and wondered if her students were ashamed of their leader.

As afternoon faded imperceptibly into evening, Subadwan took her third bath of the day. Odd to think that water could be anything other than joyful. Now it was becoming an irritant.

With no warning there came the sound of clattering boots, and the harsh note of shouting voices. Subadwan raised her head to look over the side of the pool and saw emerging from the far tunnel a squad of Triaders, dressed in orange and black. There came the sound of screams and splashing water.

At first Subadwan simply did not recognise them as

intruders, despite the uniform and the guns. Such a thing at the Baths was impossible.

Somebody pointed at her and yelled. There were five intruders, fuzzlocks shorn, armed with the black rifles used by the squad who had forced her out of her Archive. Subadwan clambered out of the pool and grabbed a green towel, which she wrapped herself in.

'Don't move!' came the order. The Triaders were running to her.

Subadwan tried to ignore the cries of running bathers. She looked for any means of escape, running around the pool so that the enemy were on the opposite side.

'Stand still or we fire!' yelled the leader, swarthy skinned and with a rasping voice.

Subadwan stopped. Five rifle muzzles pointed at her. 'Gaya save me!' she wailed.

Now both pools were empty of people, apart from a group cowering at the furthest end. Subadwan waited for the Triaders to approach.

One of the pool pyutons began to move. Another followed suit. Seconds later every one was clambering out of the water. Slack-jawed the Triaders watched, their eyes wide in horror, two of them crouching and stumbling backwards. The other three stood firm.

The pyutons hobbled on their amputated legs like possessed mannequins, their bodies shuffling from side to side as they ran, their stub arms flailing. Seven surrounded Subadwan while the others formed two phalanxes and closed on the Triaders in a pincer movement.

Rifles were raised. 'No shooting!' Subadwan shouted. 'Leave the Baths now.'

The first shot was fired and a pyuton was thrown

backwards, sparks spitting from a hole in its neck. The other pyutons charged, emitting eerie howls, thin and high, like the cries of Swamp owls emerging from the mist. One of the pyutons protecting Subadwan pushed her down, and Subadwan crouched low.

Now black bullets the size of fists, trails smoking, were flying everywhere. They burst out with a grumbling '*phut*'. Pyutons were falling, all the time trying to strike Triaders. The pyutons from the other pool were charging over, and the sight of them bouncing and leaping on their amputated limbs, sacrificing everything for speed, made Subadwan groan with horror.

'Stay back!' she called to them. A black mass flew over her shoulder. Something sharp like the claws of a bird raked her cheek. 'Stay back! The pyutons are winning.'

And they were. Two Triaders lay still. The body of a third lay twitching at the pool edge. The other two were trapped. Firing a series of bullets this pair ran, jumping over pyuton bodies, then disappearing into a tunnel.

Slowly, heads bowed, the surviving pyutons returned to their poolside places. Liguilifrey approached. 'What happened?' Subadwan asked her.

'I don't know. The first thing I saw was the squad running in.'

Liguilifrey's eyes croaked, and Liguilifrey turned to listen.

'It's only Calminthan the Laverwoman come to examine the bodies,' she said.

Indeed Calminthan was approaching, two bathers accompanying her. Subadwan studied the battle scene. Eight pyutons lay still. Two others sat wounded, helpless, their eyes closed. The wall behind them was chipped and splatted with what looked like ink spots, black and slimy, slowly sinking to the floor. Little black lumps with twitching, extended claws lay everywhere.

Folding her arms across her chest to calm her trembling, Subadwan walked to the pyuton bodies. 'What do we do with these?' she asked Calminthan.

'They will have to go to the Cemetery.'

A man's voice said, 'We will take care of them.'

Subadwan turned to see eight cloaked and hooded figures walking towards them on bare feet, single file, as if in ritual. Their hands were clasped in front of them. Subadwan could not see their faces since their hoods were voluminous. Druids, she thought.

The leading druid stopped only a yard from her. 'We will take these pyuterkin to their resting places.'

'Who are you?' Subadwan asked him.

'The pyutonic undertakers of the Cemetery.'

The other druids were already picking up pyuton bodies. Subadwan wondered, as she looked on in awed silence, how they knew what had happened here. How had exactly eight come? Marshalling her courage, she said, 'I'd like to know your name.'

The druid had been about to kneel at the side of the unclaimed pyuton. He looked up, and Subadwan saw the faintest outline of a dark face. Wishing she had not spoken, she swallowed, and looked away. But the druid stood and said, 'Are you the Lord Archivist of Gaya?'

'Yes.'

The druid knelt before her. 'I am Hedalgwadey. It is our appointed task to inter Cray's electronic sisters.'

'Why are you kneeling?'

In kneeling, he seemed to speak to her belly. 'Lord Archivist, though we owe you no reverence, I offer you anyway the honour of the druids, since we were once a part of your Archive. Long ago, the druids abandoned Gaya and travelled their own winding path, their own macabre and necromantic path, which led to the Cemetery. I kneel now in an alien country before an alien sovereign.'

'This is something I wanted to know,' Subadwan said.

Hedalgwadey continued, 'Lord Archivist, the circumstances of druidic separation are not known to me, unless they are concealed in tribal memories that I may not impart even to you. Your own Archive should possess the memoirs, unless they have been dispersed to the electronic substrate of the city.'

'How did you come? You eight?' She reached out to touch Hedalgwadey's cloak.

He leaned back. 'Druids may only touch and be touched by pyuterkin, Lord Archivist. As for our arrival, we can hear something of the future on the fluctuating bands of our cosmic radios, which tune in to the afterlife. That is how my kin know who to carry to the Cemetery. And now I must leave and perform my work.'

Hedalgwadey lifted the last pyuton and settled her over his shoulder. The druids marched away, again in single file, Hedalgwadey last. He turned before entering the tunnel. 'We will meet once more,' he said.

When he had gone, Liguilifrey clung to Subadwan, trembling. 'I couldn't see them,' she said, 'not one single druid. Only the druid's voice came to me.'

'Gaya's love, your eyes must be broken.'

'They're perfect. It was the druids I couldn't see.'

Subadwan pulled away to look into Liguilifrey's face. She had no eyes, but artificial spheres had been inserted under her eyelids for cosmetic reasons. Yet Subadwan saw the fright on her face, and for the first time she wondered how the avian pyuter could see for her friend. 'You only heard him? Did you hear their cloaks rustling as they arrived?'

'Yes, yes. It was like a visitation of ghosts.'

'I don't know what to say.' Subadwan glanced up at the pyuter perched on Liguilifrey's shoulder. It stared down at her, head cocked, beak open to reveal a yellow tongue. 'I just don't know what to say. Druids are invisible to pyutons. But I've got to get back to my Archive.'

'Why?'

'Didn't you hear what Hedalgwadey said? I've missed something there. I must find out what, before Tanglanah returns. Unless . . . unless the key to all this is the headmerger, with all its secrets.'

Gripping Subadwan's hands, Liguilifrey said, 'You mustn't leave the Baths.'

'Tanglanah has secrets. She's trying to entice me into experiencing an abstract country. Perhaps I should put on the headmerger and never take it off . . . it mustn't be stolen.'

'And will you experience this abstract country?'

'No.'

Liguilifrey sighed. 'But what if you change your mind, and Aquaitra takes over the Archive?'

'I'm *not* going to do it. As for Aquaitra, she may think she runs the Archive day to day, but she would never challenge my wisdom. She daren't. I still have a little time.'

'How much?'

Subadwan drew away. 'Umia dared break Baths law. He must be desperate. I wonder if there is more to it than just wanting me a member of the Triad. But whatever scheme he plans he will try again.'

'To invade the Baths?'

'We must be vigilant. Next time his agents will enter by stealth.'

Liguilifrey hesitated, then said in a timid voice, 'So you will stay here for fear of Umia's agents?'

Subadwan sighed. 'I suppose I'll have to for now.'

13

HEDALGWADEY'S VISIT

One night, Dwllis received an entirely unexpected visit from the druid Hedalgwadey. As usual, Hedalgwadey was cloaked and cowled, and even in the light of the Cowhorn Tower's central chamber his face was concealed. Despite Dwllis's obvious consternation, Hedalgwadey spoke as if everything was normal and his visit was a natural consequence of events in the Cemetery. It turned out that this was in fact the case.

'Do you have news for me?' Dwllis asked.

'What is news?' Hedalgwadey conversationally replied. 'That which was in the future and which has just occurred. But we druids hear faint echoes of the afterlife, which for all of us is a place of the future, and so we are, after a fashion, soothsayers. Time spreads. Sometimes we become disorientated.'

'My good man, why are you here?'

'Since your visit to the Cemetery I have taken an interest in you. I have heard your rumour on the radio frequencies of the afterlife. I believe that you have an appointment.'

'Who with?'

'Why, yourself.'

Confused, Dwllis said, 'How can that be?'

'You have seen visions in the lens. I would guess the lens to be personalised to you, for it is attracted to the Cowhorn Tower, and you claim to have seen yourself in it.'

'On occasion.'

'We druids punt across the Swamps, listening, ever listening. We wish to make the future more certain by listening to its possibilities. I have seen parts of your future. There seem to be two paths, one trod by you, one by another, and depending on circumstance one of these paths will come about, and its walker triumph. But that is all I have heard. I am here to make you aware of your position.'

'I was already aware of it,' Dwllis said haughtily. 'But you say you travel the Swamps?'

'Yes.'

'Do you not worry that ordinary Crayans will find you out?'

'Not at all,' Hedalgwadey replied. 'Even if you were to report me, nobody would listen. Social inertia takes care of that. It is believed that the Swamps are a deadly region, and rightly so. People would mock you even if you were to relay tonight's discussion.'

'But you do enter the city. What if you were found out?'

Hedalgwadey gently shook his head. 'You are thinking out of key. Everybody carries in their mind some concept, some tenet, that they never question. For example, nobody ever asks why Noct owns the prime memoirs of the city, and yet Noct represents all that is bad. Is it Noct's sombre shadow that enfolds the city? Nobody asks.'

'Are you saying that nobody can truly overcome the

many authorities under which they live, in order to become a free person?'

'Not quite. Some people have attained that enlightenment. One such was somebody I knew, Seleno, Querhidwe's predecessor, who had a gift for upturning the most stable of concepts. There was a character out of place in this city – an outsider, as I considered her. What a great tragedy was her death.'

'In what sense?'

'The loss of genius is always tragic. Luckily Querhidwe continued the gnostician augmentation programme—'

Dwllis gasped. 'You know of that?'

'A few facts only. With certain lodes, Querhidwe managed to improve the ability of some gnosticians to mentally model themselves and their environment, that being the basis for consciousness. It seemed to her that they remembered the founding of Cray.'

'Then the gnosticians arrived before the founding of Cray?'

'Possibly. But whence they came, nobody knows.'

Dwllis considered what he had heard, and thinking of his frustration in not being able to communicate with the gnosticians, he wondered how feasible it would be to devise a pyuter translator. It was a bizarre thought, but could the musical warble of the creatures be considered a language? Could he translate it as he might translate Old Crayan? Perhaps even Seleno herself had missed the possibility that the gnosticians were already conscious.

'I live with a terrible dilemma,' he told Hedalgwadey. 'The Reeve is considering a gnostician purge, and I have had to lie about earlier purges, saying there were none, when in fact there were a few.

Yet I feel it is my duty to protect these kindly creatures, since they are alive, and quite possibly intelligent. What you have told me makes me feel even more that I must understand these creatures, before it is too late.'

Hedalgwadey observed, 'There are often gnosticians in the city. The streets would flow violet with their blood.'

'You know of this?'

'It is a distinct possibility.'

Appalled, Dwllis shivered. 'It must not be. And now I begin to see a pattern in the strange events that have surrounded me. Somebody in the Archive of Selene wishes to augment the intelligence of the gnosticians, perhaps so that conversation may take place. It may be that the gnosticians were here before the founding of Cray, which is all there is of the human world. Might it be that some secret fact needs to be prised out of the minds of the gnosticians, and that is what is being searched for?'

'It is a possibility.'

'Then I too must speak with one such – perhaps Crimson Boney – before all is lost.'

'That will not be easy.'

But Dwllis was not to be put off his stride. 'And there is the question of the Querhidwe's fishtail, that was passed on to me by yourself. That marks me out as a part of these events.'

'I believe it does.'

'Do you remember what Tierquthay was told by the voice from the world after this one? He was told to continue the work of Querhidwe.'

'That is not remarkable.'

'But who are these inhabitants of the afterlife?'

Hedalgwadey paused before saying, 'We consider

them the operators of the radio stations that broadcast from the afterlife, unless their minds are themselves the broadcasters. Their whispering thoughts we use to create symbolic abstracts of the future. But they do not like us.'

'So you do not know who they are?'

'Not yet.'

And with that, Hedalgwadey departed.

Dwllis mulled over what he had been told. Fear took him as he realised that his life was no longer his own, solely his own at least, and he saw dreadful visions of what, out of control, he might do. He was scared of himself. It reminded him of his childhood in Cochineal Mews, decades ago now, when in an austere and arid house he had dreamed of the Cowhorn Tower surrounded by flights of black birds, and then, compelled by a desire so strong it terrified him, had spent hour after hour walking around the place, trying to pierce its gloom. Days long since gone. In a straight-jacket he had been brought up, he realised that now, trained by distant women, distant adults, to keep quiet, keep calm, keep his self locked away in a box, away from the dangerous probing of other human beings. For human contact was dangerous. Was he, as Cuensheley claimed, a misanthrope?

He would have to keep a rigorous watch upon himself. There was no knowing what he might do.

Once again, Tanglanah and Laspetosyne stood in the golden room, an image of Greckoh before them.

Tanglanah called for constructive interference, then added, 'Greckoh, do you hear me?'

There came the sound of Greckoh's mandibles rattling, and then, 'Yes, I do.'

'The deed is almost done. Soon, Subadwan will decide she must experience our abstract country of Gwmru.'

'How soon, how soon? There is so little time remaining.'

'Very soon. Subadwan has the ability to manipulate the abstract fabric of Gwmru, through the power of her imagination. She is a Gayan with the strength to do the deed – and the accoutrements of her position. Now she owns the shell, we can focus what we can of Gwmru upon her mind. It is just a matter of trapping her, of fooling or persuading her—'

'Fooling or persuading? You have not yet decided?'

'No,' Tanglanah admitted. 'We have a mountain to leap off, not a hillock. I will make my final decision when we force Gwmru to impose itself upon the city, and I have seen how she reacts. But she is gullible and she imagines that she has worth. Such characters can be manipulated with ease since they are susceptible to pleasant words. I foresee no difficulties with Subadwan.'

'Have you penetrated her secret?'

Tanglanah hesitated. 'Our plan is twofold. The gnosticians must have tribal memories of our arrival—'

'*Have you penetrated her secret?*'

'No, Greckoh, and do not call it *her* secret, for it is the secret of Zelenaiid, our ancient enemy.'

The mandibles clattered as if jostled by a gust of wind. 'Forget niceties! Zelenaiid feels for these flimsy humans, and so only the chief Gayan can find her. That is clear! Our plan may be twofold, but enticing Subadwan into experiencing Gwmru is the mainstay.'

To this, neither Tanglanah nor Laspetosyne gave an answer.

'She will suspect nothing,' Laspetosyne ventured.

'What then of the lunar plan?' Greckoh asked.

'The return vehicle is almost complete. It is coming out of orbit and will soon hover a hundred miles or so above the city. Laspetosyne will send images at a later date.'

'I was thinking of Selene's Archive.'

'Ah,' Tanglanah said, as if remembering a guilty secret. 'They have greatly increased network defences since we tried to send in our data thieves, and this has halted progress. Tierquthay is continuing Zelenaiid's work, as you asked him to, but I do not know what stage his faction has reached.'

'Let us hope it is advanced, and that the opposing faction will not halt it. Gwmru is being eaten away. Abstract data is becoming corporeal at a frightening rate thanks to this plague of glass. Soon the living software that supports Cray will become a lump of dead hardware.'

'Spare us your nightmares,' Tanglanah remarked. 'There is one other point, Greckoh, which I cannot now put aside. We can see neither Zelenaiid nor her defences, and the fact is that Subadwan may also not be able to see. What shall I say to her when Gwmru is upon the city? What shall I tell her to look for when neither you nor I know? I think it would be wise to strengthen our lunar plan, by persuading the lunar Archivists to secretly bring the most intelligent gnostician into the Cemetery. You and the others could then attempt to speak with it.'

'The gnosticians can speak now?'

'I do not know for sure,' Tanglanah admitted, 'but it is possible. The problem is that entry into the Archive is too risky for either me or Laspetosyne. Data trawling takes too long. The solution is to bring a suitable gnostician into the Cemetery.'

Greckoh replied, 'The druids would never allow it. Only pyutons and invited humans may enter the Cemetery.'

'We will have to risk the wrath of the druids. The chosen gnostician could be clothed, disguised—'

'It is far too risky,' stated Greckoh. 'We must leave the augmented gnosticians in Selene's Archive and invade it when one is ready to be spoken with. This is our critical time, the time for which we have waited centuries, and we must not make a single mistake. It would take only one insightful druid to notice your prospective gnostician event for the plan to fall into ruins.'

'They may already have foreseen the event,' Tanglanah observed.

'If you forget the event it will never enter the mind of any druid.'

'I suspected you would find the idea difficult,' Tanglanah said, 'but in the fabric of spacetime events can happen simultaneously. If we were to provide an event momentous enough to camouflage the minor gnostician event at the Cemetery, then . . .'

Greckoh considered. 'What did you have in mind?'

'A violent explosion, or some such disaster. This would mask in the minds of the druids any future interview you might hold with a gnostician.'

Some minutes of silence passed as the insectoid being considered all it had heard. Then it said, 'Would that those cursed druids had never appeared.'

'It was inevitable once Zelenaiid released humans here,' said Tanglanah. 'Gwmru is too vast to be hidden. Pyuter technology inevitably led to experimentation with radio, and a minor predictive ability ensued. But what of my idea?'

'We waste time discussing the secondary plan. I cannot stop you from trying your idea, and if I can speak to an augmented gnostician through Cemetery weirding then I will.'

'If we cannot find Zelenaiid, then we do need to hear those ancient tales.'

'Enough of tales. I worry that you do not spend enough time on Subadwan.'

Tanglanah relaxed, as if happy with her reply. 'Subadwan will do as I require.'

Without further comment Greckoh began to move away. When the black mass had become a spot, a dot, and then vanished, Laspetosyne turned to Tanglanah and said, 'Why did you not mention Subadwan's truculence?'

'I suspect that only an adept of Gaya's mysteries can discover Zelenaiid, for that cursed enemy left secret knowledge with Gaya after the demise of our interstellar vehicle. How then could I reveal Subadwan's independence? If I described her as flighty and wayward, Greckoh would report it to the others and there would be dissent. We might then never find out how Zelenaiid perverted the creation of Cray with her flaw.'

'But we are bodies, Tanglanah. We can ignore Greckoh and the others and do as we like. We can ignore their opinions.'

'Yes, we are corporeal, forsaking the infinities of Gwmru, but our freedom is limited. None of the others can compel us, but they can persuade us. And do not forget that we two must undergo a physical journey once the vehicle is ready, unlike the others. We will have hardships to endure.'

'Will we?'

'We have sacrificed part of our potential for the sake of the others,' Tanglanah said, 'but that is right and noble. Laspetosyne, I am four thousand and eighty-four years older than you. It took me the duration of your life just to comprehend the meaning of intuition, let alone experience its joys. But now I think I see how this strange story is playing itself out.'

'How?'

'I believe that we have all made a cosmic mistake. I believe that for our art to succeed – for us to live in harmony with our environment – we must all become embodied. Minds and bodies are not separate entities, not dual creations, rather they are one. If we are truly to complete our art then we must all become bodies. We must feel the world, not intellectually appreciate it, and so acquire intuition. We must burst out of infinity to sweat, bleed, feel warmth and icy chill, and rain.'

Laspetosyne replied, 'Those thoughts shock me, and they will shock the others. I cannot agree with you.'

'There is a reason for your disbelief. You know less than me. You do not understand the meaning of guesswork. I now suspect that it is a mistake to idolise the mind at the expense of the body.'

'I cannot agree,' said Laspetosyne. 'There are three of your class, Greckoh being one other – but you fail to mention the third, who is Zelenaiid. You sound as if you are following her thoughts!'

'No, Laspetosyne. Zelenaiid is the cause of our predicament, of our enervation. Somewhere in the Cray we made there lies her flaw, that she, the queen of glass, created before she vanished into Gwmru. That flaw is the key to our survival. No, Zelenaiid remains the eternal outsider.'

'So you say. But we created Cray to be our perfect environment. We made the hardware of the city and the software of Gwmru. If we all become bodies we will be forced to experience Gwmru as an illusion, as if we were puny humans ourselves.'

'We are greater than humans.'

'Yet we rely on Subadwan, who is human.'

Tanglanah turned to face Laspetosyne. 'Do you not see the consequences of my line of thought regarding Subadwan? In Gwmru lies our answer. We cannot hope to match her clarity of thought because of our familiarity with Gwmru. Suppose then that as the signals of Subadwan's body desert her for the artificial illusion of Gwmru, her powers desert her also? She is the Lord Archivist of Gaya, the personification of Earth's memoirs. If her powers desert her in Gwmru and Zelenaiid remains hidden, what will become of us on this dismal planet?'

'Cray will become a glass shell, and all its intricacies turn to useless lumps of memory.'

'And we will *die*.'

14

CRIMSON BONEY

Vitrescence was worsening. The foundations of the Rusty Quarter houses showed dim spot, the characteristic sign of infection, while much of the Empty Quarter was now dark and sharp, with shards covering every street, the skyline an encircling row of knives. The Water Purification House standing on Feverfew Street had not yet succumbed, but everybody knew that soon it would. Elsewhere, the Cold Quarter was in some sectors a continuous sheet of cracked glass, gloomy and deadly, a place that only the mad and the dead did not leave.

Because the consequence of glass was cuts and blood, the fervour displayed by the followers of Selene lessened a little across the city, despite the continuing transformation of the Spacefish. And at last Noct's inevitable answer arrived. From the smoking factories of the Nocturnal Quarter came black plastic ladies on sticks, thousands upon thousands of them, idols superior to previous efforts in that they could be filled with water by an act of trepanning and squeezed, thus making the image weep black tears. It was noted, however, that although these idols initiated waves of high spirits to counter the lunar acolytes, they were of poor manufacture, since when squeezed the black tegument came off to stain hands and fingers. Many people wondered if this was an omen of strife and secret discord in high circles, since to certain clerks these inferior products would constitute an act of schism . . .

Dwllis was far too busy to notice any of this. One day at the Cowhorn Tower he was disturbed by noise at the door, and upon investigating he discovered Crimson Boney jumping up and down and trying to get inside. Dwllis let him in, shutting the door after making one round of the tower's circumference; the gnostician had no lunar follower, so far as he could see.

At once he was confronted with the problem of communication. For some weeks now he had realised that the gnosticians were important to the Crayan scheme of things, the words of Hedalgwadey making this hunch even more plausible. Despite Umia's threat he desperately wanted to sit down with Crimson Boney and chat. It would solve so many mysteries.

Working for Lord Archivist Subadwan had displaced his other activities. Now, a gnostician at his side, he felt the overwhelming urge to create a translator. Vivid, dreamy minutes passed as he considered the problem, oblivious to the creaking of the tower, the pattering footfall of the gnostician, to the purr and burble of on-line pyuters.

Pyuters. That was the key. It was the only way. He would have to create a pyuter powerful enough and with enough memory to become a translation machine. It could be done. An inner certainty drove him. The fact that he was the only person in all of Cray to consider gnosticians an already conscious species made him puff up with pride.

Hours of reverie passed. Thousands of discrete thoughts entered his mind.

'I'll do it,' he suddenly said, standing. 'I'll crack this damnable thing once and for all.'

Crimson Boney showed no sign of leaving. This both worried and reassured Dwllis: because of the connection with the Archive of Selene, and because he felt a bond was forming between himself and the gnostician. All Crimson Boney did was eat leaves from his backpack and drink water.

And now Dwllis worked with intensity. Touring the Cowhorn Tower, he realised that none of his pyuters would be able to hold the abstract architecture required for something so complex as translation. One avenue remained. City wall pyuters featured vast memories. Unfortunately they were electronically and physically connected to the networks. Dwllis would have to steal one.

Placating Crimson Boney with food gestures that the gnostician seemed to understand, Dwllis departed the Cowhorn Tower, keeping his visitor inside. For some hours he strode the streets, hunting northerly sectors even to the edge of the Stellar Quarter, until he found what he wanted – a wall pyuter in a dark alley, untouched by glass. The few houses opposite seemed unoccupied. He walked past it a few times, popping a fresh lump of qe'lib'we into his mouth. The previous user had carelessly left the liquid screen undrained, and now it was a slimy mess patterned with soot, dust and glass splinters. Checking again for people walking along nearby Wool Street, he took from his toolkit a crowbar and some wedges. Risking damage, he levered one side of the pyuter away from the wall, inserting the wedges. So far so good. Two more pulls on the crowbar, a loud *crack!* that penetrated his earmuffs, and the pyuter was loose. Dwllis pulled it out, bit off the optical fibres, poured away the screen, then ran.

He had succeeded in pulling off his crime. He did not know what the penalty might be if he was discovered, but he did not care. The niggling thought that he had descended from perfect citizenship to common criminality he shrugged off.

But the niggling thought was true. He had been, by choice and with pride, a man of unsoiled repute and selfless integrity. People laughed at his stiff ways, but he had right on his side. Until he broke into the Archive of Selene . . . until he stole a wall pyuter . . .

The thoughts vanished like dust sucked into a vent. He ran on. All that mattered was speaking with Crimson Boney.

Back at the Cowhorn Tower he first tried to reassure the gnostician, realising after some minutes of Crimson Boney trying to examine his pockets that the object of the search was the food he had signed earlier. What did they eat? He looked inside the gnostician's bag, finding dried blue leaves from a plant he knew grew alongside the lane leading up to his tower. Outside, torch in hand, he found this plant. Though winter was approaching, its kissleaves were touching the kissleaves of adjacent plants, so that the whole area was cross-fertilising. No fruits here, then: they would appear in spring. Dwllis hunted up and down the lane, trying to recall the dishes Cuensheley set before gnostician guests at the Copper Courtyard, looking for a plant with kissleaves shrivelled and plump fruits. But it was not the season. There: a yellow-leafed ball-plant, its runners underground. One-handed, torch stuck in his armpit, he plucked three fruits and took them to a grateful Crimson Boney.

All night he spent working with the stolen pyuter, evacuating the electronic dross, cleaning the memory of images, recalculating response times, finally recreating optical links to the tower system so that his own sub-systems could colonise the pyuter. He set the device in a barrel of bio-gel. The plan was for the pyuter to recreate itself. Once receptive, it would first experience the environment he had devised, then, as he and the gnostician tried to communicate, the sub-systems would evolve into an abstract ecology devoted to the translation of human and gnostician words . . . if such words existed.

When the optical links grew, the environment appeared. The pyuter rejected nothing, accepting knowledge of Cray, of Dwllis and the gnostician, and of the concepts of language. It became as a year-old child, ready to speak.

Dwllis began collecting oddments from his rooms. He sat next to Crimson Boney and showed him a shoe. 'Shoe,' he said. 'Shoe?' He stared at the gnostician, waving the shoe in front of the creature's dark eyes. Above these eyes, a wide mouth slobbered with the remains of yellow fruit: below, tentacles shivered.

The gnostician made a sound. Dwllis squeezed a bulb on the end of a wire to alert the pyuter to what he hoped was a gnostician word. Later on, when the system became intelligent, he wanted it to perform this task itself, as it evolved an understanding of the rules of gnostician sounds.

'Cloth,' he said, waving a cloth. 'Cloth.'

Crimson Boney took the cloth and drew it close to his tentacles, before emitting a grunt.

'Glass.' A squeal.

'Plant.' A purr.

'Metal.' A musical whine.

And so the process continued. With no feedback from the pyuter Dwllis was forced to continue until he ran out of objects, at which point he paused for rest. The pyuter had already developed a level into which he could not inquire, a level below the symbolic, like the invisible molecules that made up a visible chunk of plastic. But despite the intense needs that he had programmed into the pyuter by means of its environment, it was not acting autonomously. Groups of symbols were floating through its electronic core, but not joining. It must need more data.

Suddenly Crimson Boney began a continuous speech like a squealing song, and he paced up and down the chamber, head bobbing and hairs erect as if he was declaiming to an invisible audience. 'Are you all right?' Dwllis pointlessly said, following with more questions along the same line. Crimson Boney seemed upset, and although Dwllis could not tell if this guess was correct, he did have the eerie sensation of strong emotions coursing through the body of the gnostician.

And then the barrel burst.

He had not noticed sub-systems evolving with manic speed. The barrel burst and a solid block of quivering gel emerged. This was an autonomous protein structured by artificial DNA, appropriated, so it was said, from the depths of the Swamps by Noct's dark aquanauts. Noct alone knew what it could do.

Crimson Boney stood still, tentacles rigid, eyes slitted, frozen in a pose of tension.

With the plastic struts of the barrel cast aside, the bio-gel, holding the pyuter firm like a child holds a doll, expanded into a column five feet tall, becoming translucent. Inside, filaments snaked with time-lapse speed, growing into nodules, and then into a range of shapes like organs. Dwllis was reminded of what he had seen at the Cemetery. Something here was growing. The pyuter was becoming its brain, held in what looked like the chest of a person.

It *was* a person. Now the image had come to mind he saw that two legs were forming, two arms, and a head from which yellow hair sprouted.

The thing was turning into a pyuton. Outer layers were now opaque, pink skin just like his. The face was appearing, with nose and mouth. The eyes were black as night, as if declaring that the pyuton had no soul, and they seemed to stare with macabre intensity at Dwllis, until, much to his relief, a brown iris and a bloodshot white appeared. Creaking and squeaking, the body stretched and filled, its skin drying. And it was Etwe.

Dwllis had never expected to see her again. Seeing her here, naked, made him tremble and he wanted to run away, though he could not. Nor could Crimson Boney, who, likewise, was fascinated.

Tentatively she moved. She twirled about, took hesitant steps. Then she spoke to Dwllis and a musical babble simultaneously emerged from her mouth, giving her words that electronic tinge of two sounds modulating one another.

'Dwllis . . . we speak . . . you, me . . . me, you.'

Crimson Boney approached Etwe with tentacles twitching. The holes at the side of his head flexed. It seemed to Dwllis that he spoke back in the gnostician tongue.

Etwe said, 'Yes . . . I speak you . . . you, me.'

This, Dwllis realised, was his translator. It had become autonomous in a most fiendish way.

'Metal,' Etwe said, 'string, head, leg, plastic, silicon, nose.' As she spoke these words their equivalents, or what Dwllis presumed must be their equivalents, were spoken in the musical gnostician tongue, and he was both appalled and astonished to see Crimson Boney running around the chamber to fetch examples of these substances.

'Etwe, are you really here?' he said.

Etwe looked at him. 'I never go . . . not go . . .'

She had returned. What would Cuensheley say?

He tried to get a grip on himself. Severely, he said, 'Etwe, tell me the route to your room upstairs. Now!'

She looked at him, looked up at the ceiling, but was not able to reply coherently. 'Go up . . . up plastic . . .'

So this was far from a complete translator. The one-year-old child had developed a year or two. Dwllis felt some relief at this. The last thing he wanted was Etwe around again, if this was Etwe. How had the pyuton formed so? Had Etwe been spying on him through the networks, waiting for her chance to pounce, to become once again his servant? The thought was dreadful. But at least he had some time in which to think. Of course, the work of translation would have to continue; Etwe's brain must grow and mature. Yet somehow he would have to squash Etwe out.

Dwllis considered the wider picture. Tierquthay had been told by the radio voice from the afterlife that the work of gnostician augmentation was one key to understanding the threat of vitrescence and the luminophagi. In a matter of days, he might be able to question a gnostician directly. He and Cuensheley would not need to break into Selene's house again. He was close to finding out some answers.

A knock from outside. He bustled Etwe into a side room and ran for the door, opening it to find Cuensheley, lumod in one hand, basket in the other.

'Hello,' she said.

'Good morning, what d'you want?' he asked, a trifle brashly.

She frowned. 'I thought we'd arranged for you to have deliveries every other day, as you're not going to live with me.'

Dwllis smelled a yeasty smell from the basket. 'Indeed, we did. It is my damnable memory.'

Cuensheley looked into the tower. 'Aren't you going to let me in, then? Is that the loper you were telling me about?'

'Yes, that is Crimson Boney.'

'How's the translator going?'

'Oh, most well,' Dwllis said. Desperate, he mentally scrambled for a way to force her away from the tower. If she saw Etwe, all his benefits would vanish.

'Are you all right?' she asked again.

Dwllis kissed her on the cheek. She smiled and kissed him back. He said, 'I am most well, Cuensheley. What say we go for a walk into the city? I have not had much of a chance to see you of late, being beset by the Reeve's orders.'

'There is something wrong, isn't there? You're practically stuttering.'

Dwllis swallowed. 'Truth be told,' he began, 'I may be worried about ... about the amount of this damnable sponge I am chewing. You are getting me into bad habits.' He took the basket from her and stepped out. 'Come along.'

Cuensheley jumped inside. 'No.'

Dwllis re-entered the tower. There stood Etwe.

Cuensheley rounded on him. 'You liar.'

Dwllis mustered his sternest tones. She must not get another word in. 'It is not as you think,' he began. 'This is a new pyuton. I know not where it—'

'She.'

'Where *it* comes from. It appeared mysteriously from my translator barrel. It is not the old Etwe. I have no interest in this pyuton except as a translator, as my translation routines are within its brain. That is the truth. If you disbelieve me, it is your fault. Speak to it. The damned thing can hardly string a sentence together.'

'I didn't realise speech was something you wanted from Etwe,' Cuensheley viciously said. The jealousy was plain in her flushed face. 'So this isn't Etwe?'

'It is the form of Etwe, with the brain of a low-standard pyuton.' Dwllis looked away, the tension he felt making his limbs tremble.

Cuensheley approached Etwe and said, 'Well, well, so you never left the tower after all. That's what happened, isn't it?'

Etwe replied, 'Tower . . . up . . . go up plastic.'

'Do you see what I mean?' Dwllis triumphantly asked.

Cuensheley shrugged, making for the door. 'There's something going on. Maybe this pyuton isn't the vacuous fool you used to entertain here, but she looks the same—'

Dwllis's restraint shattered. 'Don't talk to me! If I say she is not Etwe then she damn well is not! Don't you accuse *me* of being a liar, you damned . . . nuisance.'

He turned away, ashamed, the anger gone as if a switch had been thrown inside his mind.

Cuensheley approached and tried to hug him, but he pushed her away and stared silent at the bare wall. Again he had been goaded into a scene.

Cuensheley touched his arm. 'Where does all this anger come from?'

'Never you mind.'

'I do mind. I want to know why you're so angry, why you shacked up with a pyuton, why you won't have anything to do with me. I *want* to know.'

'Being angry is wrong. It is negative and bad.'

'You were brought up by a guardian,' Cuensheley said. 'I suppose it was a lesson you learned.'

'It is common sense. Now go. I may come see you in a few days, but do not look out for me.'

Cuensheley, face grim, made for the door. On the step she turned to say, 'Don't think you've got off the hook by making me feel guilty. You lied to me. What else have you lied about? The interment at the Cemetery? The Archive of Selene, maybe?'

Dwllis could find no answer to these accusations and, though he wanted to stand up for himself, he remained silent.

Cuensheley uttered a grim laugh. 'The only true fool is he who rejects the sincere advances of another.'

'Is that then what this is all about? You cannot bear for me to reject you?'

Cuensheley shrugged. Her gaze turned to the nocturnal scene outside. In the wordless pause, the clamour of the city entered Dwllis's speech-amplifying earmuffs as a low rumble, and he watched the changes on her face, cursing himself again when he realised how beautiful she was. Then she said, 'Maybe it is. I

know more about your feelings than you imagine. I'm
not the guilty one here.'

She departed. Dwllis shut the door immediately and
returned to the chamber off the hall, in which Etwe
stood. Crimson Boney lay on a divan.

Dwllis stopped to observe them both. Somehow, the
remembered picture of Cuensheley at his door over-
laid the real Etwe: he saw drifting blonde fuzzlocks
trailing rainbow ribbons, a figure somewhat more
slender than it used to be, two bewitching blue eyes, a
classic oval face. For a moment he realised that he was
a fool to ignore Cuensheley. There was nothing to fear.
Then the insight vanished, crushed by the acquired
behaviour of forty desolate years.

Abruptly he turned and hurried up the stairs to his
own chamber. There he tore off his clothes and,
automatically, put them out for Etwe to wash. 'What
am I doing?' he asked himself. He was not that old
Dwllis. He never could be again. His previous, perfect self had been shattered by Cuensheley. He must
either face the new circumstances or withdraw. And
he knew only cowards withdrew.

He slept until evening.

He took pains in dressing, choosing his pale violet
undershirt, black padded jacket, black kirtle with blue
leggings and a pair of stout plastic shoes. The leggings
and his socks were almost impossible to put on
one-handed, but he persevered. Cuensheley's locket he
threw into a corner, but in the end he put it in his
pocket. Then he returned to work.

An intense twelve hours followed. Eschewing simple
nouns, he tried to coax from Crimson Boney and the
translator – he refused to call the new pyuton Etwe –
any simple sentence, but the task of finding gnostician

words for such abstracts as 'the', 'a', 'it' and the like was too difficult. Symbolic systems were linking, but there were many levels of organisation yet to go.

He refused to give up. Though he and Crimson Boney shared simple nouns they were yet to communicate in depth. And yet he knew that Crimson Boney was aware of his purpose. The gnostician wanted to talk. As time passed, Dwllis wondered what had made Crimson Boney leave the Archive of Selene and rush to stay at the Cowhorn Tower. The image of a pike came to his mind.

15

THE HISTORY OF THE EARTH

When he was ready, Dwllis insisted that he go to the Baths alone. He did not want Cuensheley around when he presented Subadwan with what he had discovered.

He had never been to the place before. He considered public bathing a decadent and unnecessary waste of time, particularly if, as he had heard, persons of both sexes bathed naked. He found himself worried about entering the Baths because the potential for embarrassment was great, and he feared embarrassment almost as much as he feared anger. Embarrassment was equivalent to shame: to ostracision.

At the entrance he shouldered past lunar students and pushed through the double doors. High walls painted pastel blue and decorated with maps of starfields greeted him. The hall floor and ceiling were tiled, and the sound of his motion, and that of the shutting door, reverberated for many seconds. 'Hello?' he said. As he waited he noticed skittering at his feet a pair of bathkins – small, lithe creatures kept here to ensure the building remained free of pyuter vermin expelled by the bursting blisters of Westcity.

A woman approached – a lesser, Dwllis judged. 'Hello?' she said. 'What do you want?'

'Good afternoon my good woman,' he replied. 'I am here to speak with the madam Subadwan.'

'I'll go get her.'

'No matter,' Dwllis said, following, 'just lead me to her if you would be so kind.'

'She expecting you, eh?'

'She is indeed.'

Dwllis was led to a chamber set with luxurious divans, in which Subadwan sat. 'Thank you, Calminthan,' she said as the woman departed. Subadwan looked wan. Her clothes were fresh and pressed but they lay awkwardly, as if the body underneath was recovering from injury, and her whole manner was of a tired, dejected woman.

'Good afternoon, Lord Archivist,' Dwllis began. He indicated the bank of memories under his arm. 'This case contains the stories you asked me to collate.'

'Thank you,' Subadwan said. 'What, um . . . what did you find?'

'Some curious things.'

Subadwan nodded. 'Well, tell me some of them.'

Dwllis sat opposite the Lord Archivist, opening his case. The screen edges formed themselves, their plastic strips dovetailing and merging to create four corners. Into this space Dwllis poured liquid to make the screen. Random rainbow pixels shimmered, then expanded like oil on water to form the opening screen. Dwllis pressed pads, said, 'Begin,' then watched numbered red circles appear. He requested number one.

'Beginning my research,' he said, 'I saw that there

had been worship of Gaya before Cray was built. Did you know Gaya was somehow related to an Emerald Goddess? Emerald being a word used to denote a variety of green.'

'How could humans have been here before Cray?'

'It only makes sense if my theory of a previous city is followed,' Dwllis replied. 'This earlier city is implied by the antique memories that I collate, but it remains mysterious.'

'Does this Emerald Goddess appear in any of the tales of Cray's origin?'

'No. That story speaks vaguely of stellar fish. But it is clear that five hundred years ago worship of the Emerald Goddess changed, splitting into three large factions and a fourth smaller one.'

'These factions,' Subadwan asked, 'what were they?'

'They seem to be linked to age. One was the faction of the Chthonic Aspect – deep, underground, with a young idol central in the imagery. The second was of the Vivid Aspect, with a middle-aged idol. The third was of the Wise Aspect – old, profound, perhaps a little sad. The fourth faction was the runt, as it were, and was devoted to the Male Aspect.'

'That could be the druids,' Subadwan said.

Dwllis had considered this possibility already, but thought it unlikely. 'Possibly,' he said.

'Tell me more of these idols.'

Dwllis selected new information via his screen. 'The Chthonic Aspect was perhaps the most dangerous of the four. It seems to represent the darkness of the pre-formed mind, the unconscious perhaps, with its primal desires, raw sensations, and its simple outlook. This idol is young, dark-skinned, recently entered into puberty, with a manner of arrogance – yet she was deadly, and at the same time sombre.'

'Noct,' Subadwan said.

Dwllis stared at her. 'I am sorry, Lord Archivist?'

'Noct,' said Subadwan, louder. 'Sounds like Noct.'

Dwllis looked down at the pyuter screen. 'If your guess is correct, then what is to follow must be put into a new framework. Noct she is. The Chthonic Aspect . . . which means that Noct is the sister of Gaya.'

Subadwan did not seem shocked. 'I realise the implications. Do continue.'

Dwllis did. 'The Vivid Aspect – which clearly is Gaya – was the middle-aged aspect, pinkly voluptuous, begging your pardon madam, with a vital and overly emotional outlook. Her sigils and fetishes were blue.'

'Green,' Subadwan corrected.

'Green?'

'Gaya's blue was originally green.'

'Quite fascinating. Now, the Wise Aspect—'

'Selene.'

'—was old and pale, with a round face. Wrinkled, she was, with white sigils. She was skilled in the telling of tales with profound meanings. Yes, Lord Archivist, Selene that would be. It would seem that Noct, Gaya and Selene are all sisters, descended if you like from the early, pre-Crayan Emerald Goddess.'

'And the fourth faction,' said Subadwan, 'the Male Aspect, was that tiny bit of masculinity within the Emerald Goddess. A druid once told me that his sect was derived from mine. At the time I believed him only with my mind, not with my heart, but now . . . Gaya love me, how the Triad would change if that fact became known.'

'Reeve Umia would suppress it instantly,' Dwllis said.

'He would. But only we two know at the moment.' Subadwan paused, then added, 'We two are custodians of dangerous knowledge.'

Dwllis's mind spun with possibilities. 'Lord Archivist,' he said, 'I bring knowledge too of the Emerald Goddess, gathered, as was all the previous material, by my predecessors. The Emerald Goddess was ancient, fat and fertile if I might be so bold, and she represented the very Earth we stand on. Your religion is the spiritual successor of that most ancient of cults.'

Subadwan nodded. 'I am the rightful leader of this city! All religions should accept Gaya as pre-eminent.' Subadwan stood and began to pace around her divan. 'Noct has with her arrogant thrusting taken over this city, made it her own. Noct and the Triad are one, aren't they? It should be Gaya and the Triad are one. This constant darkness is her sombre spirit. We have to bring her down to make Cray a place fit for everyone to live in.'

'I would not advocate war,' Dwllis said nervously.

Subadwan sat. 'I can't help wanting to do something to make Cray better. It's a horrible city. Often I hate it, I can't help that. Gaya save me, to think that I left my father and then became the Lord Archivist of Gaya. What an irony!'

Dwllis was alarmed at the course the conversation was taking. He had expected Subadwan to be shocked, but he had not expected quite this conclusion. The thought of Subadwan and the Archive of Gaya attempting a coup made him shudder, especially with the Archive of Selene so volatile and agitated by the arrival of Pikeface. 'Madam,' he said, 'you have two enemies of considerable power, namely this upstart demagogue Pikeface, whom I consider far more dangerous than the doddery old Tierquthay, and of course Reeve Umia, who has the entire weight of the Triad behind him. Surely you must accept your position as it is now?'

'We'll see,' Subadwan replied.

When Dwllis departed the Baths, he began to walk west. Only minutes had passed before a knot of chanting, jumping, flailing Selenites barred his way. 'The moon is gone! The Spacefish is here! Selene to the fore! Come down pale Selene and cover us all with light! Oh, ecstasy! Oh, ecstasy!' But from the centre of this mob a more sinister figure emerged.

Pikeface. Gulping convulsively, Dwllis looked up at the towering man. Truly he was a hideous sight. It was easy to ignore the steely muscles, the shimmering blue-black cloak and the armour, and instead gaze at the fish face emerging bent over from the cloak's neck. Those baleful eyes, the toothed maw, the slick skin reflecting light storms in the plastic street below. Dwllis stood frozen as a bathkin before a carnivorous pedician, waiting for the pounce.

'Who are you?' Pikeface demanded in an astonishingly loud voice.

'I am the Keeper of the Cowhorn Tower.'

Pikeface laughed. 'Have you come to challenge me or aid me? Speak quickly.'

Petrified, Dwllis found one iota of courage. He replied, 'I am just a man of Cray, and I demand right of passage!' And with that he ran. They did not stop him, but Pikeface laughed again and Dwllis heard him call out, 'We are kin against authority!'

He ran all the way along Peppermint Street, his composure lost, until at the junction with Culverkeys Street he paused to look back, to see that no pursuit had been made. Gasping for breath he made at a more sedate pace to the Cowhorn Tower, where he locked himself in.

Crimson Boney and the translator sat in a side room. Dwllis ignored them and made for his own chamber, where he changed all his clothes and perfumed his sweating body with peach-scented talc. Then he sat and considered the afternoon's events.

When evening arrived he left the Cowhorn Tower, leaving Crimson Boney to talk as much as he could with the translator, for he wanted urgently to speak with the gnostician. He made for the Copper Courtyard, cool, calmed, but carrying unease among his thoughts. There Cuensheley sympathetically received him, and offered him free drinks, and accommodation for the night should he require it.

He told her of the day's events, omitting only his encounter with Pikeface. She was more concerned at what she called his suicidal defence of gnosticians. Dwllis, irritated by her prejudice, stood up as if to leave.

Cuensheley said, 'I'm going to bed. You coming?'

Dwllis attempted a casual laugh. 'No. I must return to the Cowhorn Tower. Soon, Crimson Boney will be conversing with me.'

Cuensheley kissed him, and he left. In the streets gnosticians were making merry, following a jaunty procession down the street. At the head one group carried a yellow disk, while another carried a giant kissleaf. Dwllis had seen the ritual before. Soon, the kissleaf would be punctured, and the clay fishes that the gnosticians carried would joyfully be cracked into two. He shrugged to himself, uneasy with such symbolism.

But as he approached the Cowhorn Tower his thoughts turned to Pikeface. Kin, he had been called. Why? He knew not. At the door of the Cowhorn Tower he paused, turning to look out over the city, Subadwan's words in his mind: 'It's a horrible city. Often I hate it . . .'

Dwllis both loved and hated it. He felt part of it. Yet its odious alleys, deafening din, its shameful regime and decadent morals were aspects that he loathed. He slammed the door shut.

Aquaitra pondered long over whether she should follow the instructions just sent by Subadwan. The Archive was losing its coherence as if Gaya was fading, and it seemed to her that her Lord Archivist was the cause of this problem. She was remote and, if she admitted it to herself, ineffectual. The Archive could only last a short time if its leader was exiled.

Yet they had been friends for years. Since the young Subadwan had escaped the ethical clutches of Noct's pyutons, she and Aquaitra had found pleasure and solace in each other's company. It was not an especially close friendship, but it was steadfast, and both, without saying it, had thought it could last until the end of their days.

Not so. Now all was changed. Subadwan had gone, had accused her of absurd misdemeanors, had become involved in a deadly affair.

Still, Aquaitra felt bonds. She would do as Subadwan had instructed and collect shells from the beach.

Dawn was approaching. She walked south to the edge of the city, then descended to the beach by way of a wriggling column of bronze plates, worn and dented over the years by many boots. Around her grew sharp plants, leafless now, their scarlet stems slick with tiny razors, while between these globular black masses expanded – the aerial roots of deeper plants that drew sustenance from geological sources.

The beach lay all around her. For a few moments she studied its dead surface. Few people ventured here since the sands were considered unsafe, the haunt of agnosticians ejected from their tribal homes, of suicidal gnosticians who ended their lives in the surf, slashing their throats with shards of glass, and of unspecified sea monsters that on occasion rose up from the depths to lay single eggs the size of a cart.

Not the place for an Archivist. Aquaitra, glancing this way and that, tripped lightly away from the cliff face and began to search for glass shells.

There did not appear to be many about. Because they seemed to serve no purpose they were ignored by most, but some with an eye for beauty collected them, displaying them like trophies on bookshelves or hanging them from wire to make prettily tinkling mobiles.

For a moment Aquaitra stood straight and cursed Subadwan for asking this ridiculous favour. She could see the advantage of comparing Tanglanah's gift with another, but why ask her? Sighing, she continued the search.

After half an hour she thought there really were

none, but as she turned to gaze over the sea at rosy dawn clouds she saw half buried in ochre sand what looked like glittering fingers, curved as if part of a buried corpse.

It was a shell. Aquaitra plucked it from the sand and brushed off the debris. It was the size and shape of her own hand, perfectly transparent, with flaws at its hinge that sparkled like opals. She put it to one ear and, when she turned to minimise the noise of the crashing sea, heard a babbling brook that seemed to leap down over clacking stones. Suddenly inspired, she dug again and found the other half of the shell.

She turned to face the beach and placed a shell over each ear.

Ghostly apparitions clouded her vision as the strength of the sonic disturbance mesmerised her mind. It was as if an alternate world had imposed itself upon her consciousness. For a while she stood swaying, as the half-hallucinations flickered and shimmered across her senses, manifesting as colours, brief smells of perfume and blossom, and then a taste at the back of her tongue like bitter lemons. And after a few seconds there was heat on her back, something brushing the fine hairs on her arms, and then a hand stroking her hair.

She pulled the shells away. Reality shocked her, and she staggered as if rudely shaken from a dream. In her hands the shells seemed innocent.

Yet as she looked a miracle happened. Hundreds of shells appeared out of the air and, as one, thunked a few inches to the yielding sand, precisely as the sun rose above the horizon and through a rent in the gloom sent amber rays to make the beach glitter. To

Aquaitra the vision was a cosmic strip of diamonds. Frightened, she climbed to the top of the cliffs. Turning again, she saw that already many of the shells were sinking into the sand or being muddied by surf.

16

GWMRU

Was that Liguilifrey's eyes in the bathkin's pink, wet mouth? The creature slunk along a corridor, stomach to the floor and eyes wide, its orange fur bristling. Subadwan stopped. It *was* the avian pyuter, ripped and shredded by tiny teeth.

Subadwan made to catch the creature, but, agile as an insect in flight, it darted around her hand, slipped by, and disappeared into the maze of tunnels around the Osprey Chamber, giving a mewling cry as if in triumph.

Subadwan was suddenly frightened. She ran to the front of the Baths, where she found Liguilifrey sitting calm, bath towels in her lap, a stick of perfumed plastic poked into a lapel hole. But her pyuter eyes were perched upon her shoulder.

Relaxed, Subadwan approached. 'I thought I saw your eyes, caught like vermin by one of the bathkins.'

'My eyes are fine,' Liguilifrey said, smiling.

Absent-mindedly, her train of thought broken, Subadwan gazed at the avian pyuter. With something of a stern gaze it turned to her. It just stared. Subadwan shivered. The eyes were beady bright, the beak sharp as

a needle, and when it opened its mouth to squawk its
tongue was . . . black?

Her muscles acted with reflexive speed. She slapped
the thing off Liguilifrey's shoulder, causing the
masseuse to shriek, clasp her face, and fall to the floor.
The eyes' wings were raised, as if for flight. Yelling,
Subadwan tried to kick it aside, to disable it, break it,
but it jumped, flapped, then rose. It seemed huge.

Subadwan knew instinctively that it was a beast
of Noct. Now it was three feet high and growing,
expanding, hissing, eyes fiery and beak a foot long
like the serrated scimitars of the Triaders. Its
taloned wings created evil-smelling gusts of air, and
its feet clawed with glinting steel and flexed with
spasmodic fury. Subadwan retreated. Liguilifrey lay
on the floor, rolling about with her face in her
hands, groaning.

She had only heard of the shape changers. Deadly
spirits they were, pyuterdriven carbon and silicon,
their brains wired to know only greed. Some were too
wild to tame: they were shoved into the pyuter
networks like banshees forced into Cemetery mud.

Subadwan carried no weapon. She did not know
how to defend herself. The beast screeched and began
a diving attack.

'Gaya save me!' she cried.

From out of the marble wall a white creature leaped
as if spring-loaded, with fangs of aluminium and eyes
of beryl.

'Gaya save me,' Subadwan repeated.

The two beasts fought. The Noct spirit shed black
blood that spurted like hot wax, solidifying where it
hit cool marble. The Baths creature seemed hard as
titanium, but it was slower. It hunched down and

lashed out, whereas the Noct beast attacked with chaotic fury, with talons, razor beak and wings. When the opposing bodies clashed, sparks fountained into the air, sparks that soon gave the atmosphere a smoky, fetid cast, so that after some minutes of screaming battle there was little Subadwan could see except turbulent smoke.

Then there was only silence. Liguilifrey appeared, pulling herself blind along the corridor. Subadwan took her by the hands and dragged her away. 'What happened?' Liguilifrey gasped. 'I'm blinded.'

'Gaya love me, you can't see anything?'

'Nothing.'

Subadwan groaned as she pulled her friend away. The smoke was clearing, allowing her a view of a body strewn like rags on the tunnel floor, surrounded by sooty debris. The Baths creature was gone.

Liguilifrey was clearly in shock, and Subadwan sat her up against a wall. 'Your eyes must have been substituted by the spirit of Noct,' she said, glancing back at the damaged corridor. 'No doubt the thing would have pounced on me when it was ordered to. I told you Umia would do his utmost to capture me.'

'But I'm blind, Subadwan, I'm blind.'

Subadwan hugged her friend. 'I know. We'll have to evolve another pyuter for you as soon as possible. In my Archive there are nano-machine tanks that can create the bodies of pyuters from DNA recipes. I control them, even though I'm stuck here. We'll get you eyes, Liguilifrey.'

'But they were connected to me.'

Subadwan glanced at the face of her friend, and wondered just what the link had been. 'If eyes can be made once,' she said, 'they can be made twice.'

Liguilifrey seemed unhappy, but she made no further comment. Subadwan left her and returned to the scene of the battle. The rags had sublimated, leaving only a dark stain in the shape of a pedician. Shuddering, Subadwan returned to Liguilifrey and guided the masseuse to the Osprey Chamber, where they both sat.

Liguilifrey said, 'What will you do now?'

'What will you do?' Subadwan countered.

Liguilifrey was passing through shock. But she had no tear ducts. Her voice was thick with emotion and she waved her head from side to side, as if trying to sense the room around her by means of echoes. 'I'll have to call in Calminthan,' she said. 'We'll have to arrange new procedures.'

'I'll try to help,' said Subadwan. 'I'll call Gwythey now.'

But her second deputy was not answering, and the Archive help screen seemed different somehow, as if it has been tampered with. For some time Subadwan ricocheted around the city networks trying to contact her Archive, but every system seemed scrambled, and some of it was meaningless static.

Returning to the distressed Liguilifrey brought on a little desperation. If something had happened she ought to be at the Archive. A quick visit should be safe, so long as she left the Baths in disguise.

But she possessed the headmerger. It contained vital information. She would have to put it on. She could not risk losing it.

Comforting Liguilifrey, she robed herself, taking a hood from stock, and light shoes in which she could run if need be. There were no weapons inside the Baths, but she took an epidermal scraper which could be used as a blunt dagger. Thus equipped she made for the front doors.

The streets outside were crowded despite it being early, and they overflowed with lunar jetsam.

A tall figure stood on the opposite side of the street. Tanglanah.

She was waiting with pyuton patience, arms folded. Subadwan pulled her hood down, but she had been spotted.

Tanglanah approached. Angrily, Subadwan said, 'What are you doing here? Didn't I tell you we wanted nothing to do with you?'

'I must have misheard,' Tanglanah answered.

Subadwan, lost for words, just wanted to lash out. 'I want you to leave me alone. I'm not interested in your Archive. What is safekeeping, anyway? Have you bothered to explain it to your followers, or do they just listen with deaf ears?'

Tanglanah paused long enough for Subadwan's alert senses to capture and record the hesitation. 'Safekeeping is important.'

'I know that.'

'We preach the wisdom of safety.'

'You're floundering,' Subadwan accused, mocking Tanglanah in words and in tone.

'No,' Tanglanah insisted. Again the pyuton paused, before saying in a quiet voice, 'Why be so harsh? Are we not both of an exalted order? We should work together, you and I.'

Subadwan managed a laugh, though she felt only apprehension. 'So you're not going to tell me why the safety of Crayans is so important to you?'

'I will if you want me to, but I do not think you really want to know.'

'I do want to know, but it can wait.'

'That smacks of contrition,' Tanglanah remarked.

'It might do had I sinned. But I think I'm entitled to enquire about your little library of fantasies.'

'It was the timing that stood out.'

Subadwan shrugged. She was almost enjoying the tussle. 'It would stand out to one whose plans were coming to fruition.'

'If you still do not trust me, do not joust with me.'

'So now you're trying to make me feel inadequate. I have many powers, Tanglanah.'

This remark, casually uttered, made Tanglanah again hesitate for some time. Then she said, 'Do you have the shell I gave you?'

'Not on me.'

'It matters not. You do possess it.'

'Yes . . .'

Tanglanah is afraid of me, Subadwan realised. Into her mind came other tiny clues to the dark, yet conscious, being inside Tanglanah's alloy skull. She understood that, despite the pyuton's social poise and intelligence, she, small Subadwan, had influence. Yes, Tanglanah was old and she was only twenty-five, but she possessed qualities the pyuton did not.

'I don't trust you,' she told Tanglanah. 'As we speak my deputy is looking for glass shells, so I can test yours against real ones.'

And then . . .

Subadwan slid into a Crayan landscape, as if into a pool of water. Behind her the Baths shimmered into nothingness, leaving a plastic field covered with darkness. Above, a blue, green and white disk sailed high. All around stood the familiar buildings of Peppermint Street and, a little way off, Arrowmint

Street: dark streets, not flashing with motes at the speed of light, though some were marked with signs glowing like fluorescent paint under an ultraviolet lamp. And yet most disconcerting was the quiet, as if her amplifiers had broken. Silence unnerved her. All she could hear was the soughing of the wind, and far off the sea, ghostly and discomfitting enough to make her shiver.

She waited for something to happen.

Nothing did, and there was no sign of Tanglanah.

After a minute she noticed that nearby a ball of air was flexing, glittering red, then transforming – and Tanglanah appeared from it, seated and with eyes closed, like a coal from a fire. She rose in one balletic movement. 'We are here,' she told Subadwan.

Subadwan answered, 'It looks like Cray.'

'Does that surprise you?'

'Can't you tell I'm surprised?' Subadwan replied. 'What have you done? What's happened to Cray?'

Tanglanah said, 'This was not of my doing. Gwmru has imposed itself upon the city.'

'But what's happened?'

'Cray is a city composed of memory. These memories are organised in subtle ways, following their own rhythms, some of which are ancient. Every now and again, two sundered halves interfere constructively, and this is the result. A new Cray has temporarily appeared.'

'How long will it last? Am I safe?'

Tanglanah ignored the questions. 'I must go now. I have much still to see.'

Subadwan felt free to goad and press Tanglanah to the limits of endurance. 'You *must* have seen this before if you're as old as you say you are.'

'I did not say how old I was.'

'You were too frightened,' Subadwan retorted. 'I know you're hiding something.'

'Very well,' Tanglanah said, 'if age interests you, know that I am five thousand, seven hundred and thirty-two years old.'

This declaration was unexpected. Subadwan did not hide her reaction. There was no point. 'Who are you?' she asked, wondering why she had not thought to ask that question before.

'I am graceful Tanglanah, Lord Archivist of the Archive of Safekeeping. That is who I am. Now let us walk awhile.'

They began to stroll westward down Peppermint Street. It was eerie walking down a street devoid of people. Subadwan found herself unable to imagine five thousand years, she who had been indoctrinated into the belief that Cray was five centuries old, but she did feel some awe at the presence by her side. Tanglanah had always emanated mystery, and the knowledge she had just gained made the pyuton still more mysterious.

'You've wanted me to experience this for some time, haven't you?' she said.

'My original bargain was for us to help one another,' Tanglanah said. 'Let me be plain. I will show you Gaya if you will show me what I seek. That is all.'

'What exactly is it you're looking for?'

'I do not know. That is the problem. I have lived here so long—'

'So that's why you told me your age,' Subadwan interrupted, realisation dawning. 'I *need* to know because of my task.'

'My problem is that I am too familiar with Gwmru to see its flaw.'

'Flaw?'

'Some presence invisible to me lives here. You must locate it for me. Your fresh human eyes will spot it. In turn, I will show you Gaya, for I know exactly where Gaya is.'

Subadwan nodded. 'So, will you follow me around the city, or do you want me to search alone?' She indicated the glowing signs. 'Do I follow these?'

'We all search alone,' Tanglanah said, softly.

Subadwan waited for more, but there was nothing. 'I'll just go then,' she said, realising that Tanglanah could see nothing of the luminous tracks.

At the bridge over the river she turned, to see that Tanglanah had gone. She felt cold. The still air, the calm, the hush, these symptoms of a city either at peace or dead did nothing to calm her nerves. Apprehension made her jumpy. Most alarming was the lack of people, despite the number of houses and buildings built off the street. Far off, she could glimpse the roofs of landmarks: the chimneys of Westcity Power Station, the spires of the Water Purification House, far, far to the east the spiral ramparts of the Archive of Vein Extraction. Oddest was her view of the Swamps, here just a watery bog with a clear river running from it, snapping fish swimming like dark arrows.

She did not know what to do. This presence: was it real? Was it a trap?

She looked beyond the walls of the city. Northward loomed a hill with vertical cliffs, a rough geological cylinder, casting and covered by shadow. The plateau at the top, however, showed tiny lights – blue, purple, glittering white, all moving, as of a camp of people. Subadwan watched for a few moments, estimating the number of lights at a dozen.

Faint, at the limits of hearing, she thought she detected voices.

As she surveyed the city she decided that the fluorescent marks were worth following, particularly since they seemed invisible to Tanglanah. She crossed into Westcity, then, at Culverkeys Street, turned south, taking the turning into Hog Street and crossing the river once more, then walking along to Min Street. There was not one soul in sight. The sound of her own footsteps, a sound inaudible in Cray, unnerved her, and she slowed as she turned into Violin Street, the circular roads of officialdom just a few minutes away.

She stopped to listen. Ahead she saw the curvaceous roof of the Archive of Noct, here missing its pale plant cover, though none the less frightening for that. She inched forward, noticing that the luminous marks were coming to a focus.

Footsteps. She heard pattering footsteps.

Subadwan wanted defence. The thought flashed through her mind, and then a glass shield lay in her hand.

Light but strong, the transparent shield, she realised, had been conjured by her mind. In the same way she had saved herself from death by flying. Subadwan understood then how powerful a single person could be in the abstract country. Imagination was the key. Without imagination, Gwmru's inhabitants could not survive. Could this in fact be Tanglanah's secret problem?

Voices: two of them.

Subadwan, skin itching, hairs twitching, felt she needed a weapon. She felt unsafe. Into her left hand the shield shifted, while her right acquired a titanium-tipped glass lance.

Two figures careered into the street from an alley. Subadwan stared, too startled to move. One was a black dome of an insect with clattering mandibles. The other was Tanglanah.

'She has vanished!' Tanglanah said.

'Is she lost?' asked the other.

'It must be Zelenaiid's malign influence. What shall we do?'

'All is not yet lost. You must return to Cray and examine this portion of Gwmru from your Archive. Looking from the outside is the only answer.'

There was a flash and Tanglanah vanished. Creaking and clacking, the insect turned around and skittered back up the alley. They had not even looked at her.

With the pair gone, Subadwan hurried on down the street to the Archive of Noct. Her suspicions were proved correct. The street marks coalesced into a glowing disk.

It was a repulsive structure, and always had been. Here it looked much the same as in reality. An accretion of buildings linked by black bridges, it seemed to have been smeared with dark Swamps mud by Noct's own gargantuan hands. Nothing of brickwork could be seen, only this smooth, yet hard, covering, a sort of toughened porcelain. Subadwan, who knew the place well, had always entertained the macabre belief that the inner building had acquired a skin that at some time it would slough off, to reveal a swarming, seething mass of blanched architecture. She shivered as she recalled the dank dungeons, with their white fungi, white insects, and pale, empty-eyed lesser slaves.

She walked around to a side entrance, listening

first, then shoving open the door with her boot. Inside, shadows concealed all. Desiring light Subadwan felt the weight of a headlamp, as worn by the street repairers of Cray, settling upon her brow, and this illumination allowed her to see that apart from minor alterations the inside of this section was the same as in Cray. Dreamlike sensation plagued her: this version of the Archive was like the real, yet subtly different. She explored a few rooms, then made for the interior chambers.

The layout had not changed. The central chamber, with its two-hundred-foot groined roof, black-on-black bas-relief walls, shuttered windows high up, and its sinuous, crepuscular statues slowly burning from the head down to disperse scented smoke, was as before; a reverberant chamber, shadow spawned and shadow kept, dusty and smelling of musk. But something, shrouded by dark mist, was sitting on Noct's podium.

The creature shifted, groaned, then stood. Subadwan froze, irrationally hoping that she had not been seen, though her lamp beam stabbed through the gloom.

It pounced. She was knocked to the ground, helmet, shield and lance sent flying. Glass smashed. A creature panted above her, holding her down with its paws. Warm alcoholic breath made her cough.

'Don't kill me!'

As her eyes became accustomed to the dark the panting became a thrumming, and she saw a pale beast like a bathkin, with twitching whiskers and slitted eyes. It had no tail. Again she cried, 'Don't kill me.'

'Who are you?' came the hissing response.

'Subadwan of Gaya.'

The creature let her go, padded away, then sat and began licking its paws. Subadwan noticed that one front paw had been lopped off, and around it the abstract substance of Gwmru distorted and twinkled. Eventually it said, 'Did Greckoh send you?'

'Tanglanah did.'

'Tanglanah. I see. Do you know who I am?'

Subadwan remembered the invisible presence mentioned by Tanglanah. She kept her silence.

'I am Zelenaiid. Tell me, Subadwan, do you carry the secret of Gaya with you?'

'I don't know. What is it?'

'I don't know either, but I know what it does. You must have followed my ancient sigils to get here.'

'The fluorescent marks? Yes. Tanglanah couldn't see them.'

'Of course,' Zelenaiid said. 'That was how I planned it.'

'Planned?'

Zelenaiid padded up close. 'You have come at an opportune moment, Subadwan. Events are coming to a conclusion.'

'Events?'

Zelenaiid said, 'Long ago, sixteen electronic beings arrived here from another world, one orbiting a far-off star. They had become convinced that their environment was wrong, and because it seemed unsuitable to them they decided to locate a new, alien environment, in which they could create a home of perfection. They planned to live in this home. They used memories of their previous home, and they envisaged that one day it would be complete. It would be perfect. This search for perfection of environment they called their art.

Now I was one of those sixteen, but I was considered an outsider because of my dealing with human beings. We travelled in a vitrified vehicle designed by me. But when we arrived here we clashed, as we had during the voyage. During a desperate tussle I destroyed the vehicle, just as the others were completing their new home – Cray, as you call it. They transmitted themselves down through the medium of Gwmru, but in the process they managed to trap me. Caught, I had no option but to hide myself. I have patrolled this abstract Archive since that time.'

'Five centuries.'

'Five centuries. But I knew my time would come once more. I altered the city created by the others, this being my final deed before I concealed myself. That alteration became a flaw. A glass flaw. Cray's vitrification is my doing. But because it is a wholly artificial city of metal and plastic bursting with ancient memories, Gwmru – with which it is occasionally coexistent – is also dying. It is for that reason that Tanglanah and the others are desperate to find me or to discover the truth of the flaw. Their plans have failed and they are enervated. They are so weak they are themselves losing their abilities.'

'What is this flaw?' Subadwan asked.

'I know that glass is its symptom. Since my alteration was made in the space of milliseconds I could not know how it would manifest. I set up the initial conditions, but from then on the flaw ran unchecked. However there is one point. Since I envisaged salvation for the humans that I had brought, the full manifestation of the flaw must involve a vehicle of some sort.'

'A vehicle?'

'You see, Subadwan, I guessed that my erstwhile kin would fail here. I understood that if they retained an intellectual view of their world they would fail to live in harmony with their new environment. To succeed in their art, they need physical bodies. Now they know they have failed. They wish to return home, as do I. And if they do that the whole human population of Cray will be left here to die. I cannot allow that since I am responsible for humanity being here. Hence my plan . . . such as it is.'

Subadwan frowned. 'If you don't even know the entirety of the flaw, it's not much of a plan.' She glanced at Zelenaiid. Claws flicked out from three pale paws. 'But I suppose your hand was forced.'

Zelenaiid said, 'You are part of the others' plan. You must think carefully on what they have told you.'

Subadwan thought back to the labyrinthine discussions with Tanglanah. 'Tanglanah said I would find something of Gaya here. That was a lie, wasn't it?'

'In part. I encoded a secret into the Archive of Gaya so that a human being would, one day, find me, when Cray was coming to the end of its life.'

'But you don't even know what your secret is!'

'I know what it *does*, Subadwan. I created an artificial reality that would see the world through Gayan eyes. The light from the star shining upon Cray is different to that of the other star. I left signs and clues that could only be seen in that otherworldly light—'

'The headmerger!' Subadwan cried.

'Headmerger?'

'I wear it now.'

'Then that headmerger is the manifestation of my

secret,' said Zelenaiid, 'and it is why you saw the signs and they did not. Did they try to follow you here?'

'Yes, but they could not see me, and they could not see the fluorescent signs.'

'My aura protects you, while the headmerger filters what you see.'

Suddenly, Subadwan understood. 'Tanglanah guessed something of what you did! They assassinated my two superiors to get me in the position that would give me access to everything in the Archive of Gaya – and that meant the headmerger.'

'I intended that somebody should come here, Subadwan, and it has turned out that you are my chosen one. Now you must help complete my plan.'

'How?'

'First, you must trust me. The survival of humanity is dear to me. Through the clashes with my erstwhile kin vitrification came about, and through my earlier deeds human beings were brought here. So I am responsible. I will tell you something. Recently, I became aware that the glass plague was reaching a climax, and that my former kin were trying to escape their fate. Therefore I briefly controlled a pyuton known as Seleno, so that the final phase of my plan could begin. As ever, an element of chaos pervaded what I did. I cannot say how it will have come out. But one of two paths will emerge, and you, Subadwan, and all the human beings of Gaya, must be on that path.'

There came a pause in the conversation. Eventually, Subadwan asked, 'What do I do now?'

'Return to Tanglanah and say you have completed your task.'

'What shall I say?'

Zelenaiid considered. 'Tell her that you found an

iceberg, but that it melted under the warmth of your breath. This will make her think. The metaphor will tantalise her, but she will not be able to come to any conclusion.'

'And how do I return to Cray?'

'Greckoh, Tanglanah and the others will have expended vast effort to bring the separate halves of Gwmru into constructive interference, so that Gwmru can impose itself upon Cray. Doubtless Tanglanah pretended it was a natural occurrence.'

'She didn't say exactly.'

'Whatever she said, it was a lie, or a perversion of the truth. You will possess a glass shell. Such objects are the corporeal components of abstract systems known as flags. You have been marked in Gwmru with such a shell, and its memories will focus upon you, and all others who are so marked. You see, Subadwan, what they wanted was a suitably endowed human – you, as it turned out – to experience Gwmru. Now you must trust me. Return to Tanglanah and speak as I suggested. You cannot return to Cray until they cease their effort. When you are out, search for the two paths emerging from the chaos.'

Subadwan quailed. 'I'd better go now, then.'

Zelenaiid purred in reply, then handed over what seemed to be a glass cylinder. 'Keep this razor shell,' she said. 'It will act as a weapon when Gwmru is upon you. But use it sparingly, for it will not last.'

Subadwan left the Archive of Noct. With no other option she began to walk north up the main streets of Eastcity, through the Plastic and Cold Quarters, until she reached the wall and an open gate. There she passed out into the frosted steppes surrounding Cray, where the landscape was radically different. A lifeless grey plain, pitted, gouged and cratered lay before her, the upthrust cylinder like a flat-topped hill not far away, on its top the busy glow of numerous lights. These lights surrounded what looked like a giant vegetable. Standing silent, she thought once again that she could hear voices.

Walking for ten minutes brought her to sheer cliffs. There was no way up. Subadwan did not want to call out for fear of meeting more creatures, but some inner sense suggested to her that Tanglanah was working up there. She took to considering how to ascend.

Soon she had the answer. If she could in utmost need desire a shield and lance, she could now desire a flying machine. She jumped as, to one side, a bat landed with a crunch of gravel, its steel claws finding little purchase, causing the machine to twist and turn before coming to rest.

Wary, she observed it. Bats were Triader mounts. But this had been created by her own mind. It must be safe.

She squeezed into the cockpit and pressed an activation pad. Dust whipped out as the bat took off, its biomotors whirring like fans, the stretched black fabric of its clawed wings humming under the tension. Subadwan's stomach gyrated as the bat, responding to hand controls in her sweaty grip, rose, then levelled, then swung to the right and began a slow ascent to the level of the plateau. She turned it around and headed for the lights.

Her flight was brief. There were figures on the plain, working frantically on the vegetable under the glare of a hundred lamps. When they spotted her they pointed. Suddenly, wing fabric ripped. The bat fell. Seconds later Subadwan hit the ground, conscious but winded. She struggled from the wreckage to see a dozen or so figures running towards her, one of them Tanglanah.

She was free when they reached her. She felt angry. This anger, she knew, would defend her if they tried to attack her or restrain her. She felt no fear.

'Stop!' she cried as they closed. Tanglanah halted, as did the others. They were a bunch of geriatric women, some mutated into beasts, others with animal heads, all of them tainted with the aura of age and exhaustion. Far off, the black dome on legs was making its way towards the group.

'Have you succeeded?' Tanglanah asked.

'You shot me down,' Subadwan retorted.

Tanglanah cared nothing for Subadwan's state. 'What was it you saw, Subadwan?'

'I only explored.'

'What did you find?'

Subadwan felt pressurised, wondering if Zelenaiid was using her as some kind of messenger. 'Nothing much,' she replied.

Tanglanah uttered a single disbelieving laugh. 'Nothing? Then it is for nothing that my kind live up here on this inaccessible plateau. What did you *find*?'

'If you must know I found an iceberg in the Archive of Noct. But it melted in my hot breath. So I left, and concentrated on Gaya.'

Tanglanah seemed almost savage in reply. She pointed to the setting disk in the sky. 'There is Gaya! We must depart, leaving five hundred years of failed experiment behind. Your people are doomed—'

'No!' Subadwan automatically yelled out.

'They are doomed to remain here.'

'What will you do?' Subadwan asked, closing in on Tanglanah.

'We have failed here. We shall depart in the Spacefish.'

'Leaving us?' Subadwan asked.

'Of course. You humans will die, since the networks and the data that we support will falter, then cease working.'

Subadwan felt a tremendous anger welling up inside her. 'I won't have it. Gaya love me, I will not have it!' Her anger boiled over. The nearest woman was small, dark-skinned, carrying a lute. Subadwan ran, lunged, and hit. The woman collapsed.

There were groans, gasps. Subadwan looked down at her victim. The body was melting, and yet it seemed to be running against the flow of gravity in three dimensions, as if along cubic runnels, faster and faster, until with a sigh there was nothing left. They were all weak as parchment, Subadwan realised, in an abstract bondage caused by the deterioration of Cray.

Except Tanglanah, who approached and stood in front of Subadwan: and now Subadwan felt afraid. 'You have killed one of our kin,' Tanglanah said.

'You killed two of mine. And *they* were flesh and blood. These kin of yours are only electronic lumps, aren't they?'

Tanglanah winced.

Subadwan continued, 'Do you think I never knew? Rhannan and poor Aswaque didn't have the required skills, so you killed them and allowed me to become Lord Archivist.'

'I deny it.'

Subadwan felt a tight, bitter hatred of Tanglanah. For all these weeks and months she had suspected the pyuton, guessing about the traps, and yet she had been strung along until she was in too deep. She had hoped

some good intentions lay within Tanglanah, but now
the pyuton was revealed as utterly callous. For all her
conscience, for all her sincerity and desire to care,
Subadwan now felt a primitive, desperate urge to
equal the score. Knowing that it was wrong, that it
was childish, she none the less took advantage of
Tanglanah's hesitation and with cursing fury lunged
out at the nearer women, hacking at the two-headed
dog-woman, kicking a pale-skinned midget. Both
melted just as the first had. Delayed emotion made her
choke with fear and horror.

With immense force Tanglanah slapped Subadwan
across the face, flinging her to the ground. There was
blood on the rocks. Subadwan, choking, saw some of
the other women running away. Tanglanah turned,
and called, 'Come back! She is but human! I can kill
her now, and then we must fly down to Cray. Come
back!'

Subadwan kicked out, but Tanglanah was tall and
heavy, entirely different from the others because she
had manifested in the real world, and was no longer
solely electronic. Subadwan knew she had to escape.

But Tanglanah had other plans. Subadwan found
herself restrained by a glowing spider's web. 'I will
complete my relationship with you later,' Tanglanah
said, the irises of her eyes spinning with rainbow
colours, 'but for now stay here, and consider the fact
that you are a triple murderer.'

'Double murderer,' Subadwan sneered back.

Tanglanah departed. The other women, now joined
by the black-domed creature, continued to work at
their vegetable dirigible, a green and brown bladder
that looked as if it was to be inflated. A wicker basket
lay nearby. From thin air the women pulled objects

and tools, creating reality from their imaginations just as Subadwan had when creating the bat. She knew that was her only chance for escape.

But the emotions within her were too violent. Furious, frightened, and awed, she was too upset to think. Realising that these emotions must be spent, she hammered at the ground, screamed, shouted, and clawed at the webbing. After a few minutes, and with tears upon her cheeks, she stopped, exhausted. Tanglanah looked across at her, but then turned away.

A knife. She needed a knife. One appeared in her right hand. She slit the webbing at ground level. The knife vanished.

She estimated that the women and their dirigible were a hundred yards away. Already the vehicle was moving, rising at one end. There was not much time left.

It became clear what they intended doing. They would fly away and leave her on the plateau, landing in Cray and searching or possibly destroying the Archive of Noct now that they had guessed Zelenaiid's location. Then a chill thought struck her: how could she depart Gwmru? She still did not know.

The dirigible wobbled in the air, a few yards above the ground, with the basket dragging along under-neath. Slowly, as if their bones ached, the women embarked. At length, only Tanglanah remained, and she boarded last.

The dirigible was floating away. Subadwan crawled through the rent she had made and stood defiant. When Tanglanah noticed, thunderbolts flashed through the air.

Just missing. Subadwan ran to one side. The bat appeared. She leaped in and took off, the smell of ozone and burned hair in her nostrils, sparkling light all around. Diving dangerously, she dropped behind the cliffs, so that the plateau stood between the bat and the dirigible. She had to stop them. If she did not, they might find and kill Zelenaiid.

The dirigible, she had noticed, descended as soon as it floated over the edge of the plateau. Its balloon was large. If she could keep her height, she could perhaps come upon them from behind and above.

Her plan worked at the beginning. Flying around the hill to the other side she saw that they were below her, some way off, floating above the Cold Quarter and descending rapidly. She pounced. Tanglanah could throw thunderbolts: so could she. She had no idea what they were, but they came from her anger and her desperation. Three blasts and the dirigible was burst, the occupants of its basket falling. Thunderbolts leaped up at the bat, one hitting its right wing. Subadwan was jolted around her cockpit.

Tanglanah's panic-stricken voice sounded through the gusting air to her. 'Manifest! Manifest!'

The bat was falling fast. She tried to control it by forcing it to fly to the left, but the flapping fabric brought only chaotic descent.

'Manifest!' Tanglanah urged once more.

'We must not,' a voice cried. 'Are we to become lumpish aeromorphs? We must not forsake our abstract grace!'

'Bring destructive interference!' cried the black dome. 'Release the grip on Cray! Do not manifest.'

But the smoking shapes of four aeromorphs appeared around the dirigible. Then Subadwan glimpsed a plummeting black shape. It was the domed creature, Greckoh. Seconds later the bat stalled, hit the roof of a building, and smashed through.

She awoke. Dust and smoke all around.

Dark. She remembered where she was – the crash site.

Her limbs ached and she tasted blood in her mouth. But she could move, so she clambered out of the wreckage and struggled to the nearest door.

Tanglanah would be searching for her, if she had survived. Subadwan knew she would have.

She stepped out into a crowded street. Gwmru was no longer imposing itself upon Cray. She ran back to the Baths. She felt dizzy. Real bats swooped and swirled above her.

At last . . . inside the Baths.

Tanglanah was nowhere to be seen. But whatever had happened, Subadwan knew she was in danger. And yet she could not leave the Baths.

This was the most dangerous dilemma imaginable. At any second Tanglanah might appear, yet outside Umia's nocturnal agents lurked.

Minutes passed, and became hours. Tanglanah did not appear. Reluctantly, Subadwan decided Tanglanah must have more important matters in hand, and she wondered what they might be.

17

GNOSTICIAN

Umia strode about his spherical chamber with violent movements. He was upset and his advisers were offering different views, worsening his dilemma, torturing him further.

Gaijin said, 'O Reeve, hearken to me, to me alone. Why the difficulty? The use of sonoplasts harms all. You heard from your pyutonic deputies how flasks of the bacterium transmute themselves. All substances do! Sonoplasts equal your failure.'

But Lune countered, 'Umia, Gaijin's way is the way of the vague, the frightened, the unbalanced. It is knowledge that will help you decide, and the only knowledge you have is that gained by the laboratories of your deputies, of Ciswadra and Heraber. The sonoplasts are ready. Set free the bacteria.'

As Umia held his head in his hands, sitting bent over as if about to vomit, Gaijin retorted, 'Gnostician power is against your power, O Reeve, for millions of gnosticians you cannot remove. Noct will support you. Noct's pale lips and pale eye will tell you the truth, that gnosticians will never do.'

Lune said, 'Free the sonoplasts, Umia—'

Umia burst out, with hoarse voice and staring eyes, 'What shall I do?'

'Somebody is approaching,' Lune warned.

'I want to kill every cursed gnostician! They are the invaders surrounding my city! They play with the glass that is killing us off. Shut up, the both of you!'

'Hither comes a personage,' Gaijin dared to say.

It was a Triader deputy who entered the chamber, the fins on her swirling cloak flapping. 'I bring the final report—'

'Read it, read it,' Umia angrily demanded.

'The sonoplast-freighted bacteria are ready for dispersal. One hundred flasks have been loaded upon bats, and may leave at your command, providing that command comes within six hours – at which time the flasks will be transmuted, and may leak. Heraber counsels caution. The bacteria transmute all substances, not just glass, and this fact must be considered before the irrevocable deed of release is performed. This is an artificial bacterium, pyuter created, and so resistance will vary greatly. That is all, Reeve Umia.'

Umia stood tall and took a deep breath. 'Release the bacteria immediately. We will have an end to the luminophage plague. We will have an end to spreading glass. I will be loved for my deeds, the people will respect me for firm command. Yes, that is how it will go. Begin a purge on gnosticians! Those who will not leave the city must be forced out or killed.' Umia paused. 'We will call it redesigning. Rebellious gnosticians will be redesigned. They are a scourge upon Cray. Now leave me, and send in my director of spies.'

'One final matter, Reeve. Should we make public the release of the bacteria?'

'Of course not! Will Crayans understand the theories behind these bacteria? Just do it, and speedily!'

Gaijin spoke when the chamber door was shut. 'O Reeve, you have done ill.'

Lune disagreed. 'This may be the beginning of a new Cray. Or an end. Do not let the whingeing Gaijin mix up your mind, for only a small number of people know of the bacteria, all of them trustworthy.'

'I predict the end,' Gaijin responded. 'Death will come.'

Umia spun on his metal leg. 'Quiet, you two,' he ordered. 'I *will* have quiet to think.'

After a minute, Gaijin's voice: 'A personage is here.'

Balloydondra, Umia's spymaster, appeared. 'Reeve, you requested my presence,' she said in her suave voice. She was tall, dark, with a brash manner. The fins on her grey velvet cloak were embroidered with gold and sequins, while its lining was covered with an overlapping scale pattern picked out in pale blue.

'I did,' Umia said, voice grim. 'Your agents failed in their duty. How now will we winkle Subadwan out of the Baths?'

'Never fear,' Balloydondra said, with a wide smile. 'The next agent will succeed.'

'You said that before. I can have you sent to the mad bats, you know. I can have you pushed into their wire pens so you fall into the blood and guano, while you watch them soar, dive, then fall upon you. Do you want their chromium fangs in your flesh, eh, eh?'

'No, Reeve.'

Umia began pacing around the statue of Noct. 'What then is this new agent?'

'Reeve Umia, the problem we have faced is that the

Baths have their own defences, that we cannot overcome. Therefore we must be crafty.' Balloydondra
took from her pocket a sheet of clear plastic, thick,
with a faint blue tinge, two feet on a side. 'This is a
dedicated pyuter,' she explained. 'We have designed it
to attach itself to a swimmer, then hypnotise the victim
in a barely audible voice into walking out of the Baths
of her own free will. An agent will introduce this
pyuter into the water when Subadwan is swimming,
loosing it as the two pass close, so that the pyuter
makes for Subadwan. When she hears the voice, she
will become temporarily hypnotised, and fall into the
waiting arms of your people outside the Baths. It
cannot fail, Reeve.'

'It had better not,' Umia said, 'or you will become
hang-glider fodder. Is that clear?'

'Very clear.'

'Then you may go.'

The spymaster departed, leaving Umia to his seething
thoughts. But Gaijin butted into these thoughts, saying,
'You have Noct on your side, O Reeve.'

Lune said, 'Light is good and always has been. Light is
the ancient symbol of goodness. Cast aside your torment,
Umia, cast it aside with doubt, pain, and other terrible
things.'

Umia sat hunched at the feet of the statue of Noct. 'I
will never leave Noct!' he roared. 'How dare you
suggest that? Would you have me follow the foul
Subadwan, and change my inner self?'

Gaijin interrupted, saying, 'Ignore Subadwan. She is
a trifle. There are others who wish to use her.
Concentrate instead on your city.'

'No,' Umia said, 'the order has gone. Even I cannot
reverse it now. And the bats are flying, raining doom

upon Cray. Oh, Noct, black mother Noct, what have I done? Have I done right or wrong? All I can see is greyness, all around. Greyness . . . greyness . . . perpetual darkness, that is the answer. That is why I live here, isn't it? Answer me, Gaijin!'

'If it must be, it must be. The fate of many will change in scant days.'

Umia kissed the statue's feet. 'Gaijin, I must remain the Reeve of Cray. I am the Lord Archivist of Noct. I will remain aloof.'

Gaijin replied, 'The aloof may become the dead.'

Dwllis and Cuensheley sat in the quadrangle at the Copper Courtyard, a plastic table set with tankards between them. It was late afternoon and the courtyard was empty. Lamps strung from the ceiling net were dim, the pink globes interspersed with white. The copper floor gleamed. In the opposite corner, Ilquisrey was sweeping up dust and dirt with a broom.

'Crimson Boney must stay at the Cowhorn Tower,' said Dwllis. 'Now Umia has made this barbaric declaration of gnostician purges, all the augmented gnosticians are in mortal danger. Doubtless there will be a raid on the Archive of Selene by those grotesque noctechnes.'

'It's risky harbouring Crimson,' Cuensheley pointed out. 'All Umia wants is the gnosticians out of the city. That's not much to ask.'

'It is symptomatic of inhumanity. Umia equates vitrescence with gnosticians. I am close to speaking with Crimson Boney. The translator made sentences last night. Why do you not come along now and see the progress? Maybe tonight that gnostician will speak to us properly for the first time.'

Cuensheley agreed. They walked down to Sphagnum Street, Cuensheley with her hand in Dwllis's. He felt unable to disengage himself because she had assented to his wish.

Sphagnum Street was quiet. Houses southward were becoming dark and glassy as the luminophages spread. Dwllis noticed that light storms speeding through the street plastic were avoiding infected areas, so that instead of a straight river of light it now meandered, coloured yellow, orange and red at the edges, as if internal infection had begun. Soon, he realised, the fabric of the Copper Courtyard and the Cowhorn Tower would be at risk. He wondered if the Archive of Gaya had succumbed to luminophage attack.

They found Crimson Boney and the translator in a small chamber full of antique memories, sitting and talking. Dwllis reminded Cuensheley that its name was not Etwe, and she looked at him with distaste. Dwllis sat next to Cuensheley on a couch. At the moment he was not interested in arguing with her.

'Translator,' he said, 'tell Crimson Boney who we are.'

Cuensheley asked, 'How can that translator be getting more sophisticated when you're not here to oversee it?'

'Shhh,' Dwllis replied, one finger at his lips. 'The routines are constantly evolving. All I needed to do was start things off.'

Then the translator said, 'Crimson Boney knows who you are. You are Dwllis and Cuensheley.'

'Translator, go into simultaneous translation mode. Crimson Boney, I – we – want to know why you ran from the Archive of Selene to my tower.'

Crimson Boney musically answered, and the translator did its work. 'Because pain arrived. People not nice to me. They came at me with bright tools. The others also feared.' Crimson Boney began to tremble, visible skin darkening to purple: a recalled emotion?

'He's really talking,' Cuensheley said.

'Until recently the thought did not cross my mind either,' Dwllis replied. 'But somebody in the Archive of Selene thought it might be possible, and so the augmentation programme began, started by Querhidwe's mystic predecessor, Seleno. Gnosticians are intelligent, Cuensheley. They are conscious like us, but they are wholly different. You see, the barriers to communication were too great to overcome, so nobody ever thought to consider them anything other than clever animals – because they have no cities, because their technology is simple. Until I arrived, nobody considered the possibility of consciousness, of morals. And all because of prejudice.'

'Could Umia know?' Cuensheley asked. 'I mean, why this ban against gnosticians? Why declare it now?'

Dwllis sighed. 'Because he is afraid.'

'But why augment gnosticians in the first place?'

'At first I did not know, but now it is obvious. Do you not see? Somebody desperately wants to speak to gnosticians. The gnosticians know something important – something concerning Cray, I would wager.'

Crimson Boney, noting the pause in conversation – another indication of his intelligence – continued. 'Before people try to hurt me, they tell me with

the-quick-moving-hands to come to you, to bring you
exuded memories of the city. They say you important
link in their plan.'

Sign language, Dwllis thought: primitive, but
workable. 'Who told you this?' he asked. 'Selene's
scribes?'

'The people of the moon. They say they disturbed
something. They used to go into the Cemetery and
make a seeing lens, then come back and tell me new
things to do. They made the clearness in my head. I
like what they did, but now they don't like me, and I
run away to nice man Dwllis, who gives me fruit to eat
amongst poor ripped up kissleaves. Plants cannot
multiply without kissleaves. We only eat fruits off
plants.'

Dwllis nodded. Cuensheley, gripping his arm, said,
'How could you be part of their plan?'

Dwllis had no answer. But Crimson Boney said, 'I
sorry I bite off fingers. You frightened me.'

'You bit off his fingers?' Cuensheley said. '*You?*'

Dwllis sat back, appalled. Now he understood part
of the story. He said, 'They weirded the lens
deliberately. They knew it was something to do with
me. The moment Crimson Boney came here, the lens
came too. What train of events have I begun?'

Cuensheley hugged him. He felt cold and numb.
The story had come together in his head as a dreadful
realisation, but much was still obscure. And yet, with
a clarity he had never felt before, he understood that
some pivotal event had occurred in the Archive of
Selene.

These realisations made him speechless for some
time. He sat still, thinking, looking alternately at
Cuensheley, who stared at him face blanched, and at

Crimson Boney, who sat with twitching tentacles, gazing at him with heavy lidded eyes.

'I had thought,' he eventually said, 'that with Crimson Boney here, speaking to us, we would not have to break into the Archive of Selene again. But now I wonder if that is wrong. And Pikeface. He knows something about me.'

'Pikeface?' Cuensheley said, wincing.

'Pikeface bad man,' said Crimson Boney. 'He had his own plans, not moon plans. He against nice white lady.'

Dwllis nodded with passion. 'You are correct, Crimson Boney. Pikeface is different. The key to all this lies with the lunar memoirs.'

'The key!' Cuensheley exclaimed. 'The fishtail Querhidwe bequested to you. It must be to do with that.'

Dwllis had forgotten about the silver fishtail. 'That may well be correct,' he said. 'But how can we find out?'

Cuensheley gently shook Dwllis, saying, 'What is it you've not told me about Pikeface?'

Dwllis told her of his meeting with Pikeface and what he had learned from it. 'These events include me,' he mused. 'Some seem to revolve around me.'

'And the Spacefish, that once was the moon,' Cuensheley said. 'What is it? It's getting closer and closer.'

'I do not know what it is.'

Crimson Boney said, 'I do not know why dear moon changes.'

Dwllis caught a strange inflection in this sentence, though he at once realised that it may have been a poor translation. 'It is your moon?' he asked.

'Always it has been our dear moon, for hundreds of generations, back into early days, early years.'

Dwllis's mind spun. *Hundreds* of generations? 'Do you mean you remember life before you came here?' he asked.

'We have always been here.'

'For how long?'

'For ever.'

Dwllis sat back, glancing at Cuensheley. 'What do you make of that?' he asked her.

'I don't really know. Ask him again.'

Dwllis said, choosing his words carefully, 'For how many years have you lived on Earth? When did you arrive?'

'We have lived here for all time.'

Dwllis shook his head. 'There are fanciful tales of the origin of Cray . . .' He hesitated before striding over to a pyuter, where, in silence, he called up a file of data. As he returned to sit, the disembodied voice of his rig spoke.

'The founding of Cray. Standard version. And it happened that a great shoal of fish swam through the air with much thrashing of tails. And from the ocean a fish, strong and shining, leaped, and then split into two, its front half landing west of the river, its rear half landing east. And from this flesh the city made itself. And so it was.'

'No city until five centuries ago,' Crimson Boney confirmed. 'You arrive. You come here. Ancestor tales say it is truth. They saw the storm of lights in the sky from the new moon that exploded. They saw everything. They saw the fish, saw the head giblets fall with a splosh into the river, saw the nasty green fishtail fall to one side.'

Dwllis shook his head. 'You may think me eccentric, but I believe Cray was built on the remains of an older city.'

'Something feels wrong,' Cuensheley muttered, head bowed in thought.

'Nonsense,' Dwllis declared. 'Have no fear. The puzzle is simply solved. Crimson Boney, from where did the architects of this city come?'

'From the sea.'

Dwllis nodded. 'The gnosticians came here some time ago, that is all. Perhaps they even saw the founding of the city.'

Tired, Cuensheley stood and said, 'I'm going back to the courtyard.'

'I must work here awhile. I will see you without fail tomorrow morning.'

She departed, head bowed, as if upset. Dwllis turned to look at Crimson Boney. The gnostician turned his gaze elsewhere.

Rhythmically chewing, he decided he must set up a special room for his guest, since Triad threats of gnostician redesign meant the life of Crimson Boney, and of the other augmented gnosticians, hung in the balance. He alone could provide a haven. He departed to harvest fruit from the profusion of plants growing outside the tower.

At the door he met Coelendwia, about to start the evening's shift. 'Good evening to you, sir,' the Triader guard said.

Dwllis paused to look the man up and down, realising that he no longer needed protection. The lens had not appeared for some time, and Dwllis suspected its time was over. 'A good evening to you, my man,' he replied.

'Everything all right with you today, sir?'

Dwllis nodded.

'Terrible thing, this purging,' Coelendwia conversationally added. 'I've witnessed some nasty scenes, I can tell you. Things I wouldn't tell my mother, if you get my meaning.'

'It is an evil day that one species can be persecuted for so small a reason as the whim of the Reeve.'

'Whim, sir?'

'Whim it is Coelendwia. There is no evidence to link the gnosticians with Cray's difficulties. It is merely speculation by Triad officials.'

Coelendwia huffed and puffed, and looked embarrassed. 'I wouldn't like to say, sir. The Reeve has never been wrong before, has he? He must know what he's doing, him being Lord Archivist and all.'

The talk of gnostician purges irritated Dwllis. He imagined them being herded up, slaughtered . . . no, no, it did not bear thinking about. He had to stop it. He felt that he had the right to do this since he knew what nobody else knew. He had to declare the truth of the gnosticians to every Crayan.

'I will not hear such immoral talk,' he told Coelendwia in staccato tones. 'These creatures do not deserve such treatment.'

'Yes, sir.'

'Incidentally, the lens has departed this locale, so your services are no longer required. You may leave.'

Coelendwia took a step back. 'I see, sir. I didn't know it had been dealt with.'

'I don't think it will bother me any more.' Dwllis began to search the surrounding bushes for succulent yellow fruit.

'Well, it's goodbye then,' Coelendwia said.

'Pardon?'

'Goodbye, sir. Good luck and all that, sir.'

'Yes, yes, goodbye.'

Dwllis hurried over to a spray of fruit and plucked them, putting the smaller ones in his pockets, twisting off a few blue leaf sprays that he had noticed Crimson Boney was partial to before returning to the tower. Inside, all was quiet. He told the translator to reassure the gnostician while he prepared a room. This room he cleared of human detritus, leaving only cushions, such as the agnosticians made for their more intelligent kin out of dead bracken and cloth. He placed the food on a tray, moved the tower's four potted plants into the room, then gestured for Crimson Boney to enter. This the gnostician did, followed by the translator.

Crimson Boney's head began bobbing and his eyes and mouth widened in an expression Dwllis thought, from earlier observation, might be happiness.

'Nice man, nice room,' came the translation. Crimson Boney took one of the fruits and said, 'Good fruit. Soon the orange sister fruit will ripen, and I will take those.'

'I will get them,' Dwllis confirmed. 'This must be your home for now. A terrible purge is in operation, and you are not safe in the city. Besides, I need you here.'

'I stay here,' the gnostician said.

'I want to rescue your other friends from the Archive of Selene, but it is too perilous.'

'Only I departed,' Crimson Boney said. 'The others caught, put back in the cells of the moon. I come here to be safe. No friends out in the lands, now I am different.'

Dwllis felt a momentary sadness as he realised the

truth of this simple statement. Crimson Boney had been elevated, his biological family no longer his social family. Without the other augmented gnosticians he truly was all alone. These thoughts, and the recurring images of purged gnosticians, made him all the more determined to save the race from Umia's madness, but it struck him that Selene's Archivists might wonder whether their loose gnostician had left the city or not.

'I shall leave you for tonight,' he said, images of a break-in passing through his mind. 'I think you are safe here. If you need anything, rouse the translator and come to my chamber, or have the translator come.'

'It will be.'

Dwllis led the translator out then shut the door. For a second he felt the gaze of the pyuton as a physical force. Disconcerted, he felt his face become hot as the embarrassment continued, for it did not look away. He said, 'Translator, you may discontinue for the night.'

'I don't want to.'

He was not prepared for this.

'I don't want to, Dwllis,' the pyuton repeated.

Dwllis confronted the translator. 'You will do as I say,' he demanded, turning to walk away.

'Am I valuable to you?' he was asked.

'You are a translator. That is a valuable skill indeed—'

'But do you value *me*? Your Etwe?'

Dwllis froze. Hearing that name uttered by this pyuton, this *unknown* pyuton, was dreadful beyond nightmare. Stuttering, face flushed, he replied, 'You are not Etwe. You are my translator. Now do as I say or face the consequences.'

But the impasse continued, for pyuton Etwe answered, 'You can't destroy me, I'm too valuable. Dwllis, do you know how pyutons commit suicide?'

'Nonsense, nonsense,' Dwllis muttered, hardly able to speak for the chaotic emotions welling up inside him. 'Suicide? Never heard of it. Silly—'

'Oh, it can be done. Do you know what I am? Yes, I'm Etwe, but am I a standard pyuton? You can't take the risk, Dwllis. But don't worry, I won't harm you or your work. Though you mustn't call me just "that translator" or "that pyuton" any more. I'm your Etwe. You must call me Etwe.'

'You *are* a translator!'

'Or I will spread myself amongst the networks like cooking oil on a pond, never to be seen again.'

'Nonsense!' It was all Dwllis could think to say. 'No pyuton can do that.'

'If you reject me, Dwllis, my Dwllis, if you push me away, I will never take another love. We were a pair you and I, a perfect pair. I won't lose what we had, I won't. You'll sleep with me, like we used to. I've not changed, and yes, you'll call me Etwe in the night and I'll feel your breath upon my neck. And in the daytime I'll do all your interfaces like I used to. There must be quite a backlog by now. It'll be just like old times, except you won't order me about so much—'

'Quiet, translator,' Dwllis yelled. 'Quiet!' He had listened to the softly spoken litany in horror, memories of the old days brought to his mind, though he tried to push them away.

'If you don't, Dwllis, I'll kill myself. If I can't have you life's not worth living.'

Dwllis spluttered, 'What cheap network story did you steal that from? For the final time, you are just a translator. Go away and say nothing until I activate you tomorrow. Is that clear enough?'

Etwe hesitated. 'Then I'll do it,' she said. She brought a chunky looking optical cable out from her hip pocket and walked over to the public access interface, a scarlet box screwed to the wall. 'I designed this interface,' she said, pointing to it with the end of the cable. 'If I plug myself in I can copy out low level groups of symbols, disabling every layer above. In just nanoseconds I'll disperse to the electronic winds.

She made to plug in the cable.

'No,' Dwllis said, moving towards her. 'No, do not do that.'

And Etwe smiled. Dwllis stopped short, horrified at how human she had become. This was a nightmare, nothing but a nightmare. 'How can you be Etwe?' he desperately asked.

'I would never leave you,' she replied. 'Did you really think I would? I had to come back. I've been monitoring the Cowhorn Tower systems for some weeks now, waiting for my chance. And now I'm just too valuable for you to risk losing. Crimson Boney is your only link with the gnosticians, not to mention him being a fugitive from Triad law. We shall never part again, darling.'

A little of the shock had now departed. Dwllis began thinking of how to destroy this electric freak and yet retain the knowledge entwined with the old Etwe character. Could it be done? No choice: it had to be possible, else he was ruined. But almost immediately he realised that disentangling the strands of what was, for all intents and purposes, a mind would be impossible. It was as impossible as excising the Old Crayan tongue from his own mind. This Etwe pyuton would have to die. More trouble, more danger, and all because of one blackmailing pyuton. The idea of having to sleep with the damnable machine, once the source of happy fantasy and secret joy, was now abhorrent. The idea repelled him, made his belly squirm and his heart thump.

And yet he knew his thoughts were unrealistic. In truth there was only one option left open to him, and that was controlling Etwe, retaining her translating abilities because he needed them so urgently. He ground his teeth together with frustration. He would have to reinforce the master and servant relationship if he was not to lose all that he had achieved.

All these thoughts passed through his mind as they stepped into the tower hall and then ascended stairs to the upper levels. Dwllis wondered what he could do. Already it was bedtime.

Cuensheley must save him. And yet she must not know what had happened. He needed her help. This was not the time for her to walk off in a huff.

'I shall check the tower locks,' he said, 'then conclude the day's work.'

'Don't be long,' Etwe replied, and the words carried an extra threat not lost on him.

He returned to the ground floor. He thought of Coelendwia, but outside, he remembered, no guard stood. 'Where are you when I need you?' he growled in irritation to the spot where Coelendwia used to stand.

He popped a lump of qe'lib'we into his mouth – the third of the day. Then he thought of memories. He could claim that a new horde had been discovered. Having gathered together a bag of antique memories – memories that Etwe had never seen – he sent a conciliatory message to the system screen in the chamber where Etwe awaited, checked his appearance in a mirror, then hurried out of the tower with the bag click-clacking at his belt.

As he hastened down the short stretch of Sphagnum Street that led to the Copper Courtyard alley, he noticed that the city seemed quiet. Others had made this claim. For some minutes he stopped, ear-muffs half off, but it was difficult to tell without decibel meters and microphones. He hurried on, wincing and looking aside when he came across the vermin-eaten bodies of two gnosticians, who doubtless had been murdered by a noctechne squad.

Cuensheley was pleased to see him, despite the lateness of the hour, and he had to emphasise that he had not come to stay with her. 'I have a severe difficulty at the Cowhorn Tower,' he said, glancing at her to see how she responded.

Immediately she picked up clues. She could be frighteningly intuitive at times. 'I wondered why you came. Something to do with us? With drugs? A woman?'

'I need the use of a room for a few days – day and night. Would you mind?'

Cuensheley frowned. 'I can't find you any space in the store room, so there's nowhere to stay except in my room.'

'What about that room opposite Ilquisrey's, along the hall?'

'Certainly not. All my private things are in there.'

Dwllis sighed. 'Then I shall have to sleep with the stores.'

'You can't,' Cuensheley began, but she hesitated, as if floundering for a reason to back up her statement.

'Don't take advantage of my predicament,' Dwllis warned.

'Why can't you live in the tower?'

'Er . . .'

Suddenly Cuensheley came alive, as if transported by undercurrents of emotion. 'I might have known. Etwe. You're involved with her again, aren't you? Aren't you? What's she done, reported you to the Triad?'

'Most assuredly not,' Dwllis replied. 'In fact—'

'It is Etwe, isn't it? You're a hopeless liar, Dwllis, despite all this silly manners nonsense. It's as clear as water.'

Dwllis, tempering his anger with the small measure of apprehension he felt, replied with some dignity. 'If you must know every little fact about me, Cuensheley, I am being blackmailed by that damnable pyuton. Damn them all! The old Etwe managed to hijack my original pyuter for her own purposes. That is the truth and no lies. Now, that store room?'

'You're not sleeping in the store room,' Cuensheley said in surprised tones. 'You're sleeping—'

'In the store room.'

'In my room, on the floor. That suit you?'

'You are exploiting me,' Dwllis said, exasperated. 'I come to you for aid, and you take advantage of me. You have not one good reason for disallowing me the use of the store room.'

'I have.' She hesitated. 'It's damp and cold.'

Dwllis laughed.

Firmly – very firmly – Cuensheley said, 'You either take it or leave it. Ilquisrey and I can kick you out if you make trouble.'

Dwllis, wanting to rant, but unable to, pondered

the unfairness of his predicament under the flashing
eyes of his tormentor. Of course, he had no choice. He
had no other friends in Cray, nor any Archive to plead
with. Just this woman.

18

The Aeromorphs Descend

When Dwllis awoke, Cuensheley was gone from her bed. He could hear her clattering pots and pans downstairs while she talked with Ilquisrey, the two voices interspersed with laughter, as if they were telling one another the night's tales. It was not without displeasure that Dwllis heard them, for he envied the ease with which Ilquisrey spoke to her mother.

Cutting a slice of qe'lib'we from the lump on Cuensheley's bedside table, he got up. Best to start the day with a shot of confidence.

He dressed with care, as usual. First washing and powdering his body, he stepped into pure white underwear, then spent half an hour choosing the day's clothes. For some minutes he gauged the effect in a mirror, trying his fuzzlocks on and off the shoulder, before tying them up with a ribbon and going downstairs.

'What a pity you have no shaving facilities,' he told Cuensheley.

Ilquisrey remarked, 'Why, do your legs need doing?'

Dwllis ignored the jibe. 'What is all that light on the ceiling?'

They looked up to where he pointed. 'Something

outside,' Cuensheley said, shrugging.

Dwllis thought it must be reflecting in through the high windows from outside. He unlocked and opened the side door, to be greeted by an unusually cold breeze.

The alley, and the small portion of Sphagnum Street beyond, were brighter than he had ever seen. Light-mote storms raced up and down like flooding rapids, sending out coloured froth up dead-end passages. Sphagnum Street itself was almost too bright to view. Dwllis walked down the alley. A few locals stood as bemused as he. 'What has happened?' Dwllis asked them.

'You be careful,' he was told. 'City's going mad, I tell you. It happened just now, streets flashing like the sun itself was underground.'

Another voice came. 'People saying there's four aeromorphs flying about streets, attacking people.'

Dwllis looked up at the sky but it was too dark to see much, though he did notice that the Spacefish, now four times as big as the moon it had replaced, had turned so that its head was turning away from Cray. This sight worried him. He ran back to the Copper Courtyard and told Cuensheley what he had learned.

'Umia's doing, I'll be bound,' Ilquisrey said.

Dwllis nodded in agreement. 'It is some foul means of populace control,' he said, 'or perhaps of frightening the gnosticians left in Cray into submission. I must do something.'

'What can you do?' Cuensheley asked.

Suspicious of the new Etwe to the point of paranoia, Dwllis found himself wondering if she would leave the tower and seek him out. He put the ghastly thought out of his mind. 'I must decide what to do about the gnosticians,' he declared, popping a fresh lump of qe'lib'we into his mouth. Umia has pushed things too far. I must show the public that they are sentient, conscious just like them. There will be an outcry, and the purges will cease.'

Cuensheley shook her head. 'Far too dangerous. You'll be arrested by the Triad.'

'I must do it,' Dwllis said, 'but there is one way of avoiding Triaders. I will speak as the guest of an Archive. If I can persuade somebody – Subadwan, let us say – that this task must be done, then I can take shelter inside the Archive if trouble should arise.'

'But not even Subadwan is safe in her own Archive.'

'She is a special case. If I speak in the Archive of Gaya, or any other—'

'Not Noct, of course,' Cuensheley interrupted.

'Not Noct. It is a simple matter of declaring the truth, then fading into the background. With the city in its current state, all will go well.'

Cuensheley disagreed, but Dwllis was not to be stopped. She tried to pull him away from the side door as he made to leave, but he tugged himself free, saying, 'It must be done. I will not stand idly by.'

'You'll be arrested for sedition, you idiot.'

Dwllis ignored her. But his forthright mood was dampened when the speech amplifiers in his ear-muffs caught shouts and screams close behind, and he turned to see people running, falling and struggling through cables and pipes, smashing panes of vitrescent wall in their haste.

An aeromorph was in pursuit. It had descended from the sky and changed into a more compact shape. It sailed through the street on a tide of smoke like a gliding aerician, catching and crushing people, then wriggling through street debris to the next victims. Dwllis managed to hide behind a steaming duct as it roared by. He coughed as the stink of ozone enveloped him.

Now travelling with caution, he hurried along the painfully bright Feverfew Street before following alleys and passages east, past the Archive of Safe-keeping, and then along Peppermint Street into Eastcity. At the bridge he saw, far off to the south, the sparkling shape of another aeromorph, bigger perhaps than the one he had just seen, flicking itself up and down through the air as if trouncing some band of hapless Crayans. At his feet, the bodies of two gnosticians lay.

The Baths were empty. Dwllis was not surprised by this, given Cray's circumstances. He convinced Calminthan that he must see Subadwan, and was led into an ante-chamber close to the main entrance, where he waited.

Presently she arrived. She looked paler than ever, tired, exhausted even, her eyes lustreless and surrounded by dark circles. 'Keeper,' she said, taking his left hand in greeting.

'Good morning, Lord Archivist,' he responded. 'I trust you are well?'

'I'm rather tired. I hear the city streets are glowing bright?'

'They most certainly are. It is damned curious. But more extraordinary are the aeromorphs—'

Now her face was blanched. 'I know what they are.'

'You do?'

'Yes, Keeper. I need your help.'

'Madam,' Dwllis politely replied, 'I require assistance also.'

They both sat on the chamber's only couch.

'Electronic beings from the abstract realm of Gwmru are sustaining Cray,' said Subadwan. 'I tried to stop these electronic beings regaining their powers. The bright streets indicate the hyperactivity brought on by my failure. They're going to leave the Earth.'

Dwllis sat back. 'Is that not a good thing?'

Subadwan recoiled. 'They hold the key to Cray! The gnosticians hold another. But if those beings leave, humanity is doomed, and the gnosticians will take over everything.' Her voice became a wail as she cried. 'These electronic beings aren't even from Earth. They're aliens from another star!'

Dwllis coughed and leaned forward. 'Madam, I must ask you to keep an immense secret. I look after a gnostician at the Cowhorn Tower, one mentally augmented by Archivists of Selene. He can speak. He told me what happened when Cray was founded.'

'The gnostician can speak?'

'Most assuredly. This is why I require your aid. The people of Cray must understand that our Reeve's purges are murderous. I have to speak out.'

Subadwan, her face expressing surprise and distaste, said, 'Won't that be dangerous?'

'Could I speak in your Archive?'

Subadwan breathed in deeply, then sighed a long sigh. It seemed to Dwllis that she was wrestling with her conscience. 'You're inviting trouble,' she said, glancing up at him.

'It must be done, Lord Archivist. I have no choice.'

Subadwan moved closer, and said, 'Dwllis, we've got more important things to do, far more important things. Tanglanah and her kin want to leave the Earth. If they do the software of Cray will die, and then everybody in the city. Except the gnosticians, that is, who seem to prosper here.'

'But—'

'Listen to me! I killed three of these electronic creatures. Four others have now manifested in the real world – they are aeromorphs – in order to escape death. Tanglanah and Laspetosyne manifested earlier. That leaves six still inside Gwmru. We've got to stop them leaving.'

'Madam, how?'

Subadwan exclaimed, 'I don't know. We have to pool our resources, our knowledge. Tanglanah and her kin support the city networks, maybe they even created them. We're on the verge of being made extinct, don't you see?'

'I do see, damnably well, but I have no answers.' Dwllis glanced up at the ceiling of the ante-chamber. 'The head of the Spacefish, I would wager, now points directly to these beings' home star.'

Subadwan began fretting and fidgeting. 'I need your help, Dwllis.'

'Lord Archivist, listen. I will go away and consider our options. You are correct, we must pool our resources. But I have my own difficulties, for I am not, at the moment, what you might term a free man. Is there a private line upon which I can call you at need?'

Subadwan told him the code of her line, then Dwllis, with a polite bow, departed. Taking great care, he journeyed west across the city, returning to the Copper Courtyard. The streets were almost empty: word of danger had spread. Dwllis felt alone and vulnerable, glancing back every few seconds, trying to pierce flashing green and yellow street after-images.

It was in Hemp Street that he noticed a curious thing. A vitrescent house stood covered by a sickly yellow substance, a substance attacking both plastic and glass. The darkened aura of the house was negated, vitrescence reduced. He was tempted to touch the substance, to analyse it, but decided not to. Small, translucent ochre blobs in the street gutters he realised were dead vermin, apparently victims of the same substance attacking the house. Worried, he hurried on.

There was a call awaiting him when he arrived. 'From Pikeface,' Cuensheley said, fearfully.

Complete silence.

'P-Pikeface?' Dwllis eventually said.

At the network screen in Cuensheley's study he took the call. The ghastly fish face stared at him. 'This is Dwllis, Keeper of the Cowhorn Tower. Can I be of assistance?'

Pikeface said, 'You must speak with me.'

'What about?'

'Selene's time is come,' Pikeface continued. 'You must be part of the transformation of Crayan society. Noct is to be overthrown. You know that. Come join us, before it is too late.'

Dwllis had no idea what this mutant man was saying, but he suddenly remembered the size of crowds commanded by Archivists of Selene, and a thought came to him. 'If I were to join you,' he said, 'I must be allowed to address your congregations.'

'On what subject?'

'Gnosticians. With particular reference to the purges.'

Pikeface considered. 'That can be done.'

Dwllis cheered inwardly. 'Good,' he said. 'I shall attend tonight's lecture. You will allow me to address the people, and then we shall converse further.'

The link was severed after farewells. Dwllis immediately called Subadwan. 'Hello?' she said, face fuzzy on a poor line.

'I no longer require your assistance,' he announced. 'I shall be speaking tonight from a podium at the Archive of Selene.'

Subadwan's face fell. Visibly upset, she said, 'Very well, go lunar. But don't reveal our secrets.'

'Have no fear, madam, I am confidentiality personified. I was brought up with manners, you know.'

With that, the link was broken, and Dwllis sat back to consider what he had done; and what he would do. He knew little of Gwmru and almost nothing of the Archive of Safekeeping, but that did not matter, for at the moment he was more concerned about Crimson Boney, Etwe, and tonight's speech. Rousing himself from reverie, he sat and began to jot down ideas.

That evening the Archive was all a hubbub. A congregation of some thousands had packed into the central hall to hear Pikeface. Dwllis sidled in just before the lecture was due to begin.

Standing stern upon the podium, arms folded across his massive chest, Pikeface waited until every voice was silenced and every pair of eyes stared up at him. Then in a voice so quiet Dwllis had to put one hand to his ear, he began to talk, and an atmosphere of mesmeric attention overcame the hall, as Pikeface slowly worked his way to almost apoplectic grandeur.

'For who am I, other than Pikeface?' he demanded of his rapt audience. 'The Moon is no more! The Spacefish is upon us. Oh, ecstasy! Lose your terrestrial bonds and follow me, for I can take you away from this city, from vitrifying Cray, to a better place. We are doomed to approach our destiny in space!

'It is I, only I, who was born to approach destiny with a stern heart and an unblinking eye. I, a fish, the ancient symbol of authority, can lead you away from the fragmenting hulk you call a city! For there is no other. Listen to me, and listen to what you already know in your hearts. For if there is one thing that is true, it is this. There are two paths to take: one right, one wrong. All of you have a duty to make the right choice. And follow me!'

Rapturous applause. Dwllis shivered as the spell was broken. Pikeface walked down, ignoring the tumult. Dwllis had witnessed a true demagogue tonight, and he did not like what he had heard.

At the end of Pikeface's speech various people were due to speak. Dwllis was second on the list, and as his moment approached he walked to the lectern. Nerves overcame him. Serried ranks of round faces stared up at him, and he dropped his page of notes, which caused some merriment amongst the congregation. Pikeface sat to one side, the doddery figure of Tierquthay next to him. Dwllis glanced across at them before speaking.

'I am Dwllis, noble Keeper of the Cowhorn Tower,' he announced. His voice seemed to have deserted him. He coughed. 'I am here tonight—'

'Take that biscuit out yer mouth!' someone shouted. He had forgotten the small lump of qe'lib'we that he had been chewing during the service. For a moment he smelled the yeasty odour of the drug, on his breath, his hands, his clothes. The stuff was beginning to rule his life.

'Plug yer mouth in!' came another call.

General laughter. Dwllis looked at his boots to spit the drained qe'lib'we out, then coughed again. 'People of Selene,' he said, 'Crayans all. Ahem.' He noticed that a man in the audience had a streak of ochre splashed across his forehead.

'Gerron wiv it, yer fat dandy!' somebody yelled.

'Fop features!' called another.

Much laughter. Dwllis took a deep breath and began to speak loudly. 'My Crayans, I am here to speak about gnosticians. In particular, I wish to impress upon you all how murderously appalling these purges are. Why, they must be stopped.' He was warming to his subject now, forgetting his debilitating nerves. 'I am here to tell you all that gnosticians, although they do not speak our tongue, and indeed seem so different to us, are in fact sentient folk just like ourselves.'

At this, the congregation began to murmur. Dark glances and silent looks of antagonism were sent up to him on waves of lunar fervour. 'My good people,' he continued, 'it is a damnable shame that these purges should continue. Why, when you see a dead gnostician in the street, do you not wonder if it is capable of feeling, even of proper thought?'

They did not like this. Pikeface was on his feet. A baying had been set up at the back of the crowd. Dwllis, with horror, realised that he might have made a mistake.

'I can prove that they are conscious,' he shouted. 'It is the truth, I say!'

Boos and catcalls now, and from the back a hand-thrusting mass salute of mob aggression.

Dwllis made one final stand. 'Do not let ordinary thought rule your lives. The gnosticians are like us, and may not be killed with impunity, for such is murder! Defy the purges!'

Glowing yellow crescents began to hit him, thrown by jeering lunar acolytes. Pikeface roared. 'Begone, wretch! Leave or feel my wrath.'

Dwllis ran down the aisle. A few in the crowd tried to trip him, but he moved too quickly, dodging the yellow crescents. A man tried to throw a punch at him, luckily missing.

Dwllis staggered out of the Archive, a crowd of twenty on his tail. Two dark-cloaked figures sprang upon him. He could not hear what they said over the din of the city. Then a smoke bomb was thrown. Fumes everywhere. He tried to resist, but the two attackers dragged him down an alley. Coughing too much to oppose them, he wriggled, but could not get free.

A woman's voice in his ear: 'Stop twisting, you idiot.'

Cuensheley. Dwllis got to his feet, to be tugged along the passage.

The other woman shouted, 'Fop features!' That was Ilquisrey.

They ran to the end of the alley. Dwllis turned, seeing no pursuit. They hurried on, up the glittering Broom Street, up Marjoram Street, along Peppermint Street, then made at a more sedate pace back up to the Rusty Quarter, pausing only to cower amongst piles of glass shards when an aeromorph swept by on clouds of ozone.

Cuensheley had handed him ear-muffs. *Idiot*, she signed.

Fop features, Ilquisrey added, an expression of fury on her face. *Can't you get anything right?*

Dwllis refrained from signing an answer. At the Copper Courtyard he left them without a word, throwing only an expression of distaste in Ilquisrey's direction.

Worse was to come.

Turning off Sphagnum Street, he saw orange-suited Triaders crowded around the door of the Cowhorn Tower. Concealed behind a spray of blue leaves he watched as the scimitar-wielding bullies dragged Crimson Boney out, shortly followed by Etwe. Etwe they kicked up the path to the Swamps with what seemed a chorus of jeers.

Crimson Boney, struggling, was held by two Triaders. A third cut off his head with a single scimitar stroke.

Dwllis could not hold back a cry of pain, of horror. City clamour camouflaged him. Shocked to the core he stood staring. The Triaders gestured to a dark-robed man who emerged from behind dense foliage. Smiling, he now shook the hand of the Triader butcher. Dwllis recognised him as the grandson of his predecessor.

Umia had acted. Dwllis had been replaced.

Sickened, too stunned to move, Dwllis watched as the grinning Triaders jogged down the path and then, after looking up and down the street, hurried south. Dwllis was left with a chill in the pit of his stomach and the dread image of the execution.

He stood still as rock for ten minutes. The locale was deserted. Illuminated cracks between the tower's exterior tiles indicated that the new Keeper was exploring his territory. Dwllis shivered and cursed as he imagined what would be found. Doubtless he would be reported and then hunted down.

But Crimson Boney lay dead. Gnosticians, Dwllis knew, did not bury their dead. Instead their out-city dwelling agnostician relatives, they who nurtured the pod-born gnostician infants for the first three years of life, dealt with matters of the deceased. Agnosticians made globular glass coffins in which all bodies were encased, gnosticians' and their own.

Dwllis ran up to the tower and pulled Crimson Boney's body into undergrowth, returning for the head, which had been kicked aside. Hidden, he wrapped the corpse in his cloak, before dragging it down to Sphagnum Street. A few starving outers signed at him, but otherwise he remained unmolested as he pulled his load up to Marjoram Street, and then along to the gate. The snoozing Triader sentries did not notice him.

He left the corpse under a tree, knowing that soon an agnostician would spot it. On the ground around him lay broken clay fishes. For some minutes he pondered the gnostician ritual of breaking a clay fish when entering the city – fish that were reformed and carried outside when leaving – and the images of Crimson Boney's legend returned to his mind. What was the clue that he had missed?

With no home, his only option was to return to the Copper Courtyard, a prospect he did not relish. But it had to be done. If he was not yet a fugitive he was certainly no longer an independent. Cray records would be amended either with the word lesser, or, more likely and more devastating, the term outer. His social position had been ruined. There was no going back.

He pushed the attention-pad at Cuensheley's side door. Tears came to his eyes, not for himself, but for

Crimson Boney. The gnostician had been a friend. Dwllis had enjoyed the company of only a very few friends during his life, and Crimson Boney he had hoped to come to know. That was impossible now.

Cuensheley invited him in, hugging him when she saw his tear streaked face. 'What's happened?' she asked, over and over.

After wordless sobbing, Dwllis, half ashamed at himself, half uncaring that he had wept, described what had happened. Cuensheley, though she shed no tears, was moved. They hurried up to her bedroom.

Chewing welcome qe'lib'we, Dwllis agreed that, as he was now homeless, he would have to stay with Cuensheley. To her credit she did not crow at this news, nor even smile. But Dwllis dreaded the consequences. It was as if he was being assaulted from all sides: pursued by an amorous Cuensheley, wanted by the Triad for sedition, chased by Pikeface and the lunar mob for perfidy. In one evening he had been destroyed, and he knew that never again in his life would he hold the high status of his years so far. He was but a disadvantaged beggar now, no better than the wretched urchins praying for alms outside the Archive of Gaya.

19

THE EYRIE

Now that the truth of Tanglanah and Gwmru had been revealed, Subadwan found life in the Baths almost unbearable. Dwllis had deserted her for lunar places, Aquaitra she hardly trusted, and there were at least two people who wanted her either captured or dead. Only Liguilifrey and Calminthan did she trust.

On static haunted city network screens she watched pictures of the four aeromorphs pillaging the streets. Many outers had died. In the air, bats flown by the Triad's foremost pilots engaged the aeromorphs in combat, losing decisively owing to the resilience and agility of the aeromorphs. Through nocturnal days many aerial battles were fought, always ending in a fountain of chiroptera sparks and aeromorph victory. Below, entire streets were turned to shattered lanes through which Crayans struggled, hands wrapped, faces masked against glass. The alleys around the Baths were themselves vitrifying.

Then there were the reports of a new plague. Vitrified houses were transmuting, becoming ochre yellow. None of the official stations reported it, but many local broadcasters illegally operating on the wire noted and mentioned the phenomenon. And they reported human susceptibility. Subadwan's stomach turned when she saw a close-up of a human body, yellow tinted yet translucent, solid like a statue of a torture victim.

One evening, she spent hour after hour bathing. Other bathers were few in number, too frightened to risk the streets. Subadwan, swimming around the pool periphery, fretted as she considered what Tanglanah might be doing.

She realised that Umia would have an answer. It was her only option. Decision made, she left the pool and dressed in her city one-piece, hurrying along to the outer doors, where Calminthan, an expression of curiosity on her face, watched her leave. By chance friends of Umia were in the street, and soon she was walking alongside them down Buttercup Street, and then Malmsey Street.

The lack of people made her notice the subdued din. Some Crayans had stopped wearing ear-muffs, and it was said that vitrescence was now spread wide enough across the city for it to affect the noise produced by machines and electronics. If that were true, then half the city must have succumbed. Certainly, many houses, even along Malmsey Street, were darkly glittering like obsidian shells. But some were covered in another substance, this ochre keratin, and these houses were notable because outside their fronts lay the sallow corpses of vermin, animals, and even some people. It seemed the ochre plague attacked everything it touched.

Soon Subadwan saw ahead the Archive of Noct: her old home. She smiled to see it again. Inside, she was led through dark corridors, up wide flights of steps carved from black-silver, and along passages dusty with the effluvia of incense burned down below, until she was pushed into the spherical chamber of Umia.

He stood waiting for her. The men at her side unbuttoned her one-piece and ripped her vest off her back.

Except that it was not her vest. Instantaneous mental adjustment changed her perspective. She saw Umia, his chamber, smelled its rank odours. She saw the statue of Noct. Why had she come to this place?

She had been tricked. She spat at Umia, and said, 'So you managed to violate the privacy of the Baths a third time.'

'Indeed,' Umia said.

Subadwan sneered at the old rogue. How he had performed his trick she did not know, but she did know that her life hung in the balance. She buttoned up her suit. 'Gaya save me,' she said. 'Don't tell me you still want me on the Triad?'

'It is the law. The Lord Archivist of Gaya must be one of the five.'

'It's an abomination,' Subadwan replied. 'I'll never serve under it. I'm human! And Gaya represents freedom.'

'The freedom of the deluded,' Umia remarked. He sat at a desk with some difficulty, as if he was tired.

'What are you going to do with me, you vile lump of dirt?'

Umia smiled, shook his head, and looked up at the statue of Noct. Nervously Subadwan looked also at the figure, then down at the malodorous garden below. Rumour had it that the bodies of enemies made fine compost.

'You leave me no choice but to tell you that you are no longer the Lord Archivist of Gaya.'

'What?'

'This morning I received an application from one Aquaitra of Gaya, claiming the title of Lord Archivist and asking me when the next meeting of the Triad might be.'

Subadwan could not help but laugh. 'I don't believe it. It's a trick. Just another—'

'It is true, Subadwan. You have just refused for the final time the lawful post of the Lord Archivist of Gaya. One has supplanted you who accepts this post. I draw the obvious inference.'

'Prove it,' Subadwan simply said.

'I do not have to. Your status no longer warrants it.'

Subadwan, confusion mounting in her mind, shook her head. 'All right, if that's the case, you can free me. You don't need to bully me any more.'

'And neither am I obliged to let you loose into the city.'

Subadwan stepped back as if physically struck. Her body went limp. The spherical chamber, the entire building, seemed to close in around her tiny frame. 'What then?'

Before Umia could reply a commotion at the door disturbed them. Heraber, Umia's deputy, struggled with a blue-gowned woman, who when she sprang into the chamber was revealed as Aquaitra.

'Lord Archivist!' Umia said, startled. He looked about him, as if for support, and took a step backwards.

'Reeve,' Aquaitra said, 'I apologise for my wild entrance, but I had to see you. I have a claim on Subadwan. I must have her!'

'Have her?' Umia seemed helpless, as if unable to cope.

'Indeed!'

Umia waved his deputy away, then turned to face Aquaitra. 'What claim do you have on Subadwan?'

'Subadwan is a former Lord Archivist of Gaya who departed us in an indecent manner. Our laws dictate that she must answer to a Gayan court, to explain her behaviour.'

Subadwan stared astonished at her friend. 'Aquaitra, it's me,' she said. 'Don't you recognise me?'

'Quiet,' Umia demanded.

Subadwan ignored him. 'Aquaitra,' she implored, 'you know this is Umia's doing. He forced me out of the Archive and he tricked me into coming here. Can't you see that?'

Aquaitra sent her a cold glance. 'You deserted, Subadwan. That deed has to be dealt with.'

Umia coughed, trying to return the conversation to himself. 'Subadwan is mine,' he explained to Aquaitra. 'I am the Reeve of Cray and when Cray's laws, which override those of your establishment, are broken I have the authority to say what happens.'

'I will have her,' Aquaitra repeated. 'You are free to watch from the public chambers of our Archive, if you wish.'

Dumbfounded by Aquaitra's confidence, Umia began to flounder. 'I am the Reeve. I will speak with my advisers on the matter. Subadwan's fate will be postponed for now.'

'But—'

Umia had regained the initiative. Calling for Heraber, he turned away from Aquaitra and refused to listen to her pleading.

Subadwan meanwhile stood in shock, her gaze alternately on Umia and on the flushed and angry face of her former friend.

'Aquaitra . . .' she whispered.

Heraber had emerged to lead Aquaitra away. Umia called for the three burly Triaders who had brought Subadwan into the Archive of Noct.

'What will you do with me?' Subadwan asked.

'You used to come here, daughter of Brynnon. You remember the place known as the Eyrie, I imagine?'

'You're not putting me up there?'

Umia glanced at his Triader henchman. 'Take her away.'

The three Triaders grabbed her without ceremony, hurting her wrists and shoulders, tugging her so her joints clacked. She cried out in pain.

'Enjoy the next few decades,' a chuckling Umia called out.

Subadwan struggled, but her captors were labouring pyutons with muscles like coils of steel. In their grip she stood no chance. High up she was taken, feet dragging through dust-choked passages, thumping up crooked stairs. She was lifted through a series of trapdoors, until at last she was thrust in front of a door.

It was unlocked with a giant fishtail, and she was cast into the room beyond.

One of the Triaders joined her. 'We are not barbarians,' he said. 'Twice a day food will be sent up here by lift, water too. That circular trapdoor covers a hole. The hole is your lavatory. You can see there are basins here for washing.' He unbuttoned the mid-section of his suit and for a ghastly moment Subadwan thought he was about to assault her. But he brought out a slim tube from some inner hip pocket. 'This is an infinite pen. It will never run out. You can use it to write on the walls, or perhaps to decorate them. But remember you'll be here for the rest of your life.' He grinned. 'So don't finish too early.'

Another Triader popped his head through the door. 'If you get bored, think of Gaya, eh?'

'Bye, now.'

The door slammed shut. With a clunk its mecho-magnetic lock was set.

Subadwan gazed witless at the room around her. It was four yards square, a sash window fused shut at one end – the west end, judging by the lamp-encircled area of blackout that must be the Empty Quarter. From this highest tower of the Archive she could see most of Westcity across a strip of roof and a balustrade. A dome-shaped skylight gave her an almost panoramic view of the heavens. And there, as if to taunt her, hung the Spacefish.

Objects were few: four basins, some cloths, one chair with an old cushion, and she had the pen and the clothes she now wore. How would she wash her clothes?

She did not really believe she was here. The interview had been so quick. She could scarcely remember the walk down from the Baths.

She checked the two exit points: the lavatory hole and the lift door. Both were made of steel, the former too small to squeeze through, the latter tall, but too narrow. No chance of escape, then. She had heard of the Eyrie in her childhood and knew its reputation. Most probably there was more than one room designated so, since at any one time the Triad would have more than one prisoner suitable for solitary confinement.

Sitting in the chair, she passed a difficult night. When the red clouds of dawn came she saw through the window the silken wings of bats roosting upside down from the balustrade, their glittering control panels twinkling, the rusting mouths of their engines gently fuming. Behind inch-thick panes of glass twitched eight black escape routes. Perhaps the sight of them was part of the torture.

The bats snuffled, fidgeted, then, as the gloomy dawn turned to pitch-black day, they slept. Subadwan watched them, then turned away. She did not know what to think.

Food arrived, as promised. On a scrap of a cuff she wrote 'I accept Triad membership,' putting it into the lift before the automatic door closed.

The food was fair – parsnip bricks, mint mash, peach granules. There were eight brass pitchers of water tall and narrow enough to pass through the lift door. With a sigh Subadwan realised that her new life had begun. When she lifted the lid to the hole there emerged the smell of anaerobic decay.

The day passed slowly. The shifting Spacefish, just visible as a glowing crescent through the grimy air, allowed her a sense of passing time. When her evening meal arrived there was no note. Nobody came to reply to her message.

How long would she be forced to remain here? A week? A month? She could not imagine a solitary month. Yet they had said she would be here for the rest of her natural life.

Next day she received her visitor, but it was the last person she expected to see.

Her father arrived alone. In one hand Brynnon held the unlocking fishtail, in the other lay a Noct text. He was of ordinary looks, but he had a way of grimacing and pulling at the hairs of his beard that caught the eye. He looked at her in silence, then shut and locked the door, cracking the fishtail in half then putting the pieces in separate pockets.

'Hello, father,' Subadwan said, wearily. Already the grim expression on his face had caused emotions within her – fear, anger, perhaps a little excitement. 'Have you come to release me?' she asked, trying to settle her face into neutrality.

'Only the Lord Archivist has the power to release you,' Brynnon replied. He stared at her. 'You can be candid with me. You can relax.'

Why had he said that? Normally he would launch straight into his complaint. Subadwan felt the weight of his vexed looks upon her. She could not relax, not ever, for past experience had taught her that at some point, sooner or later, he would lash out like an angry animal. She tried to think of something unimportant to say.

He spoke as she drew breath. 'Why are you here, Subadwan? What crime have you committed?'

The assumption of guilt irritated Subadwan. She could feel the force of sarcasm rising within her. 'I think I'm guilty of free thought. It's difficult to say with Umia, isn't it? You'd know, of course.'

'Free thought? But Noct understands free thought.'

'Oh, yes, free thought from useless books.' Already Subadwan could feel her annoyance increasing, and her desperation. 'Umia wanted me to join the Triad. I refused.'

'Why?'

'Because the Triad is just a tool of the Archive of Noct. I'm not going to be the stooge of a dictator.'

Brynnon sniffed, as if giving her words short shrift. 'Better a living stooge than a half-living Eyrie captive, surely? You realise, of course, that the chances of you being let out of this place are slim?'

'I'm not stupid.'

He shrugged. 'Perhaps that was always your problem. You have an excellent opinion of your own intellect.'

'Not quite so good as the opinion you hold of your own.'

'So is it to be like this between us?'

'Gaya love me, *you* started it.'

He actually smiled. As if reminiscing – though Subadwan could tell he was acting – he said, 'That was always what you used to say when you knew you were wrong. You started it.'

'Go away, Father, if you're determined to be an utter fool.'

His tone hardened. '*Father* is it? Subadwan, you won't be telling me to go away in a few years . . . if I come to visit you.'

'If? So you're just going to ignore me?'

'Umia could not have acted wrongly. Besides, the law says the Lord Archivist of Gaya—'

'I know all that,' said Subadwan. 'Go away if you can't even be original.'

'I was just trying to point out that I follow the law.'

'There's a higher law than Crayan Law,' Subadwan said.

'Trite nonsense.'

Subadwan glared at him. 'What about Baths law?' she asked.

That took him by surprise. Subadwan awaited the burst of anger. He replied, 'How clever you are now you are one whole quarter of a century old. Well, I shall just leave you to consider your actions for the next quarter of a century.' Now he was tugging at his beard, his eyes flashing. 'Perhaps then you will have something different to say to me.'

He reassembled the key and made to leave.

'If you're still alive then,' Subadwan said, calculating her words for maximum effect.

'I will be,' he retorted, 'if only to see how much you have changed.'

Brynnon unlocked the door and departed.

As the rest of the day passed, an inner sense told Subadwan that Brynnon would be the last visitor she would entertain for some time. Well that at least gave her something to think about.

She toured her prison, looking for cracks in the plastic, looking around the lavatory hole and the lift door, checking the seals of the sash window and the skylight.

Night arrived. Standing tip-toed on the chair she studied the sky. The aeromorphs were low. She counted them. One, two . . . seven . . . a few more to the east: eight and nine.

For an hour she examined the heavens, counting and recounting the aeromorphs until, as if her unconscious mind had for some time been on the verge of solving a puzzle, a sudden understanding came. The synthesis of facts.

There were thirteen aeromorphs. Now four had descended from the sky. How could it be otherwise? She herself had experienced part of Gwmru inside an aeromorph, led there by Tanglanah.

The electronic beings were somehow connected to the aeromorphs. And if these flying machines were destroyed, then maybe. . .

Escape was essential.

20

TO BE A BEGGAR

Every morning Dwllis woke to a fresh lump of qe'lib'we taken from Cuensheley's inexhaustible supply. This morning was no different. Hearing him move about the room, Cuensheley awoke. She smiled at him. 'My outer addict,' she said.

'Good morning, Cuensheley. My status is no joke.'

'Don't be so fussy. Come here.'

Dwllis laughed. 'Why?'

She threw the bedclothes off and sat up. Dwllis had seen her naked once or twice before, an unavoidable intimacy caused by sharing a room, but this action was different. A direct, lusty look shone in her eyes. Dwllis felt his heart begin to pound with distrust and apprehension.

'Come here, I said,' she repeated.

He sat, not moving. She crawled over to him, caressed him, and kissed him. For some minutes he half enjoyed her attentions. Memories of Etwe lay far away. She straddled him and with surprisingly deft movements stripped off his gown. Dwllis knew what she wanted.

He tensed. 'Relax,' she said, one hand upon him,

the other upon herself. 'Relax, Dwllis . . .'

But he could not. Once he realised there was no going back, that she intended to seduce him all the way, he clawed at her, trying to roll himself up into a ball. But she was a strong woman and she was on top of him. She resisted; she demanded. In sudden panic Dwllis yelped and struggled free of her, leaving her wide-eyed and astonished on her hands and knees.

'How dare you?' he said. 'What do you think you were doing?'

'I should have thought it was obvious. What's the matter?'

He was hastily putting on his underwear. 'I gave you no permission, did I?'

She looked at a loss. 'Permission? Don't you want to be my lover now you've left Etwe?'

'I never said so.'

'Words aren't everything. Honestly, if I'm so distasteful to you, why didn't you sleep somewhere else?'

Dwllis gasped at her audacity. 'It was you who forced me into this room. I wanted to sleep in the other room.' He threw on some city clothes, snatched at random.

She seemed angered. 'I thought we agreed you couldn't go there, you idiot. What's this all about? Am I too old for you, or what?'

'We have a mild friendship, that is all. I do not need you if you must know. I hope never to have to come here again, and I hope I never see you again.'

Then he approached her and from her neck ripped the silver fishtail given to him by Querhidwe. With no further word he turned and departed, slamming the door; the only emotional gesture he allowed himself. At speed he descended, leaving the Copper Courtyard by the public exit, Ilquisrey's earmuffs, grabbed from a table, upon his ears.

Some streets away he paused. He was in Red Lane. He hurried down to the Damp Courtyard and bought a peppermint soda. Then he congratulated himself on his escape.

So the day passed. He stayed in the Damp Courtyard. He realised that he had, under the stress of the moment, dressed in the first clothes to hand. They were an inelegant mixture of garments that ordinarily he would have scorned. Now he felt embarrassed to be seen in public.

He truly was a street outer now, with no home and no friends, very little money, no possessions, and no prospects. A certain amount of shock dulled his thought – he did not consider himself one of the ragged urchins he so often saw, despite the possibility that he might become one – and so when he was ejected from the Damp Courtyard in the evening he thought himself somehow different to the beggars and the half-dead alcoholics.

It was cold for the time of year. Normally the city was suffocatingly close, but now the air was cool. It was quieter, too.

Drifting south, he ended up in a vitrified doorway on Feverfew Street. An aeromorph rushed by. There was just enough time to hide beneath a clot of plastic that had accumulated in one corner. Seconds later the glass around him shattered and he was covered in fragments. He crawled out. The house seemed unsafe so he ran off down the street, dodging pipes, ducts, ducking under swaying tubes that hissed out steam.

The whole length of the street was one mass of

glass, shattered in places, elsewhere a crush of darkly gleaming surfaces. Only the street plastic was untouched, except at the edges where vitrification was taking hold. At the further end he saw a flickering illusion of reflections, concealing the exit and the buildings there, and for some seconds he was dizzily hypnotised by the lights, the glass, the twisting refractions, so that he had to crouch down to steady himself.

And, as he wandered south, he noticed that the ochre disease was spreading. He stumbled across human bodies, all hard as marble and translucent like medical models, their organs dull internal shapes. Everywhere lay the small sallow corpses of urban animal life. Afraid that such a condition might be contagious, Dwllis touched nothing.

He felt tired. It was late evening. From a sleeping outer stretched half across an alley he stole a hat, the better to disguise himself. He realised there were more street people than there used to be, doubtless the result of vitrification. Where could they go? Where could *he* go?

In the end, rather ashamed of himself, he found a clear doorway set deep into an old plastic house on Five Street, just behind the Water Purification House. With rumbling stomach and dry mouth, he tried to settle himself.

Sleep came much later. Hunger, thirst, and fear of discovery by aeromorphs jangled his nerves, seeing slumber off except for two snatched hours around dawn.

Then the withdrawal symptoms began. Automatically he reached into his pocket for his film-wrapped lump of qe'lib'we, to find nothing, not even an empty wrapper from which he could lick the crumbs. Fear gripped him. Qe'lib'we he could not do without. The damnable Cuensheley had enticed him with larger and larger doses. He would have to go back and plead. It would not be easy.

Dizzy from deprivation, and with an itching, stinging sensation along his veins, he made his way to the Rusty Quarter, approaching the Copper Courtyard from a narrow passage to the south, so as not to attract attention. The public entrance was lit 'open', and he saw Ilquisrey inside serving a young couple. He opened the door and entered the quadrangle.

Ilquisrey turned and saw him. Her face darkened and she ran at him, grabbing a tureen spoon on the way. Dwllis withdrew. At the door she yelled at him, 'You said you weren't coming back! Get away! If you ever come back here again I'll slit your throat with my own biscuit knife.'

Dwllis, at a safe distance, replied, 'I did not wish to speak with you, but with your mother.'

Ilquisrey's fury was tangible. 'Didn't you hear what I said? She never wants you here again. Never, d'you understand? I'm warning you, you fat, bald fop, if I ever come across you in the streets you'll feel my blade go straight through your heart – if you've got one. Now get out of our alley!'

Dwllis had no choice but to leave. Withdrawal symptoms worsened as depression struck. He felt as if every artery and every vein was itching. In addition, hunger and thirst made him giddy, made his stomach hurt, and he felt a dull tiredness.

The appearance of Etwe was a relief. She saw him first, in an alley off Marjoram Street. 'Dwllis,' she called, 'I've been looking for you around here since the Triaders came. Are you all right?'

'No,' he croaked in reply.

'How long have you been wandering?'

'One day.'

'Come to the Swamps,' she said, helping him to walk. He felt better for the attention. 'We'll get some water.'

'Swamps water? I can't drink Swamps water. Do you have any triad tokens on you?'

'None. But there is a way to filter the water.'

Dwllis retched in reply. At the Swamps wall he collapsed. From a low bush with achlorician-stripped leaves Etwe plucked a spherical fruit, which she broke in half, using one half as a basin and the other to filter water from the gelatinous liquid. 'It's all right,' she said, 'there aren't any bodies here. Drink it, it's safe.'

Dwllis had no option. Quickly he drank the water, trying not to taste it, but breathing out he caught an odour of rancid dust in his mouth, which made him retch once more. He began rubbing his hand up and down his arm in an attempt to soothe the internal itching. 'Damnable woman,' he muttered. 'Damnable woman threw me out.'

'You should have stayed with me,' Etwe remarked.

He looked up at her. He felt confused. Was this a new enemy or an old friend? And Cuensheley: was she lost forever, or had her vicious daughter lied? He did not know, and he possessed no energy with which to find out.

'I must have qe'lib'we,' he said in phlegmy tones. 'I shall die if I do not. Perhaps tomorrow.'

'It would be better to give up now,' Etwe advised. 'We are outers with no—'

'I am an outer,' Dwllis interrupted sourly, 'but no pyuton is offered that status. You always have the option of returning to that damned Triad Tower.'

'Not necessarily. I want to help you.'

'Indeed.'

Dwllis started rubbing at his legs. He found that he could not put them in a comfortable position. If he rested them, one or the other would itch internally, would ache, and he would be forced to move. It was a constant torment.

'I do want to help,' Etwe insisted. Her long blonde hair brushed across his face as she moved closer. 'How could I return to Triad Tower when you are here, with no food or friends? It would kill me inside, Dwllis.'

Dwllis looked up at her. The words sounded sincere. Repressed memories of pyuton happiness came to mind. Etwe would be a useful assistant, he realised, not subject to the wear and tear, the hungers and needs, of the real world; somebody he could use to get what he wanted.

'Very well,' he said. 'I need food urgently. How can we get some?'

'Steal some. Or get into an outer group.'

'An outer group? What is an outer group?'

Etwe, a smile on her face, sat at his side. 'Cray's outers don't just wander in singles, or pairs. There are some organisations. We could join one to get food.'

'I have had *enough* of people,' Dwllis said. 'People have let me down, as always.' He ruminated on his troubles for a minute.

'I know what is best for you,' Etwe replied.

Dwllis could not believe his ears.

Speechless, he stared. She seemed just like the old

Etwe. Even the voice was identical. But where did this disobedient streak come from? 'What exactly are you?' he demanded. 'How did you spoil my translation work, and how did you get this body?'

'That is my affair. Content yourself with the knowledge that I am back to look after you, like I did in the old days.'

'I damned well shall not.'

Etwe did not lose her sweet reason. 'You have no option. You are destitute, an outer, with no idea how to find food. You have enemies, but no friends and no money. You need me.'

'I have my pride.'

'And pride kills.'

Dwllis slumped. All she had said was true. He knew it, or half knew it, for full admission cost too much. Of course he could not admit that to her face. He said, 'What, out of curiosity, do you suggest that we do?'

'We must find a safe house in which to shelter. I shall go out and look for food.' She stood up. 'Follow me.'

Meekly, Dwllis followed his pyuton saviour down to Sphagnum Street. 'Let us try to find somewhere in Cochineal Mews,' he said. 'I used to live there. I know it well.'

Etwe agreed. The further part of the mews, abutting on to Sphagnum Mews, was vitrified and showed evidence of the ochre plague, but the near end was clear and clean. Here they found an old pumphouse, empty, desolate, but suitable for their needs. It was a two-roomed ruin with cracking plastic and rusty floors. They found plastic shavings, old clothes and pieces of dead vegetation which they made into bedding. Dwllis, ashamed at what he was being forced to do, felt an incoherent, dull anger at all the world. The withdrawal symptoms did not help. Now he was shivering, fidgeting, unable to keep still for the dreadful ache of his limbs. He suffered simultaneously from fatigue and hyper-alertness.

To keep his mind off his body he began to talk to Etwe about his childhood in Cochineal Mews. 'I was a quiet boy, you know. I never played with the other fellows like I was supposed to. Instead, I went around collecting odd twigs and bits of stone and nicely shaped fragments of dead buildings. I used to arrange them all in groups, you see, in order. I always loved order as a boy. I was a compulsive arranger of things. I suspect that's when my interest in Cray's history began. I remember realising all these things that had happened that nobody cared about. I saw that they were all jumbled up, all these old facts and events and things, and I wanted to do something about it. I can remember lots of things about my childhood. It was always too hot, but I never complained. It was a tight household, ours, with certain rules that you had to follow, but the trouble was nobody ever told me what they were, and I had to find them out by experience. They were good times, though. I don't mind now that it was so . . . difficult. Nothing was ever easy for me. Even arranging my pieces of twig and suchlike was frowned upon. I remember thinking that there must be ten rules for things not to do for every rule that said you could do something . . .'

And so eventually he fell asleep, in Etwe's arms.

When he awoke next morning, he was rolling about the floor, limbs and head aching, itching, driving him to the edge of madness. He craved his drug, but his mind was too clouded to think of schemes to get some. All he wanted was for some to arrive. Etwe shone in his thoughts like a beacon.

'Get qe'lib'we,' he managed to croak.

She offered him water and broken biscuits. 'Forget the drug,' she said. 'I found these packets behind the Glyptographic Courtyard with other rubbish. They're old, but edible.'

Dwllis scoffed the stale crumbly biscuits. Nausea rose in his guts, but he managed to hold the meal down. The food brought the focus of his clouded mind back to his body, making the craving for qe'lib'we worse, centred on his stomach, as if a cold pit lay there, waiting for warm drug-laden digestive fluids to appear. He rolled around some more, then made the effort to stand, encouraged by Etwe in a cooing voice. He failed.

He saw no future. He would die soon. He felt as though his circulatory system was being dissolved from the inside.

Lying desolate on the floor, the city around him only half real – a shadow of its former self – he began chewing at the fingers on his left hand. It dulled the ache. Etwe tried to stop him, and this led to fights, one-sided fights, since he was far too weak to resist her. So he took to hammering his hand and feet against the wall – it transmuted the ache to pain – until Etwe again stopped him. He yelled at her to leave him. Etwe said something about tying him up, but he screamed so loudly that she decided not to. He began shivering again, and this she could not stop. He felt he had won a victory. He shivered as much as he could. It negated some of the ache, but, more importantly, it annoyed Etwe.

Time itself became a tormentor. The red blazes of dawn and dusk were out of sight. He had no idea of the hour, of the day. Plastic delirium surrounded him. He imagined every slight sparkle, every mote of light to be a sign of the luminophages. Anything yellow he screamed at. Etwe fluttered around him. Often he thought she was Cuensheley handing him lumps of qe'lib'we, so he would crawl across to her and beg for the stuff, offering her any and every sexual service, pulling down his kirtle and underwear, until Etwe convinced him she was not Cuensheley, and he collapsed, sobbing.

The point of crisis came when he started to realise that the pumphouse was itself made of qe'lib'we. How he missed that fact before he did not know. He could smell the yeasty smell, could feel the drug giving like a plump cushion under his fingertips. But for some reason he could not rip any off, and scrabbling at the floor produced nothing.

It grew cold. Wetness surrounded him. His clothes were soaked. A woman with a bucket stood above him.

Time passed. Probably. He stared at the woman. Behind her shoulder the material from which the pumphouse was built showed a hole, and through that hole he saw a pale crescent.

That sight brought him around.

The Spacefish!

He managed to speak to the pyuton he now realised was Etwe. 'My destiny lies in the Archive of Selene,' he spluttered. He spat filthy water from his mouth. 'We must go inside. Something happened there, Etwe, and we must discover what it was.' From an inner pocket he withdrew the metal fishtail. 'Querhidwe gave me this. It is the key to my life. It must be, there is no other answer. Come on, Etwe, we had better go. Is it night or nocturnal day?'

'It is midnight precisely,' Etwe answered.

Dwllis found his mind clearing. He stood up. Tottered. His belly ached. 'Have we any food?'

Etwe handed him packets of biscuits, which he ate to the very last crumb, washing down the mouldy meal with brown water in which dead leaves and other plant debris floated. He ate and drank it all. He wanted to be as fit as possible for this last task.

'Are you willing to assist me?' he asked Etwe.

'If you say there is hope in that Archive, I must help you. But you know how dangerous it might be?'

'I know full well.' Dwllis drew himself up to his full height. 'I have been there before, you know, and know a secret way in.'

First checking the streets for aeromorphs, they departed the pumphouse. The city lay quiet. Dwllis gripped a rod of plastic, his only weapon, and wondered what lay in store.

Reeve Umia stared at his minion in amazement. 'Pikeface is here to see me?'

The minion nodded.

Umia repeated, 'That ghastly creature is *here*? To see me?'

The minion nodded again.

Umia sent the minion away. Alone again, he staggered back to the statue of Noct, where he fell in abasement. 'Noct, save me. I did not request the presence of that lunar mutant. Why is he here? What will he say to me?'

The disembodied voice of Lune replied, 'Umia, there is nothing to fear. This is a creature of Selene.'

'But Gaijin is gone. What shall I do? Dear Gaijin is gone, and there is only you to advise me.'

'Gaijin is not gone,' Lune replied. 'Gaijin now has other plans that do not include talking with you. But Gaijin is a black creature with no heart. We are well rid of her.'

'But what shall I *do*?'

'My advice is not to panic. The rumours of this creature cannot all be true. He is here to bully you, that is all. But you must not allow him to manipulate you. The Archive of Selene has split asunder, and Pikeface comes from the wrong side. Has Iquinlass contacted you?'

Umia shook his head in muzzy confusion. 'Who? I recall the name, I think.'

'Do not let Pikeface get the upper hand!'

'Yes, yes . . . not take the upper hand.' Umia pressed a pad on the control panel of a pyuter. 'Send the lunar messenger in.'

Seconds later the door into Umia's spherical chamber opened. Pikeface entered. The door shut with a snap.

Umia could barely look at the dreadful head. It slowly bent this way and that, as if trying to hypnotise him. Then Pikeface examined the layout of the chamber, studying the statue, the plants below, the furniture, the pyuters, all without moving from the door.

'Why did you request this personal interview?' Umia asked.

Pikeface approached. Umia smelled fish. He gagged. The merciless yellow eyes stared down at him.

Pikeface took a final look around the room, and

then answered, 'I have come to have words with you.'

'Why didn't you just use the networks?'

Pikeface stared on. Lacking eyelids, he did not blink. Again Pikeface turned to study the chamber. He walked away, strolled around the circumference, then knelt down with a barrage of creaking armour to peer upon the pale garden. His body was immense. Umia watched, fascinated, horrified, repelled by this gargantuan presence and yet unable to look away.

Pikeface approached. 'So the legend is true?'

'What legend would that be?'

'That the Reeve of Cray lives here alone, never to leave, at the centre of his hierarchical web.'

'That is true.'

Pikeface's head slowly swayed, to the left, to the right, to the left again, like a sly animal about to pounce. 'Then you are alone here, Umia.'

'Apart from you.'

The pike mouth opened. Umia heard a hiss. 'What is the origin of this custom?'

Umia, keen – desperate – to placate the creature, said in a flurry of words, 'Cray was founded five hundred years ago by folk enthusiastic to stem the gnostician invasion. It is thought that the city, once begun, built itself using plans contained in ancient memories. That is why I have fought the curse of vitrescence, and why I ordered the purge on those foul glasier gnosticians.'

'You stray from the topic, Umia. What is the origin of the custom of Reeve solitude?'

'It is ancient custom, of course. The legend says that if the Reeve of Umia goes amongst his people he will learn too much of them and their lives, and so become unworthy. A leader must be apart from the rabble, you understand.'

'So the Reeve must remain here. Alone.'

Umia hesitated. 'I would not phrase it like that. I have my hierarchy. The work of ruling, of administration, it goes on despite my not knowing the exact details.'

Pikeface took something from the pocket of his outer cloak. 'Do you know what this is?'

'It is a metal fishtail. Why do you ask?'

'With this fishtail I have just made myself Lord Archivist of Selene. With it I shall make myself Reeve of Cray. Somewhere in this city there lies a vehicle in which I can approach Selene, the Spacefish. I must find it. Now die, Umia.'

'No!'

But Umia flinched too late. Pikeface spun him around and stabbed him in the back several times, until he fell with a gurgle. His body twitched.

Pikeface knelt and stripped the body, then began ripping at the plastic flesh with his teeth, gorging himself on chunks of neoprene, spattering white fluid everywhere, on himself, all around, upon the plants below. He left no part of the body untouched, gobbling bioware and flesh, cracking bones, consuming the violet brain after smashing the skull with one chop of a bare hand. Ten minutes passed. The feast ended. All that was left of Umia was a steaming carcass, wetly purple and strewn with metal grit. Above it stood the satisfied, belching hulk of Pikeface.

A weak voice spoke. Pikeface paused, listened. It was coming from Umia's replacement forearm. Pikeface stamped on the metal limb until it was silent.

He turned to the statue of Noct. 'Now I will investigate you,' he said.

He pushed over the statue. Falling, it dented the metal gauze that was the dividing floor of the chamber. Pikeface took the statue and began pulling at it, tugging the arms off, gouging out the opalescent eyes, biting off the lips, pulling away the feet, then the legs, until all that was left was a pile of plastic, dark and crumbling. He kicked chunks about, but found nothing that drew his attention.

Having smashed up the furniture to his satisfaction, he descended to the pale garden. The oozing compost sucked and squelched at his boots, dragging even his formidable bulk down. He floundered about, pulling up plants but ignoring the screams of their roots, crushing kissleaves in his fingers, biting and hacking, until all was mud and debris, and a few skeletons. But still he did not find what he was looking for.

He returned to the upper chamber. No clue to the vehicle was here. He strode to the door.

A force sent him reeling. He tried again. He failed again. Something invisible, inaudible, was barring his exit.

He had not damaged the pyuter rigs because of the data they might hold. He pressed a communications pad.

'This is the new Reeve of Cray. The old Reeve, Umia, is dead. I am the new Reeve and my orders will be obeyed because Noct is thrown down. Turn off the force field. Turn it off by all that is sacred in the beams of Selene's light.'

But still Pikeface could not leave.

'Turn it off!' he bellowed into the communications rig.

The door was open. Scribes were gathering outside, staring in at the chaos. Pikeface tried to run at them. The force field hurled him back. One of the braver scribes grabbed the door and pulled it shut.

Pikeface lay alone in the chamber.

21

THE TRUTH

Dwllis and Etwe crouched at the rear of the Archive of Selene. The glowing crescent sigil was dim. Behind them a sheer glass wall stood, where once plastic and metal sheeting had been. The unaccustomed cold made Dwllis shiver.

'Which is the grille you pulled off before?' Etwe asked.

Dwllis tried to remember. It seemed so long ago. His head had cleared somewhat but his mind was snoozing. Caught by feelings of uncertainty, he began to sense qe'lib'we withdrawal symptoms once again. 'That one,' he said firmly, standing up and walking over to the grille he had pointed at. 'Yes, this one.' It was pretend decisiveness, but it was enough to mitigate his symptoms.

Etwe joined him and helped him pull away the rusty grille. They slipped into the Archive.

Dwllis recognised the store room that he and Cuensheley had entered, pointing out to Etwe its yellow glowing floor, the pieces of broken plastic crescent, and the only door. 'Just out there, go left, then down the stairs, and we will be in the research area,' he instructed Etwe.

She led the way. The Archive was silent, though a faint humming could be heard, as of an engine rumbling far off. Dwllis doubted the place would be empty, but it should at least be quiet.

He had ascertained from Etwe that the Spacefish was presently below the horizon. 'Soon,' she had said, 'it will be only a few hundred miles above the Earth. They say it'll just hang above the city, as if by magic. The noctechnes say they'll shoot it down.'

They crept down the corridor that led to the gnostician room. Dwllis was worried to find the door open, hinges broken, and more so when he saw no gnosticians inside, nor any pyuters. 'Something bad has occurred,' he said. 'I hope there hasn't been a massacre.'

Etwe paused for thought. 'It's possible that they were all transported out of the city,' she suggested.

Dwllis tried to remember what he knew of the augmented gnosticians. 'I think they said they had no friends outside,' he whispered.

'Sshhh!' hissed Etwe.

Dwllis heard gnostician voices. They followed the corridor down, arriving at a number of cells containing one gnostician each. He saw one that reminded him of Crimson Boney. 'Speak to that one,' he urged.

With Etwe translating, Dwllis learned what had happened. 'The fish-faced man has killed the old high man and assumed his place. All is chaos. The place is feverish with plots. The fish-faced man said we were bad creatures and we must not speak to one another. He had muscle men drag us to these cells. You must let us free!'

Dwllis was tempted. 'You say Pikeface is the new Lord Archivist of Selene?'

'Yes. He is a selfish man. He doesn't act nicely to us. We helped moon folk with their plans, and this is how we are repaid. It is a bad thing.'

Dwllis rattled the doors, but they were steel shod polythene. Too tough. 'I cannot force these cell doors,' he said, 'but we will continue to explore, and maybe find a set of fishtails.' Experimentally he tried his own, but it did not fit in the lock groove. 'We will be back, I promise. I tried to fight the purges but I was almost killed for my trouble. Don't worry, I am on your side.'

'Hurry back,' was the gnostician's only reply.

They explored the remainder of the cell sector, finding nothing. Returning to the main gnostician room, Dwllis paused to look inside, hoping to spot a clue.

A hiss, something whisking by, and he was pulled against the wall. He struggled; he was caught. He looked to his right to see Etwe also caught, although the thin black wires that entangled her had missed one arm and she was trying to struggle free. On the ceiling a full moon, creamy yellow, faded up into brightness, and he looked down at his body to see a tracery of wires binding him to the wall. No hope of escape.

He felt his withdrawal symptoms returning again, but he could not even fidget. All he could do was stamp his feet. 'Escape, escape!' he called out to Etwe, since she at least had one arm free.

'I am trying to pull the cords away,' Etwe replied.

Bootsteps. Dwllis put all his efforts into shaking himself free, but in vain. He looked to his left to see a solitary woman approaching, an Archivist judging by her white gown and yellow hood.

'Oh, it's you,' she said.

Iquinlass. She pulled the hood from her face.

'It's you,' she repeated.

'Madam Archivist,' Dwllis began, 'we intended no harm—'

'Dwllis, I need your help urgently.' Iquinlass slapped at the wall, and with whipping sounds the wires retracted. With a white fishtail she opened a concealed door on the opposite side of the corridor. 'Quickly,' she said, gesturing them with windmilling arms into a room.

It was a tiny room, just six feet square, illuminated by a glowing crescent wall-lamp. Inside stood one divan, one rig of pyuters, and a number of plastic incense tripods. Iquinlass shut the door.

They all sat. 'What's happened?' Etwe asked.

Iquinlass addressed Dwllis. 'I have no choice but to tell you this,' she began. She was on edge. Her face told of fatigue, her eyes of dismay. 'Pikeface has assassinated Tierquthay and become Lord Archivist. He went to see the Reeve, but he hasn't come back yet. There were two factions: Pikeface and Tierquthay; Querhidwe and myself. Now I'm alone and I don't have any allies, and to make things worse I don't know the full story. Querhidwe never told me it all.'

'What story would that be?' Dwllis asked.

'The story of you and Pikeface. I don't know where Pikeface originated from, but I believe you were born here.'

Etwe and Dwllis chorused, 'Here?'

'Yes, in this building. I was only a human child from Gaya when you were born, but Querhidwe, she was a pyuton, much older—'

'But I was born here? Why? How? Of whom?'

Iquinlass sighed. 'I don't know exactly. Only Querhidwe knew. She carried on the work that her predecessor started. I've been trying to find out who –

what – Pikeface is, but, well, it's not easy. You see, we saw something of the future surrounding you two, and that created the two factions; one supporting you, one supporting Pikeface. There were terrible arguments. Anyway, that's the reason my faction stirred up the lens. We tried to make you see the part of yourself encoded into the fate of Cray. You see, Querhidwe thought that part of your future dead self lay quiescent in the city.'

Dwllis shook his head. 'I cannot understand even one word of this, Madam, not one single word.' He looked at her, as if by the force of his helpless stare he could wring the answers out of her.

'I know how you feel,' Iquinlass said in sincere tones. 'I feel as if the whole city is on my shoulders. I don't know what to do. And now you turn up, and force me to act, to tell you . . .'

She seemed close to tears. Dwllis asked her, 'Did you know that Querhidwe sent me a silver fishtail?' He brought it out and held it up on its chain.

Iquinlass stared. Her expression changed from misery to excitement. 'So that's what he lost. The liar!'

'Explain,' Dwllis demanded.

'Tierquthay told me he had lost the fishtail of an old box, but I always suspected it was more important than that.' Iquinlass took the fishtail from Dwllis's trembling hand and held it under the lunar lamp. 'This is the activation key of the lunar orb. Look at the fine sigils engraved into it. Querhidwe must have given it to you to thwart the enemy faction.'

'But what will it do?'

Iquinlass stood. 'We must find out. It could be crucial.'

'But—'

'Pikeface left the orb in the main shrine. Nobody

has dared touch it, but if Pikeface isn't here . . .'

Through a maze of corridors Iquinlass led them, her pale cloak fluttering, until, having climbed a claustro-phobic spiral staircase, they emerged into the auditorium in which Dwllis had attempted to make his address. On the cushion of the central throne, basking in the light thrown by a thousand yellow sequins, lay the orb.

'We believe it is a relic from the birth of the city,' Iquinlass said, leading them towards it. 'I'm not sure I should touch it.'

'Ordinarily,' Etwe said, 'this would never be left by whosoever rightfully held it?'

'Never. Querhidwe carried it everywhere. So did Tierquthay. It is distilled moonbeams, the very quick of Selene. But Pikeface maybe has other, more impor-tant concerns.'

'Then you must use the fishtail.'

Iquinlass hesitated. Overcome by events, Dwllis sat down to watch.

'Hurry,' Etwe said.

At the top of the orb was a narrow slot, into which Iquinlass placed the fishtail. Immediately the orb fell apart into hemispheres, revealing a green fishtail almost the size of a hand. Iquinlass picked it up. With a snap the orb reformed itself.

'Another fishtail?' Etwe said.

Iquinlass nodded, then handed it to Dwllis. 'Querhidwe must have wanted you to have it.'

'I wonder what it is,' Dwllis said, closely examining the fishtail.

'Two factions are struggling,' Iquinlass said. 'And there will be one of two outcomes. This fishtail must be a sign from the past.'

'We struggle in the dark,' Dwllis observed.

'We can guess something,' Etwe said. 'If Querhidwe knew that the orb never left the hand of its rightful owner, she intended Dwllis to receive this green fish-tail when somebody of her own faction was Lord Archivist.'

Iquinlass considered. 'Or, she arranged that he would receive it under the present conditions.'

'How could she guess that Pikeface would treat it differently, simply leaving it alone?'

'She knew Pikeface's character,' Iquinlass said.

Dwllis looked up. 'I think Querhidwe meant it for me to thwart Pikeface.'

'How do you know?' asked Iquinlass.

Dwllis shrugged. 'I just know it. Pikeface knows something of me. He accosted me once in the street and called me his kin.'

'Then he is ahead of us,' Iquinlass said, 'and worse things may yet happen. Come, we had better leave this place, in case he returns.'

They returned to the secret chamber. Dwllis voiced his desire to free the augmented gnosticians. Iquinlass at first spoke against him, suggesting that it would not be wise to defy Pikeface in this way. A bargain was struck. Iquinlass would set the gnosticians free if Dwllis and Etwe would consent to live in a room off Tode Lane, just behind the Archive; for Iquinlass, now she had found Dwllis, wanted him close by. Dwllis said nothing of his personal circumstances and agreed.

So the gnosticians were freed, leaving the Archive by way of the store room, each heavily cloaked and armed with glass shards in padded hilts.

Iquinlass then led Dwllis and Etwe to the house in Tode Lane. It was narrow, one lower and one upper room, the former full of lunar oddments. 'You must live up here,' Iquinlass said, kicking debris to the sides of the dusty room. 'There isn't much soundproofing, but the city is quieter, so you probably won't need ear-muffs.'

Dwllis looked out through a perspex window to the street below. Mixed emotions sobered him, made him fear the future. He said, ' "Tode" is Old Crayan for death, you know. I wonder if that is an omen.'

'Calm yourself,' Etwe said. 'Omens exist in the minds of the imaginative. We'll survive here, with Iquinlass's help.'

'I had better go,' Iquinlass said. She pointed to a plastic chest. 'I keep food and water in there, for my own use. You'd better tuck in.'

'Will we be found here?' Dwllis asked.

Iquinlass shrugged. 'In the event of trouble, there is a ladder behind this rear door.'

Having indicated the door, concealed behind cloth hangings, she made to depart.

'Wait,' said Dwllis. 'There is one last point. This predecessor of Querhidwe, who I have been told was known as Seleno – who was she? If we knew what plans she laid we might progress.'

'She was a gifted pyuton. Seleno was her assumed name, but what her real name was, I don't know. Once or twice I remember her calling herself Silverseed, but she would never explain why.'

'Then she is buried in the Cemetery?'

'Yes. Her barrow is marked with three symbols, a fishtail of red, a whole fish, and a blue and brown disk marked with wispy, white patterns.'

Dwllis considered this. 'It seems to me that Seleno knew something of the future. I believe she knew that the moon would transform into the Spacefish long before it happened. I believe she knew something of me, and my fate.'

Iquinlass nodded. 'That is probable, but still too much is mysterious. The disk is a representation of Gaya, for instance.'

'Why should she have such a symbol on her barrow, when she was of Selene?'

Iquinlass shrugged. 'She must have had some connection with Gaya. The bloodied fishtail must be her own personal sigil, the meaning of which we cannot now guess. The whole fish must represent her self.'

Dwllis sighed. 'Would that the afterlife had not become closed off, which, if the druids are to be believed, is the case. We might have tried to listen for Seleno's ghostly thoughts.'

Iquinlass departed. Dwllis felt exhausted by the rush of events. His withdrawal symptoms were lessened, and he felt, if not heartened, then at least less desperate. Too tired to think, he lay on a rug and fell asleep, the green fishtail secure underneath his body.

He awoke to find Etwe at his side. He looked out across the western parts of the Old Quarter, down to the river. All was glass flecked with ochre, smashed and shattered under the influence of earth tremors. A few lamps gleamed, and the streets themselves were bright, but it was easy to tell where people lived and where luminophages lived. He told Etwe, 'I must go and meet Subadwan.'

'I'll come with you.'

They stepped out into the street. Now that the four

aeromorphs were abroad, few Crayans were up and about.

They had not gone far when Dwllis overheard the conversation of two delinquent outers in Broom Street. He stopped to stare at them. One said, 'What are you gorping at?'

'Did you just say to your friend that Reeve Umia was dead?'

'Yer. What of it?'

'And Pikeface is the new Reeve?'

'Yer.'

Over and over Dwllis asked himself, how could it be? Only the Lord Archivist of Noct could become Reeve. Was this then the nature of Pikeface, that he was a spy heretic?

At length, Etwe said, 'We must find Iquinlass. She must be told what's happened.'

Dwllis shivered. He felt demoralised again and the thought of qe'lib'we returned. Immediately, he felt his legs tingling inside. He said, 'Is that not taking a risk, seeing as Pikeface is on the loose, and is now our Reeve?'

'Possibly. But Iquinlass is our only hope.'

'Iquinlass will already know.'

'We have to talk more about Pikeface.'

Dwllis shrugged. 'I suppose so.'

Using only the darkest, narrowest alleys, they made their way back to the Archive of Selene, where Etwe asked a recorder if she could speak with Iquinlass. The reply was not promising. 'Archivist Iquinlass is unavailable, and will be for some time.'

'Is she ill?'

'She is unavailable.'

Dwllis, peering out from behind a pillar to lipread,

felt crushed. Unavailable: that was surely meant to indicate captured, under suspicion of betrayal, or worse. Etwe joined him, and they stole off into a dark passage.

'What do we do now?' Dwllis asked.

'I am uncertain.' Etwe responded.

'Subadwan told me that Tanglanah is trying to leave the Earth – her first stop the vehicle that is the Spacefish.' Dwllis mused on. 'Further, how could details of my personal self have been encoded into the memory fabric of Cray? That I do not understand . . . which is ironic, since I have spent so much of my life piecing together fragments of memory.'

'I think we should speak to Subadwan,' Etwe said.

They began to walk north along Hog Street. Around them, the glass-scape of Cray stretched. This entire street was a lifeless row of glittering silica, smashed in places to leave piles of fragments upon the street plastic. The lights below caused the debris to flicker like a hallucinogenic phantasm.

The perpetual refractive display meant that they did not see the aeromorph until its groaning engines warned them of its proximity. They ducked into a doorway, but too late, for the machine seemed to have sensed them, smoke pouring out from its vents.

Suddenly a figure ran out from a passage. Although the aeromorph had no obvious eyes, it seemed to detect the newcomer, shifting its body with a storm of hissing and clunking. Then the figure, a stout man wrapped in rags, ran off, and the aeromorph tried to follow him. It failed. The man had darted into an alley between two metal buildings, and despite the smashing and pushing of the aeromorph it was unable to follow. In the confusion Dwllis and Etwe ran back the way they had come, to enter another street lined with vitrified pipes and cables, and so continue their journey.

Back in the alley, Coelendwia emerged from the bent and smoking metal structures between which he had hidden, satisfied that he had saved Dwllis and Etwe from the maw of the aeromorph.

Still the city collapsed around Dwllis and Etwe as they struggled on. Because foundations were succumbing to vitrescence and the ochre plague, the supporting structures of many buildings were weak, resulting in earth tremors. Even as Dwllis and Etwe stepped across Culverkeys Street and into the maze of ochre-splattered alleys to the east of the Blistered Quarter, they felt the ground around them shake. And they heard answering tinkles of noise as glass buildings cracked, shattered, and fell. Around them, fragments tumbled from high turrets, a sequence of razor cloudbursts. They hurried on, dodging the keratin corpses of ochre plague victims, ever alert for the marauding aeromorphs.

They did not expect what followed. From a dark side alley, two masked and cloaked figures emerged. Dwllis at first took them to be druids, but he soon saw they were women. Then one brandished the club she was carrying.

Dwllis stepped back, hands raised, fear making him tremble. But the pair ignored him and faced Etwe, the second woman also raising her club, and when she did this Dwllis thought he recognised her aggressive posture. Surely it could not be . . . ?

'Ilquisrey?' he said.

The first woman cursed, but Dwllis, still confused by the attack, did not immediately recognise her voice. Then the pair struck out at Etwe.

'Halt!' Dwllis shouted. 'What do you want? Is that you, Ilquisrey?'

They ignored him and continued to batter Etwe, who had knelt down, trying to protect her head. Dwllis sprang forward and grabbed the arms of the first woman. He recognised Cuensheley.

Ilquisrey thrust him aside, but he managed to pull off the mask, revealing Cuensheley's face. Her expression of fury was softened by the tears streaming from her eyes. 'What is going on?' Dwllis asked her in a shocked voice.

Cuensheley refused to answer, instead pulling away from him. But Ilquisrey confronted him, and said, 'I'll never forgive you for what you did to my mum.'

'It is none of your affair,' Dwllis replied. 'Keep out of this—'

'Don't bluster at me! You deserve a beating yourself, you heartless . . . heartless . . .'

Fury made her incoherent. Dwllis turned from her to face Cuensheley. 'Your daughter put you up to this, didn't she?'

'Why did you do it?' Cuensheley replied.

'Do what?'

'Why did you leave her!' Ilquisrey shouted.

Dwllis said to Cuensheley, 'Nobody leaves what they are not with. You presumed upon me, and that was unforgiveable. Do you believe that violence can solve your problem? Do you believe that your tears will persuade me to return to the Copper Courtyard, and forget all the things that have been done to me?'

'Like care for you when the gnostician bit your hand?' Ilquisrey harshly said.

Cuensheley gestured for her to be silent, but instead Ilquisrey stomped away, smashing at the plastic and metal around her, until she was gone. Then Cuensheley told Dwllis, 'I am an innocent in all this. I did not deserve the treatment you meted out.'

Dwllis felt a haughty mood come over him. 'You flatter yourself,' he replied. 'You are no more innocent than your unspeakable daughter. Go away, and never trouble me again. I don't expect to see either of you again.'

Cuensheley stared at him, before anger returned to her face. 'You're no better than a pyuton yourself,' she said, before walking away. And Dwllis understood that at last he had rid himself of her for ever.

22

BAT

Subadwan approached the window, trying to attract the attention of the fat, pseudo-sentient bats that hung just outside. Soon one was pawing at her window. Subadwan waved at it, not knowing what else to do. She neared the window and tried a high-pitched whistle.

With sapphire claws it scratched a circle in the glass, then punched it out. Subadwan jumped back, saving her feet from being sliced off. She clambered out, ensuring her skin did not touch the sides, pulling her clothes to her body so that they were not ripped by the glittering razor edges of the hole. Outside, the bat followed her to the edge of the balustrade. The other bats ignored them. Inside the cockpit she saw an extended finger of pyuter controls – pads and knobs mostly – and behind that the glinting golden disk of an aeronautic pyuter.

Apprehensive, but encouraged by the bat's obsequious manner, Subadwan settled her slim body into the clinging bucket seat, which in response wrapped itself around her. The seat was warm, like a bed wrap. 'Hello, bat?' she said. None of the controls were labelled – unlike the bat she had imagined in Gwmru.

'Hello, mistress,' came the buzzing electric reply.

'I am your new pilot,' Subadwan said, hoping she was not pushing her luck.

'Where do you want to go, mistress?'

'The Baths. And don't speak to any other bats, please.'

'I will do as you say. Please give me the flight plan.'

Subadwan hesitated. Her scheme felt as though it was faltering, and doubt took her. 'Flight plan?'

'Yes. The aerial route, if you will, mistress.'

Subadwan said, 'Fly directly there.'

With a jerk and a pop of its engines the bat flung itself off the edge of the Archive roof, and frigid air swirled around her body. Automatically, she tensed herself as the Nocturnal Quarter appeared below her, that dark mass twinkling at the edges with lights, criss-crossed with luminous veins, impenetrably black at its centre. Noticing the faintest remnants of violet cloud to the west, she guessed it was early evening.

Vistas of glass glittered below her like a frozen sea. Towers rose up splintered like transparent icebergs.

Swiftly, descending in minute increments, they flew north, arriving above the Baths after only a few minutes in the air. Subadwan directed the bat to land in a deserted courtyard behind the main building, which it did, faultlessly. 'Wait here,' Subadwan said, clambering out of the enveloping seat.

'I will, mistress,' said the bat.

Subadwan added, 'Don't obey anybody else's command. Just do as I say.'

'As you say.'

Subadwan peered into the alley that connected the quadrangle and the rear courtyard of the Baths. Nobody about. She passed along the splintered alley, through the courtyard, which was also empty, then crept along the passage leading around the Baths to Peppermint Street and the front door. Along the street a few Crayans trudged, nervously looking over their shoulders, stepping around splotches of ochre that seemed to be infecting the street plastic itself. Seeing this, Subadwan, with racing heart, examined her own boots to find splatters of ochre gel. She pulled the boots off. The stuff had not eaten through. Weak with relief she thanked Gaya, then tip-toed to the front door, noticing with a shiver of horror that the marble base blocks were turning to glass.

She could hear voices reverberating around the Baths as she hurried inside. From a rail she grabbed a green gown, the hood of which she pulled over her head. It was an imperfect disguise but better than nothing. It worked, since nobody stopped or even looked at her, and soon she was at the entrance to Liguilifrey's room.

She tapped at the door.

'Who is it?' Subadwan wondered if Liguilifrey was alone. 'Who is it?' Liguilifrey repeated, louder. Subadwan pressed her ear to the door but heard no voices.

'It's me,' she said.

The door opened. Subadwan touched, then hugged Liguilifrey. In seconds she was inside. 'It's only me,' she said, over and over again, as they clasped one another.

Liguilifrey was overjoyed to have Subadwan back. 'Some sort of mental trick took me away,' Subadwan explained, 'some trick of Umia's.'

'He's dead,' Liguilifrey said, proceeding to update Subadwan on extraordinary recent events. In reply she told Liguilifrey everything she knew about Gwmru, and about what would, if she did not stop it, happen soon.

Liguilifrey did not believe that something awful was about to happen to Cray and its citizens. 'You need help,' she remarked. She hesitated. 'I'm afraid Aquaitra is the new Lord Archivist.'

'I'd guessed that,' Subadwan lied, her heart sinking. She had hoped Umia's words to be part of a ruse. She took a deep breath. 'But I need help now. This is urgent!'

'How will you destroy the aeromorphs?'

'I'll explode them.'

'Flying in a bat?'

'Yes,' Subadwan said. 'It's quite tame. Anyway, it's all I've got, isn't it?'

'The street aeromorphs will attack you,' Liguilifrey warned. 'Umia sent out bat fighters when they came, and not one of those aeromorphs was destroyed.'

'I'll have to be careful,' Subadwan said, shrugging. She glanced down at her stockinged feet. 'Got any boots my size?'

Then an idea. The ochre plague. It attacked substances.

She asked Liguilifrey, 'This yellow plague, is it still infecting everything?'

'It's a terrible thing. I daren't go out. And if it's not yellow goo, it's vitrescence.'

'That's the answer,' Subadwan said. 'Thank Gaya! One blob of yellow stuff on each aeromorph and they'll transmute. Problem is getting the stuff up there. A gun holding it would soon transform.'

'You want a goo gun?' Liguilifrey said. 'Mogyardra will make you a goo gun.'

'Who?'

'My old guardian, if he's still alive. He was an armourer who used to be a Triader, before the Triad demoted him to lesser status, on account of his cheating his accounts and stealing living parts for rifles.'

'Find him, find him,' Subadwan urged.

Liguilifrey turned to the dusty audio-rig at her side. 'Find Mogyardra,' she said. Flute music began, the bass part detuning by a quarter tone. Liguilifrey frowned, then said, 'Then look under weapons.' After some seconds a baritone voice sang out a code. 'Call him,' Liguilifrey instructed.

Liguilifrey, still blind, asked Subadwan to put water in the rig screen. It lit up, and at the same time the face of an aged man peered out from within the ripples. 'Mogyardra?' said Liguilifrey.

'Is that really you, Liguilifrey?'

'It is! You're still going, you old duffer.'

'You dotty old termagant,' the old man replied, his creased face stretched into a smile. He plucked at a discoloured beard and moustache. 'What are you doing calling me at this hour?'

'We urgently need to borrow your skill at weapons manufacture. This lady here is Subadwan of Gaya, and she needs you to make a special gun. Come on over to the Baths.'

'Expect me in half an hour.'

He arrived on time. Mogyardra was a small man, only a few inches taller than Subadwan, and just as slim, though where Subadwan gave the impression of small-scale dynamism, Mogyardra was decidedly frail. He possessed the mysterious aura of a solitary pyuton. However he entered the Baths armed with a rifle, a dagger and a miniature pistol. Liguilifrey said they had not met for over a year, but they got on as if yesterday they had spent all night talking in the quarter's courtyards. They spoke, laughed, then returned to Liguilifrey's chamber.

'Where's your eyes?' Mogyardra asked.

'Gone for ever.'

Subadwan added, 'Some time ago, Mogyardra. But on to this rifle we need made. You know the ochre plague? We need a gun, or more likely more than one, to fire gobbets of plague stuff.'

'What for?'

'To kill aeromorphs.'

Mogyardra nodded. 'Unorthodox, but it would provide me with an excellent challenge.'

'You love a challenge, don't you?' Liguilifrey said.

'I do, I do. So, four projectile rifles. How would you load the gobbets of ochre gel?'

Subadwan began, 'Well . . .'

'Isn't that your problem, you dimwit?' said Liguilifrey.

He grinned. 'I suppose it is.'

Mogyardra stood up as if the meeting was already at an end. Subadwan said, 'This is vitally important, Mogyardra. I can't tell you how important. More rests on your inventiveness than you can imagine.' She wondered how far to trust this particular Crayan. Liguilifrey said he was trustworthy, but . . . 'We might need more than four guns, though,' she added.

'How many exactly?'

'If they only last for one shot each, um . . . a few more at least.'

This made Mogyardra frown. 'What are you planning to do, if I may ask?'

Subadwan hesitated. She looked at Liguilifrey, but

her friend did not see her glance, and offered no help. 'Cray is in peril. I have to bring down all the aero-morphs.'

'Impossible.'

'I've got a bat to fly in.'

'Mine is not to wonder why. I'll do my best, Archivist, that's all I can do.' With that, he departed.

Liguilifrey consoled Subadwan. 'He won't sleep tonight. He can't resist a challenge. We'll hear from him at dawn tomorrow, and like as not he'll have built a prototype. Don't worry.'

'I can't help it,' Subadwan said.

She slept soundly that night, despite her fears. Dozing next morning she dreamed of flying high above Cray on the back of a black aerician, guns spitting fire, killing aeromorphs, watching them cart-wheel, drop to the ground, and burst in an explosion of kissleaves that fluttered, scented, to the earth. She had never dreamed of scent before.

Liguilifrey woke her. 'He's here.'

'Wha?' Subadwan muzzily replied.

'Mogyardra. I told you we'd hear from him.'

Dressed in robe and slippers Subadwan followed Liguilifrey to the fore hall, where an impatient looking Mogyardra awaited. In his hand was a black tube. He exhibited the excitement of a small boy as he explained to Subadwan the principles of his invention. 'This is a projectile tube. The difficult part was the expulsion of the plague gel. I've made a sort of flipping tongue, which will expel the substance at speed. See, you just bend down, activate the tongue' – here a black tongue emerged to scrape the floor – 'and make it suck the substance back down to the base of the tube. Then you press this button to fire it. Try it out today?'

Subadwan nodded. 'The sooner the better.'

'I ought to stay here to guard the Baths,' Liguilifrey said.

'Mogyardra and I will go,' Subadwan said. 'You stay here in case of trouble.'

Apprehension made Subadwan's stomach churn. If it went wrong, the end of Cray could follow. And if Tanglanah discovered what was going on, the same. But she had Gaya on her side, even if Aquaitra had assumed the role of Lord Archivist.

Outside, the vitreous street was deserted. They hurried along to a tiny alley called Sand Passage, where Mogyardra spotted a patch of ochre on a wall. There they waited, crouching down in the shadows. With Peppermint Street the thoroughfare from Eastcity directly into the heart of Westcity's Blistered Quarter, they did not have long to wait. One of the aeromorphs came flying along the street. Subadwan noticed how careful it was to move centrally down the way and not touch anything, and she realised that it knew of the ochre plague.

'Shall I do it?' said Mogyardra.

Subadwan nodded. Placing the nozzle on the ochre patch, he activated the tongue. The aeromorph rumbled by. Mogyardra leaned out and fired.

'A hit!'

Subadwan, her heart thumping, leaned out of the passage. The aeromorph had stopped only a few yards away. For some seconds it lay quiescent like a confused beast, before an extraordinary transformation began. The soot-blackened outer plates of the aeromorph fell away to reveal a latticework interior of pipes, ducts and cables, all gleaming metal and coloured plastic, with gouts of black oil and clouds of

steam spurting from exposed vents. The aeromorph
seemed to shiver, and more of its exterior fell away, so
that the street became littered with piles of metal and
smoking plastic. What remained – half its original
volume – was an almost humanoid form twenty feet
long, wracked with spasms. Subadwan realised that
the thing was trying to rid itself of all traces of the
ochre plague. Yet it seemed to be panicking. Bolts,
cables and fragments of metal were flying in all
directions as the aeromorph shook itself into an ever
smaller form, until all that remained was a recumbent
figure like a dying pyuton.

Subadwan understood that it *was* a dying pyuton.
This was the transformation that Tanglanah and
Laspetosyne had undergone to become pyutons; but
they had endured it in their own time, and without
stress. Now Subadwan understood the potential of her
plan. If she could destroy the remaining aeromorphs
she would bar the surviving beings of Gwmru from
manifesting. Forced to stay in their abstract land, they
would continue to sustain Cray while they lived
within it – and they would not depart since they would
not leave Tanglanah and Laspetosyne behind.

Again Subadwan looked out into the street. She saw
an oil-covered pyuton, its glittering innards visible as
if it had been unable to create a skin. It tried to climb
to its feet, but failed. With a screech of metal its limbs
fell off and its torso disintegrated. There were a few
sparks, a few oily bubbles, and then nothing.

Subadwan turned to Mogyardra to say, 'It works!
Leave the gun, you might catch the plague. We've got
to run back to the Baths.'

Despite his frailty he was not entirely decrepit, and
in seconds they were out of Sand Passage and

navigating the alleys around Print Street and the shattered remains of the Indigo Courtyard.

'We need more guns,' Subadwan said, 'as urgent as anything you've ever done.'

'You return to the Baths,' he said, 'and I'll set to work.' Subadwan watched him vanish into the maze of passages.

Back at the Baths a fretting Liguilifrey awaited. 'Did it work?'

'Yes,' Subadwan crisply replied. 'Now, there's not a moment to lose. I'd barricade the Baths if I was you. Tanglanah might suspect me.'

Liguilifrey agreed, her face showing her worry. 'I suppose you're right, but it's vitrifying!'

'This is life or death,' Subadwan replied. 'The Baths should hold out until I've finished.' But despite her words she inspected the foundation blocks at the front, to find the glittering street outside partially visible, as a river of light through a smoked window.

By evening Mogyardra was ready. In a rucksack they packed the stubby rifles, before leaving to creep down Peppermint Street. Here, they planned to ambush the other aeromorphs.

Cray now was almost an empty city. The sweating, dancing, yelling lunar hordes were a sight of the past. The city was lined with impassable lanes, choked to the eaves with glass shards. Pipes and cables dangled: dead. The networks were shutting down. A few outers banded together, but even they were leaving the city to take their chances outside.

'One comes!' hissed Mogyardra. Subadwan peered out, her head at ground level, to see an aeromorph hurtling down the street from the direction of the Baths. She could hear the clink of its metal plates as convulsively it attacked anything, human or animal, that moved.

'Get ready,' she said.

Mogyardra tensed.

'Ready!' she said, her voice more urgent.

He lay at her side and aimed down the street. The aeromorph sped by and he fired. Subadwan was not certain, but she thought he had scored a hit. 'Success?' he asked.

'Let's run,' she replied. 'I think you got it. C'mon!'

Over the dull sound of the city came the distinct sound of glass smashing as the aeromorph thrashed about, the knowledge of its doom contributing to its violence.

'Two to go,' Mogyardra said, grinning.

'Don't get too confident,' Subadwan warned.

But Mogyardra exuded excitement. 'Those awful beasts are intelligent. They understand their fate well enough.'

They decided to make east. Subadwan, disconcerted by Mogyardra's attitude, tried to calm him down, point out the risks, but though he listened he retained the fervour of a boy killing helpless animals for fun. In the privacy of her fearful mind Subadwan prayed for a swift conclusion.

In an alley off Jessamine Street they waited. The hours dragged by. Passers-by Subadwan questioned, while Mogyardra hid in a doorway. Nobody had seen any aeromorphs for some time, but there were rumours of the remaining two in Westcity, killing and smashing in the courtyards and quadrangles of the Stellar and Rusty Quarters. Subadwan and Mogyardra discussed moving west, but were dissuaded by the eerie silence.

The night passed by. Cray was cold now that its
many buildings and factories had stopped generating
heat, and even though they were wrapped well, they
shivered. Worried, they decided to investigate the area
from which the smashing sounds had emanated, to
find, illuminated by dawn's red streamers, the motionless remains of an aeromorph.

They made west along passages and through
deserted quadrangles, crossing the river, then scurry-
ing through glassy lanes east of Culverkeys Street,
until they were peering out on to it. In a passage they
made their hide.

Morning became afternoon became evening
became night.

It was shortly before midnight when Subadwan felt
a breeze on her face and heard the characteristic
rushing noise of an aeromorph flying towards them.
She peered out. It wound its way along the street, as if
hunting.

Subadwan instructed Mogyardra to load up with
plague gel. He did so. They stood and shrank back
into a doorway as the aeromorph skulked by, then
Mogyardra darted out, leaned into the street, and
fired at the thing's aileron. A hit.

'Run,' he said. 'It's already thrashing.'

Plastic was battered and glass shattered. The third
aeromorph knew its body was infected. They hurried
back to the Baths, at once afraid and full of joy.

Subadwan, having decided what next to do, put her
case. 'The final one has either gone away, or it's in
hiding. There's no time to search for it. I've got to go
for the aerial ones before it's too late.'

Mogyardra agreed, after a pause for thought. 'I
suppose so, though it's a dreadful thing.'

Subadwan tried to ignore the glint in his eye. 'How will you load that gel?' Mogyardra asked. 'It transforms all it touches.'

Subadwan had given this problem some thought. She wanted to infect every aeromorph in one trip because flights from and to the ground would attract attention and leave her vulnerable to attack – either from the Archive of Safekeeping, from the missing street aeromorph, or from other aeromorphs. She replied, 'I'll load in flight.'

'One jolt of the elbow by a gust of wind and you could infect yourself. It's too risky.'

'No option. Give me those tubes.'

They were standing in the yard behind the Baths. On the wide, plastic rear wall, two plagues were fighting it out – the left half glass, the right half ghastly yellow. Mogyardra handed over the remaining tubes, then, using a spatula, scraped some of the gel off the wall and dropped it into a thick pot that he had made. Its two-inch sides would take some time to transmute, time enough for Subadwan to complete her mission. Returning to the bat, into which Subadwan had climbed, he closed the pot lid and dabbed a spot of resin upon its base. Then he stuck the pot to the inner board of the bat.

'Good luck, brave Archivist,' he said. He handed her a laser rifle for emergencies.

Subadwan told the bat to rise. 'I'll return,' she said. 'Gaya save me, I have to. Goodbye!'

The bat rose, leaving a whirlwind of dust and a coughing Mogyardra. Then Subadwan was gliding over rooftops with a bitterly cold wind tearing at her skin.

The skies were deserted. On a normal day at least

one or two bats would be circling the Archive of Noct, riding the thermals, but now there were none. Nor were flying carpets transporting Crayans. Not one aerician flew. A feeling of complete solitude took Subadwan, as if Cray had deserted her now that the end was near, and she was its last remaining citizen, armed only with the knowledge of what might be and a desperate plan. As she ascended she looked down upon twinkling glass and a hundred sparkling streets. It all seemed miles away.

She had told the bat what she intended doing. 'Set a flight plan that'll visit each aeromorph in turn,' she had instructed. 'The brightest ones first, then the others. Hover close above each one. I'll be firing out the window. If you sense an attack, tell me first, don't jog me. Then we'll scoot away.'

Already the first aeromorph was close. Subadwan opened the pot lid and loaded her first tube, watching, disgusted, as the tongue licked up a dab of plague gel. A pad winked red: 'loaded'.

The aeromorph engines were noisy, clouds of sooty fumes pouring from their underside vents. The metal monstrosity hovered poised like a steel hawk, polished flanges to either side reflecting light from the city, its own lamps golden bright. The bat ascended, banked, then performed a tight circle, bringing it only a few score yards above the aeromorph. Subadwan fired. She had to guess the effect of the wind, but she hit. The plague bullet spread itself over an aileron fin.

'Go!' Subadwan yelled. 'Next one!'

Now speed was essential. If the actions of the third street aeromorph were anything to go by, somebody was aware of her plan. What followed would be a mad dash from aeromorph to aeromorph.

Bats could fly at speed. Just thirty seconds passed before Subadwan was hovering above a second aeromorph. Tube loaded, she fired. Another hit.

Hardly believing her luck, she urged the bat on and loaded a third tube. Seven aeromorphs remained. The wind roared by as the bat sped on, banked, then circled the third target. Gripping the tube, knuckles white, Subadwan aimed, then fired. A hit. 'Go, go!' she yelled.

Disbelief shocked her. She could not accept that she would complete her task.

Then she saw something rise from below.

It sprang up from the Swamps. It must have been lurking there. Subadwan urged the bat on. Risking all, she loaded a fourth tube. Holding it in her right hand, she grabbed the laser rifle with her left. Through the left window she fired, at random, not to hit, trying to drive the aeromorph away.

The bat followed instructions, and even improved them. 'Don't worry!' it told Subadwan. It hovered above and to one side of the fourth aeromorph, trying to keep the metal craft between itself and the street aeromorph. Subadwan fired the tube, her projectile just catching the edge of a fluke.

The street aeromorph wriggled by. 'On, on!' she urged the bat. She turned to fire again.

The aeromorph followed, then sent out a missile, hitting the bat's right wing. A shudder vibrated through its body. Subadwan heard, 'I'm damaged,' then, 'descending!' then a lurch to one side. Sparks flew into her face. The stink of burning plastic swept by on gusting wind.

She saw the city laid out below her. As they fell the aeromorph followed, spiralling, as if damaged.

The streets turned black.

But the Swamps were a pool of radiance, glowing white, shivering with coloured light. An instantaneous effect.

'Emergency landing,' the bat warned.

Subadwan threw out the pot, just in time. The tubes and the laser rifle she hugged to her body.

She stared at the Swamps as they soared over. The city all around was illuminated, revealing a ring of sparkling glass, and inside this ring a single mass of optical spillover shone, bisected by the river, spotted here and there with darkness. Subadwan knew it must be too late. A transition had occurred. Electronic beings had journeyed. She had surely been beaten. As the bat wavered across the eastern half of the Swamps she had to raise one hand to her eyes to prevent painful blindness.

The bat crash-landed. Subadwan was thrown out. Winded, she managed to rise to her feet. Sparks fountained, and then the engine, with a screech, detonated. She was thrown against a wall. The air stank of smoke and fumes. Choking, she stumbled away.

She thought she was somewhere between the Cold and Plastic Quarters. In an uninfected quadrangle she rested, checked her clothes for signs of ochre plague, then sat to think.

Had she failed? She remembered that shortly after Tanglanah's electronic kin decided to act, the streets of Cray became brighter. Now, all light had been transferred, as if at the flick of some cosmic switch, into the Swamps. Clearly another abstract journey had taken place, most likely involving the surviving beings.

So her plan must have forced them into a hasty

decision. It was the only answer that offered her some
hope.

She must make for the Baths. Tanglanah and
Laspetosyne were neither aeromorph nor abstract. At
any minute they might leave Earth for the Spacefish.
Subadwan ran.

The radiant Swamps painted the undersides of low
cloud with silver, a pyrotechnic display enhanced by
atmospheric dust. These clouds seemed extra-
ordinarily close. Every detail of their lower surfaces
were visible, like maps. To the north, above the
Swamps, fainter clouds billowed – dust, grime and
smoke, layer upon layer upon layer, moving under the
influence of heat and gravity. Subadwan felt dis-
located, as if she were in some other city, a city gone
quiet, emptied, with a luminary at its heart.

And then all light was switched off. Subadwan's
gaze flicked upwards, to the patch of clear sky containing the Spacefish. A multitude of lines and points
had appeared – white, blue, purple, a tracery criss-
crossing the surface of the Spacefish. And the city was
wholly dark.

Cray was black and the Spacefish was illuminated.
Another transformation: another abstract journey.
The surviving electronic beings of Gwmru had com-
pleted their task and left Cray.

Did Tanglanah and Laspetosyne remain? Subadwan
struggled in an agony of confusion. The darkness
smothered her, pressing down into her mind.
Everything was closing down, everything was stopping.

The beings she fought to control held the future of
humanity in their abstract hands. A sudden sense of
the abyss between them and herself came to
Subadwan's thoughts. How could she persuade them

to stay? All she knew was that she must do something.

Ambient light was low but her eyes were adjusting to it. The danger was ochre plague. Subadwan stopped. She needed light but all she possessed was the laser. She thumbed it down to lowest power and aimed it at the sky. A blue beam lit her way. Excepting shadows seen against windows, not one Crayan did she spy on the way. In this meagre light she made it across to Peppermint Street.

Already the Baths seemed different. Vitrification had taken hold. Gingerly, Subadwan pushed open the glittering remains of the door and crept in. A crack: a splinter: and then the double doors shattered all around her.

'Madam!' a voice said. 'Where have you been?'

It was Dwllis.

23

GLASS

When the streets of Cray lost their light, Dwllis and Etwe were standing outside the Baths, about to enter.

Dwllis spun around, as if the light had been sucked away and by looking he could discover where it had gone. Darkness lay all about, but to the north something glowed, something vast, brightly kaleidoscopic. From his position in the street he could not make out what it was, but he knew that it must occupy an area of the Swamps. Something had happened – something momentous.

'Come inside,' he told Etwe. 'There is awful danger afoot.'

The Baths were lit by glow-beans in string bags, enabling Dwllis to find his way through the interior of the building. He heard no human voice, no echo of conversation, not even the clink or thud of another footstep. Glass blocks, massive and bowed out under the pressure of glass above, lay all around. Little of marble remained. Frightened, he called out, 'Is there anybody present?'

Now he heard something above the lapping of the nearby pool. Etwe said, 'That is a light footfall, I think.'

'We will await its owner.'

The owner was Liguilifrey. Dwllis identified Etwe and himself, then said, 'Is Subadwan of Gaya here? I need to speak with her, most urgently.'

Liguilifrey shook her head. 'I daren't think where she is. She's trying to shoot the aeromorphs, destroy them—'

'Destroy them? Did she say why?'

'They're related to these beings of Gwmru that she's struggling to control.'

Dwllis, apprehension in his voice, said, 'But madam Sabadwan is not even in contact with you?'

'No.'

Dwllis turned to Etwe. 'Then we have an obstacle in our way. There is only one option. We must go to Tanglanah.'

As they turned to leave Liguilifrey said, 'But Dwllis, it is this pyuton Tanglanah that she is struggling with.'

'I see,' Dwllis said. 'Etwe, should we wait here? Subadwan may not arrive—'

From nearby came the sound of smashing glass. They waited, silent and apprehensive. Dwllis walked forward a few steps, but then a figure leaped out of the tunnel: Subadwan.

'Madam,' Dwllis cried, 'where have you been?'

'Stay calm,' she reassured them, hurrying over.

'But what have you been doing?' Dwllis asked.

In a tumble of words Subadwan replied, 'The aeromorphs are bodily houses for Tanglanah's kin in Gwmru. I infected a few of the aerial ones with the ochre plague, hoping to force the beings to remain in Gwmru and sustain Cray, but I may instead have forced their hand. It might be too late. Dwllis, we have minutes left. Those beings are leaving the Earth for ever. They've transmitted themselves from Cray to the Spacefish. We've got to stop them.'

'How?'

'Only Tanglanah and Laspetosyne remain physical. I think they will be trying to reach the Spacefish. We've got to keep them here.'

Again Dwllis said, 'How?'

'We've got to hold them hostage, force the others to stay until human life is secured.'

Dwllis shook his head. 'Madam, it is surely an impossible task. I believe an historical event is upon us. But as for Tanglanah and Laspetosyne, their powers are beyond us.'

'Don't give up!' Subadwan said. 'In Gwmru, Zelenaiid told me that she had imparted a flaw into Cray when it was formed, but that she did not know exactly how the flaw would manifest. Vitrification is part of it. She told me that one of two paths would come to pass. Pikeface is on one of those paths, and you are on the other. I believe Tanglanah is still searching for knowledge of that flaw. She is trapped in Cray with Laspetosyne.'

'A path,' Dwllis mused.

Subadwan nodded. 'That was the point of the gnostician augmentation programme. Zelenaiid initiated it as Seleno. The gnosticians keep ancient memories in their minds.'

'Then Zelenaiid did not recognise their conscious state,' Dwllis said. Vainly, he tried to recall Crimson Boney's description of the legend of Cray. 'The gnosticians mimic old events with their rituals,' he explained. 'The split fish represents the physical origin of Cray. What was it that he said? There was a fire in the night sky. A fish jumped out of the sea and split into two, one half on each side of the river.'

Etwe concluded, 'The head giblets flopped into the river.'

'The Swamps!' Dwllis exclaimed. 'That is where the street lights coalesced. Hedalgwadey thought it to be a great bioprocessor – the brain of the fish in the symbolic gnostician story. Of course! I see it now. The Swamps are the source of the flaw, and doubtless they are the source of the luminophages, and thus the glass plague. And from the Swamps Pikeface emerged, like the corporeal manifestation of that place.'

'Zelenaiid guessed some of this,' Subadwan said.

'Who then is the key to the flaw?' said Dwllis. 'That even I do not understand.'

Subadwan replied, 'It must be you or Pikeface. You must go to the Reeve's chamber and confront him.'

Dwllis shook his head. 'You are asking too much of me.'

'What about your green fishtail?' Etwe began.

There was a smashing of glass from above.

Everybody ducked, then ran from the fall of shards. Dwllis bumped into a wall. In the gloom he saw two figures alight upon the floor as though they had jumped from the domed roof above. With superhuman effort they leaped upright, their arms circling in flourishes as if they had performed a gymnastic feat, before they stood upright by the side of the pool. Tanglanah and Laspetosyne.

Instinctively Dwllis ran, Etwe alongside him, as the tinkling cacophony smashed around them. From the corner of his eye he saw Subadwan flee. Liguilifrey stayed put, crouching head bowed on the floor.

'Halt!' Tanglanah cried.

Shards had hit Dwllis. Both arms were bloodied,

and blood ran into his eyes. His jacket sleeves and tails were shredded. 'What do you want of me?' he called out across the pool.

'Remain still. We have come for you.'

Dwllis looked about him. Much of the wall around him was glass – dull, gleaming glass. The nearby exit had sagged and cracked, making escape impossible. Before him, the perfectly calm surface of the pool lay.

From both sides the pyutons approached. Dwllis said, 'What do you know of me? What do you want of me?'

'We heard all we need to know,' said Tanglanah, indicating the roof. 'Either you or Pikeface is the key to Zelenaiid's method.'

They were closing. Dwllis looked wildly about him. Under his feet glass cracked, making him jump. The Baths were collapsing. Fault lines sprang out.

'Stay put,' Tanglanah said.

'It is dangerous,' Dwllis replied, temporising.

They were just yards away. Dwllis panicked. He feared those deadly eyes, those beatific expressions. Holding his nose he leaped into the water.

Glass smashed all around him. The surface of the pool had vitrified, forming a crust like ice on a frozen pond. Arms windmilling, he trod water, trying to keep his head in the air, conscious of the swathes of blood billowing around him. He gasped for air, but he knew he must not swallow water, replete as it was with a myriad glass splinters. Tossed by water currents, the flickering fragments reflected gleaming light through crimson clouds as they sank to the bottom.

Less than a minute passed before he surrendered to

the impassive pyutons. They hauled him from the pool
like children recovering a broken doll. He collapsed to
the fractured floor.

Tanglanah pulled him to his feet. 'You will come
with us. Do not resist.'

She dragged him away while Laspetosyne instructed Etwe not to follow. They did not tend to his
wounds, rather they clouted him when he tripped,
searched his clothes, and confiscated the green fishtail.
Then they tied his hands behind his back and put a bag
over his head. Bleeding from many cuts, Dwllis
tottered through the streets until his whole body
began to sting and throb. The metallic taste of blood
filled his mouth. His breath came hoarse. The chilly
air made it worse.

The torment continued for some time, stopping
only when they entered a building. Bootsteps echoed.
Smoke made him cough. He was forced onward, until
Tanglanah said, 'Stop here. I will see whether he is in.'

A door was hammered open with a single blow.
Dwllis was thrust forward.

Sound told him that he was inside a large chamber.
Released, he stood silent, tense, waiting.

Then Pikeface spoke. 'What business have you with
me?'

'This is our moment, Pikeface,' Tanglanah replied.

'Who is that man?' he answered.

'You do not know?'

Pikeface did not reply. But neither did Tanglanah.
Dwllis felt a surge of hope. It was as if everybody in
the room knew nothing of the future: nobody, perhaps
not even Tanglanah, knew what to do.

'You do not fool me,' Tanglanah said. 'Laspetosyne,
take the bindings and the sack off.'

Laspetosyne obliged, caring nothing for Dwllis's wounds. He gasped as the ropes rasped his stinging flesh. When the bag was removed he found that he was inside a spherical chamber of two hemispheres, below his feet a mass of rotting, broken vegetation, around and above a mass of broken equipment. Only one pyuter showed indicator lights. Four people stood in the chamber.

'My kin,' Pikeface said to him.

Tanglanah turned to Dwllis. 'Pikeface knows you are his brother.'

Dwllis felt a surge of disgust. 'How could that beast be my kin? The word means nothing to him. Pikeface is as ignorant as yourself. Face the truth, Tanglanah. You are lost here and you know not what to do.'

Tanglanah confronted him. 'All I lack is the method. Zelenaiid tried to ruin our plans, and she failed. How can one such as you stop us?'

'I am unable to stop you,' Dwllis agreed. 'So, Tanglanah, if you wish to leave the Earth then leave. Or can you not?'

Tanglanah turned again to Pikeface. 'It is only the method I lack, only the method. Pikeface, I know a vehicle lies somewhere.'

'I do not know, and I have looked. I am but the Reeve, condemned to remain inside this chamber.'

Dwllis felt passion upon him. 'You have ascended to become Reeve and you have no city to rule. That is the truth of all this, is it not, Pikeface? Our futures were deliberately tinkered with. Yet it is you who has attempted most and lost the most, for here you stand, the ruler of nothing. And that is tragic.'

Tanglanah turned to Pikeface. Dwllis, gasping for

breath, saw – or thought he saw – the confusion in her stance.

Silence. The four stood in silence.

Then Tanglanah said, in tones lacking all human warmth, '*I will have my way*. No human will stop me, nor will Zelenaiid's dead hand.'

Dwllis scoffed, the elation of his superiority loosening his tongue. 'Fools! You pyutons are half dead by virtue of not being *human*. What can you tell me of death?'

Tanglanah stared at Dwllis. He shrank back, wondering what he had said. 'That is the answer,' Tanglanah softly said. 'It is not a matter of being *led*. Here we have the two actual creations. One is human, one is not – the eternal opposition of this city. Laspetosyne, we are free at last!'

Dwllis swallowed to ease his aching throat. Tanglanah took out the green fishtail and, walking over to Dwllis, slapped it into his right hand, saying, 'This is yours.' Dwllis stared.

'What is that?' Pikeface immediately asked.

'It is mine,' Dwllis answered, studying the fishtail, giving little attention to Pikeface. Glinting in pale light, it seemed undamaged.

Tanglanah had moved to the door, there to shut it. 'Hand that fishtail over,' Pikeface demanded.

Dwllis looked up. 'It was a gift to me.'

'I *will* have it.'

Pikeface strode over. Dwllis stepped backwards. Tanglanah barred the exit, forcing him to run to the edge of the chamber. He knew that the moment Pikeface laid a hand upon him he was a dead man. He must run.

Pikeface showed a good turn of speed. Dwllis ran

round the edge, Pikeface closing, ever closing, trying
to cut him off.

It was hopeless. Dwllis stopped, held the fishtail
fins outwards, threatening Pikeface.

Pikeface stopped a yard away. He turned to
Tanglanah and said, 'Nobody thwarts me. Tanglanah,
you have failed.'

Dwllis saw the broad back before him. Just that
broad back. He stabbed forward. The fishtail slid like
a dagger into his opponent.

Pikeface uttered a deafening cry. He fell to the
ground.

Transformation followed.

First, Pikeface's legs merged, forming one limb a
yard in diameter, leggings ripped off by twisting flesh,
torn by razor protrusions that grew out of his ankles
and knees. These protrusions softened, becoming
flukes, not unlike the aerial flukes of the aeromorphs.
Then Pikeface's piscine head thrashed, bent, doubled
over, and became a blunt dome, coloured pink, inlaid
with designs of red and yellow.

He expanded. At ten feet tall, he flipped up upon
his lower limb and stood upright. His arms shrank,
then disappeared. Every item of armour and clothing
was now torn asunder, revealing prickly flesh here
and there turning black. No trace of Pikeface
remained: this was a thing, a device, still transforming, becoming blacker, its head expanding and
turning green.

Now the body was becoming slimmer, while the
base was thickening. Dwllis saw before him a pillar
twelve feet tall, slim waisted, black rooted, pink
topped, its body marked with spirals, dots, curls,
dimples and pimples.

With form set, it expanded further, emitting a chorus of creaks and groans, and when its bulging top hit the roof there was a cracking and dust fell. Dwllis ran for the door. Tanglanah opened it but stopped him leaving, holding him firm with one hand. Laspetosyne stood near.

The chamber began to collapse as the thing expanded still further. Tanglanah dragged the struggling Dwllis away, but stayed as near as she could to the transforming object. Dwllis peered upwards. It must now be twenty, maybe thirty feet tall. The black roots at its base were thick, metallic, and the top was ovoid, green-shrouded, but pink tipped.

To Laspetosyne, Tanglanah said, 'Do you see that bud on the lower root? Pluck it off.'

Laspetosyne, dodging falling rubble, did as she was told. She returned holding a lump of plastic the size of a pyuter.

Dwllis stared at the still-expanding object. 'What is it?' he asked.

Tanglanah ignored him at first, muttering to herself, 'Of course, of course, a throwback. Of course!' Then she answered Dwllis's question. 'It is a flower.'

'A flower?'

'It is an astromorph,' Tanglanah replied. 'It is akin to the aeromorphs, though distantly related. Zelenaiid, desiring humans to travel with us, created an astromorph. In this and in others like it she hoped a journey could be made – against my wishes.'

Tanglanah held the lump of plastic in front of Dwllis. 'With this, another astromorph could be made, and another, and another, and another. But I must halt that process. Only two may depart.'

Dwllis frowned. 'Flowering plants?'

Tanglanah threw the bud to the floor and made to stamp upon it.

'*Stop!*'

The voice was loud. Everybody swung around to see Subadwan, a laser rifle in one hand, a black tube in the other.

24

ASTROMORPH

When Tanglanah and Laspetosyne entered the Archive of Noct, Subadwan shivered. There was nobody else about. She hesitated over entering, having been incarcerated here so recently. But she forced herself to proceed. She dared not lose the pyutons.

She followed tracks of soot and dust, guessing, as she passed through the central chamber, that they were making for the Reeve's chamber. She was correct.

From behind a pillar she saw Tanglanah and Laspetosyne, Pikeface and Dwllis, all four of them engaged in conversation. She heard the debate, saw the deeds. Pikeface's transformation she watched. She saw the roof collapse, and she saw Laspetosyne breaking something off the transformed Pikeface. She heard the ensuing conversation. A little more became clear in her mind.

She raised the laser and thumbed it to full power. In her other hand she held one of Mogyardra's black tubes, though it was not loaded. When Tanglanah moved to stamp out the possibility of human beings departing the Earth, she yelled, 'Stop!'

All three swung round.

'Stop,' she repeated, still louder. 'If anybody moves I'll fire. That includes you, Dwllis.'

'Laspetosyne and I will stay put,' Tanglanah said. 'Do not fire upon us! What do you want, Subadwan?'

Subadwan replied, 'Just you. You won't be leaving. In fact, I'll give you a choice. You either stay here with us or take every last Crayan with you. We are not being left here to die.'

Tanglanah stood perfectly still for a minute. Rubble fell, crashing to the ground, dust swirling down on cold gusts of wind. The Reeve's chamber was open to the sky. Shivering, Subadwan waited.

At last, Tanglanah spoke. 'I cannot make the decision without consulting Greckoh.'

Subadwan frowned. 'Where is Greckoh?'

'She awaits me in the Spacefish.'

Subadwan shrugged. 'Then you are separated?'

'Not at all.'

Subadwan shook her head. 'I couldn't trust you. You must realise that.'

'I understand perfectly. Fortunately, there is a simple solution. Laspetosyne will contact Greckoh, during which time you will train your laser upon me. Laspetosyne will return with Greckoh's decision. If we try to entrap you, then you may fire at me. But we are sincere. You won't be harmed.'

Subadwan felt confused. Detecting a trick she asked Tanglanah, 'What will Laspetosyne do?'

Laspetosyne answered, 'We retain a few meditational capabilities, such as you witnessed Tanglanah performing when Gwmru imposed itself upon the city. A mental call can be made.'

Subadwan considered. The prospect of losing

Laspetosyne did not worry her. If Laspetosyne failed to return within a specified time, she would hold Tanglanah hostage. Would Tanglanah sacrifice herself for Laspetosyne? Highly unlikely. More believable would have been the reverse situation.

She threw a glance of disrespect across to Laspetosyne. 'I'll give you five minutes,' she said.

Tanglanah told Laspetosyne, 'You must ask only one question. Ask Greckoh if humans can leave with us. The answer must be one of either yes or no.'

'I will ask,' Laspetosyne said. She stood relaxed, and her head drooped so that her chin touched her collar bones. To Subadwan's dismay, Tanglanah adopted a similar position. She twitched, rifle ready, expecting a leap, a pounce, but Tanglanah stayed quiet as if embracing sleep. Subadwan waited, skin prickling, too afraid of a trap to do anything.

'What is happening?' Dwllis asked.

Subadwan called out. 'Tanglanah? *Tan*glanah?'

'Is she in a trance, too?'

A minute passed. It might have been less. Time's passage flew unreal.

In the time of an eyeblink the Archive became a tumble of wreckage – cracked, melted, blistered. Subadwan, shocked for a few seconds, realised that Gwmru had imposed itself upon the city, and she knew who had forced it: Tanglanah and the rest of her kin.

Dwllis stood at her side. The transmuted Pikeface was now more like a new shoot bending gracefully in a breeze, and she smelled a sweet perfume off its leaves. As for Dwllis, he too seemed different. He was frailer, smaller, bent over at the shoulders just enough to give the impression of weakness.

She looked up. From the Spacefish figures descended.

Subadwan counted them. Six.

As they closed Tanglanah and Laspetosyne reappeared. Tanglanah laughed. One of the six, Greckoh the black insect, approached her.

'We have succeeded,' Tanglanah said. 'Kill them! I will prepare the astromorph.'

In seconds, Subadwan and Dwllis faced the six electronic beings. Greckoh was at the front, the other five – a motley collection of mutated beast-women – seething with anger behind. Laspetosyne looked on from the side, the static energy of her fury raising her hair into a cap of spikes. Subadwan stepped backward. She raised her weapons.

The black tube was gone and the laser had been replaced with Zelenaiid's razor. Quivering with fear, Subadwan raised the glass shell, but she could find no words of warning. Failure seemed close.

'We have destroyed the abstract Archive of Noct,' Greckoh hissed through chattering mandibles. 'You will not find us so flimsy this time, *human*.' She spoke that word as if referring to the most insignificant creatures imaginable.

Subadwan was too shocked to reply. She reached for Dwllis's hand, grasped it, and stood firm. He too remained silent.

One of them, a woman with a dog's head, leaped forward as if unable to restrain her anger. Instinctively Subadwan, eyes closed, lashed out with the razor.

Silence. She opened her eyes.

Her attacker had been transformed to glass. She hung inches away from Subadwan. Subadwan punched with her left fist, and the vitrified object smashed into a thousand pieces.

'Madam,' Dwllis said, 'your foot!'

Subadwan's right foot had been transformed also.

But Dwllis continued, 'Madam, this is an abstract world! Your glassy foot is but a metaphor. Destroy them all!'

Greckoh and the others had been staring at their lost comrade, but now, roaring and screaming, they leaped forward. Dwllis shrieked and staggered back, but Subadwan stood her ground, lashing out at the flailing creatures, turning them to glass with each hit, but losing her own self. Every transmutation lost her part of a limb.

Flashing seconds passed. Subadwan stood panting before a pile of shards. Laspetosyne, Greckoh, and a woman with talons and a hawk's head stood close. Dwllis lay gibbering some yards behind.

Subadwan glanced down at her body. The entirety of her right leg and the left foot of her Gwmru-self had vitrified. She was fading. She tottered, unable to stand still.

'Cowards!' she yelled. 'Come and get me!'

Laspetosyne ran towards the astromorph, but the two abstract beings leaped forward, parting to attack from left and right.

Without thought, Subadwan grasped the shell in both hands and split it. She threw: left, right.

Both halves hit. She staggered to the left to smash the hawk-woman, but saw that both her own hands were now glass. With no other option she punched, and both the image and her own hand shattered into flying shards.

Greckoh she punched with her other hand. Now all her limbs were fragmenting under the stress. She collapsed to the floor.

Laspetosyne was at the astromorph. 'Shutdown!'

she called. 'Shutdown! Destructive interference!'

A rumbling began. It emanated from the base of the vehicle. Subadwan saw translucent pink leaves spiralling out from the conical green case at the top. Laspetosyne forced her way into the astromorph.

'It's launching!' Dwllis yelled.

Subadwan watched as the rumbling grew ever louder, knowing it was too late. Dwllis ran to her and dragged her away, but she fought him off like a wild animal. As he looked at her in horror and began to stumble away across the thrumming ground, she followed him, crawling as best she could.

The astromorph engines, if engines it had, gave a wheezing whine. Subadwan and Dwllis stopped retreating. They could see the pink head of the vehicle through the ruined roof of the central chamber. A lattice of pale rootlets had grown in the air around the astromorph, out of empty space, or so it seemed. With a final wheeze the astromorph, its roots gripping the rootlet scaffolding with dazzling speed, ascended into the air above the Archive. There it paused. A tower of rootlets appeared around it, rising high into the heavens, disappearing from view in the direction of the Spacefish. With a roar the astromorph lifted itself away, climbing the tower faster than a bullet from a rifle, so fast that every pink lamina became detached and floated to the ground.

Subadwan, tears in her eyes, hardly able to speak for the loss in her heart, said, 'I don't understand, I don't understand, I don't understand . . . Oh, Gaya, I don't understand.'

Dwllis stood at her side staring, as she did, at the wisps of rootlet that twitched, hardened, then fell out of the sky, fragmenting as they did to form a rain of delicate wafers that smelled of sweet perfume and corrosive fumes. 'I do,' he said. 'You see, madam, those things known as flowers never evolved around or in Cray. We have just seen the most arcane expression of our heritage: a flower. Those pink leaves are called petals. Pikeface was no fish-man, he was an ancient flower. Damn it, we have all been fooled, madam, every last one of us.'

And then Gwmru was shut down, and they were left amidst the real ruins, the freezing, dusty, filthy ruins of the Archive of Noct.

25

THE END

Three figures struggled north through the dead city, cloaked against the bitter wind that snaked through empty lanes – a wind no longer heated by the effluvia of a hundred factories and ten thousand machines. Around them, all was gloom. Streets were dark plastic, buildings were shattered or diseased, and only occasional noises disturbed the silence. No mechanisms. A few creeping people. Whispering gnosticians came to scavenge for glass splinters. Vast plains of glass spread to the south, deeply dark, cracks showing up like storms of brown lightning, while to the east the Swamps bubbled and stank. They too were dark.

Frost twinkled on every exposed surface.

Above, a tiny Spacefish gleamed in a turbid sky, like a distant salmon leaping the interstellar gulf.

Two of the figures, Dwllis and Etwe, stood upright, Etwe pushing an improvised wheelchair in which Subadwan's shrunken body lay amidst polythene cushions. What remained of her left leg stuck out in front of the wheelchair. Her wrists were bandaged with black cloth. Lacking hands to steady herself, she bounced and jerked as the wheelchair was pushed along crumbling streets.

She glanced to one side to see a supine figure in a doorway. For a moment she saw a face amid the rags, and it seemed to be Aquaitra. Then the moment passed, and she was pushed onward.

They entered the Cemetery and began to negotiate its ruts of frozen mud, at length encountering a few druids sat against a barrow, tired and hungry druids with no hope in their faces. Normally they would have challenged the newcomers, but now there was no reason to do so.

Subadwan approached one of them. 'We're looking for a radio. Do you have one?'

The druid glanced at his colleagues, then said, 'You'll have to get inside a barrow. But you are wasting your time, for the broadcasts of the afterlife have ceased.'

'Is there a barrow?'

The druid shrugged. 'That one over there?' He pointed to an incomplete granite barrow. 'Just heave the front stone over.'

This they did. Inside, the body of a pyuton lay, dust and grime gathered upon her. The radio to which she was attached showed a blue indicator, signifying internal batteries still good.

Etwe and Dwllis knelt by it. Etwe said, 'I would have come here to rest, had Cray not been left to die. This would have been my place of resting.'

Dwllis heard but was too intent on tuning the radio to make any answer. 'Have we got the correct band?' he asked.

Etwe looked. 'I think so.'

Then: a sound, as of abstract trees moving under the breath of an abstract breeze.

'That is it,' said Dwllis. 'That is the Gwmru
broadcast, the whisper of all those shifting memories.'

But it was faint. The sound of Gwmru was barely
audible over the cycling, phased white noise of the
carrier wave. For almost half an hour they listened,
before the sound faded, crackled, and then, with a
resonant sound as of a door closing, died for ever.

MEMORY SEED

Stephen Palmer

There is one city left. And soon that will be gone, for the streets of Kray are crumbling beneath a wave of exotic and lethal vegetation as it creeps south, threatening to wipe out the last traces of humanity. In the desperate struggle for survival, most Krayans live from day to day, awaiting salvation from their goddesses or the government. Only a few believe that the future might lie in their own hands.

Zinina, having fled from the Citadel, determined to discover what secrets are buried beneath it . . .

Arrahaquen, daughter of a member of the all-powerful Red Brigade, whose privileged position makes her insurgency all the more dangerous . . .

Graff-lin, channelling the prophecies of the Eastcity serpents, and racing against time to infiltrate the city's computer networks before they collapse . . .

And a man, deKray, whose sudden appearance accompanies a startling sequence of events . . .

Memory Seed is Stephen Palmer's first novel.

LITTLE, BROWN AND COMPANY ORDER FORM

Little, Brown and Company, PO Box 50, Harlow, Essex CM17 0DZ
Tel: 01279 438150   Fax: 01279 439376

☐ Memory Seed	Stephen Palmer	£5.99
☐ Consider Phlebas	Iain M. Banks	£6.99
☐ Excession	Iain M. Banks	£6.99
☐ Rendezvous with Rama	Arthur C. Clarke	£5.99
☐ Sundiver	David Brin	£5.99
☐ Midshipman's Hope	David Feintuch	£5.99
☐ Mid-Flinx	Alan Dean Foster	£5.99

Payments can be made as follows: cheque, postal order (payable to Little, Brown and Company) or by credit cards, Visa/Access/Amex. Do not send cash or currency. UK customers and BFPO please allow £1.00 for postage and packing for the first book, plus 50p for the second book, plus 30p for each additional book up to a maximum charge of £3.00 (7 books plus). Overseas customers including Ireland, please allow £2.00 for the first book plus £1.00 for the second book, plus 50p for each additional book.

NAME (CAPITALS) _____

ADDRESS _____

_____

_____

☐ I enclose a cheque/postal order made payable to Little, Brown and Company for £ _____
or
☐ I wish to pay by Access/Visa/Amex* Card (*delete as appropriate)

Number [ ][ ][ ][ ][ ][ ][ ][ ][ ][ ][ ][ ][ ][ ][ ][ ]

Card Expiry Date_____ Signature _____

SCIENCE FICTION AND FANTASY — MONTHLY

interzone is the leading British magazine which specializes in SF and new fantastic writing. Among many other writers, we have published

BRIAN ALDISS	GARRY KILWORTH
J.G. BALLARD	DAVID LANGFORD
IAIN BANKS	MICHAEL MOORCOCK
BARRINGTON BAYLEY	RACHEL POLLACK
GREGORY BENFORD	KEITH ROBERTS
MICHAEL BISHOP	GEOFF RYMAN
DAVID BRIN	BOB SHAW
RAMSEY CAMPBELL	JOHN SLADEK
RICHARD COWPER	BRIAN STABLEFORD
JOHN CROWLEY	BRUCE STERLING
THOMAS M. DISCH	LISA TUTTLE
MARY GENTLE	IAN WATSON
WILLIAM GIBSON	CHERRY WILDER
M. JOHN HARRISON	GENE WOLFE

interzone has also introduced many excellent new writers, as well as illustrations, articles, interviews, film and book reviews, news, etc.

interzone is available from specialist bookshops, or by subscription. For six issues, send £16 (outside UK £19). For twelve issues send £30 (outside UK £36). Single copies: £2.75 inc. p&p (outside UK, £3.20, US $5.50).

American subscribers may send $30 for six issues, or $56 for twelve issues. All US copies will be despatched by Air Saver (accelerated surface mail).

....

To: **interzone** 217 Preston Drove, Brighton, BN1 6FL, UK

Please send me six/twelve issues of *Interzone*, beginning with the current issue. I enclose a cheque/p.o./international money order, made payable to *Interzone* (delete as applicable) OR please charge my Mastercard/Visa

Card number

Expiry date   Signature

/		

Name ....

Address ....

....
If cardholder's address is different from the above, please include it on a separate sheet.